Texas Cattleman's Club

HEIR APPARENT

JANICE MAYNARD   **JOANNE ROCK**   **CAT SCHIELD**

MILLS & BOON

Published by
Mills & Boon
An imprint of Harlequin Enterprises (Australia) Pty Limited
(ABN 47 001 180 918), a subsidiary of HarperCollins
Publishers Australia Pty Limited (ABN 36 009 913 517)
Level 19, 201 Elizabeth Street
SYDNEY NSW 2000
AUSTRALIA

MIX
Paper | Supporting
responsible forestry
FSC
www.fsc.org FSC® C001695

® and ™ (apart from those relating to FSC®) are trademarks of Harlequin
Enterprises (Australia) Pty Limited or its corporate affiliates. Trademarks indicated
with ® are registered in Australia, New Zealand and in other countries.
Contact admin_legal@Harlequin.ca for details.

Printed and bound in Australia by McPherson's Printing Group

CONTENTS

Texas Tough
Janice Maynard

USA TODAY bestselling author **Janice Maynard** loved books and writing even as a child. After multiple rejections, she finally sold her first manuscript! Since then, she has written sixty books and novellas. Janice lives in Tennessee with her husband, Charles. They love hiking, traveling and family time.

You can connect with Janice at www.janicemaynard.com, www.Twitter.com/janicemaynard, www.Facebook.com/janicemaynardauthor, www.Facebook.com/janicesmaynard and www.Instagram.com/therealjanicemaynard.

Books by Janice Maynard

Southern Secrets

Blame It On Christmas
A Contract Seduction
Bombshell for the Black Sheep

The Men of Stone River

After Hours Seduction
Upstairs Downstairs Temptation
Secrets of a Playboy

Texas Cattleman's Club: Heir Apparent

Texas Tough

Visit her Author Profile page at millsandboon.com.au, or janicemaynard.com, for more titles.

Dear Reader,

Thanks for buying a copy of *Texas Tough*. We may not all live in Texas, but we've certainly had to be tough this past year. I hope you and your families are well and that you are looking forward to better times ahead.

May the summer be filled with sunshine and possibilities!

I'm grateful for each of you...

Fondly,

Janice Maynard

To "romance lovers" everywhere.
You help keep the human spirit alive.
Thanks for your support of the genre and
your dedication to characters and stories.
There would be no books without you!

One

Abby Carmichael was a Starbucks and bright-city-lights kind of girl. What was she doing out here in this godforsaken section of Texas? Maverick County was flat. So flat. And the town of Royal, though charming enough with its wealthy ranchers and rough-edged cowboys, didn't even *have* a storefront for her usual caffeine fix.

So far, she'd been in Royal less than a day, and already she was regretting her current life choice. That was the trouble with being a documentary filmmaker. You had to go where the stories took you. Unfortunately, this particular assignment was smack-dab in the middle of the old Western movies her grandpa used to make her watch.

She pulled off onto a small gravel side road, dazzled by the glorious sunset despite her cranky mood. Flying did that to her. Not to mention having to drive a rental car where all the buttons and knobs were in different places.

Taking a deep breath, she concentrated on losing herself in the moment. All she needed was a hot bath and a good night's sleep. Then she'd be good as new.

Grudgingly, she admired the stunning display of colors painting the evening sky. The orangey reds and golds caught the tips of prairie grasses and made them flame with faux fire. New York City *had* sunsets, but not like this.

While she watched the show, she lowered the car windows. It was June, and plenty humid. The air felt like a blanket, dampening the back of her neck.

At least the heat didn't bother her. Gradually, the peaceful scene smoothed her ragged edges. She'd left her cameras back at the hotel. This excursion was about relaxation and mental health, not work.

Suddenly, she noticed a lone figure far-off on the horizon, silhouetted against the glow of the quickly plummeting sun. The phantom drew closer, taking on shape and form, moving fast, paralleling the road. It was a rider, a horseman. With the sun in her eyes, Abby could make out nothing about the cowboy's features, but she was struck by the grace of man and beast and by the beauty of day's end.

As the horse drew closer, Abby could hear the distinctive *thud, ka-thud* of hooves striking the raw dirt. Something inside her quivered in anticipation.

Grabbing her phone, she jumped out of the car, ran down the road to get closer and began videoing with her cell. That was often how she processed information. Give her a lens, even a phone lens, and she was happy.

The man's posture was regal, yet easy in the saddle. As if he and the animal were one. Soon, they would be past her.

But without warning, the rider pulled on the reins abruptly. The horse whinnied in protest, reared on its hind legs and settled into a restless halt.

A deep, masculine voice called out across the distance, "You're on private property. Can I help you?"

For the first time, it occurred to Abby that she was entirely alone and far from civilization. *Vulnerable.* A frisson of caution slid down her spine, and some atavistic instinct told her to run. "I have Mace," she warned over her shoulder as she walked rapidly back toward her car.

The man's laugh, a sexy amused chuckle, carried on the breeze. "Mace is good, but it's no match for a Texas shotgun."

Her heart bobbled in her chest, her breath hitching as she moved faster and faster away from him. She had come farther than she realized. Surely, the man was joking. But she didn't plan on finding out.

She jumped into her car, executed a flawless U-turn and gunned the engine, heading back toward town.

Two hours later, Abby was still a bit shaky. Her room felt claustrophobic, so she grabbed her billfold, pocketed her key card and went downstairs. Maybe a drink would calm her nerves. She wasn't normally so skittish, but everything about this place felt alien.

Not the hotel. The Miramar was lovely. Comfortable. Just the right amount of pampered luxury. And still in her budget. She *could* have stayed at the lavish Bellamy, but Royal's premier five-star resort was too high-profile for her needs.

At the entrance to the bar, she paused and took a breath, soothed by the dim lights and the traditional furnishings. The room was filled with lots of brass and candles and fresh flowers. And almost *no* people. The bartender looked up when she walked in. He was an older man with graying hair and a craggy face. "Plenty of room at the bar," he said. "As you can see. But feel free to take a booth if you'd prefer."

"Thanks." Abby debated briefly, then sat down at the booth in the corner. It was private, and she felt the need to regroup. She was well able to handle herself in public, or even wave off the occasional pushy male. After all, she was a New Yorker. But tonight, she just wanted to unwind.

The bartender came around to her table, pad in hand. "What can I get you, young lady? The appetizers are on that card right there."

She smiled at him. "No food for me, thanks. But a glass of zinfandel, please. Beringer if you have it."

"Yes, ma'am," he said, walking away to fill her order.

When the man returned with her drink, Abby took the glass with a muttered thanks. "I needed this," she confessed. "I was driving outside of town, and some macho cowboy on a horse threatened me with a shotgun. It was scary."

The bartender raised a skeptical eyebrow. "Doesn't sound like Royal. Folks around here are pretty hospitable as a rule."

"Maybe," Abby said, unconvinced.

When the man frowned and walked away, she realized belatedly that either she had insulted his fellow Texans, or maybe he thought she was an interloper dressed a tad too casually for the Miramar. Whenever she flew, she liked to be comfortable. Today, she had worn a thin flannel shirt over a silky camisole with her oldest, softest jeans and ankle boots.

Oh, well, it was late, and the bar was almost empty. She hoped no one would even notice her...

Carter Crane yawned and stretched as he sauntered into the Miramar and headed for the bar. He should be on his way home for a good night's sleep, but he had just finished a late evening meeting with a breeder, and he was feeling restless for no good reason he could pinpoint.

At thirty-four, he'd thought he would have a wife and maybe a kid by now. But he had gambled on the wrong woman and lost. His fault. He should have seen it coming.

The gorgeous summer weather made him feel more alone than usual. Maybe because this was the time of year for socializing. Carter hadn't *socialized* with a woman in far too long. A year—or maybe a year and a half?

He worked hard enough to keep his reckless impulses in check. Mostly.

Tonight, he felt the sting.

There were other more popular watering holes in Royal, but he liked the private, laid-back ambience at the Miramar.

He grinned at the bartender. "Hey, Sam. I'll have a beer, please. The usual." Carter's dad had known Sam since the two men were boys. Now his father was enjoying the good life in a fancy condo on Miami Beach.

Sam brought the frothy beer and set it on a napkin. "Food?"

"Nope. I'm good."

"How's the herd?" the older man asked.

"Best one yet. Barring tornadoes or droughts, we should have a banner year."

"Your dad says you work too hard."

"It's all I know how to do," Carter said. "Besides, he was the same way."

Sam nodded as he rinsed glasses and hung them overhead. "True. But not now. He misses you."

"I didn't realize you kept in touch."

"Now and then," Sam said.

Carter changed the subject. "You won't believe what happened to me earlier tonight. Some crazy tourist lady threatened me with Mace. On my own property."

"How do you know she was a tourist?"

"Who else would carry Mace?" Carter scoffed. "Royal is a safe town."

"Maybe she didn't know that. And the way *I* heard it, you threatened her with a shotgun."

He gaped. "Say what?"

Sam pointed. "Little gal's over there. You probably should apologize. It rattled her."

Carter glanced over his shoulder. "Looks like she enjoys being alone."

The bartender shook his head, eyes dancing. "Come on. I'll introduce you, so she won't think you're hitting on her."

Sam didn't wait. He poured a glass of wine, swung around the end of the bar and went to where the woman sat, half shielded by the high wooden back of the banquette. "This one's on the house, ma'am. And I'd like to introduce you to Carter Crane. He's one of Royal's fine, upstanding citizens. I think he has something to say to you."

Carter felt his neck get hot. The woman eyeing him warily was visibly skeptical of Sam's assessment. "May I sit for a moment?" he asked.

After a long hesitation, the woman nodded. "Help yourself."

He eased into the booth, beer in hand, and cut to the chase. "I was the one you saw on the road outside of town. I was kidding about the shotgun," he said quickly as her eyes rounded. "It was a joke."

The woman looked him over, not saying a word. Though her perusal wasn't entirely comfortable, Carter seized on the excuse to do his own inventory. She was slim and young, almost too young to be drinking alcohol, but maybe her looks were deceptive.

Her hair was long and brown and wavy, her eyes a rich brown to match. She wasn't wearing a speck of makeup, except possibly mascara. Even then, her lush lashes *could* be real, he supposed.

It was her complexion, however, that elevated her from merely pretty to gorgeous. Light brown with a hint of sunlight, her skin was glowing and perfect.

Carter felt a stirring of lust and was taken aback. Ordinarily, he preferred his women sophisticated and worldly. This artless, unadorned female was the rose that didn't need gilding. She was *stunning*.

He cleared his throat. "As Sam said, I'm Carter Crane. I own the Sunset Acres ranch. Most days I'm proud of it. Others, I curse it. What's your name?"

The tiniest of smiles tilted her lips. "Abby Carmichael. And I knew you were kidding about the shotgun."

"No, you didn't." He chuckled. "I've never seen a woman move so fast."

She lifted her chin. "I was in a hurry to get back to the hotel, because I needed to pee. It had nothing to do with you."

He laughed again, letting the blatant lie go unchallenged, charmed by her voice and her wide-eyed appeal. "I think I recognize the accent," he said. "You're from back East, right? New York? My college roommate was born and bred in Manhattan."

"I don't have an accent," she insisted. "You're the one with the drawl."

Carter shook his head slowly. "I never argue with a lady," he said.

"Why do I not believe that?"

Her wry sarcasm made him grin all over again. She might be young, but she was no naive kid. "What brings you to Royal?" he asked.

"I'm doing a documentary on the festival—Soiree on the Bay."

He grimaced. "Ah."

She cocked her head. "You don't approve?"

"I don't *not* approve," he answered carefully. "But events like that bring hordes of outsiders into town. I like my space and my privacy."

"The festival takes place on Appaloosa Island."

"Doesn't matter. People have to sleep and eat and shop. Royal will be a madhouse."

"You're awfully young to be a curmudgeon. How old are you, forty?"

He sat up straighter, affronted. "I'm thirty-four, for your information. And even a *young* man can have strong opinions."

"True…"

From the twinkle in her eye, he saw that she had been baiting him. "Very funny," he muttered. "But since we've broached the subject, how old are you? I guessed seventeen at first, but you're drinking wine, so I don't know."

"Didn't your mother tell you never to ask a woman her age?"

"Seventeen it is."

"Don't be insulting. I'm twenty-four. Plenty old enough to recognize a man with an agenda."

"Hey," he protested, holding up his hands. "I only came over to say hello. And to assure you that you're in no danger here in Royal."

"I can handle myself, Mr. Crane."

"Carter," he insisted.

"Carter. And because I'm a nice person, I'll forgive you for the shotgun incident, if you'll do me a favor."

He bristled. "There *was* no shotgun incident, woman." Was she flirting with him? Surely not.

She smiled broadly now. The wattage of that smile kicked him in the chest like a mule. "If you say so…"

"What kind of favor?" He wasn't born yesterday and wasn't going to give her carte blanche.

"A simple one. I'd like to see your ranch. Film it. And interview you. On camera."

"Why?" He was naturally suspicious. Life had taught him that things weren't always what they seemed. "I have nothing at all to do with the festival. I don't even care about it. Period."

She shrugged. When she did, one shoulder of her shirt slipped, revealing the strap of her camisole and more of her smooth skin. His chest tightened as did parts south.

The fact that her expression was matter-of-fact didn't jibe with his racing pulse.

"My documentary about the festival will be punctuated by scenes from around Royal. To provide local color. Since Royal is home to the famed Texas Cattleman's Club, it only makes sense for me to include ranching. You're the only rancher I know, so here we are."

"My days are busy," he muttered, sounding pedantic, even to his own ears. "I don't have time for futzing around with movie stuff."

Her jaw dropped. "Do you have any idea how patronizing you sound? My job is no less important than yours, Mr. Carter

Crane. But don't worry. I'm sure I can find another rancher to show me the ropes."

Like hell you will. The visceral response told him he was wading into deep water. "Fine. I'll do it," he said, trying not to sound as grumpy as he felt. This artless, beautiful young woman was throwing him off his game. "Give me your contact info."

Abby reached into her wallet and extracted a business card. It was stylish, but casual. Much like the gal with her hand extended. He reached out and took the small rectangle, perusing it. "I'll call you," he said.

"That's what they all say," she deadpanned.

"I said I would, and I will."

"I appreciate it, Carter."

The way she said his name, two distinct syllables with a feminine nuance, made him itchy. Suddenly, he was in no great hurry to head home.

"I could stay a little longer," he said. "Since you're new in town."

The rosy tint on her cheekbones deepened. "How chivalrous."

"May I buy you another glass of wine?"

The woman shook her head. "I'm a lightweight. But I wouldn't say no to a Coke and nachos. Though this place might be too upscale for comfort food."

"I'm sure Sam will rustle some up for us," he told her.

"I love how you do that."

Carter frowned. "Do what?"

"Talk like a cowboy. *Rustle some up.*"

He leaned back in the booth, feeling some of the day's stress melt away. This unexpected encounter was the most fun he'd had in ages. Though he was likely destined for a cold shower and a restless night. "Are you making fun of me, Ms. Carmichael?"

"You can call me Abby," she said.

"Don't move…" He went to the bar, gave Sam their order and came back. "I told him we wanted fried pickles, too."

His companion wrinkled her nose. "Ew, gross. Don't you care about your health?"

Carter hid a smile as he took off the noose around his neck. He removed his jacket, too, and stretched his arms over his head, yawning. "Do I look unhealthy to you?"

Two

Not fair, Carter Crane. Abby would have choked on her pickle... If she'd been eating one. Which she wasn't. Her face heated and her pulse stumbled as she drank him in from head to toe. The man was eye candy, leading man material, drop-dead *gorgeous*.

Carter Crane was a lot of male. In every way. When she had seen him earlier on horseback, she'd barely had the time to digest what he looked like, much less what he was wearing. But she was pretty sure it hadn't been this expensive navy sport coat, pristine white button-down and tailored dress pants. Not to mention the patterned crimson necktie that he had shed so quickly.

The fact that he managed to wear cowboy boots without looking even a smidge ridiculous told her he was the real deal.

Underneath the soft cotton fabric of his shirt was a chest that went on for miles. Hard, with ripped abs. She'd bet her gym membership on it.

Summer-morning blue eyes were bracketed with tiny lines from squinting into the sun. His hair was brown and tousled, as if he had just tumbled out of bed and run his hands through the silky strands.

She downed a gulp of the Coke that Sam had just set on the table. "I have no medical training," she said primly. "You might be at death's door for all I know." When she thought her expression wouldn't give her away, she sat back and gave him an even stare. "I'm not a doctor, but you look fine to me."

He raised an eyebrow. "*Fine?* That's the best you can do?"

Humor lifted the corners of her lips, despite her best efforts to take him down a peg or two. "You know what you look like, rancher man. You don't need me to stroke your ego or anything else."

Carter blinked and quirked a brow. "Umm…"

Suddenly, she heard the blatantly suggestive comment she had made. Unwittingly, but still… "Moving on," she said briskly, trying to pretend she was not embarrassed. Or interested. Or *turned on*.

Her companion didn't call her out on her faux pas. Instead, he leaned forward on his elbows and offered her a pickle. "You're a filmmaker. Surely you sample the local cuisine when you travel. Come on, Abby. At least try one."

Against her better judgment, she opened her lips and let him tuck the crispy slice in between. She bit down automatically and felt the flavors explode on her tongue. The sharp bite of the pickle and the tangy seasoning of the outer layer were utterly divine. "Oh, my…this is good."

Carter sprawled in the corner of the booth and scooped up two for his own pleasure. "Told you," he said as he chewed and swallowed.

Abby was mesmerized by the ripples in his tanned throat. She turned to the nachos in desperation. Apparently, New York wasn't the only place in the world with good food. "These are amazing, too."

Carter offered her a napkin, his gaze intense. "You have cheese on your chin," he told her quietly.

Abby quaked inside. This was getting way too personal, way too fast. She needed to put on the brakes. "Tell me about your family." She blurted out the request.

Carter ran a hand across the back of his neck, eyeing her with undisguised male interest. Abby was interested, too, but they had just met, and she certainly wasn't going to invite him upstairs to her hotel room.

Finally, he sighed. "Not much to tell. I'm the older of two kids. One sister. My parents retired to Florida, leaving me in charge of the ranch. It's been in our family for five generations. Sunset Acres is not only in my blood, it's part of me."

A squiggle of disappointment settled in Abby's stomach. The last thing she needed was to get involved with a man who was wedded to a plot of dirt in this remote, flat, rural landscape. "Did you always want to be a rancher?"

He shook his head slowly. "When I was ten, I wanted to be an astronaut."

"Seriously? Wow. That's cool. Why didn't you go that route?"

"Several reasons. Turns out, I'm claustrophobic. But more to the point, one of my ancestors fought with Davy Crockett at the Alamo. Walking away from a couple centuries of family history wasn't an option." He signaled Sam for another round of drinks.

They were the only customers in the bar now. Abby glanced at her watch. "Should we go? Maybe Sam wants to shut down."

Carter shook his head slowly, his gaze still focused on her mouth. "We have another hour," he said.

Those four words were innocuous, but the handsome rancher's tone was not. Suddenly, Abby wanted to take off her shirt. She was far too hot. The camisole was not indecent. But such a move might signal something she wasn't ready to signal.

"What shall we talk about?" she asked in desperation, her hormones melting into a puddle of heated sexual attraction. "Politics? Religion. Something easy?"

Carter leaned forward and touched the fingernail on her pinkie, barely any contact at all. "I want to talk about you."

* * *

Carter wasn't the kind of man to press a female who wasn't interested. He'd been taught by his daddy to respect the fairer sex. And truth be told, women usually came on to him, not the other way around.

If Abby had been uninterested, he would have paid the check and walked out of the bar. But she *was* interested. He'd bet his prize stallion on it.

Still, he gave her an out. "Should I go now?" he asked gruffly. "Am I making you uncomfortable?"

She stared at him, pupils dilated slightly, as he rubbed her fingernail. He'd never done such a thing before. Ever. In fact, in the cold light of day, this move on his part would probably look dorky and dumb.

But right now, they were connected.

Her chest rose and fell. "No," she whispered. "Don't go."

His hand shook. So much so, that he pulled it back and tucked it under the table out of sight. It wouldn't be good for her to realize how close he was to begging for a night in her bed.

One-night stands were indulgences he had given up long ago—about the time his father began handing over more and more responsibility for the ranch. Carter was not a selfish twentysomething anymore. He was a landowner, a wealthy rancher and a respected member of the community.

For Abby Carmichael, though, he might make an exception.

He cleared his throat, trying to focus on anything other than the fantasy swirling in his head. "As I recall, you never answered my question about where you're from."

"You were right about that. New York City. I went to film school at New York University, and I still live with my mom when I'm in town. Apartments are ridiculously expensive."

"So I've heard. NYU. I'm impressed. Isn't it hard to get accepted?"

She grimaced. "Definitely. But I had two things going in my

favor. My father is Black, and my mom is white, so I ticked the biracial box."

"And the other?" he asked.

"Daddy is a filmmaker out on the West Coast. He and my mom are divorced. I spent summers with him growing up and got the movie bug. He asked a couple of his influential friends to write recommendation letters for me. So here I am," she explained.

"Why documentaries?"

"We're a visual society. As much as I love books and believe in the power of the written word, there's no faster way to touch someone's heart or change someone's opinion than with a well-framed documentary." She spoke with intensity.

"What piqued your interest about Soiree on the Bay?"

"Well, you talked about family legacy—" She smiled, her face lighting up. "I can claim one, as well, though not so long-lived. My grandmother was at Woodstock. In fact, she supposedly got pregnant with my mother there. Gave birth to her when she was barely eighteen. Music is in my blood, and in any big gathering like that, there are fascinating stories to tell. Lots of stories. I want to capture this festival from beginning to end."

Carter had lost his appetite for nachos and fried pickles. What he wanted now, *needed* now, was far more visceral. "I love your passion," he said slowly. "I'm sure that comes across in your work."

Pink stained her cheeks again. "I hope so. And you'll let me film you? Please?"

With Abby's big brown eyes staring at him hopefully, he felt churlish for turning her down. But he sensed that a yes from him right now would ensnare him in something he wasn't sure he was prepared for, neither the movie project nor the woman who wasn't going to stick around.

"I'll think about it. I promise."

He saw her disappointment, but he held firm.

"Well, thank you then," she said. "For the nachos and Cokes.

And the conversation. But I should get some sleep. The time change is hitting me." She yawned, proving her point.

They both slid out of the booth at the same time, suddenly standing far too close. Carter's throat constricted. He wanted to grab her up and kiss her until her body went limp with pleasure.

He shoved his hands in his pockets. "Welcome to Royal, Abby Carmichael. I hope you enjoy all we have to offer…"

Abby left the cowboy standing in the bar, his hot gaze giving her second and third thoughts about being reckless. It wasn't vanity on her part to think he would have accompanied her upstairs. There were enough sparks arcing between them to pretty much guarantee the sex would be explosive.

But once she was in her room, she knew she had done the right thing. She was really tired, and she had a meeting tomorrow that was very important. Lila Jones, from Royal's Chamber of Commerce, was going to welcome her to town and even give her a tour of Appaloosa Island.

Abby hoped she would also be able to do some preliminary filming.

As she showered and crawled into bed, however, it was hard to keep her mind on work. When she closed her eyes, Carter Crane was there with her, laughing, flirting, teasing. It had been a long time since she had met someone so intriguing, so different from the men she knew in New York. Or even California for that matter.

Carter was his own man. A Texas rancher. That meant something in this part of the world. Still, even aside from his ranching expertise and land holdings, she knew he would stand out anywhere in the country. Carter had a commanding presence, an innate confidence that was very appealing and sexy. And though his intense masculinity was flavored with a tinge of arrogance, the arrogance wasn't off-putting.

After the *interesting* evening she'd had with him—starting out on a deserted stretch of highway and ending in a dimly lit bar—she might have tossed and turned. Fortunately, exhaustion claimed her, and she slept long and deeply.

When she awoke the next morning at 6:00 a.m., her batteries were recharged, and she was eager to jump-start her day. After heading out for a run and then taking a quick shower, she couldn't deny feeling bummed when she glanced at her phone. Not a single text or missed call. Would Carter agree to let her film him? He had promised to think about it. But without a time frame. He might keep her dangling indefinitely.

She would give him forty-eight hours. After that, she would assume his answer was no. Which meant she would have to find someone else. Handsome ranchers might be a dime a dozen in this part of the world. Who knew?

When she stood at the window for a moment and looked out over the heart of Royal, she had to admit it wasn't so bad after all. Though it wasn't quite big enough to be called a city by her standards, it was definitely a very nice, large town. The broad main thoroughfare was landscaped with flowers and ornamental trees, and in the distance, she could make out the shape of the venerable Texas Cattleman's Club.

There were clothing stores and restaurants, bars and banks— even an intentionally retro country emporium. In her research, she had learned that the schools were rated highly, and in addition to all the wealthy cattle barons, the town was home to artists and potters and other creative types.

It wasn't New York City or Malibu, but she could see the appeal.

A tiny alarm beeped on her watch.

Grabbing up her roomy leather tote, a water bottle and a rain jacket just in case, she headed out to meet her tour guide.

Lila was right on time, waiting at the curb in front of the hotel. She jumped out of her car. "It's wonderful to see you again, Abby. Welcome to Royal."

Abby shook the other woman's hand. "Thanks. I'm happy to be here." As they got settled, she took stock of her companion.

She had met the other woman in LA and knew she was about her age, maybe a little older. She reminded Abby of the actress Zooey Deschanel.

Lila waved at the back seat. "I have snacks when you get hungry."

"Thanks. I appreciate your taking me out to the island today. But tell me again why I can't just stay there for the length of my project?" This was going to be a heck of a commute. Three hours each way.

Lila chuckled. "Well, first of all, you have to get used to Texas. Everything is big out here in the Lone Star State. Big ranches, big egos, big open spaces. It's fairly common to travel by helicopter or small plane. You'll find landing strips just about anywhere you want to go."

"But I can't stay on the island?"

"Not realistically. It doesn't have everyday amenities. There are some huge mansions out on the western end, but the rest of it is undeveloped. That's why the Edmond family decided it would be the perfect spot for Soiree on the Bay."

"And Mustang Point?"

"Mostly private residences for the super wealthy. Mustang has a ton of water sports, but I promise you, living in Royal while you do this project will be far more reasonable. Not to mention the fact that all the people you'll need to interview for your documentary live in Royal or just outside of town."

They had been driving for twenty minutes when Lila pulled the car into a gravel parking lot. Abby's stomach pitched. She was a frequent flier on coast-to-coast routes. But the tiny prop plane sitting on the narrow strip of tarmac looked flimsy and unimpressive.

Lila didn't seem at all concerned. She hopped out and greeted the young pilot. "Hi, Danny. Thanks for running us out to the Point."

The freckled kid ducked his head bashfully. "Happy to do it,

Miss Lila. I need flying hours to keep my license up-to-date, and Daddy said not to charge you a dime."

"I'll add my thanks, too," Abby said.

Soon, they were airborne. Abby took out her camera and aimed through the tiny plane window. The result was not great, but it helped her get a feel for the landscape.

Lila watched with interest. "What kind of camera are you using? It looks fairly portable and light."

Abby sat back in her seat. "Twelve pounds. It's a Panasonic DVX200. Pricey, but it shoots great 4K resolution and has up to twelve stops of dynamic range."

"I'll pretend I know what you're talking about," Lila said, laughing.

"The camera was a gift from my dad when I graduated. He was really hoping I would follow in his footsteps."

"And now here you are."

"Yes. After you invited me to film the festival, Dad hooked me up with somebody at Netflix who might be interested in a documentary about Soiree on the Bay, but I'll have to find a strong human interest angle."

"A hook as they say?"

"Exactly." Abby tucked her camera back in her bag. Incorporating Carter's story would add depth and local color, but she wasn't holding her breath. "What's on our schedule for today?"

Lila tapped her phone and perused what was clearly a calendar. "We'll catch the ferry out to Appaloosa Island. It's a quick, fifteen-minute ride. On the island, Jerome will meet us. He acts as a groundskeeper for several of the landowners, and he's arranged for me—and by extension you—to have the use of a golf cart anytime you come out to the island. You'll just call him in advance, and it will be waiting. Today, we'll do an informal tour and answer any questions you might have."

"I really appreciate you giving up a huge part of your morning and afternoon to do this."

"No problem. It's my job, of course. And besides, any chance to get out of the office is a plus."

As the small plane touched down, Abby glanced at her watch. The trip had taken an hour and a half. So, better than the three-hour drive she'd been expecting, but still not quick. She was going to have to be very disciplined about planning her shooting schedule. Much of the groundwork would have to be done in Royal.

She grabbed her things, thanked the young pilot and followed the other woman out of the plane. The ferry dock was a quarter-mile walk. Though a small line of cars sat waiting to cross, foot traffic was almost nonexistent. Abby and Lila boarded and made their way inside the air-conditioned cabin.

Abby frowned as she thought about the logistics. "How is this going to work during the actual festival?"

Lila uncapped her water bottle and took a sip. "It won't be easy. The organizers are planning to add four more ferries. And parking on the island will be limited. Festivalgoers who want to have their personal vehicles on-site will pay a hefty premium in addition to their ticket price."

"So part of the cachet of the festival will be that it's hard to access…it's *exclusive*."

"Exactly."

At the end of the brief ferry ride, Lila waved at an older man with deeply tanned skin and grizzled salt-and-pepper hair. *That must be Jerome*, Abby guessed. He sat in one golf cart alongside a second cart with a much younger driver.

The younger man jumped down and slid onto the seat beside Jerome. The groundskeeper tipped his hat. "That one's all yours, Ms. Lila. When you ladies are done for the day, just park it right here and leave the keys under the seat."

Abby's eyes widened. "Isn't that dangerous?"

The other three chuckled. "Safe as going to church," Jerome said. "You little gals have fun."

Lila motioned toward the back of the golf cart. "Toss your things in there and hang on. Not everything has been paved yet."

The sun was hot and directly overhead, but a breeze danced off the water. Trinity Bay was idyllic, deep blue, touched with whitecaps. No wonder the Edmonds had acquired this private island. It was exquisite.

Abby looked around with interest as the small vehicle lurched into motion. The festival grounds were larger than she had imagined. And far more upscale. This would be no Woodstock with music lovers lounging on the grass.

Lila narrated as they wound among the structures that smelled of new wood and excitement. "The two main stages will anchor the event with headliners. Big names. Crowd-pleasers. The scattering of smaller venues you see will be home to quirkier bands. The kind of musical groups that in five years might become household names."

"And over there across the main pathway?" Abby curled her fingers around the top edge of the golf cart. Some areas had been prepped for sod, but others were covered in wood chips. The golf cart bumped and jolted.

"Those are the wine bars and pop-up restaurants. Each will have a celebrity chef."

"Wow." The logistics of putting on an enormous music festival—on an *island*—boggled the mind. There was so much to coordinate: food shipments, the sound equipment, a medical presence, seating—presumably chairs and benches. The portable toilets... Abby definitely wouldn't want to be the person in charge. The whole thing could be a smashing success or a raging headache fraught with disaster.

Lila eased the golf cart onto a small point surrounded by water on two sides. "I brought fruit and cheese. And a bottle of wine. You hungry?"

"Actually, I am."

Lila wasn't a huge talker, which Abby liked. It was peaceful to sit in silence, watch the water and enjoy the simple pleasures of an alfresco meal.

Without warning, a vision of Carter Crane popped into her head. The handsome rancher was no doubt neck-deep in cattle ranch business in the middle of a busy workday. Maybe Abby could convince him that his routine was exactly what she found fascinating. There was only so much video she could take here on the island before the festival got underway. But to immerse the viewer in the flavor of Texas, she would need solid footage of what it meant to be from Royal.

Lila yawned. "Do you want to get some preliminary shots? I can check email on my phone or maybe grab a quick nap. Take your time."

"That would be great." Abby finished her light lunch and slid out of the golf cart, going around to the back to retrieve her camera. For the actual festival she would need her tripods. Today, though, she wanted to shoot the mood of the unoccupied island.

The bay was an obvious star. Out in the distance, sailboats glided along, pushed by the wind. Abby was sure she saw a dolphin break the surface in a carefree arc. When she had what she wanted from the water, she turned to the land.

Some of the empty structures would be dramatic in black and white. She paused for a moment, listening. Trying to envision what the energy of the crowd would sound like… Imagining the steady thump of the bass. The sharp twang of an electric guitar.

Steadying the camera on her shoulder, she panned from left to right. And caught a cowboy dead in the middle of her viewfinder.

Three

Carter enjoyed catching Abby Carmichael off guard. She had incredible confidence and self-possession for someone so young, but he had managed to rattle her. He saw it in her eyes when she lowered the camera.

"Carter," she said, her gaze wary. "What are you doing here?"

He hid a grin by rubbing his chin. "I was in the neighborhood and thought I'd drop by." He took a moment to enjoy the picture she made. Being a filmmaker was a physically demanding job at times. Abby must have dressed for comfort and professionalism, but her choice of clothing flattered her.

She wore an ankle-length, halter-neck sundress of a thin gauzy material that hinted at the shape of her body. The colorful fabric made him think of Caribbean islands and cold drinks with tiny umbrellas. Abby's beautiful wavy hair was down, despite the heat. The breeze fanned strands out across her golden-skinned shoulders.

She chewed her bottom lip, clearly convinced he was up to no good. Maybe she was right. "We're miles from Royal," she said. "And I have it on good authority that your little cows are a demanding lot."

He laughed softly, suddenly very glad he had come. "None of my cows are little, city girl. Besides, I told them I wanted the day off."

She frowned. "Your cattle?"

"Nope. My staff."

"Oh…" She glanced back over her shoulder. "I should go. Lila will be waiting for me."

He reached for the camera. "Here. I'll carry that. I'd like to say hello."

Abby surrendered the video equipment with obvious reluctance, but she fell into step beside him. "You know Lila?"

"Everybody knows *everybody* in Royal. Besides, Lila is big news lately. She enticed a celebrity Instagram influencer—whatever the hell that is—to come to Royal and promote the music festival. Next thing I knew, the gossip was flying, and Lila was engaged to Zach Benning."

"I've heard about Zach, and I did notice the gorgeous ring on her finger. Sounds like a fairy tale."

Carter grimaced. "Don't tell me you're one of those."

Abby stopped abruptly. "What does that mean?"

He faced her with the camera tucked under his arm. "A dewy-eyed romantic. I thought documentary makers were more realistic." Though he had to admit that her soft brown irises were pretty damn gorgeous. A man could dive into those eyes and get lost.

"You think romantic love is fiction?"

"Yes," he said baldly. Perhaps his response was harsh, but he knew better than most men that romance was little more than a charade.

Abby continued walking, her expression thoughtful. When they approached a golf cart parked by the water, Lila Jones got out and waved. "Hey there, Carter. What brings you to Appaloosa Island? You're several weeks early for the festival."

He kissed her cheek. "You know I'm not a festival kind of guy. But I haven't had a chance to congratulate you on your engagement."

Lila blushed. "Thanks."

Abby studied them both. "How long have you two known each other?"

Carter shrugged. "Forever... Folks in Royal tend to put down roots."

Lila's brows drew together. "I might ask you two the same question. Abby, I thought you only got into town last night."

"That's true. But I went for a drive, and on a dusty secluded road, Carter here threatened to shoot me."

"No, no, *no*," Carter protested. "The truth is, Abby isn't as innocent as she looks. The woman tried to Mace me."

Abby's eyes danced. "I don't think that's a verb."

Lila put her hands on her hips. "I'm missing something."

Carter lifted his face toward the sun, feeling more carefree than he had in a long time. "Let's just say that our first meeting was dramatic and our second far more cordial."

"I need to hear the whole story," Lila insisted.

"I'll fill you in on the way back." Abby took her camera from Carter and tucked it into a cushioned bag. Then she climbed into the cart and glanced over her shoulder at him. "We have to go. Our ride is picking us up in twenty minutes."

Carter lifted a brow, looking at Lila. "Danny getting in practice miles?"

"You bet."

"Abby?" He touched her arm briefly, feeling the insistent *zing* of attraction. "I was hoping I might persuade you to drive back with me. When we get to town, I'll take you to dinner."

"I came with Lila," she said, her face giving nothing away.

Lila shook her head slowly. "Carter has a gorgeous black Porsche. It's by far the better offer."

He smiled at the woman in the passenger seat. "You said you wanted to interview me. Now's your chance."

"I said I wanted to *film* you."

"Yes, but the interview should come first. I've been reading up on how to make a documentary. I wanted to be ready."

Abby's lips parted, almost as if she felt the same magnetic sexual pull and wasn't sure what to do about it. "I don't want to abandon Lila."

Lila pooh-poohed that idea. "Go with Carter. You and I will have plenty of time together. I don't mind at all. Honestly."

Carter gave both women his most innocent smile. "Abby?"

"Okay, fine." She exited the golf cart with a graceful swish of skirt and a flash of toned thigh. "Let me grab my stuff."

Lila intervened. "Better yet, why don't we just give Carter a ride back to the dock? It's too hot to walk around with no shade."

"I'll take that offer," he said. The golf cart had two rows of seating, so he slid in behind the women. Abby reclaimed her spot in the front. If he leaned forward, he could kiss one of her bare shoulders. That thought had him shifting uncomfortably on the seat. Maybe spending three hours in the car with the delectable filmmaker wasn't such a good idea after all.

He had parked the convertible adjacent to the dock. The ferry was moments away from pulling out. Because there was no room in his small sports car for a second passenger, Lila and Abby exchanged goodbyes, and Lila boarded on foot.

Carter helped Abby in, started the engine and, when instructed, eased his vehicle onto the ramp and into the ferry. Because the ride was so short, they stayed in the car with the windows down. Abby had her camera out shooting the seagulls chasing the boat. He suspected it was a ploy not to have to converse with him.

Was she nervous? Carter wasn't. Well, not exactly. He would describe it as being *on edge*. His senses were heightened, and truth be told, he rarely reacted this strongly to a woman he had just met.

When they reached Mustang Point, Carter and Abby greeted Danny and said goodbye to Lila. Then they wound their way back to the highway. Carter still had the top up. The blistering heat was too much right now.

He adjusted the air and glanced at his silent companion. "You okay?"

Abby smiled, playing with her large hoop earring. "Yes. This is a very nice car."

"I'm glad you like it. When we get closer to Royal, there's a two-lane road that turns off the main drag but still leads into town. It's the old highway actually. I thought we could put the top down then and enjoy the view."

"Sounds good."

Carter gripped the wheel, wondering why he had taken the day off. He never played hooky in the middle of the week. In fact, he had been known to work six and seven days in a row. The pace wasn't healthy, but ranching took up most of his life.

It was just him. All day every day. Carrying the weight of a family legacy. He wasn't complaining. He knew he was lucky beyond measure.

But Abby Carmichael was the best kind of interruption.

"How old were you when your parents divorced?" he asked quietly. His own mom and dad were heading for their forty-seventh anniversary.

Abby sighed. She had kicked off her sandals and was sitting with one leg tucked beneath her. "I was five. So I don't remember a lot. But as an adult, I finally understood why the marriage unraveled."

"Oh?"

"My mother was an Upper East Side society princess," she explained. "My grandparents owned tons of real estate, and Mom had the best of everything growing up. She met my father during a spring break trip to Jamaica."

"Her parents didn't approve because he wasn't in their social circle?" he mused.

"They probably didn't, but that wasn't the tack they took in opposing the relationship. My father's family was wealthy, too. They were bankers and lawyers in Jamaica. Daddy was a musician when he and Mom met, but he was studying to be a filmmaker. Mom says her parents weren't impressed with the odds of success in that career."

Carter looked over at her before returning his eyes to the road. "Were they right?"

"Yes and no. It took my dad years to break into the industry. And it meant going where the jobs were. If he'd had a wife and kid in tow, it might never have happened."

"Did your grandparents give in?"

"Sadly, no." She sighed. "My mother wanted a cathedral wedding with all the frills. In the end, she had to settle for a Vegas chapel."

"Did her parents ever come around?"

"When she got pregnant with me...yes. But maybe my mom and dad were too different from the beginning. Even sharing a child couldn't keep them together."

"I'm sorry, Abby," he said quietly. "It must be hard to have them on opposite coasts."

When he glanced at her again, she was staring straight ahead, as if the road held answers. Her expression—what he could see of it in a quick glance—was pensive. "I've learned to be happy anywhere. I love both of them, and whatever animosity there might have been during the divorce evaporated over the years."

"Have you thought about where you'll settle? For the long haul?"

She shot him a look of surprise. "I don't know that I *will* settle. Living out of a suitcase doesn't bother me."

"But surely you see yourself putting down roots eventually."

"Maybe."

"Don't you want kids someday?"

"Do *you*?" Her question was sharp. "Why do people ask women that? I bet never once has anyone tried to pin you down on the fatherhood question."

"Well, you'd be wrong then," he said wryly. "My mother

brings it up regularly. I'm a terrible disappointment to her. And I have ten years on you, so the pressure is mounting."

"I guess you're glad they don't live here anymore."

"Not really," he said. "I miss them. But they deserve this time to spread their wings. The ranch always tied them down."

Abby heard the clear affection in his voice and experienced the oddest moment of jealousy. She loved her parents—of course she did. And she got along well with both of them. But the three of them weren't a family unit. Not like the close bond Carter evidently had with his mom and dad. Abby and her parents were two halves of a family that somehow didn't add up to a whole.

She let the conversation drop. Carter didn't seem to mind. It was a beautiful day for a drive. In a strange way, she felt very comfortable with him. Well, that was true as long as she ignored the palpable sexual undertones.

Without meaning to, she dozed. When she jerked awake and ran her hands over her face, she was embarrassed. "Sorry," she muttered. "I was sleep-deprived coming into this trip. I guess I'm still catching up."

"No worries. You're cute when you snore."

"I *don't* snore," she retorted, mildly offended, and also worried that he wasn't joking. Carter didn't answer. He kept his eyes on the road, but she could see the smile that curved his lips. The man had great lips. World-class. Perfect for kissing.

To keep herself from fixating on his mouth and his jaw and all the other yummy parts of him, she looked at the view beyond the car windows. Fields and more fields. Cows and more cows. It was all she could see in any direction.

Carter shot her a sideways glance. "What?"

Abby frowned. "I didn't say anything."

"No. But you were thinking really loud. You can say it. You don't like Texas."

It seemed churlish to agree. "That's an overstatement."

"Is it? You're missing the skyscrapers and the world-class ethnic food and the museums and Broadway."

"Maybe. But that doesn't mean I'm criticizing your home. You love it here."

"I do. But I've traveled, Abby. I know what the world has to offer."

"May I ask you a question?"

She saw him frown slightly. "Of course."

"Why did you come to Appaloosa Island today?"

His chest rose and fell as he sighed deeply. "The truth?"

"Yes, please."

"You intrigue me, Abby. My personal life has been pretty boring for the last year and a half. The pool of available romantic partners in Royal—for someone like me who has always lived here—is finite. You're new and different, and I wanted to spend time with you."

Her stomach flipped. Here was an übermasculine man, not a boy, stating unequivocally that he was interested. What was she going to do about that?

"Does this mean you're willing to let me film you at your ranch?"

He winced. "I'm still debating."

"So, what you're dangling is carte blanche as a videographer if I consent to get better acquainted with you?"

He grimaced. "This isn't a negotiation. One has nothing to do with the other."

"Well, if you let me film you, we'll be spending *lots* of time together."

"I'm not interested in being cast as some token rancher for your viewers. I am who I am. It's nothing exotic."

"For a city dweller, this lifestyle you've chosen has a certain je ne sais quoi."

"That's what I'm talking about," he grumbled. "There's nothing romantic and exciting about sweat and dirt and cows."

"Familiarity breeds contempt. You don't see yourself as an outsider would."

He shot her a look. "I thought you were doing a documentary about Soiree on the Bay."

"I am. But I'm beginning to realize that the town of Royal and the Texas Cattleman's Club may be as much or more interesting than a music festival that hasn't even happened yet. You see, I've picked up a lot from Lila about how things work around Maverick County. I'm still after the human interest angle."

"Well, good luck with that."

Carter pulled off onto the side of the road. He reached across her lap and opened the glove box. "Here. If I'm putting the top down, you'll need this."

This was a narrow silk scarf, clearly expensive. It was deep amber scattered with tiny navy fleur-de-lis. When he leaned close, Abby inhaled his scent. Probably whatever he had shaved with that morning. Lime… And a hint of something else.

Her pulse beat faster. It was a relief when he straightened.

She pulled her hair to the nape of her neck and secured the ponytail with the scarf, knotting it tightly. The wind would still do a number on the loose ends, but she didn't mind that.

She watched as Carter hit the button and made sure the top retracted slowly. Then he climbed back into the driver's seat and gave her a grin that caused her knees to quiver. "Ready?"

Abby nodded, her heart beating more quickly than the moment warranted. "Hit the pedal, cowboy."

The next hour took on a surreal quality. The open road. The wind in her face. The man beside her. With a sigh, Abby leaned against the headrest and closed her eyes. Clearly, there was more to Carter than she'd first thought. This busy, successful rancher who was willing to blow a whole day chasing down a woman who might or might not sleep with him had layers. Interesting layers. *Irresistible* layers.

Texas roads were straight and flat, and Carter drove with confidence. Never once did Abby have any qualms about her safety. For the first time, she understood the appeal of a fast, sexy car and an adventurous man behind the wheel.

When they arrived in Royal, she was windblown but content. She touched Carter lightly, her fingertips registering his muscular forearm and warm skin. "I'm hungry," she admitted. "So dinner sounds great. But I should change first."

He eased into a parking spot and turned to face her. His blue eyes reflected the sky. "Only if you want to. Your dress is beautiful." He paused. "And so are you." His gaze roved from her face to her breasts and back up to her eyes, making her shiver despite the heat.

Her throat tightened. Were all cowboys so direct? She licked her lips, telling herself they were dry from the hot summer breeze. "Um…thank you. But I'd feel more comfortable if I could shower and change."

"Whatever you want. It's still early. An hour and a half? I'll make a reservation at Sheen. It's a newer restaurant. I think you'll like it."

"How dressy?"

"Anything similar to what you're wearing."

At the hotel, Carter pulled up under the portico and they both got out of the car. He retrieved her belongings from the back seat. "I'll run out to the ranch and be back to pick you up around six thirty." Casually, he kissed her cheek. "See you soon, Abby."

She stood and watched as he gunned the engine and sped away around the corner.

In the elevator, she barely recognized her reflection in the mirrored glass. Her cheeks glowed with a deep rosy hue. Slowly, her smile faded.

She was getting off track. She had come to Royal to make a documentary and get her career on solid footing. Flirting with a sexy rancher wasn't on the list.

Even so, as she showered, washed her hair and changed into another dress, nothing could block Carter from her thoughts. Or erase the feel of his hot lips burning against her skin.

He was dangerous. Why would she get involved with a man, even temporarily, whose worldview was so different from hers?

She would have to tread carefully. Needing him for her documentary was one thing. Tumbling into his bed was another entirely.

Four

Going home to the ranch was a mistake. Too many people needed to ask Carter too many questions. By the time he escaped the inquisition, showered and changed, he barely had enough time to make it back into town to pick up Abby at her hotel at the appointed hour.

As he drove to get her, he thought about the day. He'd had fun. Honestly, that was never high on his list these days. Responsibility, yes. Hard work, definitely. But fun? Not really.

Abby made him want things. Lots of things. Sex, of course. She was real and beautiful, and he couldn't deny the powerful attraction. But it was more than that. She represented a time in his life when he still had choices. At her age, he'd been actively working on the ranch, but had still entertained the idea that he might ultimately do something other than be a rancher.

Unfortunately, his dad had suffered a heart attack when Carter was twenty-five, and soon after, his life was mapped out for him. He hadn't minded. He loved the ranch. But it had been a shock to go from his carefree postcollege days to being the top dog.

And then there was the whole thing with Madeline. His gut clenched. He'd been wrong about her. *So wrong.* Was Abby too much like his ex-fiancée? Did he have a type? Was he setting himself up for embarrassment and hurt again?

The unpleasant thought was one he didn't want to dwell on, especially since his libido was firmly in the driver's seat. He shoved the past into a locked box where it belonged and concentrated on the evening ahead.

Abby met him in the lobby. She had changed into another sexy outfit, this one more sophisticated, but no less flattering. The sleeveless, knee-length dress was white jersey knit. It clung to her body in ways that probably should be outlawed in the presence of red-blooded males. The bodice plunged in a deep vee, where a gold necklace dangled. Again, her shoulders were bare, her hair was loose and she wore white espadrilles with three-inch cork heels. The laces crisscrossed around her ankles.

He closed the distance between them. "You look amazing," he said. When he kissed her cheek lightly, she seemed flustered.

The restaurant wasn't far away. Over dinner, they spoke of less personal topics. Abby was funny and smart and well-informed. He should have expected that from a woman who spent time on both coasts. She might only be twenty-four, but she had grown up in a privileged atmosphere with a top-notch education.

Carter liked the fact that she challenged him. The conversation was stimulating and wide-ranging. She kept him on his toes. And underneath their back-and-forth was a slow, molten sexual awareness.

He knew it was too soon to sleep with her. He thought she wanted him, but a man needed to be sure. On the other hand, maybe he could speed things along with a little cooperation.

Over dessert, he played his best card. "I've decided I'm willing to let you do some filming at the ranch, within reason. How about coming over for lunch tomorrow?"

Abby wrinkled her nose. "I'm glad to hear that, but I already have plans. Lila has arranged for me to sit in on a meeting of the advisory board for the festival. I think we'll be at the Texas Cattleman's Club."

"Ah." Now he was really frustrated.

"I could come the next day," she said, perhaps reading his mood. Big brown eyes focused on him intently. She reached across the table and patted his hand. "I appreciate the invitation, Carter. Really, I do. But this meeting is important."

"Of course it is," he replied. "I understand."

"May I make a personal observation?" she asked quietly.

He stared at her, trying to read her thoughts. His fingers itched to tangle in her hair, to pull her closer and press his lips to hers. To hold her and trace the curves of her body beneath that soft, clingy dress. "Personal?" The word came out a little hoarse.

Abby nodded. "If you don't mind."

So polite. So incredibly enticing.

"Sure," he said. "I have no secrets."

When she swallowed, the muscles in her slender throat moved visibly. For the first time, he realized she was not as calm as he had imagined. "I get the feeling," she said, "that you want to sleep with me. Am I way off base?"

After nearly choking on his tongue, he found his voice. "Are you always so direct?" Her question rattled him.

"I don't play games, if that's what you mean. Most men and women make things too complicated."

"What happens if I say yes?"

"Well…" She stared at her hands clasped on the white linen tablecloth. "I'd probably explain that it's too soon." She looked up at him from beneath her lashes.

His breathing hitched. "So, you're saying there *is* a hypothetical date that might *not* be too soon?"

Her smile was slow and mysterious. "Precisely. I like you, Carter. A lot. But there are things to consider."

"Such as?" He would bat them all down one by one.

"I've never in my life slept with a man I've known only two days. Or two weeks for that matter."

He felt his advantage slipping. "Is there a *but* in there?"

"Not really. The problem is, you and I have nothing in common, and I'm only going to be in Royal for a limited time. I don't know if I'm willing to do short-term with you. It might be better to settle for flirting and friendship."

"Nope," he said, scowling. "Not a choice. I have friends, Abby. You don't fall into that category."

"Acquaintances then? Or business associates?"

Was she taunting him? The fact that he wasn't sure frustrated him. Or maybe it was the need pulsing in his gut. "I don't have to label anything, Abby. We'll be who we are. If that leads to sex, I'm all for it."

Abby trembled. Had she ever met a man who was so earthy and civilized at the same time? Carter wasn't rude or crass, but he took no pains to hide his sexual desire. For *her*. She was both flattered and intimidated. Could she hold her own with so much testosterone? Carter was a man who knew what he wanted and wasn't shy about going for it.

She suspected that a woman in his bed would find incredible pleasure. And she wanted him. No question. Still, sex and men had been tripping up women for millennia.

In her adult life, she had been disappointed by a few guys. She'd misjudged a couple of others. Not once had she faced heartbreak. Maybe that said something about her tolerance for risk. She always calculated the odds for success in any situation.

Carter Crane might turn out to be her weak spot. The strength of her desire for him was enough to make her put on the brakes. It would be dangerous and indulgent to embark on an affair when she was in the midst of a possibly career-changing project.

"Fair enough," she said. "No labels. No clock. No expectations."

His grin was tight. "I'm expecting plenty, gorgeous. But you'll have to make the call. Agreed?"

She nodded, her stomach fluttery. "Agreed."

"Dessert?"

"Yes, please."

Because looking at Carter was making her rethink her sensible approach, she scanned the restaurant. It was beautiful, made almost entirely of glass. An interested patron could observe a chef at work or track the sunset.

Sheen was hugely popular, not only because it was new, but because the food was spectacular. Every table was full. Over strawberry crepes slathered in real whipped cream, she eyed her dinner companion. Although earlier he had tried to convince her she didn't need to change for the evening, she was glad she had.

It was true that some diners had come in casual attire, but at least three-quarters of the men and women around them were dressed in what Abby would call special occasion clothes. The clientele ranged from the occasional high school couple on a date, to clusters of business associates, to folks like Carter and Abby enjoying a night out.

She was sad to see the evening end. Being with the ruggedly handsome rancher made her feel alive and intensely feminine in a way that was novel and exciting. Still, she was cautious. He could coax her into bed with little effort on his part. That knowledge was sobering.

If she wasn't ready for such a rash decision, she needed to limit her exposure to him.

She licked the last dab of whipped cream off her spoon and set it on her plate with an inward sigh of appreciation for the pastry chef's expertise. "I should probably get back to the hotel. I still have some prep work to do for my lunch meeting tomorrow."

Carter's face was oddly expressionless. "Of course." He dealt with the check and then escorted her between tables to the front door.

The night was perfect. A summer moon. A light breeze. Unfortunately, the trip back to the hotel was quick. Carter parked the convertible just around the corner from the main entrance beneath a dim streetlight. He'd kept the top up this time.

She jumped out, bent on escaping her own wants and needs. Carter met her on the sidewalk and put a hand on her wrist. "A good-night kiss? Or is that too much to ask..."

Her legs trembled. "I'd like that," she said.

When his lips covered hers, it was like jumping off a cliff into unknown waters. Her stomach shot to her throat and dropped again, leaving her woozy and breathless.

He held her with confidence. One big male hand settled on the curve of her ass. She made a small noise, somewhere between a whimper and a moan, when he pulled her more tightly into his embrace. Her arms curled around his neck.

His body was hard everywhere hers was soft. She smelled the scent of his skin, trying to memorize it. How had she known from almost the first moment that he was the one? Not *the* one as in gold rings and white picket fences, but the one who could reveal everything she had kept tightly furled inside her.

Carter's reckless passion burned through her inhibitions, her ironclad caution. They were on a public street just off the central thoroughfare, somewhat secluded this time of night, but in plain view of anyone who might happen by. Truthfully, he could have taken her against the hood of the car, and she might not have protested.

When she felt the urgent press of his erection against her abdomen, she knew one of them had to keep a clear head.

Though it pained her to do so, she put a hand against his chest and pushed. "Carter..."

To his credit, he released her immediately.

They faced each other in the shadowy illumination from overhead.

"Do I need to apologize?" he asked gruffly.

It was impossible to read his expression. "No. Not at all. Thank you for dinner. I enjoyed our evening. And thank you for driving me home this afternoon from the island. I'm touched that you gave up an entire day for me."

He shook his head slowly, his jawline grim. "I'm beginning to think I'd do just about anything for you. Which makes you a dangerous woman."

She traced his chin with a fingertip, feeling the late-day stubble. "I like that. No one's ever called me dangerous before."

"You don't have a clue..."

Was he feeding her a line? Spinning a tale of a man made vulnerable by sex? How could she believe that?

She knew she was attractive in a casual, understated way. The male sex responded to her. But she was no femme fatale, luring unsuspecting men into reckless behavior. That was a ludicrous notion.

Still, she wanted to trust his words, wanted to believe that he felt the same urgent pull she did. Pheromones were a powerful thing. That didn't mean she and Carter were kindred spirits. It only meant they wanted to jump each other's bones.

With reluctance, she made herself step back. "Good night, Carter."

His eyes glittered. "Good night, Abby."

Turning her back on him as she walked away felt risky, but she had to get inside.

"I'll make sure you get to the door," he said, following her at a short distance.

"It's only a few steps." She picked up the pace.

"A gentleman doesn't drop a lady on a street corner."

By the time Abby made it to the portico where the doorman stood, her heart was pounding. Carter had lingered on the sidewalk. She felt his gaze on her back as she headed for the double glass doors.

She wanted badly to turn around. But she kept on walking...

* * *

After a remarkably peaceful night, given her jumbled thoughts and feelings, Abby awoke ready to meet the day. She was determined to focus on her job and not the enigmatic Carter Crane.

Lila had offered to pick her up again, but Abby waved her off. It was time to get acquainted with the town of Royal. Besides, the Texas Cattleman's Club was only a few blocks away. Even with her camera and tote, it was easily within walking distance.

Today, she dressed in black dress pants and a cream blazer over a cinnamon silk tank. The jacket had large, quirky black buttons. When she was ready, she glanced at herself in the mirror. The only jewelry she wore was a pair of onyx studs she had purchased from an artisan in Sedona. Her black espadrilles were comfortable enough for the stroll, but nice enough to complement her outfit.

She debated what to do with her hair. Her preference was to leave it loose, but it was going to be very hot today. In the end, she twined it in a loose French braid.

When she had grabbed what she would need for the morning and then exited the hotel, she realized she was nervous. The people who would attend this meeting today were key players in Royal's high-powered business scene. It took a lot of money and influence to pull off an event like Soiree on the Bay.

Seeing the famed Texas Cattleman's Club in person was fascinating. The imposing edifice dated back to 1910, though it had been updated over the years. The large, rambling single-story building was constructed of dark stone and wood with a tall slate roof. Though once an all-male enclave, the onetime "old boys' club" now welcomed females into the membership.

Inside was even more impressive. Super high ceilings, large windows and, of course, the ubiquitous hunting trophies and historical artifacts displayed on paneled walls. Abby liked history as much as the next person, but dead animal heads weren't her thing.

The meeting was to start at ten. She had arrived at nine thirty.

After gawking in the spacious foyer, she spoke with the receptionist and showed her credentials. The woman directed her to a conference room down a broad hallway.

Lila was already there, setting out water glasses and pens and paper. She looked up when Abby walked in. "Hey, Abby. I'm glad you're early. I made up a cheat sheet for you."

"A cheat sheet?" she asked.

"Yeah, I thought you could use a head start. It's confusing when they all start talking at once. Do you want me to introduce you formally?"

"Whatever you think. Honestly, I wouldn't mind being the proverbial fly on the wall. At least until I get my bearings."

"Then we'll do that," Lila said cheerily. She handed Abby a sheet of paper. "This isn't everyone, but it's the core of the group. I copied their pictures in color and gave you a brief bio of each."

"Excellent." While Lila finished her prep work, Abby took a seat at the back of the room against the wall. The main participants would be seated around the large, beautifully polished conference table.

She had studied up on the main players already. Russell Edmond—Rusty—was the oft-married patriarch of the über-wealthy family. His money came from oil, and he owned a massive, luxurious ranch outside of town. It was his three children, Russell Jr., known as Ross, Gina Edmond and Asher Edmond, who were spearheading the festival.

When the door opened and the principals began arriving, she put aside her cheat sheet and concentrated on learning about the actors involved. Ross Edmond—tall and lanky with dirty blond hair and blue eyes—was impossible to miss. He had the innate confidence that comes with wealth.

His sister, Gina, had gorgeous dark hair and eyes and was super stylish. She looked to be close to Abby's age. That left the other Edmond sibling, Asher, who, according to Lila's cheat sheet, was actually a stepbrother. Odd, because his close-cropped brown hair and brown eyes resembled Gina's. Even at first glance, he seemed the most intense of the trio.

There were a few other people entering the room in a trickle, but it was soon clear they were either assistants or people like Lila who represented the town of Royal in various capacities.

That left only one unidentified player. According to Lila's info, his name was Billy Holmes. Somehow, he was involved with the Edmonds in planning the festival.

Abby had to admit he was gorgeous. Black hair, pale green eyes and scruffy facial hair gave him a roguish presence. He smiled. A lot. At *everyone*. Who was he, and how did he fit into this scenario?

Ross Edmond convened the meeting. Apparently, all the heavy lifting had been accomplished in earlier gatherings. Today was about tying up loose ends and making sure everyone was on the same page.

Abby listened carefully, making notes about anything she thought might have a bearing on her film.

At a lull in the conversation, Lila stood and motioned toward Abby. "I want you all to meet Abby Carmichael. She's the documentary filmmaker I've told you about. If the festival goes well, Abby's work will help lift our visibility to the next level and ensure that the festival continues for years to come."

Abby smiled and nodded, well aware that no one was particularly interested in what she had to offer. Except perhaps Billy Holmes. His grin seemed personal, and he looked her over carefully. The perusal fell just shy of being inappropriate. She had met men like him. If any female appeared on their radar, they *had* to make a good impression.

Eventually, the meeting wound to a close. There was a sense of urgency, given that the festival was only weeks away. After months of planning, everything was finally falling into place.

As Lila did her job, chatting with everyone and gathering up the materials she had brought with her, Abby was disconcerted to realize that Billy Holmes had lingered and was making a beeline in her direction.

She stood and smiled politely. "Hello, Mr. Holmes. I wonder if I might interview you in a few days. I'm sure you're a very busy man."

He reached out to shake her hand. "I always have time for anyone who wants to promote the festival."

Abby hesitated. "Well, I'm not *promoting* the festival per se. I'm a visual storyteller. Soiree on the Bay—along with the town of Royal—promises to be an interesting project. But of course, my film won't be out anytime soon."

"Doesn't matter. We want the festival to be such a big hit it will go on for years."

"You sound like a man with a vision."

"I like to think so." He glanced at his watch. "I've gotta run. How about Thursday at eleven for your interview? Would you like to see the Elegance Ranch? I live in a guesthouse on the Edmonds' property. I'll get my housekeeper to feed us."

"Sure," Abby said, wondering if she might be getting in over her head. Billy Holmes seemed nice enough, but she couldn't figure out where he fit in with the Edmond clan and the festival. Until she did, she would be on her guard.

As Billy walked out of the room, Lila joined Abby. "Well, what did you think?"

"I think people with a lot of money are a different breed."

Lila cocked her head, smiling gently. "Your father owns a Malibu beach house and your mom is a Manhattan socialite. You're hardly scraping by."

Abby grimaced. "Fair point. But you know what I mean. The Edmond family has buckets of cash. Not to mention land and influence. Here in Texas, they're practically royalty. Now that I've met several of them, I'm seeing a new direction for my film. Maybe the documentary will be less about the festival and more about the people who can pull off such a feat. What do you think?"

Lila held up her hands. "Not my area of expertise. But the Edmonds *are* fascinating, that's for sure. What's next on your schedule?"

"I've asked Carter Crane to let me do some filming on his ranch. You know, for local color."

The other woman grinned. "How was the drive yesterday? You must have made a big impression on the man."

Abby felt her face get hot. "It was a fun afternoon. I like him. And I think the camera will *love* him…those sharp cut features and strong chin."

"I'm surprised he's agreed to that. Carter likes to keep a low profile."

"I'm not sure how much latitude he'll give me. But I'm hopeful."

Lila sobered without warning, her expression serious. "Be careful, Abby. I wouldn't want you to get hurt."

Five

Abby's stomach curled with anxiety. "What's wrong with Carter? He's been a perfect gentleman as far as I can tell."

"I feel bad gossiping, but you need to know the truth. Carter keeps women at a distance, particularly women like you."

"Women like *me*? What in the heck does that mean?" She was mildly insulted. And worried.

Lila perched on the edge of the table, one leg swinging. "Carter was engaged to a woman from Chicago a few years ago. Madeline moved to Royal, and they began planning a wedding. But the next thing I knew, the festivities were canceled and the two of them were officially over. Apparently, Madeline hated life 'in the sticks' as she called it. She missed her big-city life, and she detested cows and horses and dust."

"Oh." Abby felt stupid and small. Maybe Carter was just playing with her. "Thank you for telling me," she muttered.

"I hope I haven't stepped over the line," Lila said, her expression conveying both worry and concern. "But if I weren't a happily engaged woman, Carter Crane might give *me* a few heart palpitations. He's macho and sexy and aloof. The trifecta when it comes to attracting the female sex."

"He *is* handsome."

"Maybe I shouldn't have said anything," Lila fretted.

Abby summoned a light tone. "I barely know the man. But I appreciate the information." She picked up her bag. "I'd better head out. Plenty to do. Thanks for letting me sit in on this meeting. It helped a lot."

"Sure," Lila said. "And let me know if there's anything else you need."

As Abby walked down Main Street, she tried to absorb the feel of the place. It's true that the town wasn't huge. Maverick County was mostly rural. But still, there was an upscale feel to the buildings and the businesses. Perhaps because oil money and cattle money had a far reach. Good schools. Great roads. This was no backwoods holler.

Her stomach growled, reminding her that lunch was next on the agenda. On a whim, she popped into the Royal Diner. Its 1950s retro decor and red, white and black color scheme were charming. When Abby had asked her hotel concierge for recommendations, he told her the diner was top-notch, and that the owner, Amanda Battle, was the sheriff's wife.

Now Abby slid into a red faux leather booth and tucked her things on the seat beside her. The menu offerings made her mouth water. When the pleasant older waitress stopped by the table, Abby ordered a vanilla milkshake, a tuna melt with fries and a glass of water. It had been a long time since she had indulged in such comfort food. Her mother was always dieting, and her father was a vegan.

When the meal arrived, Abby dug in with enthusiasm. Often while eating alone, she used the time to "people watch" or to get ideas down on paper. Today, she did both. With a sandwich in one hand and a pen in the other, she began filling a small notebook with her observations from today's meeting.

The Edmond siblings each had distinct personalities. She didn't know what to make of Billy Holmes. Perhaps her interview with him would uncover interesting layers. Often, people were more at ease in their home settings, so she wasn't averse to meeting him out at the ranch. He might even give her access to the Edmond family members if she decided to explore that route.

She had finished her sandwich and was nibbling on the last of her fries when she realized two women had taken the booth right behind hers—the one that had been vacant when she arrived. Abby tried not to eavesdrop, but the hushed conversation turned interesting quickly.

Though the women were conversing in lowered voices, Abby was only inches away. The words *festival* and *money* caught her attention immediately. Unfortunately, she couldn't hear every single phrase. But the gist of the topic was clear: the women seemed to be discussing the possibility that someone had taken a large sum of money from the festival coffers.

Abby's eyes widened. Not a hint about finances had come up during the advisory board meeting, nor a whiff of a problem. Were the members of the board hiding something, or was she overhearing idle gossip?

Unfortunately, the waitress brought Abby's check. There were customers waiting to be seated, so it seemed rude to linger. As she stood and picked up her belongings, she glanced at the women in the booth behind her. Neither of them was remarkable.

But what she heard stuck with her.

She spent the next couple of hours exploring Royal, filming anything that caught her fancy. Historic buildings. Quirky shop signs. Kids playing in a park. Though the town definitely possessed an almost palpable energy, that feeling was balanced by a sense that life was comfortable here. Predictable. *Enjoyable*.

Despite the fact that she was definitely out of her element, she had to acknowledge that Royal was interesting and charming. People were friendly. More than once, she found herself embroiled in a sidewalk conversation. In a community where everybody knew everybody, Abby apparently stood out.

She didn't mind the attention, not really. But after a few hours of walking the streets, she was more than ready to head back to the hotel. Getting clean, donning comfy pajamas and watching TV sounded like the perfect way to unwind.

The only irritant marring her peaceful afternoon was knowing that Carter hadn't called or texted. When he invited her to his ranch, she'd had to wave him off because of the advisory board meeting. Unfortunately, he hadn't said a word about tomorrow or the next day or the day after that.

When she got back to her room, she decided to be proactive...

Hi, Carter. Is it okay if I come out to the ranch in the morning? Seven-ish? I'd love to do some filming with the morning light. If there are no gates to unlock, I won't even have to bother you.

After a moment's hesitation, she hit Send. Then she turned her phone facedown and headed for the shower.

Carter rolled over in bed and glanced at the clock—5:00 a.m. He had no reason to be up at this hour, but he'd been dreaming. Hot, sensual, disturbing dreams.

And all because Abby Carmichael was coming out to his ranch. He slung an arm over his head and stretched, feeling the brush of cool sheets against his hot skin.

Already he knew the shape of her body, the sound of her voice, the scent of her skin. At this particular moment, he felt like a hormonal teenager about to catch a glimpse of his high school crush.

The difference was, he and Abby were consenting adults, fully capable of making rash decisions.

By the time he showered and dressed and gobbled down some breakfast, he was jittery as hell. He didn't want to be interviewed, and he didn't want to be filmed. But he *did* want more time with Abby, so he was stuck.

In their text exchange last night, she had offered to stay away from the house. Abby claimed to want ethereal shots of the stables and the pastures and the corrals bathed in warm light. She promised not to get in the way of any ranch operations.

Did she really think he would ignore her presence? Surely, she wasn't that naive or clueless. That one kiss they shared had been incendiary and left him wanting more.

He walked out back to the barn and saddled up his horse. As a teenager, he had sometimes slept until noon. Now he had come to appreciate the mystical purity of the early morning. A man could think and plan and contemplate taking risks at this time of day. The slight chill in the air was invigorating—even more so because it was fleeting.

Carter galloped along the gravel and dirt road that bisected the ranch, squinting into the strengthening rays of the sun. It was after eight now. Where was she?

And then he spotted her. She had parked her rental car at the edge of the road and was climbing the fence to get a shot of sunflowers. Carter hadn't planted them. They were his mother's legacy. But he had to admit, they made his heart swell with happiness and pride every time he passed them.

Sunset Acres had been passed into his keeping. Carter had a duty to perform. And he was working his ass off to make sure the ranch remained healthy and viable.

As he approached his visitor, he slowed the horse to a trot. Abby seemed to not notice his presence yet. She was intent on her task. With the camera balanced on her shoulder and one leg wrapped around the fence, she was perched precariously.

He didn't want to startle her.

Instead, he tied off the horse and covered the last few yards on foot.

"Abby," he said quietly. "Good morning."

After a split second, she half turned and looked over her free shoulder at him. "Carter. I didn't hear you."

"I could tell." Then he noticed her earbuds. "Ah. You're listening to music."

She shook her head, grimacing. "No." She lowered the camera. "It's a podcast."

"About?"

She shrugged. "Learning to take chances. Building self-confidence. Stuff like that."

"All set?" he asked.

"Yes."

"Then let me help you down. Camera first."

She handed it over without argument and watched him as he placed it carefully on the seat of her car. Then he lifted his arms. "Come off that fence, Ms. Photographer. Before you break your neck."

When he settled his hands on her waist, she leaned forward and let him take her weight. She was thin. Maybe too thin. But she was really tall for a woman, so perhaps that accounted for it. In the split second when he held her completely with her slender body pressed to his, his heart punched hard.

Carefully, he let her slide to her feet. She stumbled, but he steadied her.

"Thanks, Carter," she murmured.

There it was again. That odd and disarming way she pronounced his name.

"I thought you might stop by the house to say hello," he muttered, swamped by a wave of need so intense it made him tremble.

Abby swept her hands through her hair. "I didn't want to wake you. Or catch you in the shower."

"Perhaps you could have joined me."

Her eyes opened wide. A tinge of pink darkened her cheeks. "Still too soon," she muttered. But her body language was not as negative as her words. She had plenty of room to step away, to put distance between them. Yet she was so close he could feel the brush of her breath against his ear.

He had to get a grip. Clearing his throat, he focused his gaze just past her shoulder, telling himself he was imagining the strength of his arousal. It was deprivation. That's all. He needed a woman. *Any* woman. Abby Carmichael was nothing special.

"Did you get the early morning shots you wanted?" The words came out husky and slow as if he were seducing her, not asking a mundane question.

Abby nodded. "Most of them. With your permission, I'd like to come back at sunset to shoot some more."

"You could stay all day," he said, brushing his thumb across her cheekbone. "You know, shadow me. See how things work."

Her smile was rueful. "You're a man used to getting what he wants."

"Not always. But yes, frequently."

"I suppose it doesn't help my case if I admit that I want what you want."

He sucked in a sharp breath. "Not fair, Abby. Not when you're asking to take things slowly."

She toyed with a button on his shirt, one right near his heart. "I didn't expect a complication like you when I came to Royal. You're perfect for my documentary. Beyond that, I'm not so sure."

He lifted her chin with his fingertip and brushed a light kiss over her soft lips. "Why don't we let things unfold and see what happens?"

At last, she backed away. Big brown eyes stared at him. "I suppose I could do that."

"Do you ride? Horses," he clarified, since she seemed dazed.

"No."

"I could put you up on Foxtrot with me. Show you the ranch. You won't have to do a thing but hold on."

"Foxtrot?" Abby raised an eyebrow.

"He's been known to do some fancy footwork when he doesn't want to be ridden."

"Sounds dangerous."

"I won't let you fall," he reassured her.

"What about my car?"

"Leave it here. No one will bother it."

"Do you think I could film on horseback?" she wondered aloud.

"I have no idea, but you're welcome to try." He watched as she glanced from him to his horse and back again.

"Okay," she said. "It might be fun."

He ignored the jolt of jubilation that fizzed in his veins. Abby was wearing a thin, orangey-red cotton shirt over a white camisole and a pair of pale denim skinny jeans with artful holes at the knees. Her sneakers were white Keds, already stained by the Texas soil. It wasn't exactly riding attire, but he supposed it would have to do...

He held out a hand. "Shall we?"

Abby was no dummy. She knew what kind of trouble she was courting. But she couldn't stop herself. Ignoring Carter's outstretched arm, she sidled around him and headed for her car. Fortunately, the enormous horse was tethered in the opposite direction.

In the end, she decided it would be too awkward to hold her video camera and cling to Carter at the same time. For the record, she knew there would be plenty of clinging. By the time she put her camera away, locked the car and pocketed her keys, Carter had already mounted the beautiful glossy black stallion.

As she walked back to meet him, he stared at her. The intensity of his gaze was as intimate as a caress. Beneath her top, her nipples beaded. The day was heating up, but she couldn't blame her rapid heartbeat on the rising temperatures.

When she was six feet away, Carter leaned down and held out his hand, smiling as if this was no big deal. "Put your left foot on the heel of my boot to steady yourself," he said. "I'll pull you up, and you swing your right leg over."

"You make it sound so easy." She hesitated, trying to remember every movie she had ever seen where the heroine joined the hero on horseback. There weren't that many. Especially not ones filmed in the twenty-first century. "I don't want to be responsible for pulling your arm out of its socket or tearing your rotator cuff."

"You're stalling, Abby. Don't overthink it."

"Couldn't I climb on top of the fence and do it from there?"

"Where's the romance in that?" His broad grin taunted her.

Still, she paused. In the course of her dating life, she had been acquainted with a few very wealthy men. But they were generally ensconced behind corporate desks and wore suits. She had also known surfers and ballplayers and gym rats who prided themselves on their hard bodies and athletic prowess.

Carter was a disturbing mix of both wealthy confidence and masculine strength. He didn't posture or preen. He was who he was. The whole package.

Stifling her doubts, she reached out and took his hand. His grip was firm and sure. As soon as he saw that she had situated her foot as he had instructed, he tugged her up behind him. The entire maneuver took mere seconds. She landed in the saddle with a startled exhalation.

And then she looked at the ground. Her arms clenched around his waist as her knees quivered. She hadn't realized how high off terra firma she would be.

With her cheek pressed against Carter's back and her fingers in a death grip on the front of his belt, she tried to calm down.

"You okay back there?" he asked.

She wanted to hate the amused chuckle in his voice, but she was too busy relying on him to keep her from a painful death. "Just peachy," she bit out, rounding up all the sarcasm she could find and stuffing it into those two words.

Carter set the horse in motion and laughed harder. "Is it a fear of heights that's getting you, or the horse?"

The breeze whipped her hair in her face. "The horse is fine. And it's not a fear of heights. It's a fear of hitting the ground in a bloody, broken mess."

Carter laid his free hand over both of hers, stroking her knuckles in a move that shouldn't have been particularly erotic, but did in fact send arousal pulsing from her scalp to her toes.

"You're safe, Abby. I swear. Now, how do you feel about speed?"

Six

Carter was enjoying himself immensely. Abby was plastered against his back as if he could protect her from every source of harm. He didn't want her to be scared, but he liked having her close.

He gave Foxtrot free rein as Carter took Abby from one end of the ranch to the other, looking at it through her eyes, pointing out every spot that had meaning for him. From the small corral where he learned to ride as a five-year-old to the copse of cottonwood trees where he had his first kiss a decade later, this ranch was home.

Occasionally, they stopped, and he lifted Abby down, taking advantage of the situation to flirt with her while he showed her a new barn or an old steer—the saddle shop or the historic bunkhouse. Abby was enthusiastic, but always in the context of her documentary. Never once did he get the impression that she saw things through *his* eyes.

A Texas ranch was a novelty to her, perhaps even beautiful in a certain context. But Abby was a city girl. It was a truth he'd do well to remember.

Eventually, they both gave in to hunger—for food. He dropped her off at her car, and then rode ahead to show her the way to his house.

When they went inside, Abby's genuine praise soothed some of his disgruntlement.

"This is gorgeous, Carter! I love it."

As she wandered from room to room, he followed her, remembering the choices he had made with a designer. Comfort had always been his first priority. And natural light. Lots of windows. Furniture made for sitting.

Abby skittered past the door to his bedroom with comical haste and went on down the hall to explore the laundry room, the workout room and the small in-ground pool outside, just past the breezeway. When they doubled back to the living room, she smiled at him. "This is the perfect house for you. I see your stamp on every bit of it."

"When my parents moved, and I took over, they gave me their blessing to remodel extensively. At the same time, we all went in together to design a large guesthouse about a half mile from here. We're a close-knit family, but they didn't want to cramp my style when they came to visit."

She sobered. "Lila told me about your fiancée…or ex-fiancée, I should say. I'm sorry. I wasn't prying."

His jaw tightened. "You're saying she volunteered the information? And why would she do that?"

Abby chewed her bottom lip, visibly uncomfortable. "She warned me that you were not in the market for a relationship. That you'd been burned."

He slammed his fist against one of the chiseled wooden support beams. "This whole damn town needs to mind its own business."

"But they won't. Not according to you."

He exhaled, not really sure why he was so pissed. "No," he said curtly. "They won't." He turned toward the kitchen. "How do you feel about turkey and mayo sandwiches with bacon? My housekeeper comes in three time a week and keeps my fridge stocked."

"Lucky you." Abby seemed as glad as he was to move on to other topics. "And yeah, a sandwich sounds good," she said.

They ate their lunch in the small breakfast nook, enjoying the view from the large bay window. Carter was extremely aware of the woman at his side. Her scent. The sound of her voice. The enthusiastic way she devoured her meal.

She seemed to be a woman unafraid of indulging her appetites.

He shifted on his seat, realizing that he needed to focus his attention on something other than Abby's slender, toned arm, her hand almost touching his. "So, have you nailed down a theme for your documentary, an angle? You were hoping yesterday's meeting of the advisory board would help."

Abby stood and carried her plate to the sink. Then she refilled her lemonade and returned. "It was just business, unfortunately. I did get to meet the Edmond family and see them in action."

"And?" he prodded.

"They were nice. I like them. Tell me what you know about this Billy Holmes guy. I can't figure out how he fits into all of this."

"I've only met him a handful of times," Carter told her. "He moved to Royal a few years ago. Has plenty of money. People seem to like him."

"And he lives on the Edmond estate?"

"That's what I've heard," he replied.

"I wonder why?"

Carter shrugged. "No idea. You'd have to ask him."

"I will. He and I have an interview set up for tomorrow."

Carter tensed. He had nothing concrete against Holmes, but the other man struck Carter as a womanizer. "Are you going alone?"

"Yes. Is there a problem?"

"No. But women are vulnerable. Sometimes when you don't know a person, it's better to meet on neutral ground."

"I'm having lunch at *your* house at this very moment," Abby pointed out with a mischievous grin.

"Touché."

"It will be fine. I've taken self-defense classes since I was sixteen. I can handle myself."

Carter didn't argue, but he remained mildly concerned. Maybe he could wrangle an invitation to go along as Abby's sidekick. Even as the thought formed in his head, he dismissed it. Abby would never admit she needed a bodyguard.

He let the subject drop. "So, what now? My sister always leaves a few swimsuits here. She's close to your size. Do you fancy a dip in the pool?"

"It sounds lovely, but I really want to start interviewing you on camera."

"That again?" He groaned. "I was hoping you'd moved on from that idea. Ranchers are a dime a dozen around here. The job is nothing special."

"Maybe so. But you don't see the big picture, pardon the pun. What you do here at Sunset Acres echoes the frontier cowboys of the olden days. There's poetry in it. And tradition. This probably won't be the central focus of my film, but it could serve as a powerful backdrop. Please, Carter. It won't be so bad. I promise."

He had boxed himself into a corner. By inviting her to stay the entire day, he'd all but guaranteed that she would not give up. "Fine," he grumbled. "Let's get it over with, so we can move on to something that's actually fun. Where do we do this?"

"The great room, I think."

Instead of having a traditional living room or den, Carter had designed a large, open space that could be configured in a number of ways. Despite the ample square footage, he liked to think the cozy furniture and the artwork and large windows worked together to create a welcoming atmosphere.

Abby went out to her car and returned five minutes later with the camera, a tripod and a large tote bag. "It won't take me long to set up," she assured him, practically bouncing on her feet with enthusiasm.

"I could have helped carry something," he said. "I didn't know you had so much gear."

"Well," she replied, dumping everything on the sofa, "often it's just me and the video camera, but when I'm doing serious work, I want to have all my options available." She put her hands on her hips and surveyed the room. "I think that big leather chair will be good. Can we build a fire in the fireplace?"

His brows shot to his hairline, his reaction incredulous. "It's June. In Texas."

Abby faced him, smiling sweetly. "Please, Carter. It will make the scene perfect. We can run up the AC...all right?"

His muttered response was not entirely polite. "Sure. No problem."

As he pulled together a pile of kindling, small logs and fire starter, he was conscious of Abby flitting around the room. Once she had the camera attached to the tripod, she began unfolding filters and screens to get the light exactly as she wanted it.

It was obvious she was a pro at what she did. There was no fumbling, no second-guessing. She worked with purpose, her slender hands moving at lightning speed as she manipulated settings and angles and equipment.

At last, she was satisfied. "Will you take a seat in the chair, so I can take a look?"

He sat down, feeling stiff and ridiculous. "I don't want to be turned into some romanticized stereotype. That's insulting."

"Quit being grumpy. I would never do that to you."

She touched his leg, rearranged his arm, smoothed the collar of his blue button-down shirt. With every moment that passed, he grew more and more uneasy. And more horny.

At last, Abby was satisfied.

Almost.

She peered through the camera and wrinkled her nose. "Would you mind grabbing your Stetson? We can place it artfully on the arm of the chair or on the back near your shoulder."

He glowered, ready to end this before it started. "I don't wear a hat inside the house."

"I'm not asking you to wear it. I just want it for the ambience."

"No," he said firmly. *"This—"* he waved a hand at the ridiculous fire "—is plenty."

"Fine." Abby sulked, but it was a cute sulk.

His fingers dug into the supple leather of the chair arm. "Can we please get started? This fire is making me sweat…"

Abby could tell she was losing her reluctant subject. Carter was visibly fidgety. Was it weird that his irritability made him more attractive to her? She must be seriously messed up. Or maybe she was tired of slick guys who thought they could fast-talk a woman out of her clothes. Carter was rougher around the edges. More real.

She took a sip from her water bottle and ignored her jumpy pulse. "I'm going to ask you a series of questions. Talk as long as you want on each topic. None of this will be included word for word, but during the editing process, I'll pull out bits that complement the documentary as a whole. Does that make sense?"

"Sure."

She checked the camera once again to make sure Carter was still framed nicely, and then hit the record button. "Tell me more about how you came to run the ranch," she began, giving him an encouraging smile. She had learned that many people were not comfortable on camera, but if she got them talking, they loosened up. "You're a wealthy man. Couldn't you simply hire a manager?"

Carter grinned. "I'm pretty hands-on."

"And why is that?"

"I suppose it's what I learned growing up. My sister and I ran wild. Very few rules except for being home in time for dinner. My father worked long hours. He and my mother had a very traditional marriage. He'd come home tired and dirty at six, sometimes later."

"And why didn't *he* hire a manager?"

"It goes back a couple of generations. My dad's grandfather died in a riding accident when Dad was only seven years old. So my grandfather groomed *my* father from a very early age. Dad was used to working sunup to sundown. Those were the years when the ranch really boomed. The money was pouring in, and my father loved what he did. When my grandfather passed on, he left the entire ranch to my dad."

"That's a lot of responsibility," she remarked.

"Definitely. But my dad never questioned his role. Unfortunately, my grandfather wasn't a fan of organized education. Dad never had the opportunity to go to college. But Sunset Acres was his consolation prize."

"Some prize."

"Yes," he acknowledged. "My mom is from Royal, too. They were schoolmates. She fit right in with the ranching lifestyle, because she'd had a similar upbringing. After they got married, they spent the next two decades and more building the ranch into an even bigger operation."

"But you mentioned health issues?"

"He had a massive heart attack when I was a year older than you are. We almost lost him." A shadow crossed Carter's face. "The doctor said it was imperative that Dad cut back on both the physical labor and the stress, but my mother knew Dad too well. She realized he couldn't *play* at being a rancher. So she convinced him to retire and hand over the reins and the keys and the headaches to me. They moved to Florida and threw themselves into fishing and boating and everything else that comes with a carefree lifestyle."

"How did you cope in the beginning?" she asked.

"It was scary as hell, I'll admit it. I had a good roster of men working under me, but knowing that the decisions were all mine was terrifying."

"Did you resent having to shoulder so much responsibility?"

His jaw tightened, his gaze stormy. "Is this a documentary or a therapy session?"

"It was just a question, Carter. You don't have to answer."

"Yes," he said, the single word flat. "I did have some negative feelings at first. I was a young male adult, intent on pursuing my own agenda. I'd finished a degree in business management, but I wasn't particularly interested in settling down."

"I'm sorry. That must have been hard."

He shrugged. "I've made my father proud. That was reason enough to put aside my personal goals. And as the years have passed, I haven't regretted that decision. This ranch is thriving. It provides jobs."

"And the legacy is unbroken," she murmured softly.

"That, too."

"I assume you'll want to pass Sunset Acres on to your own children someday?"

"Next question."

Okay. Touchy issue. She checked the viewfinder again and shifted the tripod to get a new angle. "So tell me about Madeline, your ex-fiancée."

Carter rose to his feet, glowering. "Turn off the camera." The words were curt. "I don't see how that question pertains to your documentary. If you want to ask me for personal info, Abby, please have the guts to admit that you're interested."

His sharp criticism stung, particularly because it was on point.

Flushing uncomfortably, she shut off the recording. "Sorry," she muttered. "Lila told me the bare bones. I guess I wondered how your girlfriend fit into your legacy."

"She didn't. That's why we broke up."

"How did you meet?"

He prowled, his hands shoved into his pockets. "I was in Chicago with my whole family to attend the wedding of one of my cousins. Madeline was a guest. We hit it off. There was sexual chemistry. I think both of us were looking for something and had convinced ourselves we found it."

"That must have sucked when you realized otherwise."

"Yeah, it did," he admitted gruffly. "Partly because I disappointed my mom. She was over the moon that her boy was finally settling down."

"You were running a huge ranch. That seems pretty settled to me."

"It's different. I told you…she wants grandchildren."

"Ah, yes," Abby murmured.

"Are we done with this now?" He scowled at her.

"Sure. I'd like to ask you some more questions," she said. "Not personal. More about what your days are like. The actual running of a ranching operation."

He glanced at his watch. "I have a few things I need to take care of. Why don't you make yourself at home, and I'll be back in an hour or so…"

"Do you have internet?" she asked.

"Of course I do. What kind of question is that?"

"A valid one. We're in the middle of nowhere."

His expression cooled. "Only in your eyes."

When Carter strode out of the room, Abby realized that she had let her prejudices show. No matter how rural the landscape, Royal and the surrounding environs were home to an upscale roster of citizens. Money flowed like water apparently. These people were worldly and powerful.

She'd heard somewhere that Maverick County had more cows than people. That might not be true, but it was certainly possible. Still, the people themselves were the furthest thing from unsophisticated.

Even in the short time she had been in town, she had been forced to confront her expectations. It was becoming clear that her documentary would include entrepreneurs and politicians, society mavens and trendsetters. Blue bloods and old money. Not to mention the occasional upstart.

How was she going to capture all that and still frame Soiree on the Bay in an interesting way? The footage with Carter was a start, but she needed more.

With him gone for an hour, she was free to explore his house on her own, this time more carefully. She didn't open drawers or closets. *Duh.* She wasn't a weirdo. Instead, she walked room to room, soaking up the ambience.

She stopped at the threshold to Carter's bedroom. Even alone, she wouldn't trespass. It didn't take a psychologist to tell her that she was fascinated with his personal space. The man was intensely masculine, but he lived alone. What did he do with all that pent-up sexual energy? A little flutter low in her belly told her she wanted to find out.

It took considerable effort, but she made herself go back to the great room and deal with email. Her mother wanted to know how things were going, as did her dad. She gave them each a slightly different version of her time in Royal. After that, she watched the raw footage of Carter that she had just shot.

Holy heck, he looked good on camera. Broad shoulders, brooding good looks. And his occasional smiles were pure gold. Plus, when he talked, there was an authenticity about him, a sense of integrity. In the old days, people would have called him a straight shooter.

She ran out of things to do about the time she heard the back door slam. Carter appeared in the doorway, looking hot and windblown. "Any chance you'd be interested in that swim now?"

"Sure. As long as one of the suits fits. I'm not skinny-dipping with you, ranch man. At least not in broad daylight," she said, giving him a taunting grin.

The heat in his laser-blue gaze seared her. "Then I suppose I'll have to keep you here until dark. I grill a mean steak."

She swallowed, feeling out of her depth. She'd been teas-

ing about the skinny-dipping, but Carter appeared to take her
words at face value. "I don't want to drive back to Royal in the
dark," she said, entirely serious. "I don't know these roads. I
might hit an armadillo."

His face lit up with humor. "I'll take you home. One of my
guys can return your car in the morning."

Well, she had run out of excuses. What did she really want?
And was she brave enough to take the risk?

Seven

Carter wondered if Abby knew how expressive her face was. He swore he could read every emotion. She was flattered. And probably interested. But she was cautious, too. He could hardly blame her.

"I won't pressure you, Abby. All you have to do is say the word, and we can part as friends."

"Is there another category than friends?" Her smile was a little on the shaky side.

"You know there is. I want you. But only if you feel the same way. And beyond that, there's no timetable... Is there?"

She lifted one slender shoulder and let it fall. "Actually, yes. I won't be here more than a few weeks. That's not much time to decide whether I can trust you."

He cocked his head. "Trust me how? I'm no threat to you, Abs." He held up his hands, palms out. "There's no quid pro quo. I'll let you interview me some more even if you and I never knock boots. You have my word."

"*Knock boots?* Are you kidding me? Is that a Texas expression? Besides, it's easy for you to be magnanimous. You know how sexy you are. I'm not sure I can keep this professional. I'm not even sure I want to..."

"So, where does that leave us?" It wouldn't do for her to know how tightly wound he was as he awaited her answer.

She grimaced. "Let's swim," she said. "After that, I don't know..."

Fifteen minutes later, when Abby exited the house and joined him in the pool, he was damn glad the water concealed his instant boner. She was the most beautiful thing he had ever seen.

And he was wrong about her being skinny. Now that she was wearing a remarkably modest, but nevertheless provocative, black two-piece swimsuit, it was painfully clear that Abby had all the curves a man could want. Long, toned legs to wrap around his waist. A flat stomach with a diamond belly button piercing that caught the sun, and breasts that were just the right size to fill a man's hands.

His fists clenched at his sides. "I see the suit fit you."

"Quit staring," she said sharply.

With no apparent self-consciousness, she walked to the end of the diving board, bounced once and made a clean dive into the pool. When she surfaced, she lifted her face to the sun and slicked back her hair, laughing.

"The water is perfect," she said. "Do you swim every day?"

"Not always." And why was that? There was no good reason other than the fact that his waking hours were busy.

Abby began doing laps, her long legs and strong arms propelling her through the water easily. Carter followed suit, careful to keep to his side of the pool. They were completely alone. None of his staff would dare seek him out without an okay ahead of time. And since he had his phone on silent, this little bubble of intimacy was intact.

At last, Abby tired. She stayed in the deep end, treading water. Finally, she clung to the metal ladder, one arm curled around the bottom step. "This is nice."

An invisible cord drew him across the pool to where she

lazily kicked her legs. He stopped a few feet away, his heart pounding. Water clung to her beautiful skin in droplets that refracted the sunlight. Her eyelashes were spiky. Brown eyes stared at him as if assessing his intent.

"I'm gonna kiss you, Abs," he said hoarsely. "Unless you object."

Her eyes widened. But she didn't speak. She didn't move.

He was tall enough to touch bottom. Moving closer still, he brushed her arm. "Hang on, Abby."

Without hesitation, she released the ladder and curled her arms around his neck. Now their bodies were pressed together so closely he could feel the rapid rise and fall of her chest. All the blood left his head, rushing south.

Maybe he had heat stroke. His brain felt muzzy, and his hands tingled. "Abby…" With one arm around her back and the other hand gripping the ladder, he stared into her eyes. Deep in the midst of those chocolate irises he found tiny flecks of gold.

"Car…ter…" She caressed his name, infusing it with sensuality. Her lips curled in a smile. "This feels naughty."

"Hell, yeah…" He tried to laugh, but he didn't have enough oxygen.

She nipped his bottom lip with a tiny, stinging bite, then soothed the pain with her tongue. "You taste like chlorine," she whispered.

He yanked her closer and slammed his mouth down on hers. No smooth moves, no practiced technique. Only sheer desperation.

She met him kiss for kiss, not submitting, but battling. He wondered in some far distant corner of his brain if the heat they were conjuring would turn the pool water to steam.

If two people could devour each other, this was how it would happen. She was strong and feminine, her skin and muscles soft and smooth everywhere he was hard. Lust roared through his veins. He wanted her. But his conscience said, *too soon…*

After what seemed like an eternity, he made himself pull

back. Abby's lips were swollen and puffy from his kisses. Strands of her wet hair that had dried in the sun danced around her face.

He stared at her. "We should probably find some shade," he said. "How about a lounge chair with an umbrella and a cold drink?"

Abby's expression was dazed. "Sure. Water is fine for me. But you go up the ladder first. I don't want you staring at my ass."

"Too late."

That finally made her smile.

He did as she asked, lifting himself out of the pool and deliberately shaking water at her. When Abby screeched, he chuckled. The small fridge in the pool house held chilled water bottles. He grabbed a couple of those along with some dry towels that he spread on the two chaises. Abby hovered nearby, her arms wrapped around her waist. Long, beautiful hair cascaded down her back.

"Ladies first," he said.

Abby widened the gap between the two chairs by about a foot, and then settled onto the lounger gracefully, raising her arms over her head and bending one knee.

Carter took the remaining seat and lay back with a sigh. Despite his arousal, the sensation of hot sun on his wet skin was a familiar, soothing taste of summer. Behind his sunglasses, he managed to sneak a sideways glance.

Was she asleep? Awake? He couldn't decide but chose to assume the latter. "You want to tell me more about yesterday's advisory board meeting?"

She turned her face in his direction, a half smile lifting the corners of her mouth. "Business talk?"

"It's either that or carry you to my bedroom. Seemed premature."

He witnessed her startled breath, a gasp really, quickly disguised. "I think I covered everything."

"Then let's talk about *you*."

She slung an arm over her eyes, shutting him out. But he wasn't so easily dissuaded. "Seriously, Abs, you've grilled me nonstop. And if that weren't enough, Lila blabbed about my personal life. I think it's only fair that I get to delve into your psyche."

Moving her arm, she scowled at him. "Couldn't we just have sex?"

He laughed. "You don't like being interviewed any more than I do."

"Why do you think I chose to be on this side of the camera?"

"You're only twenty-four," Carter reminded her. "How bad could your secrets be?"

"Who said I have secrets?"

He exhaled, emptying his lungs so he could inhale the scent of her again. "Everybody has secrets, Abby. But you can start with your childhood. What were you like in school?"

Her profile made him ache. Vulnerability etched her features. "I was lonely mostly. That whole mean girl stereotype is based on reality. I was a biracial kid in a sea of white faces. I was an oddity. So that put me on the outside looking in. I didn't understand why until I was seven or eight. But the first day someone said a nasty thing about my father, I was done trying to fit in. My mother went to see the principal over and over, begging for adult intervention. That only made things worse."

His stomach twisted. "I'm sorry, Abby."

"It got better in high school. There was a more diverse population. Supersmart kids whose parents had immigrated to New York as children, grown up there. I gradually built a circle of intimates, classmates with whom I could be myself." She released a breath. "In fact, my very best friend is a Pakistani woman who's now a doctor at Lenox Hill Hospital in New York. She's doing a residency in geriatric medicine. We've brainstormed about me maybe doing a documentary about the social and emotional costs of increased life span."

"Wow." Carter stared at her, for the first time understanding how complex she was, how passionate and talented. "I'm impressed, Abby. You've made an amazing life for yourself."

"It suits me. I love to travel, and I don't mind traveling alone. My parents have always given me a lot of freedom. I tried never to abuse their trust."

Silence fell between them, but it wasn't awkward. They were sizing each other up, wondering about the differences in their lives and whether there was even the tiniest bit of overlap.

He honestly didn't know. A decade separated them, though that age gap was hardly a novelty. Abby was city mouse; he was country mouse. She was happiest crisscrossing the country, whereas he had deep roots in this Texas soil.

"Do you still want to film me talking about the ranch?" he asked gruffly.

Her eyes flew open, and she turned on her side. "You don't mind?"

He tried not to notice the way her breasts nearly spilled out of her swimsuit top in that position. "It wouldn't be my first choice, but if it will help you with your project, I'll do it."

Her smile blinded him. "Thank you, Carter. That's awesome." She jumped up. "I'll go change, and we'll get started."

After she left, he stared glumly at the water. Was he stupid? If he'd kept his mouth shut, Abby would still be beside him, sunbathing like a beautiful goddess, at arm's length.

Maybe his subconscious was trying to point out how self-destructive it would be to initiate a physical relationship under these circumstances. Even so, his libido demanded equal time. It was hours yet until sundown. Anything could happen.

Abby was thrilled and surprised that Carter had agreed to more on-camera time. She changed back into her clothes, twisted her damp hair into a loose knot on the back of her head and rushed to the great room to prepare for this next session. The fire, of course, had long since burned out.

Since she didn't have the heart to ask Carter to build another, she shifted his chair in front of some beautiful cherry bookcases. And she tossed a Native American blanket over the back corner of the chair.

By the time she had the scene prepared to her liking, Carter was back.

He had showered. Her twitching nose told her that. The scent of a very expensive aftershave emanated from him. Why would a man shave midafternoon? To be ready for a rendezvous later in the evening?

Her heart skipped a beat, but she focused on her work. "I'm all set," she said. "Why don't you take your seat, and we'll get started."

Carter was dressed a little less casually this time. His dark dress pants and gray knit polo shirt showcased his impressive physique. It was clear that the owner of Sunset Acres was a hands-on boss, one who spent plenty of time doing heavy chores and building up the strength to bench-press a car. Or woo a woman.

When she noticed he had chosen to go without shoes, she melted a little. Something about those large, tanned feet struck her as both masculine and boyish.

He smiled at her as he sprawled in the chair and ran his hands across his head. "I threw some potatoes in the oven. If we can wrap this up in forty-five minutes, I'll get the steaks on the grill. There's stuff in the fridge to make a salad, if you don't mind doing that."

"I'd be happy to." She peered through the camera and frowned. "I like you relaxed, but you've messed up your hair." Without overthinking it, she went to him and used her fingers to comb the thick, damp strands until she was happy with how he looked.

Carter took her arm and kissed the inside of her wrist. "I like it when you groom me, Abs."

She pursed her lips, refusing to let him see that one achingly tender kiss had her undone. "You mean like a gorilla mom with her baby?"

His jaw jutted. "I'm a full-grown man, Abby. You can count on that."

"Duly noted." She took her spot behind the camera. "Start with staff," she said calmly. "How many full-time employees do you have? What do they do? And what about seasonal and part-time?"

The camera started rolling, and Carter began talking. Despite Abby's total unfamiliarity with the topic, he managed to make it interesting. She quizzed him on herd sizes and breeds and what constituted a "good" year. She asked about weather disasters like tornadoes and hailstorms and fires, and then lesser crises like drought and floods.

The more Carter talked, the more Abby realized how deeply devoted he was to his heritage. He had to be. No one else loved it like he did.

Lastly, she touched on his family.

"They're actually coming for a visit this weekend," Carter said. "My parents, my sister and brother-in-law, and my niece, Beebee."

"Beebee?"

"They named her Beatrice, but that might stick when she's ten or eleven. At eight months, Beebee works."

Abby turned off the camera and stretched. "I have one last question, but I don't want it on camera."

He raised an eyebrow. "Oh? Should I be worried?"

"It's not about you. It's about the festival."

"Sounds serious from the tone of your voice."

Abby curled up on one end of the sofa and picked at a loose thread on the knee of her jeans. "I stumbled on something yesterday…something that might make a huge jumping-off point for my documentary. But I wanted to get your opinion."

"Go on…"

"When I was in the diner eating lunch, I overheard a conversation in the booth behind me. I wasn't eavesdropping on purpose, but it was hard not to listen. One woman was saying she heard someone stole a ton of money from the Soiree on the Bay checking account. Could that possibly be true? Nothing was mentioned in the meeting yesterday."

Carter scowled. "That's a dead end, Abby. We've talked about this. Royal thrives on innuendo and gossip. It grows as fast as kudzu. But ninety percent of the time, there's nothing to it. People don't like outsiders poking their noses in our business. You need to drop it. Find another angle. Otherwise, you'll end up alienating the very people who could help you with your project."

Abby was stunned by his vehemence. And hurt. The careless way he referred to her as an *outsider*, gave his warning a personal slant. Was that what he thought of her?

When Carter left to go put the steaks on the grill, she carried all her gear to the car and then wandered into the kitchen and began fixing a salad. As promised, she had everything at hand in the oversize, cutting-edge refrigerator. Finding a large bowl and a small pitcher for the dressing gave her an excuse to snoop through his cabinets.

As she worked, her pride still stung from his harsh rebuke. And her heart. Soiree on the Bay wouldn't be the first festival to be rocked by graft and greed. Local sponsors, both individual and corporate, had fronted an enormous amount of money to move the event forward.

Carter might not like it. In fact, she wouldn't bring it up again. But on her own, she was determined to explore this lead, tenuous though it was. Almost all gossip contained a grain of truth, no matter how tiny. She would follow this road until it petered out—or gave her the impetus she needed to put her documentary on a strong footing.

Abby didn't eat much red meat as a rule, but the steaks were extraordinary. She supposed a man who owned an enormous ranch learned early how to prepare beef. It was tender and subtly flavored. With the loaded baked potatoes and salad, it was the perfect meal.

Though Abby offered to help with cleanup, he refused. "There's not that much. And my housekeeper comes at ten in the morning."

"In that case, I should be getting back to town," she said.

Carter stilled, his back to her as he put things in the fridge. He shot her a look over his shoulder. "Or you could stay." The gleam in his beautiful blue eyes was temptation, pure and simple.

Here it was. Decision time. It would be much easier to get caught up in the moment, but Carter wasn't taking that tack. He was asking flat out. Offering her a clear choice. Be intimate with him, or choose to walk away.

He had given her everything she could ask for in terms of the interview. It was going to make incredibly good footage. But she felt no compunction to stay based on that. Whatever happened between the two of them was not going to be business.

The positives were clear. He was an honorable man, a conscientious son. A reputable landowner. Beyond that, he was sexy as hell. She knew without hesitation that he would be good to a woman in bed. Or *bad*, if she desired.

Up until this visit to Royal, Texas, she had been cautious in her love life. Her few relationships had been based on shared interests and a mutual desire for sexual satisfaction. But in every case, she had felt relief when the weeks or months were over, and she was *single* again. She'd told herself that she wasn't good at giving and receiving intimacy. Mostly, because she was too self-sufficient, too private.

Yet now, here was Carter. The man who burned away every last one of her reservations with a single look. Her body recognized him as a potential lover. But there was nothing simple about it. In fact, the urgency she felt was both astonishing and intimidating.

"Is that a good idea?" she asked, stalling for time to answer her own doubts.

"I could be convinced to come to the hotel with you." He leaned his hips against the counter and folded his arms across his chest. His face was hard to read.

She forced a laugh. "After you lectured me about Royal's gossipy grapevine? No, thanks. I don't want the whole town knowing what we do."

His expression softened. "It's your call, Abs. I won't be accused of pressuring you."

"I know that, dammit." She put her hands to her hot cheeks, mortified. "I'm sorry." Perhaps this was where his extra decade gave him the edge. He'd probably lived this scene half a dozen more times than she had. She took a deep breath to steady her nerves. "I liked riding with you this morning. Could we take Foxtrot out for an evening cruise? I want to chase the sunset, hard and fast."

A flush rode high on his cheekbones. His eyes darkened. "We can do that. Meet me in the stable in fifteen minutes."

And then he was gone. Abby sought out the guest bathroom again and tidied her hair, securing it more tightly in its knot. As she stared at herself in the mirror, she wondered what Carter saw when he looked at her. Some men had called her exotic. It was a description she didn't really enjoy.

She didn't want to be different, at least not in that way. Though she had no hard data to back it up, her gut feeling was that Carter saw her as a woman first. A sexual being. A human with hopes and dreams.

She was okay with that. Because she recognized those same aspects in him. And something about him drew her like no one she had ever met.

It struck her suddenly, that not once had she entertained the idea of taking her camera on this outing. The professional Abby was done for the day. Tonight was all about *pleasure*.

As she walked through the house and out to the barn, she

listed all the reasons not to stay with Carter. She had no clothes, no suitcase, nothing but a tube of ChapStick in her purse. Would she wake up in the morning feeling awkward and embarrassed? The answer was almost surely yes.

But even as she tried to talk herself out of tumbling into his bed, she knew the decision had been made.

The barn smelled amazing. As a city girl, she saw it as an anomaly, but one she liked. The atmosphere was earthy and real. When she saw the man waiting for her, her heart stumbled. He was wearing the Stetson this time. And riding boots.

The horse whinnied softly when Abby approached.

Carter smiled at her, an uncomplicated, straightforward look that encompassed welcome and desire and forbidden promises.

"I'm putting you in front his time," he said.

Unlike before, there were no instructions. He simply put his hands on her waist and hefted her up into the saddle. His easy strength gave her a little thrill.

Moments later, he settled in behind her, his arms coming around her to hold the reins. His lips brushed the back of her neck. "You ready?"

It was a question with layers of meaning. "Yes," she answered, her response firm and unequivocal. "I can't wait."

Eight

Carter knew the exact moment Abby unwound. Like a rag doll, all the stiffness left her body, and her spine relaxed against his chest. He held the reins with one hand, so he could curl his arm around her waist.

The large saddle accommodated both of them comfortably. Foxtrot was a strong stallion, easily capable of bearing their weight and more. As the horse ambled away from the house toward the road, Carter told himself he had to concentrate. He had precious cargo. But all he wanted to do was bury his face in Abby's hair and hope she had stayed for more than an evening excursion on the ranch.

The sunset was particularly beautiful. Just enough clouds to make striking patterns of orange and pink and gold, much like the night he and Abby had first met. Already, that moment seemed like eons ago. But it wasn't, and he'd do well to remember that.

He nuzzled her ear. "You still want speed?"

She nodded. "Definitely."

He gave Foxtrot a nudge with his knees and felt the jolt of

adrenaline as the powerful animal reached his stride. They were streaking down the road that bisected the ranch at a dizzying speed. It was a safe enough course.

Abby's delighted squeal made Carter smile. He pushed the horse faster and harder. Foxtrot loved the free rein. Even though it had been a hot day, at this hour and this speed, the wind felt chilly. He held Abby close, his posture protective.

Carter knew she was strong and independent, but she was young and new to Texas. He wouldn't let any*thing* or any*one* harm her, not even himself.

At last, they reached the far boundary of his acreage and turned around to head for home. Now Foxtrot's gallop was more sedate. Eventually, Carter slowed him further still. No point in ending the night too soon.

"Are you cold?" he asked.

"A little. But it's okay. I wouldn't have missed this."

"What would you be doing back in New York about now?"

He felt her shrug. "Maybe seeing a play. I adore Broadway. Always have. I actually thought about pursuing acting at one point."

"You'd have been good at it, I think. You have a very expressive face. And a beautiful voice."

She turned her head and rested her cheek over his heart for a moment. "Thank you, Carter. That's a sweet thing to say."

"But true."

He held her close, steering the horse in the gathering gloom.

As they neared the house, Abby whispered something he didn't quite catch.

"What was that, Abs?"

Still facing straight ahead, she reached behind her and cupped his cheek with a slender, long-fingered hand. "I don't have any clean clothes with me. Or anything for that matter."

The insinuation went straight to his head and his groin. "I can hook you up," he said gruffly. "The guest bathroom has everything you'll need. And we can throw your clothes in the washer. I'll give you one of my shirts in the meantime."

She nodded. "Then I'd like to stay the night."

Things got fuzzy for Carter after that. He had wanted her for hours. The day had been one long and wonderful—but frustrating—dance of foreplay.

Now Abby was in his arms and committed to his bed. He'd won the lottery, though he would have sworn he wasn't a gambling man.

At the stable, he dismounted and helped her down. "I have to deal with the horse. If you'll wait for me, we can take a shower together."

In the illumination from the light inside the barn, her expression was bashful. "I think this first time I'd feel more comfortable getting ready on my own. Okay?"

He kissed her forehead. "Whatever you want." He was still fixated on that one important phrase *this first time*. How many would there be? Abby had a job to do in Royal. She wouldn't be at his beck and call. And his days were plenty busy, too.

It was pointless to overanalyze things. He removed Foxtrot's saddle and rubbed him down before checking his food and water. Then he lowered the lights and closed up the barn. As he walked back to the house, he felt jittery. A shot of whiskey might be nice. But even that couldn't dull the hunger he felt.

When he reached his suite, the walk-in closet door stood open. Abby had clearly helped herself to an item of his clothing. That image kept him hard all during his shower. And when he returned to the bedroom and found her sitting cross-legged in the center of his bed, his erection grew.

She had picked out a plain white cotton button-down and had rolled the long sleeves to her elbows. Her dark, wavy hair fell around her shoulders. The shirttails covered her modestly.

But not for long…

Carter wore only a damp towel tucked around his hips. He

had a hard time catching his breath. "Did you find everything you need?"

She tilted her head to one side and gave him a mischievous grin. "Not yet."

That was the thing that kept tripping him up. Abby Carmichael looked young and innocent, but she wasn't. She was an adult, with a woman's wants and needs. Luckily for him, she had found her way into his bed.

When he tossed the towel on a nearby chair, Abby lost her smile. Her gaze settled on his sex. He saw the muscles in her throat move when she swallowed.

"Scoot over," he said, pulling the covers back and joining her. He sprawled on his side, propping his head on his hand. "You look beautiful, Ms. Carmichael. And you smell delicious."

Abby didn't move. He thought she might be holding her breath. Finally, she exhaled a little puff of air. "Your guest bathroom is stocked with lovely toiletries."

"I'm glad you approve." He ran his thumb across her exposed knee. "Are you scared of me, Abby?"

She wrinkled her nose. "No. My birth control pills are at the hotel. You'll have to wear a condom."

"That's not a problem." He slid his hand from her knee to her thigh, under the shirt. "Talk to me, Abs."

Her hands were clasped in her lap. She looked either nervous or uncertain, or both. "I haven't slept with a lot of men," she admitted. "And you're not like any of them."

"Meaning what?"

"What if this doesn't work? I've known you four days. That's not me, Carter. I'm not an impulsive kind of woman. But this chemistry between us…it's…"

"Undeniable? Explosive? Breath-stealing?"

She nodded. "All those things."

He sat up and leaned against the headboard, pulling her into a loose embrace, combing his fingers through her hair. "We'll take it slow. You tell me if I do something you don't like."

She pulled back and stared at him with those deep brown eyes framed in thick lashes. "I don't think that's going to be a problem."

With unsteady hands, he unbuttoned the shirt Abby wore, *his* shirt, gradually revealing pale brown skin that was soft and smooth and begging for his kisses. Her breasts were high and full, the tips a lighter shade than her eyes.

When he managed the final button, he slid the garment off her slender body and cast it aside. Abby watched him with a rapt expression that stoked the flame burning inside him. When he palmed her breast, she gasped.

He thumbed the nipple, watching in fascination as it furled tightly. When he leaned down to take that bud into his mouth, Abby's choked moan ignited him. He dragged her onto the mattress and lifted himself over her, giving the other breast equal attention.

Her hands fisted in his hair painfully. He suspected they were both too primed to make this last as long as he wanted, but he was going to try.

She moved restlessly as he kissed her forehead, her eyelids, her nose and finally, her soft lips. The taste of her was like a drug, clouding his brain. "Abby," he groaned.

They kissed wildly, like they had in the pool. Only now, they were in a big soft bed made for a man and a woman. And pleasure. *Endless* pleasure.

He lost himself in the kissing, his hands equally occupied learning the hills and valleys of her lithe, long-limbed body. She was soft and strong, a seductive combo.

In some dim, conscious corner of his brain, he remembered protection. Rolling away from her, he snatched open a drawer and found what he wanted. After ripping open the package, he sheathed himself, knowing he couldn't hold out very long this first time.

When he delicately stroked Abby's center, she was warm and wet and ready for him. He entered her with two fingers, feeling her body tighten against his intrusion. "I need you, Abs. I'll make it up to you, I swear."

Even then, he waited, stroking that tiny bundle of nerves that controlled her pleasure until she arched off the bed and cried out.

He entered her then with one forceful push, feeling her inner muscles contract around him, her body still in the throes of sweet release. The sensation was indescribable. He was consumed with lust and racked with the need to give her tenderness and passion in equal measure.

As he moved in her slowly, Abby squirmed beneath him, locking her legs around his waist and angling her lower body so they fit together perfectly. She was dreamy-eyed, flushed, her skin damp and hot.

"Don't hold back, Carter. I want it all."

Her words were a demand, one he was happy to meet. His world narrowed to her face. Each time he pumped his hips, he saw her react. The flutter of long-lashed eyelids, the small gasps of breath, the way her chin lifted toward the ceiling and her lips parted as she reached for a second climax.

She found it as he found his. He came for eons, it seemed, shuddering against her and whispering her name. When it was over, he slumped on top of her, barely managing to brace most of his weight on his elbows.

He might have dozed.

When reality finally intruded, it was because Abby squirmed out from under him to go to the bathroom. Carter rolled to his back and slung one arm over his face. He felt blissfully sated, but oddly unsettled.

Some things were too good to be true, and this might be one of them. Madeline hadn't been the woman for him. He could see that now with the benefit of hindsight. Losing her had wounded his pride and his dignity. The broken relationship left him lonely and afraid to trust.

Abby wasn't Madeline. Carter knew that. But she was no

more likely to hang around, so he needed to keep his head out of his ass and be smart about this.

While his lover was still occupied, he crawled out of bed and retrieved her clothes from the guest bathroom. As he turned on the washing machine and added soap, he stared at the bra and panties in his hands. They looked alien.

This was a male household.

He'd had a handful of one-night stands since his aborted engagement. Mostly out of town. Almost exclusively with sophisticated women who took what they wanted and asked for nothing in return.

Abby was different. Honestly, he couldn't say exactly how or why, but he felt it in his gut. The fact that confusion swirled in his brain warned him to take a step back.

He tossed the few items of laundry into the water and closed the lid. She was spending the night. There was nothing he could do about that. So, he might as well enjoy himself.

Abby was tucked up in his bed, snug beneath the covers when he returned to his room. The sight of her constricted his chest.

She raised up on her elbow. "Where did you go?"

"I promised to wash your clothes, remember?"

"Oh. Right. I was thinking about leaving in a little bit, but I guess I won't."

He frowned. "Leaving? Why?"

Abby shoved the hair from her face, some of it still damp. Her gaze was guarded. "You'll need to be up early in the morning. And I've already taken a lot of your time this week. I don't want to overstay my welcome."

Was there a note of hurt in that explanation? Had she picked up on his unease? Guilt swamped him. He climbed back into bed, pulling her close. "I'll let you know if you're in the way, Abs. For now, we're right where we should be."

They slept for an hour, or maybe two. Then he made love to her again. This time was less frantic, but no less stunning. He wasn't a teenager anymore. Sex was an important part of life, but it hadn't been the driving force in the last few years.

Now he craved her with a fiery intensity that took his breath away. What was he going to do about that?

When he roused the next time, he stumbled down the hall to put her clothes in the dryer. He contemplated *forgetting*, so she would have to stay longer. But he knew she had an interview lined up with Billy Holmes, and Carter couldn't be the one to sabotage her project, even if he wasn't keen on knowing Abby would be alone with Holmes.

Sometime before dawn, he awakened to the pleasant sensation of female fingers wrapped around his erection.

Abby nuzzled her face in the crook of his neck. "It will be morning soon. Are you up for one more round before I go?"

He cleared his throat, feeling like a sailor lost at sea. The only thing he could hang on to was Abby. "I think you know the answer to that."

He took care of protection once again, and Abby climbed on top with no apparent self-consciousness. Cupping her firm, rounded ass in his hands, he thrust into her warmth, feeling his certainty slip away.

Were there some things a man could make exceptions for? Some prizes worth any price? His life was all mapped out. It was a *good* life. But there was no room for self-indulgence. Abby was cotton candy at the fair, a brilliant display of fireworks on a hot summer night. But she wasn't the mundane day-to-day of responsibility.

When she leaned down to steal a kiss—her hair cocooning them in intimacy—he quickly lost the desire for self-reflection. Her breasts danced in front of him, ripe for the tasting. He took every advantage.

Her body was a mystery and a wonder of divine engineering. This was the third time he'd taken her tonight. He should have been sated and tired. Instead, he felt invincible.

When she cried out and came, he rolled her to her back and

pounded his way to the finish line, shocked even now at the effect she had on him. Was it some kind of sorcery? Or was he simply sex deprived?

Maybe there was yet another explanation he didn't want to acknowledge.

He had slept only in snatches the entire night. This time, he fell hard and deep into unconsciousness. When his alarm went off at seven, one side of the bed was cool and empty, and his lover was gone.

Abby yawned her way through a hotel breakfast in the dining room. The eggs and bacon, fresh fruit and croissants were delightful, but she didn't enjoy the meal as much as she should have. She felt disheveled and gloomy, and she didn't have the luxury of going to her room and crashing.

Billy Holmes was expecting her at eleven.

She refused to think about Carter at all. He confused her. That was the last thing she needed right now. Her documentary was still an unfocused blob. She *had* to find a sound angle if she hoped to make any progress at all.

By the time she had showered and changed into a melon-colored pantsuit with a jaunty aqua and coral scarf around her throat, she felt a renewed determination. The fashionable clothes were intentional. This documentary was her big shot. She had someone at a major studio willing to take a chance on her. The film she produced had to be rock-solid. And it didn't hurt to dress for success.

Driving out to the Edmonds' property steadied her. As she passed an ornate sign that read Elegance Ranch, she wrinkled her nose. The name was pretentious, at least to her. Billy had texted her a set of directions. That was a good thing, because the sprawling private dynasty included a pool and stables and several guesthouses in addition to the massive, luxurious main house.

She recalled from the meeting at the Texas Cattleman's Club

that Rusty Edmond, the oft-married but now-single patriarch, lived there along with his son, Ross, daughter, Gina, and stepson, Asher. And for a reason yet to be discovered, Billy Holmes lived in one of the guest cottages.

The property was completely private, surrounded by miles of ranch land. Abby stopped several times to get out and photograph interesting spots. Once she was cleared at the gatehouse, there were no other impediments. She had allowed herself plenty of extra time. Being prompt was one of her personal mantras.

By the time she located Billy's guesthouse, her nerves returned. His home was beautiful, lushly landscaped and neither huge nor tiny. How had he ended up here? And why had the family accepted him as one of their own?

When Abby rang the doorbell, a uniformed older woman with gray hair answered. "You must be Ms. Carmichael," she said. "Please come in. Mr. Holmes is expecting you."

Abby followed the woman through the house to a pleasant sunroom overlooking a grassy, well-manicured lawn.

Billy Holmes stood. "Abby. Right on time. So glad you could join me. Would you like a drink?"

"Water for me, please."

He offered her a comfortable seat and took an adjoining chair. "How are you liking Royal, so far?"

"I'm getting my bearings," she said diplomatically. "The people are friendly. And I enjoyed the advisory council meeting." She set her glass of water aside. "Would you mind if I go ahead and get set up to film our conversation? I don't want to miss anything. Unless the camera makes you uncomfortable."

"The camera doesn't bother me at all," he said, giving her a smile that was almost too charming.

Fortunately for Abby, Holmes's phone dinged. He stood and dealt with the text, leaving her a few moments to frame a backdrop and get her equipment where she wanted it. By the time she was ready, Billy returned.

She motioned to where she had situated a chair adjacent to a large-paned window. "May we get started?"

"Of course." He put his phone in the breast pocket of his jacket and unbuttoned the coat before sitting down. With the sun gilding his dark hair and his deliberately scruffy five-o'clock shadow, Billy Holmes looked every inch the bad boy.

Abby sighted her subject through the viewfinder one last time and then stepped back. "How long have you lived in Royal, Mr. Holmes?"

"Call me Billy, please. I guess it's been two and a half years now. Time flies."

"And what is your connection to the Edmond family?" she asked.

"Ross and I were college buddies. He always talked about Royal and how much he loved it. When I decided to relocate and get settled for good, I thought about Maverick County as an option. Ross offered me one of the guesthouses, and here I am."

"He sounds like a very good friend," Abby remarked.

"Indeed."

"Who came up with the festival idea originally? Was it you?"

His smile was modest. "Hard to say. Ross and Gina and Asher and I were talking one day about ways to put Royal on the map. It was a brainstorming session, a group project."

"What do you hope to achieve? The actual festival site is a long way from here."

He shrugged. "Distance is nothing in Texas. Royal will be the jumping-off point for the festival. Our main focus is luxury, whether it's food or wine or music or art. We're marketing to a particular clientele. No empty beer bottles and smelly port-a-johns. Beyond that, we want to bring people together, and also raise significant money for charity." He cleared his throat. "To that end, we're sparing no expense. We want Soiree on the Bay to be talked about for years to come."

Abby kept asking him questions for another half hour and then began winding down the narrative. Billy Holmes was good on camera, charismatic, easy to listen to… This footage would be excellent.

Before she wrapped up, she decided to take a risk. "I heard a rumor in town," she murmured, keeping her tone light. "Something about money missing from the festival account. Could you comment on that?"

Billy's expression changed from affable to calculating. He seemed tense. "Turn off the camera."

"Of course."

After she did as he demanded, Billy stood and paced, his face flushed. "Off the record? Yes, that's true. Ross discovered the discrepancy. But it's a family matter. We're handling it."

Yet Billy Holmes *wasn't* family. "I see." She didn't see at all, but she was stalling. "Is the festival in danger?"

"Of course not," he snapped. "We're full steam ahead. It's going to be epic."

Abby realized she wasn't going to get anything further out of Billy Holmes. If he had slipped before, now he was covering his tracks.

In the end, she was forced to put her equipment away and sit through a long and one-sided lunch conversation. Holmes liked talking about himself. That much was clear.

But he was being closemouthed on the topic that interested her most.

Only the housekeeper's culinary skills made the meal memorable. The quiche lorraine was amazing, as was the caprese salad.

Eventually, Abby decided she had stayed long enough not to seem rude if she bolted. "I should get back to town," she said. "Thanks so much for lunch and the interview."

Holmes stood when she did. "My pleasure." His expression was guarded now, as if he was aware he had overstepped some boundary and now regretted his candor.

He walked her to the front door and out to her car, helping carry one of her bags. Abby had left her sunglasses in the glove box. She shielded her eyes with her hand. "One other thing. I'd love to speak with a few of the charities who will benefit from the Soiree. Could you make that happen?" She was deliberately playing to his vanity.

"Of course." He preened. "You should start with Valencia Donovan at Donovan Horse Rescue. You'll like her. She has an interesting story to tell."

"Perfect," Abby said. "You'll give her my number? See if she's willing to be interviewed? I don't want to assume…"

"I'll deal with it this afternoon. If you're lucky, she might be able to see you tomorrow."

Nine

Abby was thrilled that the wheels were beginning to turn more quickly with regard to her documentary, but even so, she couldn't stop thinking about Carter. She'd written him a polite but brief note that morning, explaining that she had a busy day ahead.

What did he think when he found her gone? Was he disappointed?

Maybe he was glad. Some men didn't like complications.

When she got back to the hotel, she forced herself to concentrate on work. Between the brief footage she had shot during the advisory board meeting and the personal interviews with Carter Crane and Billy Holmes, she already had a great start. Now came the hard part of scrolling through frames and editing the sequences she knew would serve her purpose.

Billy Holmes was as good as his word, apparently. Abby got a text midafternoon from Valencia Donovan inviting her to meet Valencia and see her charity at ten tomorrow morning. That should work. After responding in the affirmative, Abby was soon deep into her storyboard. What was the hook going to be? More and more, she was convinced it was the money trail.

When her stomach growled, she was surprised to realize it was after seven. Sitting in the restaurant didn't appeal, so she ordered room service. That way she could continue working while she ate.

Two hours later, she stood and stretched. She'd made good progress. Now she could goof off and watch TV or add some new shots to her Instagram account. As a budding filmmaker, social media was essential.

She was just about to get in the shower when her phone dinged. It was Carter. Her pulse skittered. What did he want? She snatched up her cell and read the text.

Abby—Hope you had a good day. How about coming out to the ranch for dinner tomorrow night? I know my family would love to meet you. Let me know...

In the bathroom mirror, her expression was startled. Meet his *family*? Why? She scowled at her reflection, parsing his words for hidden meanings. Maybe the invitation was no more or less than it seemed. After all, not all families got along perfectly. Maybe Carter thought an outsider would cushion any squabbles.

She didn't answer right away. During her shower, she tried not to think about Carter's offer to *shower* together at his house. She had turned him down. Maybe now she regretted that. Would he have made love to her then? And again in the bed?

Thinking about sex with Carter made her hot and bothered. By the time she dried off and put on a clean T-shirt and sleep pants, she was no closer to knowing what to do.

She liked Carter Crane. A lot. He was funny and smart, and so sexy she had let him coax her into bed with embarrassing ease.

That was what worried her. If she had so little self-control around the man, wouldn't it be safer to keep her distance? This town wasn't for her. Neither was this lifestyle. She liked being free and able to go wherever the wind took her.

If she embarked on a relationship with one of Royal's premier bachelors, wasn't it possible she could end up getting hurt?

In the end, she chickened out. Her text was a monument to indecision.

Carter—I'm not sure about my schedule tomorrow. I should be able to let you know by noon. Okay???

She hit Send and tucked her phone under a pillow, too anxious to wait for his answer. Although she was finished with work for the evening, she couldn't resist taking another look at the interview with Carter. She uploaded some of the raw footage to her laptop and unmuted the sound.

Like most people, she didn't enjoy hearing her own voice. But Carter's made up for it. The timbre of his speech was intensely masculine. He looked straight at the lens, unflinching. Though he claimed to have no experience being on camera, he came across as natural and appealing. Even someone with no interest in cattle and horses would find his enthusiasm compelling.

It didn't hurt that his rugged good looks played well.

Finally, she shut off the electronics and did a few half-hearted yoga stretches. Her usual routine had been shot to heck. She was supposed to be finding a revelation or two. About Soiree on the Bay. Or ranchers in general. Or the Texas Cattleman's Club way of life.

Instead, Texas was showing her a few truths about herself.

The next morning, she hopped out of bed, refusing to think about hot, sexy ranchers and wild, incredible sex. She grabbed a croissant and coffee downstairs before bolting to her rental car. Valencia Donovan's property was a few miles outside of town, but Abby wasn't sure how far out.

In the end, she made it with ten minutes to spare. Valencia

met her at the gate with a friendly smile. "Hi, Abby," she said. "Billy filled me in about your work. How exciting. I'd love to have my organization featured in your documentary."

Valencia was gorgeous. Her eyes were the same brown as Abby's, but the comparison ended there. She was tall and leggy with a mane of wavy, golden blond hair. Her skinny jeans and multicolored peasant blouse painted a picture of free-spirited warmth.

Abby felt a little dowdy in comparison, which was dumb, because she had been perfectly satisfied with her appearance when she left the hotel. Perhaps something about Valencia was an unpleasant reminder of all the blond and perfect girls who had at times made her life a misery growing up.

In reality, Valencia was nothing but welcoming and complimentary of Abby's chosen profession and everything else. She was patient while Abby filmed various aspects of the horse rescue. After they toured the barn and met a few of the horses, the other woman sighed. "I'm in the mood for some of Amanda Battle's lemon meringue pie. What if we head back to town and finish our conversation at the diner?"

"I'm game," Abby said.

Over lunch, the two of them bonded. Valencia was funny and unpretentious. Abby learned that she had left a successful corporate career to rescue horses.

Abby took a sip of her tea. "From boardroom to horse ranch? What was the appeal?"

"I love horses, always have," Valencia said. "I had saved up enough money to buy the land, and I've begun locating horses in peril. You'd be shocked how many people think they want to own a horse and then find out how much hard work it is."

"But not Royal ranchers."

"Oh, no. The horses I rescue come from all over. I sometimes drive five or six hours to pick up an animal."

"Impressive. I don't mean to be rude, but are there enough people who care about mistreated horses to donate to a charity? Billy Holmes told me that Donovan Horse Rescue is one of the beneficiaries of Soiree on the Bay."

"I'm hoping to make the focus of my work equine therapy, in particular for children. You see, I'm very interested in providing immersive summer camp opportunities, and kids who have experienced tragedy respond well to horses. Particularly when part of their activities include learning how to care for an animal. Feeding, brushing, that sort of thing... I filled out an application and submitted it to the festival board. They must have liked my pitch."

"Do you mind if I ask how much you're going to receive?"

"Not at all." Valencia named a number in the high five figures.

"Wow! You must be very excited."

"I definitely am. I've been working on my business plan. Of course, I won't receive any money until all the ticket sales are in. But in the meantime, I'm getting everything ready on paper, so I don't miss a single moment. I'm thrilled that I was chosen."

"I see why." Abby flashed her a warm smile. "You're passionate about this project, and I'm sure that came across in your proposal. Good for you. I think it's wonderful that the money from the festival will get you started. And to know that children will benefit? You must be very proud."

Back at the hotel, Abby studied the notes she'd made during lunch. She had filmed Valencia speaking in the barn. But the footage of the horse rescue operation would be excellent B-roll. No one wanted to see a documentary that was only talking heads. Abby's narration would flesh out the woman's vision.

At one thirty, she stared at her phone, wishing she could pretend she had never seen last night's communication from Carter. If he'd sent a simple "let's hook up" text, it might have been easier to answer. She could have responded from the standpoint of purely physical gratification, nothing more. But if she went out to Sunset Acres this afternoon, she would have to interact with his family.

It didn't make sense. She knew without a doubt that Carter wasn't making a grand meet-the-parents gesture. Abby had known him less than a week. So why had he invited her at all?

The clock was ticking. To wait any longer would be unforgivably rude.

Gnawing her lip, she tapped out a long-overdue reply.

Is the offer still good? I finished up a couple of things earlier than expected.

One minute passed. Then two. When the phone finally dinged, she exhaled all the breath she had been holding. Carter's reply was not nuanced at all, darn it. No lines to read between.

Sure. Why don't you show up around five? We'll eat at six. Or I can pick you up, if you don't want to drive.

Abby was alarmed to realize how much relief she experienced.

I'll see you then...happy to drive. Can I bring anything?

Carter posted a smiley face.

You're staying in a hotel. I think that gives you a free pass. See you soon...

Abby clicked out of the text screen. Now her next question was very personal. Should she pack a bag? If she *didn't*, she'd be giving her libido a clear signal. That this was dinner. Nothing more.

On the other hand, if Carter was interested in a repeat performance of *Abby and Carter's Greatest Hits*, she would be much more comfortable with her own toiletries and a change of clothes.

Did a grown man invite his lover to spend the night when his parents were in residence? Of course, Carter *had* made a point of mentioning a guesthouse and his privacy.

On the other hand, was Abby really his lover? That sounded like a far more formal relationship than what she had with him.

They had slept together. True. But that was it. Or was it?

She changed her mind about what to wear half a dozen times. It was hot today, scorching really. In this weather, she always preferred a light, loose-fitting dress. Fortunately she had one she hadn't worn yet. The double layer of white gauzy fabric and halter neck meant she wouldn't even have to wear a bra.

That seemed like a prudent choice when the temps were nearing the hundred-degree mark. The dress had its own woven, gold leather belt. She had sandals to match. And a pair of unabashedly over-the-top dangly gold earrings.

Because she was antsy, she got ready far too early. She decided to leave anyway and drive around town before heading out to the ranch. Her camera would be in the trunk, just in case.

Friday night in Royal meant a lot of people in town. Restaurants and bars were hopping, even at this early hour. Teenagers thronged the streets, doing all the silly things adolescents do when it's summertime, and hormones are raging.

Abby had to smile. Some behaviors were universal. She hadn't dated much in high school, but she'd suffered through a couple of unrequited crushes. It had been college before she had really come out of her shell. She'd been shy by nature and inclined to stay out of the spotlight.

That was one reason filmmaking appealed to her. She could control the narrative. No one would be staring at her as long as she stayed behind the camera.

Finally, she turned the car in the direction of Carter's ranch, smiling as she recalled their first encounter. Even now, the memory of him on horseback—silhouetted against the sun— caused her heart to beat faster.

This evening's visit to Sunset Acres made her uneasy, and

she wasn't even there yet. Despite their night of unbridled sex, much of her contact with Carter up until now had been couched in terms of her project. Nothing about this latest invitation was business related.

It felt *personal.*

The last time she had seen him, he'd been asleep—his big, tanned body sprawled against white sheets, his hair mussed and his face unshaven. She had tiptoed out at the first hint of dawn, not wanting a confrontation. Cowardly? Sure. But an action and a choice predicated on self-preservation.

This time, she didn't linger anywhere on the property. She drove straight to Carter's house and parked. As she stepped out of the car, a curvy brunette with a baby on her hip came down the steps. "Hey there. You must be Abby. I'm Denise, Carter's younger sister. And this is Beebee."

Abby gazed at the infant with something like awe. Beebee was solid, her legs bracketed in rolls of baby fat. "Hi, Beebee."

The kid babbled a few nonsense syllables, but she didn't smile. Maybe she didn't approve of women who wanted to travel the world instead of getting pregnant.

Denise retrieved a plastic booster seat from her car, the kind that could be strapped to a chair. "Come on in, Abby. I want you to meet my husband and my mother. Dad is out back grilling with Carter."

Abby fell into step. "That must be a macho Texas guy thing. Grilling? I guess it's a requirement?"

Abby held open the door as Denise replied, "Not gonna lie. It's in their DNA. After all, this is beef country. At least Mom and I have convinced them to branch out over the years. There will be steaks, always, but chicken breasts, too, and fresh veggies."

"Sounds delicious." Abby's stomach growled. She'd gone easy at lunch, but now the smells wafting from the grill teased her taste buds.

Mrs. Crane was in the dining room. She was in her midfifties, attractive and fit. Carter's mom seemed pleasant enough, but Abby had the feeling that she was being assessed by her de facto hostess and maybe falling short.

The older woman grilled Abby right away. "So how long has my son known you, Ms. Carmichael?"

"Call me Abby, please. Not long at all. I've come to Royal to do a documentary on the Soiree on the Bay festival."

"Ah. But Carter has no interest in the festival."

"No, ma'am. None. But he's allowing me to film here at the ranch, so that I can showcase Royal and the ranching industry as a backdrop to my story."

"I see."

"Mama." Denise raised an eyebrow. "Behave."

Her mother gave her an innocent look. "I'm just getting to know Abby."

"Right." Denise shook her head, apparently used to her mother's tactics. She handed Beebee to the only other person in the room. "This is my husband, Ernie. Ernie, Abby."

Abby shook the man's free hand. "Nice to meet you. Your daughter is a sweetheart."

Ernie was quiet and seemed not to mind when his little one yanked handfuls of his hair. "She keeps us on our toes," he said ruefully.

Mrs. Crane's given name was Cynthia, as Abby learned when the father-son duo came in bearing a platter of shrimp, the ubiquitous steak and chicken breasts.

When Carter's gaze met hers across the room, the jolt of heat was so profound, she looked around to see if anyone had noticed. Apparently not.

Carter smiled at the room in general, though his introduction was more personal. "Abby, this is my dad, Lamar. I see you've met the rest of the clan."

"I did," she said, taking the seat Denise offered her. Cynthia had set the table earlier while her son-in-law poured drinks. Abby was surprised to see that the menu was free of any alcoholic beverages. Only tea and iced coffee and lemonade were offered.

Denise whispered an explanation. "Daddy's a teetotaler now. Doctor's orders. He's supposed to be avoiding red meat, too, but that won't happen tonight."

There were no formalities observed, though everyone was dressed nicely, and nary a paper plate in sight. Cynthia had used china and crystal and a heavy, ornate silver service adorned with the letter *C*.

Abby wondered if the Cranes always dined so elegantly or if this show was for her benefit. No one seemed to think it odd that she was in attendance. But the longer the dinner lasted, the more she wondered why she had been included.

Conversation flowed freely. Abby was questioned at length about her job and her background and whether or not she watched college sports.

Cynthia pressed delicately at times, but finally with a vein of determination. "Tell us about your family, dear."

All eyes shifted to Abby. She set down her glass of iced tea and managed a smile, even though she might as well have been on the witness stand. "I'm an only child," she said. "My parents have been divorced for a very long time, though they are on good terms. Daddy is a filmmaker out in California. My mother works at Sotheby's in New York. Her specialty is appraising twentieth-century paintings."

"Impressive." Cynthia's gaze was assessing, as though trying to read between the lines. "And is this your first trip to Texas?"

"Yes, ma'am." Abby fell into old habits. Carter's mother was a force to be reckoned with, even though his father was a big ole teddy bear.

Denise chimed in. "And what do you think of Maverick County?"

A hushed silence fell over the room. Abby frowned inwardly. This was weird. "Um, it's very different from what I'm used to. But it has a beauty all its own, I suppose."

Ernie laughed, his kind eyes dancing. "Good for you, Abby. Stand up for yourself. This family is a bit much. Diplomacy is a required skill."

There was a momentary lull in the conversation. Denise and Cynthia left the table to serve dessert. Carter's sister had made two apple pies. Apparently, both Crane women were homemakers extraordinaire.

The remainder of the meal passed without incident.

Abby noticed that Carter didn't have a whole lot to say in the midst of his boisterous family. Of course, the baby kept things lively, but even so, Carter's quiet presence was notable. He smiled a lot. And he answered when spoken to. Still, he seemed more watchful than anything else.

At last, Beebee fell asleep on her father's shoulder. Denise smiled. "We should head for the guesthouse soon. Mom, Dad... you stay as long as you want."

Cynthia gave her son a pointed look. "May I speak with you in the kitchen, Carter?"

Abby breathed a sigh of relief. The other members of his family were far less frightening.

But Denise unwittingly put a confrontation in motion. She scooped up Beebee and glanced at Abby. "Would you mind helping me change her into pajamas? Daddy and Ernie are dying to have another slice of pie without Mom noticing."

"Of course." Abby stood and followed the other woman down the hallway. They were heading away from the kitchen. But apparently, Carter and his mother had chosen to go to the sunroom instead.

Suddenly, Denise held up her hand and backed up. But it was too late. The conversation was impossible to ignore.

Cynthia's voice carried. "Why did you invite that girl tonight, Carter? What are you up to? Is this another doomed romantic alliance?"

Carter's tone was perfectly calm. "Abby is not a prospective fiancée. We're friends. I thought she might enjoy meeting my family. That's all."

"Bull testicles," his mother snapped. "You're playing games. But I must say that this one is better than your wretched *Madeline*."

Carter's reply was less conciliatory now. "At least you're being honest. It might have been nice if *one* of you told me you didn't like Madeline. I didn't find out until it was all over that my nearest and dearest had reservations about her."

"We didn't want to meddle."

"Since when?"

Abby's whole body was one big blush. She touched Denise on the arm. "I'm going to step outside for a few minutes. Please make my excuses."

Before Carter's sister could reply, Abby darted back the way she had come. She dodged the dining room and sneaked out onto the veranda and down to the driveway. In the dark, she put her hands to her hot cheeks. What had Carter been thinking? She was humiliated and confused.

After fifteen minutes, she knew she couldn't stay outside any longer without causing comment. She grabbed a thin sweater from the front seat of her car as an excuse and started to walk back inside.

As she hit the top step and took a breath for courage, the door opened suddenly. A familiar voice spoke out of the darkness.

"There you are," Carter said. "I was starting to worry about you."

Ten

Carter was pissed and frustrated. He loved his parents, but his mother could be a handful. Thankfully, Denise had whispered a heads-up to him, warning that she and Abby had unwittingly overheard the conversation between mother and son.

He turned on the porch light and saw Abby freeze when she realized it was him. "I just came to get my sweater out of the car," she said.

"No. You overheard my conversation with my mother, and you were embarrassed. I'm sorry, Abby."

He couldn't read her expression, but her body language spoke volumes. Her arms were wrapped tightly around her waist, and she had backed up as far as humanly possible without falling off the porch.

She placed her sweater with exaggerated care on the railing. "Why did you invite me to come here tonight, Carter?" she asked.

The slight tremor in her voice made him feel like scum.

"Two reasons. First of all, I wanted to see you."

"And the second?"

"I haven't socialized much since Madeline called off the wedding," he admitted. "My mother is constantly on my case to *get back out there*. So I thought if she met you, I'd get credit for dating but she wouldn't pressure me, because she wouldn't approve of our relationship."

Abby's shock was visible. "Why not? I'm delightful."

He chuckled, charmed by her candor. "I won't argue with that. You definitely are. My mother, though, doesn't see you as ranch wife material. Sunset Acres means everything to my parents, even though they've handed it over to me. They know the kinds of sacrifices that are required, because they've made those very same sacrifices."

After a few beats of silence, Abby took a step toward him and exhaled audibly. "Not that I have any interest in marrying you or having your babies, Carter Crane, but why am I not ranch wife material?"

He stepped closer, as well, reaching out to brush his thumb over her cheek. "You don't even *like* Texas, Abs. There's nothing wrong with that, but it means my mother won't start making wedding plans. That's a good thing."

"Ah."

"I didn't think she would react so strongly tonight." He grimaced. "Usually there's a honeymoon period before she starts vetting my female companions."

"Aren't you kind of old to have your mommy picking out your lovers?"

He pressed the heel of his hand to his forehead where a headache hammered. "You would think so, yes."

Abby cocked her head and gave him a steady stare that made him want to fidget. "I'm sure we should get back inside," she said. "I don't want to be rude."

"Why not? My family certainly hasn't been kind to *you* this evening."

"That's not entirely true. Denise and Ernie and the baby were pleasant. Your dad's a peach. And to be honest, your mother wasn't technically rude to me. In fact, you're the one who set this train wreck in motion."

He curled a strand of her hair around his finger. "I'll make it up to you, Abs, I swear. You look beautiful tonight by the way." His throat tightened as his body hardened. Her scent, something light and floral, teased his nostrils. "Are you wearing anything under that spectacular dress? I've been wondering all evening."

When she rested her cheek against his chest, his heart bumped against his rib cage. "That's on a need-to-know basis."

He held Abby close, linking both arms around her bare back, resting his chin on top of her head, feeling her slender body and feminine curves nestled against his flatter, harder frame. "I need to know," he said huskily. "Really, I do."

"Feel free to explore," she whispered.

It was a dangerous game they played. But he was counting on his family's guilt to give him a few moments of privacy.

Slowly, he gathered Abby's skirt in two hands, pulling it upward until his fingers brushed her bare ass. Well, not entirely bare. She wore a tiny, lacy pair of panties that barely merited a mention.

His mouth went dry. He stroked her butt cheeks, feeling the smooth skin and taut flesh. As caresses went, it was mostly innocent. He didn't trespass anywhere he shouldn't. "That answers half the question," he groaned, wondering why the hell he had started this adventure with his whole damn family close at hand.

Abby slid her arms around his neck and looked up at him with a tiny smile on her face, one that mocked his handling of the evening. "You could kiss me," she said.

The last time they were together, he had been driven by hunger and adrenaline. Tonight, he was no less hungry, but he had more control. He kissed her deeply, holding her chin with two fingers and tracing the seam of her lips with his tongue, giving her passion wrapped in tenderness.

The kiss could have stayed that way, but Abby groaned and went up on her tiptoes to take what she wanted, reminding him that she was no shrinking violet waiting for him to direct her. She was passionate and needy and generous with her kisses.

His head swam. Though the hour was late, the humid air made his body damp and hot. He wanted to strip her naked and swim with her nude.

That image broke the last ounce of control he had over his baser impulses. "God, Abby." He dragged her closer still and ravaged her mouth. Sliding one hand beneath the top of her dress, he found a bare breast. The soft skin and pert tip were a fascinating contrast.

He was rapidly reaching a point of no return. With a muttered curse, he released her and stepped back. "Did I ruin your lipstick?"

"I'm not wearing any." She reached in her pocket and pulled out a clear lip gloss, using it to soothe lips that were puffy from his kisses.

Carter winnowed his fingers through her hair, tidying away the look of passion. "We have to go back in. They won't leave until we do."

"Okay."

He couldn't blame her for the lack of enthusiasm. "I'm sorry I made you uncomfortable tonight. It won't happen again, I swear."

She wrinkled her nose. "Don't make promises you can't keep."

As he started to open the door, she tugged on his arm. "One more thing. I haven't talked to you since I interviewed Billy Holmes."

His hackles went up. "What did he do?" Something in her voice made him wonder if there had been an incident.

"Not a thing. He was a perfect gentleman. But at the end of our meeting, I told him the rumor I had overheard...about the missing money."

"Oh, geez, Abby. I told you not to poke around in that. Was he angry?"

"Actually, he said it was true."

The smug look on her face didn't even bother Carter. He was too stunned. "You can't be serious."

"The camera was off. He lowered his voice and said it was a family matter, and that it was being handled."

Carter shook his head slowly. "I have a bad feeling about this. Who on the committee is handling the actual money part of the festival?"

"Asher, I think. But he's rich. Why would he need to skim funds?"

"I don't like you messing around in this, Abby. People get squirrelly when money is involved. You could be getting yourself into a dangerous situation."

"Or," she said, excitement lighting her face, "I could have found the focus for my documentary. An exposé. It doesn't get better than that!"

He ground his jaw. "Promise me you will let this go." He didn't want to quarrel with her, but he was certain his fears were well-founded.

Abby frowned at him. "Why are you so angry?"

"I'm not angry," he bit out. "I'm aggravated." And it was true. His feelings about Abby and his family and the festival coalesced into a fiery ball of sexual frustration that churned in his gut.

Carter yanked her close, lifting her off her feet and kissing her again. He held her tightly, relieved when she wrapped her legs around his thighs. "You drive me nuts, Abby." Didn't she know how vulnerable she was?

He wanted her in his bed. Now. Naked and needy. He wanted that more than anything in the whole world.

Abby patted his cheek and kissed his forehead. "We have to go inside. Remember? Your family?"

"Hell." She was right. "Tell me you brought an overnight bag."

"That wasn't part of the invitation."

"Abby..." He was at the end of whatever stores of patience he had accumulated.

She slid down his body and stepped away, gathering her sweater and smoothing her hair again. "I did," she said quietly. "But I'm not sure why."

"Don't lie to me, Abs. Or to yourself. We may not be a match made in heaven, but between the sheets we're dynamite."

He took her by the hand and dragged her inside. They found his family gathered in the room where Abby had interviewed Carter earlier that week.

The four adults were seated around a card table playing a game. Denise and Ernie had apparently decided to linger, given the drama that had transpired. The baby snoozed on a pallet on the floor.

Denise was the first to notice them. "There you are," she said, smiling. "Would you like us to deal you in?"

Carter managed not to cringe, though he could think of nothing more dreadful. "No, thanks," he said, his tone mild. "You guys finish your game. Abby and I will hang out. Or maybe have more dessert."

Cynthia Crane stood and approached them with a contrite expression on her face. "I'm sorry you overheard our conversation, dear."

Abby didn't smile. "But you're not sorry you questioned my presence here tonight."

Wow. Carter wanted to high-five somebody. Abby Carmichael had just put his mother in her place.

The older woman narrowed her eyes. "I love my son. It's normal for a mother to want the best for her children. That said, Carter is free to invite whomever he likes to his home. I'm glad I met you, Abby. You are a very interesting woman."

There was a collective exhale in the room when Cynthia returned to the game and left Carter and Abby to entertain themselves.

Half an hour later, the house was finally quiet. Carter shot Abby a wry glance. "Now you see why we built the guest cottage."

"I do," Abby said. But her laugh sounded forced.

"You okay?" He lifted her chin with a finger, looking deep into those dark brown eyes surrounded by thick inky lashes.

Abby stepped away, breaking the small contact. "I'm fine, Carter. Really. But I think I'll head back to town. Your family wants to spend time with you. It feels weird to be sneaking around."

"We're not *sneaking*," he protested. "We're two grown adults. I want you to stay the night." Her reluctance dented his mood.

She flipped her hair over her shoulder, unwittingly drawing his attention to the spot where her throat met her collarbone, a spot he would like to nibble. Soon.

"They'll be coming over for breakfast, right?"

"Not if I tell Denise to keep them away."

"Oh, Carter. This is complicated. I don't want to get in the way of you enjoying your family. You told me they don't visit all that often."

He shoved his hands in his pockets and leaned against the door frame. "If you don't want to stay, just say so."

"I *do* want to stay." She played with her earring, pacing the confines of his living room. "But I don't want *them* to know I stayed."

"Well, that's easy. I'll set an alarm for seven. You can be on your way, and I'll pretend I slept alone. Although it's really nobody's damn business."

Humor lit her face. "As weird as this evening was, I do like your family."

He ducked and looked over his shoulder.

She frowned. "What are you doing?"

"Waiting for the lightning to strike. That's usually what I do when somebody tells a whopper. You can't honestly say you *like* my mother."

She scrunched up her face. "Maybe *like* is the wrong word. But she brought you into this world, so she can't be all bad."

His shoulders loosened, and he crossed the room to take her hands in his. "I've been wanting to get you out of this dress for hours. Swim first? Or straight to the main event?"

Abby realized that the window for changing her mind was over. Actually, as soon as she admitted she had an overnight case in her car, the course of the evening was set. Carter wanted her here, and she wanted to be here. In the end, nothing else mattered.

She snuggled up to his chest, sliding her arms around his waist. "We can swim later. Isn't there a full moon tonight? For now, I'm more than happy to see your bedroom again."

Abby realized a couple of things in the next hour. First, Carter was far less serious than the face he showed to the world. Beneath that mantle of responsibility was a man who liked to play.

And second, he knew way too much about how to pleasure a woman. The man made an art form out of removing her dress. He did it so slowly and with so much sensual heat, she was ready to dissolve into a puddle of lust by the time he had stripped her down to her panties.

They took a quick shower together, one that involved lots of soap and teasing. Then they dried off and returned to the bedroom.

Abby was less self-conscious now, more willing to let her gaze linger on Carter's aroused sex. He was a stud. No question. A very masculine man with the body of someone who did physical labor. If she were a sculptor, she would carve him, every sinew and muscle.

He scooped her up in his arms and nuzzled his nose against hers. "You cold?"

Her heart beat faster. "Not at all. Make love to me, Carter."

His face flushed with heat. "Whatever the lady wants."

For a split second, she wished she had used a different phrase.

There was no love between them. How *could* there be? She didn't believe in love at first sight, and besides, these feelings she had were physical, not emotional. Carter made her body sing.

He didn't give her time for second-guessing. Soon, he worshipped her, kissing from earlobes and eyelids to the throbbing spot at her center, making her squirm. She was close to coming already. She'd been aching for him since that moment when she had slipped out of this bed like a thief in the night.

"Now..." she begged.

He left her for mere seconds to take care of protection and came back to shift her thighs apart and thrust deep. The noise he made was half groan, half curse.

She understood what he didn't say. This was beyond words. He filled her completely, his hard sex claiming everything she offered willingly. Their joining was something more than the two of them slaking a sexual thirst. Rather, it was the kind of chemical reaction that fizzed and sparked and boiled over.

Because it was hot and urgent and not to be denied, Abby was swept up in a wave of sheer bliss. How insanely wonderful could a moment be? How *perfect*...

Carter surrounded her, aroused her and, paradoxically, protected her.

When her orgasm yanked her up and threw her into the abyss, she felt limp with joy, sated with pleasure.

In the aftermath, he pulled her against his side. She stretched one leg across his thighs and pillowed her cheek on his chest.

Abby wasn't asleep, and she wasn't 100 percent awake. She floated, wallowing in the seductive feeling of invincibility.

Carter played with her hair, his breath warm on the top of her head. "I can't feel my legs," he complained.

She pinched his upper thigh, hard enough to bruise. "I can."

"Brat."

"Bossy, arrogant rancher."

His raspy chuckle made her feel happy and warm. In Carter's

embrace, she felt like herself. With the few other men she had let into her life on a sexual basis, she had always held something back, wary of being judged.

In this bed, with this man, her world was complete.

And that was scary as hell.

Finally, she lifted up on one elbow and smiled at him. "I'm not sleepy. Can we take a glass of wine out by the pool and enjoy the moonlight?"

His gaze was hooded, his hair mussed. "Of course, beautiful. But don't get dressed. We might take a dip. There's no one around to peek."

He gave her a robe out of his closet, a hotel-style garment that was soft and plush and smelled faintly of Carter's aftershave. For himself, he grabbed a towel and tucked it around his waist.

In the kitchen, he didn't bother with the overhead light as he gathered glasses and a corkscrew. Abby was glad. These minutes felt precious and private. She wanted to preserve this bubble of intimacy, to savor every moment of it.

Outside, the moon shone down serenely, illuminating the pool and chasing away shadows. They settled onto cushioned lounge chairs. Carter opened the wine and poured. When he clinked his glass against hers, he smiled. "To new friends. And beautiful cinematographers. I'm glad you stayed."

Abby wanted to say something nice in return, but her throat was tight, and her thoughts were all jumbled. Instead, she sipped her wine and wiggled her toes, feeling the peace of the summer night wash over her.

Beside her, Carter resembled a large, lazy jungle cat. His body was completely relaxed. So much so that it took her by surprise when he spoke.

"I want to see you again, Abby."

He laid it out there. No games.

"Your family is here all week, right?"

"Yes," he said. "But they don't bite."

"I'm not your girlfriend, Carter. It would be different if I were. You need to spend quality time with them. Besides, I have several more interviews lined up this week. I'll be busy."

Turning toward her, he pinned her with his blue gaze. "The weekend, then?"

"I'm flying out to LA on Friday. My father is going to help me begin to piece together my story. He's great at editing."

"When will you be back?" he asked.

"Midweek probably," she replied. "I'm bringing some camping gear then. Since there isn't any public lodging on Appaloosa Island, I have to find a way to spend the night and get those magical early morning shots. Camping is the best solution. If I can get permission."

"And after that?"

"I'll probably go home to New York, regroup and come back to Royal right before the festival starts."

"I see." He paused. "It sounds like you consider New York home, and not California. Is that true?"

"Yes. My mother wanted my school years to be uninterrupted. But summers and holidays were a roll of the dice." Abby raised the wineglass to her lips and took a sip. "Neither she nor my father meant to make me feel bad, but there was always an unspoken tug-of-war. I think that's when travel started to appeal to me. I could go where I wanted, when I wanted, without having to answer to anyone."

"Makes sense."

"I haven't told you much about my parents," she said quietly. "They still care about each other, even after all these years apart."

"Why did they split in the first place?" he asked curiously.

"Because their lives were too different. Once they got past the wild rush of falling in love and having me, the reality of day-to-day life didn't work." She shrugged. "My mom couldn't conceive of leaving New York. But my dad dreamed of becoming a filmmaker and needed the flexibility to go where the opportunities arose. Having a wife and a little baby held him back.

Ultimately, my mother set him free to be who he was meant to be. And she found happiness and fulfillment on her own."

"Is this the part where I'm supposed to see the parallels? If so, I'm not convinced." A muscle ticked in his jaw. "I don't give a damn about the future right now. But I want to be with you, Abby."

The lump in her throat grew painfully. "I want to be with you, too."

A light breeze danced around them, ruffling the water, diluting the moon's reflection. The wine bottle was empty now. Abby felt mellow, but melancholy.

When Carter said nothing for long minutes, she blurted out the truth that had struck her tonight. "I envy you, you know."

He set his glass on the table. "How so?"

"Your family. I love my mom and dad, and they love me, but I've never had the kind of family unit the Cranes have. Even your brother-in-law is an integral part of that tight circle. I can tell that each of you would do anything for the others."

"Like taking over a huge ranch far too young?" Carter sighed. "I'm handling things now, though the first few years were tough. I grew up here, but suddenly sitting in the owner's seat was terrifying."

"Your father is proud of you."

"I hope so."

Abby was drenched in sadness suddenly. To come close to something so perfect and yet know it was out of reach shredded her emotions.

"I think I'll swim now," she said.

Eleven

Carter stayed where he was, his hands fisted on his thighs. Watching Abby shed his robe and dive gracefully into the water was an experience he couldn't describe. Her beauty in the moonlight made his heart ache.

When she surfaced, laughing, he felt something crack inside his chest, some wall of self-protection that had begun to crumble without his knowledge. Since Madeline's defection, he had put his emotions on hold, denying his needs, focusing on the ranch.

Tonight, beneath a full moon, sated sexually and slightly drunk on a bottle of very good wine, he felt reborn. Yet, at the same time, he knew nothing for certain.

Was he feeling lust and gratitude, or something more?

Abby swam and played like a creature familiar with the sea. He supposed she really was. With one home base in Malibu, she must have spent long hours on the beach, or frolicking in the Pacific.

Carter was jealous suddenly of every teenage boy and young man who had lain at her side, flirted with her, wallowed on a sandy blanket and kissed those perfect lips.

His breath sawed in and out of his lungs as if he was running full tilt. His heart pounded. He didn't know what to do. That very uncertainty was so novel, he was stunned.

At thirty-four, the world was his oyster. He had money and power and unlimited opportunity.

What he didn't have was a mate, a lover, a life partner.

With Madeline, he had seen her as he wanted her to be. His blindness had cost him greatly in terms of his pride and his confidence. Thankfully, he had ultimately realized that while she had treated him shabbily, she hadn't broken his heart.

He didn't want to make another impulsive mistake. Especially with so little time. He and Abby weren't ships passing in the night. They were high-speed trains on opposite tracks. This moment with her was nothing more than a blip.

She came to the side of the pool and waved at him. "Come join me."

He noticed that she was careful not to expose her naked breasts. The show of modesty amused him. "How's the water?"

"Somewhere between chilly and almost perfect."

"You'd better not be kidding." He dropped his towel and walked down the steps into the shallow end.

Abby stayed near the rope that marked deeper water. "It's your pool. You should know by now. Or do you never go skinny-dipping when you're alone?"

He strode through the water, stalking her, grinning when she ran out of her depth. "Stay put, little mermaid. Don't be scared."

She lifted her chin. "I'm not scared of you. But I'm not accustomed to being stark naked in public."

He glanced around the pool. "It's just us, Abs."

Finally, he was within touching distance—close enough to see the droplets of water beading on her arms, each one reflecting a tiny moon. Her dark hair floated around her, partially obscuring her bare breasts.

Was that intentional?

"Do you know how beautiful you are?" he whispered hoarsely.

She didn't respond. But a blink of her eyes could have meant anything.

He shook his head slowly. "I know you're smart and competent and career focused, and all those things strong women aspire to be. But damn, Abby, you're also incredibly lovely. The kind of lovely that makes a man wish he could paint you exactly the way you look right now."

"You're embarrassing me," she whispered.

"Oh? Does that mean you want me to stop talking?"

She nodded slowly. Even with the moon, he couldn't read the secrets hidden in her dark eyes. Carefully, he took a piece of her hair and tugged. She came to him willingly, her smile striking him dead in the chest, stealing his breath.

When their bodies met, they groaned in unison. Naked flesh to naked flesh. The water made them buoyant. He coaxed her legs around his waist.

"I like your…pool," she said, with a naughty grin.

He fondled her butt, feeling his sex flex and stir. "I like the way you're all wet and slick. Like a sea otter."

Her head fell back, and she laughed so hard one breast popped up above the water. "That's awful, Carter. No wonder you don't have a girlfriend."

He took them a few steps closer to the side of the pool. Then he kissed her long and slow. "If you're auditioning for the part, it's going really well," he muttered.

She clung to his shoulders as her smile dimmed. "I'm not an actress," she said. "What you see is what you get. Just a girl who's a friend."

The moon dipped behind a cloud, plunging them into darkness. "I want you again, Abby. Now."

"We can't, Carter. It's too dangerous."

Beneath the water he stroked her sex, entering her with two fingers. "Did I ever tell you I was a Boy Scout years ago? Always prepared?"

He leaned toward the side of the pool briefly and reached for the robe she had discarded, finding what he wanted.

Abby stared at him, mouth agape. "You hid a condom in my pocket? That's sneaky, Mr. Crane."

"Sneaky? Or very, very smart?"

He set her on her feet and tugged her by the hand. "Come toward the steps for a minute."

When he ripped open the packet and dealt with the latex, Abby watched. He liked that. A *lot*. Men had a tendency to show off for the opposite sex. He was no different.

He took her hand. "I'm ready. Are you?"

She ran her hand down his chest, stopping to toy with his navel. "I was born ready, cowboy."

They moved into deeper water. Carter scooped his hands under her hair and cupped her neck. "I'm glad you stopped to film the sunset that first night. Otherwise, we might never have met."

Now that she couldn't touch bottom, she clung to his shoulders. "I'll tell you a secret. The sunset was gorgeous, but I was filming *you*. Riding flat out. Horse and man moving as one. It was poetry in motion. I liked what I saw."

He kissed her slowly, intimately. "And now?"

"I'm super glad you dumped that skank Madeline."

This time he was the one to laugh uproariously. "Hell, Abby. If I'd been *married* to her, I'd probably have dumped her for you."

Abby smiled softly, running her thumb over his lower lip. "No," she said. "If you'd been married, you never would have looked at another female. I've learned a lot about you since I've come to Royal. You're a man of honor. A gentleman. The kind of guy all women want. But when they don't find him, they settle for less."

"You're buttering me up, Abs. I'm as flawed as anyone. For instance, right now I'd like to beg you to forget about your documentary and stay with me for a while."

She rested her head on his shoulder, her legs tangling with his. "It sounds like fun. But I know you're not serious, not really. We both see the bigger picture. Sometimes doing the sensible, mature thing sucks."

"Yeah," he said gruffly. "It does." He was done with talking. Nothing Abby had to say made him feel any better about their situation. His erection hadn't flagged, not even in the midst of a semiserious moment. In fact, holding her like this was pure torture. The moonlight. The silky water. The way Abby's body felt against his... His sex throbbed with urgency, even as his brain tried to draw out the pleasure.

Abby kissed his chin. "Take me, Carter. I want you so much I'm shaking."

It was true. He could feel the tremors in her body, could hear her fractured breathing. "Hang on, sweetheart."

He lifted her, aided by the water, and positioned her to slide down onto his swollen sex. The muscles in his arms quivered as he supported her weight. When they were joined, male to female, yin to yang, he cursed. "Damn, woman. You're killing me."

His knees were embarrassingly weak. Abby's body accepted his as if they had been designed for this exact joining. Her sex took him in and wrapped him tightly in blissful heat. The sensation was one he couldn't have imagined.

"I've never done this in the water," he said, the words breathless.

Abby pulled back so she could see his face. "Really?"

"Really."

He wasn't sure she believed him, but he was beyond talking. He'd gone into this without overthinking the logistics. Now his body was driving him to seal the deal. "Abs?"

"Hmm?" She pressed kisses along his jawline.

"I need the wall."

Her lips curved. "I can handle that."

He lurched toward the metal stairs and gently pressed Abby to the right of them against the slightly rough surface of pool.

The water was up to her chin. "Does this hurt?" He thrust into her while he asked the question, obviously not under control.

"I'm good," she said.

It was weird, weirder than he had anticipated. The water made his movements clumsy. Carter drove into her once, shifted, and then went deep again. He was close to coming, but what about the mermaid in his arms?

She had one hand wrapped around the metal steps. Her breasts pillowed against his chest. Leaning back, he reached between their bodies and found her most sensitive spot. As he thumbed it, Abby climaxed, a little cry echoing on the breeze.

Her inner contractions were all it took to set him off. He moaned and came hard. The pleasure was mind-blowing, yet at the same time, he found himself mentally cursing the way the water made it difficult to move like he wanted to...

Abby was limp in his embrace. He peeled her fingers from the step railing and put her hands behind his neck. "It looks more romantic in the movies, doesn't it?"

She rested her cheek against him. "I've got no complaints. Except that my fingers are getting pruney."

"Well, we can't have that."

With no small amount of regret, he separated their bodies. "Time to get out."

Abby refused to go first, so he dragged himself up the steps, dealt with the condom and reached down to take her hand. "Up you come."

It felt strange to be on firm ground. The night air seemed colder suddenly. Abby's arms were covered in gooseflesh. He fetched her a towel and grabbed the one on the lounger for himself.

She didn't say anything. Neither did he.

They walked back inside the house and down the hall to his room. "Do you want to shower again?" he asked, trying to be the gentleman she proclaimed him to be.

Abby yawned. "Nope. I just want to sleep."

They tumbled beneath the covers. He twined his arms and legs with hers and turned out the light.

His lover was asleep in seconds, her damp hair spread across his pillow.

Carter was not so lucky. He lay awake, staring into the darkness. An odd memory floated across his brain. Something from when he was six or seven years old. He'd heard a tale about a pearl that was so valuable, a man sold everything he had to purchase it.

At the time, he'd thought it was a stupid story. His Sunday school teacher had been a stern, no-nonsense woman who—as Carter remembered it—had little patience for wiggly boys who only wanted to be let loose outside.

He turned his head and watched Abby sleep. Unable to resist, he kissed her forehead and gently stroked her hair. Even if the merchant's actions made more sense now, Carter couldn't follow suit. The ranch belonged to him on paper, but its legacy was a joint venture, a family bond.

Even worse, he couldn't repeat the mistakes he made with Madeline. He'd met her at that damned wedding and proposed to her far too soon, without even knowing her. His impulsive behavior had doomed the relationship from the start.

But Abby was different, wasn't she? There was no artifice in her, no selfishness. And Carter was older and wiser.

The more he thought about his situation, the more trapped he felt. In that moment, he felt the sting of loss.

Abby was right there beside him, but he knew their time was short.

Sometimes life was a bitch.

Abby didn't leave a note this time. They had come too far for that. She'd set her alarm for six thirty. When it buzzed, she silenced it quickly. Carter never moved.

After she showered and dressed, she sat down on the bed at his hip. "Carter," she whispered.

He grunted and rolled onto his back, scrubbing his hands over his face. "What time is it?"

"Barely seven. I wanted to say goodbye before I left."

He sat up and frowned. "What's the rush?"

"We talked about this," she said quietly. "Your family will be over for breakfast soon. I'm heading back to the hotel."

"And did we agree on anything for when you return?"

Her smile cost her. Leaving Carter like this was a physical pain in her chest. If she'd had her wish, she would have lingered to play all day. "I'll let you know when I get back from New York." She leaned down to kiss him. The cheek seemed too casual for what they had shared. But the mouth was dangerous.

She chose the mouth anyway, her lips melding with his. Carter was warm. His big arms wrapped around her and held her close.

He nuzzled her forehead with his. "You sure you don't want to stay a few more minutes?"

"No. It wouldn't be a few minutes, and you know it. Tell your family I enjoyed meeting them. Bye, Carter."

She fled the house, perilously close to letting him sweet-talk her into staying. But she knew what was right. Family was important.

Every moment of the week that followed, she worked herself hard, researching, filming, interviewing. She had thought that she and Carter might text back and forth casually. But neither of them initiated a virtual conversation. After all, what was there to say?

She missed him terribly.

Though her personal life was a mess, her professional life flourished. Most notably, Lila arranged for Abby to have access to the Texas Cattleman's Club to shoot interior montages after hours. With patrons on-site, the permissions involved would have been too complicated.

Abby began working on a voice-over script that would narrate this particular section, touching on the history, but also pointing out how the club was central to life in Royal even in the twenty-first century.

Carter was a member. No surprise there.

When Abby had first sat in on the meeting of the advisory board, she had seen part of the club, of course. Now, with no one in residence but the night watchman, she was free to roam the halls and peek into the various rooms.

She was surprised to see a state-of-the-art day care on the premises. The center was a bright, cheerful place with murals on the walls and everything a young child could possibly want.

Lila had given her a roster of current members and oddly, Billy Holmes was included. He'd only lived in Royal a few years, and he didn't own a ranch. But other people of influence in the community were recognized for their accomplishments, so maybe Billy had been inducted based on merits Abby wasn't privy to during her short visit with him.

The night watchman himself had related how an F4 tornado a few years before had destroyed part of the town and even damaged this fine old building. The community had pulled together to rebuild Royal stronger and better than before.

At last, Abby had all the footage she needed, in truth, far more than she would ever be able to use. But she was fascinated by what seemed like a vestige of the Old West. Money talked. Here in Royal, it talked louder in this building than almost anywhere else.

When she packed up her gear and wandered back to the front lobby, she found the night watchman talking to someone familiar. Carter.

Her pulse jumped. She approached the two men calmly. "What brings you here, Carter? I thought I was the only after-hours visitor."

They made their goodbyes to the guard and stepped outside. Carter took two of her bags and carried them to the car. "I wanted to see you before you left," he said.

"Oh." She didn't know how to respond to that. "Is your family still in town?"

"They're leaving in the morning, too. Maybe you'll see them at the airport."

I hope not, she thought wryly. "Did you have a good visit?"

"Actually, yes. It was great. My brother-in-law helped me around the ranch. Dad's health is doing well, so he joined us occasionally. It was especially fun to spend time with the baby. She's changing every day."

"And your mom and sister?"

"My mother was extremely well-behaved. I think she feels guilty about what happened with you. My sister, on the other hand, told me not to let you get away."

Abby winced. "But you told her we weren't a thing?"

He shoved his hands in his pockets and leaned against the car. "I did."

"Good."

Her stomach curled with regret. She had always hated good-byes. "I should go," she said softly. "Thanks for stopping by."

"I was hoping you might invite me up to your room."

And there it was again. The insidious temptation that made a mockery of all her grown-up plans.

What could it hurt, the devil on her shoulder whispered.

He'll break your heart, said her conscience.

Five seconds passed. Then ten. "I have a very early flight, Carter. And I haven't finished packing. I'm sorry."

He didn't react visibly to her polite refusal, but he straightened and took her hand, reeling her in with ease, since she had no intention of protesting.

His mouth settled on hers, his lips firm and masculine. She breathed in his scent, trying to memorize it. He tasted of cinnamon and coffee.

"Don't forget about me, Abs, while you're gone," he muttered. "I'll miss you."

Her eyes stung with tears. "I'll miss you, too."

He kissed her again. This one almost took her down. It wasn't him she was resisting; it was her own yearning. At last, he let her go. "Keep in touch, Abby. I want to know how you're doing."

"I will," she promised.

He opened her car doors, put her gear in the back seat and then leaned down to watch her fasten her seat belt as he closed her in. "Do you need a ride to the airport?"

"No, thanks. I'll be turning in the rental car."

"Ah, yes."

Her window was lowered, letting out the heat that accumulated even at this hour. He had a hand on the sill. She put her fingers over his. "Bye, Carter. Thanks for everything."

Then she put the car in gear and drove away, looking in the rearview mirror only once to see him standing tall and alone in the club parking lot.

Twelve

Abby's father met her at the airport. He was a tall, barrel-chested Black man with kind eyes and a gentle sense of humor. Though they had lived on opposite coasts for most of her life, she had always known that he would drop everything and come to her if she ever needed him.

Her dad negotiated the horrible traffic without flinching. He truly was a Californian after all these years. They stopped at Abby's favorite seafood restaurant before heading on to the house. Over lunch, she brought up a subject that had been occupying her mind recently.

"Daddy, when you and Mom first separated, did you know you were doing the right thing?"

He seemed surprised, but he answered readily enough. "Yes. We both did. The hard part was how much I adored you. We wanted to stay together for your sake, but we knew it couldn't work. Sometimes people come into our lives for a season, Abby. Your mother and I were very happy for a time, but life shifted us onto different paths."

"I understand." She didn't. Not really. It was hard for her to imagine loving someone and then *not* loving them.

That was the last of the personal conversation, even during the drive to the coast. She sensed the introspection made him uncomfortable. After she was settled into her old bedroom, they met out on the back veranda overlooking the Pacific. Her father had done very well in his career. His neighbors up and down this stretch of Malibu were actors and producers and other luminaries.

Though the land had increased in value over the years, her father's house was relatively modest. He had no interest in re-decorating or following fashion trends. Right now, Abby was grateful. It was comforting to know that some things stayed the same.

They watched the sun go down.

She worked up her courage and took the plunge. "Daddy?"

"Hmm?"

"What would you think if Mom and I came out for Labor Day and stayed with you? Just the three of us."

He'd been watching the water; now he turned to face her. "I have no problem with that, baby girl. I've always told you that your mother is welcome here. Is something going on with you?"

"No. Not really. I just thought it would be nice for the three of us to get together. Now that I'm an adult, too."

"It will depend on your mother," he said with a wistful smile. "You know how stubborn she is. I'm sure she'd rather do a get-together like that on her turf."

"True. Well, I'll ask her, and let you know."

Afterward, her father excused himself to go make a work-related phone call. His state-of-the-art studio was upstairs. For the next couple of days, she knew that the two of them would bond over her fledgling movie.

For now, she lingered to enjoy the stars and the sultry ocean breeze.

What was Carter doing tonight? She regretted not letting him stay with her the evening before, but it would only have made things harder. He was wrapping himself around her heartstrings without even trying.

Her father rarely asked about her personal life. Maybe because he didn't want any questions in return. They loved each other, but certain lines were never crossed.

In many ways, her relationship with her mother was the same. Abby loved her parents and had always known that she was loved unconditionally in return. But her family was different than Carter's. *Very* different.

However, as much as Abby had yearned for a "normal" family while growing up, she knew how lucky she was.

The long weekend passed in a blur. Her father had a keen eye for visual storytelling. Though he was always quick to point out that it was her project, *her baby*, the suggestions he made for her documentary were spot-on.

By the time he put her on a plane for New York, she was ecstatic at how the film was coming together. And more confident, too. If this project turned out as well as she was expecting it to, she would be on her way to a promising career.

She was already almost regretting the flight to New York. It wouldn't have been a big deal to simply fly from LA to Royal. Still, even though this would be a super short visit, she wanted to swap out some of her clothes, and she also hoped to talk to her mother about Carter. If the right moment arose.

Her flight landed on time Monday afternoon. Abby took a cab from LaGuardia to Manhattan. She and her mother lived in a high rise on a quiet block of East 77th Street. Abby had never questioned her mother's finances. There was money from Abby's grandparents. And she was certain her father had paid child support. Beyond that, she only knew that she and her mother lived a very comfortable life.

When she took the elevator to the tenth floor and unlocked the door, her mother wasn't home. No real surprise. But for the first time, the apartment's quiet emptiness struck her as a little sad.

What would it be like when Abby moved out for good? Did her mother have any desire for grandchildren? Some women didn't.

Abby did some laundry and rifled through her closet to re-pack her suitcase. On a whim, she folded a beautiful, fire-engine red evening dress and added it to the pile. Lila had mentioned the possibility of some special events surrounding the festival kickoff. Abby wanted to be ready.

It was hard to admit that in the back of her mind, she was al-ready picturing herself wearing that sexy dress for Carter. Days ago, he had asked her to stay in touch. But she hadn't known what to say. When he didn't text either during their time apart, she had assumed he was busy or distracted or both.

Or maybe he had decided a clean break was the best.

Abby picked up her phone and stared at the screen. She had lots of emails and texts, but not the one she so desperately wanted.

Her fingers had a mind of their own. Quickly, she composed a message before she could change her mind.

Hey, Carter... I'm in New York now. My dad was super helpful with my film. We enjoyed catching up. Hope things are good at Sunset Acres...

It was a breezy, nonpersonal text. She almost deleted it, but then she sucked in a breath and hit Send.

Now that she was far away from Royal, it seemed almost ludicrous that she had indulged in an exhilarating, short-lived affair with a sexy, rugged Texan. The list of things they *didn't* have in common was depressingly long.

Had he already forgotten about her? Had she been an easy mark to him?

It was painful to consider. She honestly thought he was as

caught up in the magic as she was. But maybe she was kidding herself.

Her beautiful, stylish, blond-haired mother made it home at six and brought food from Abby's favorite Chinese restaurant. Both her parents spoiled her when she was around. It was nice, but despite being twenty-four years old, Abby was in that odd stage between being a college student and a fully grown adult.

In any other place in the country, she might already have her own apartment by now. New York's cost of living was exorbitant, though, and her mother had often said Abby was welcome to use this apartment as home base for as long as she needed it.

Over a combo meal of various chicken and rice dishes, Abby mentally rehearsed how she was going to present the Labor Day idea. Something about the prospect of having her mom and dad together in Malibu, with her, excited Abby. Was she re-creating a childhood fantasy? A time she barely remembered?

Her motives were murky.

Before she could make her pitch, her mother set down her glass of wine and gave Abby a nervous smile. "I'm glad you're here, sweetheart. I have something I need to tell you, and I didn't want to do it over the phone."

Abby was alarmed. "Are you sick?"

"Oh, no. Nothing like that." Her mother fiddled with her chopsticks. "The thing is… I've met someone. A nice man who works in the financial district. He came in to have a painting appraised, and we hit it off. He asked me out to dinner, and well…things snowballed. He's asked me to move in with him."

"Mom!" Abby gaped, her brain swirling. "How long ago was this?"

"Back in February. You've been traveling a lot, and I didn't want to say anything until I knew if it was going anywhere."

Abby was shocked to the core. She didn't remember her mother ever dating anyone, which now that she thought about it was highly unlikely. Maybe her mom had been discreet for

Abby's sake. Or maybe she had put her personal life on hold until her daughter was old enough to fend for herself.

"I'm happy for you, Mom. Really."

Her mother beamed. "I'd love for you to meet him, but I suppose it will have to be when you're finished with that festival project. August, maybe?"

"I'd like that."

"And about this apartment..."

"You should sell it," Abby told her. "I'll find a place. Don't worry about me."

Her mother grimaced. "I'm not going to rush into marriage. I'd rather you keep the apartment for now. That way, if things don't work out for me, I won't end up looking for some place to live."

"Are you unsure about this relationship? Is that it?"

Her mother's face glowed. "Oh, no. Not at all. Bradley is a wonderful man. We have fun together. And we laugh a lot. But I failed at marriage once. It's made me gun-shy, I guess. For now, I just want to enjoy his company and see what happens."

Half a dozen emotions buffeted Abby. Time never stood still. Her parents had been divorced for almost two decades, but this new development felt like a threat. That was dumb. After all, Abby wasn't a child anymore. Her mother deserved to be happy.

Clearly, there would be no mini family reunion in Malibu.

Her eyes burned. "Tell this Bradley person that he's found a jewel. I love you, Mom. This is wonderful news."

They both stood. Hugged tightly.

A few moments later, Abby put her dishes in the dishwasher and threw away the take-out cartons. "I need some exercise after sitting on a plane forever. You want to come with me? A walk in the park, maybe? It's too hot to run."

Her mother shook her head. "Thanks, sweetie. But I have some work to do, and Bradley will probably call in a bit. Will you be okay on your own?"

"Of course."

Abby changed clothes and went downstairs. Out on the pavement, the heat was oppressive. Instead of her usual three-mile run, she decided to walk the streets.

New York was *home*. She loved the hustle and bustle and even the crowds in Times Square. The city was huge and vibrant, and always *open*. Where else could you get a doughnut and coffee at 2:00 a.m.? Or a pizza.

The clothes shopping and the bookstores energized her. She found entertainment in the trendy boutiques and the high-end fashion empires that might not have what she wanted or needed, but were fun to explore anyway. Everything about the city of her birth was part of her DNA.

Yet, for the first time, she felt something was missing. Sex with Carter was great, but she yearned to hear his laugh. To enjoy his droll sense of humor. Her day felt empty and flat without him.

What did that mean? Was she in too deep?

She lost track of how far she walked. Surrounded by strangers, she nevertheless felt completely at home. Alone, but not lonely.

When it was time to head back, she was no closer to making a decision. Truthfully, there was no decision to make. If she wanted to sleep with Carter Crane a few more times, she could do that. He'd be happy to oblige. She was sure of it.

Why did she have to get swept off her feet by a man who lived several hundred miles away? As much as she cared for him, why indulge in something that had no future?

It was a question with no answer. Or at least not one she wanted to hear.

Even worse, Carter had never responded to her text. What did that mean? Was he done with her?

Tuesday flew by. Abby had lunch with a couple of friends. They had known each other since the beginning of high school and always managed to pick up right where they left off. Abby wanted to tell them about Carter, but she felt self-conscious. She wasn't in a relationship with him. Just because he had seen her naked, and she was crazy about him didn't mean anything was going to come of it. Carter was Carter, and Abby was Abby.

They were great in bed, but morning always came.

After lunch, she stopped in at a high-end outdoor adventure store and picked out a small tent and the most basic of camping supplies. Her family had never done the camping thing, but Abby was certain she could make it through one night in the relative wilds of Appaloosa Island. Shooting at dawn was one of her passions. The morning light made cinema magic.

She plunked down her credit card and paid an ouch-worthy premium for two-day delivery to Texas. As the day passed, she grew more anxious about returning to Royal. Would Carter expect to see her again? And could *she* handle seeing him again now that she was at least being honest with herself about her feelings?

Abby and her mother went out for dinner that evening. They even dressed up and made a celebration of it. The meal was fun and delicious and just like old times.

But the world was turning, and life was changing. Abby had to change along with it whether she wanted to or not.

Wednesday morning, her mother gave her a tight hug before heading off to work. "We'll make a date for August," she said. "Whenever you know your plans and your schedule for coming home. I'm glad the documentary is going so well."

"Thanks, Mama." Abby hugged her again. "Bradley had better treat you right, or he'll have to answer to me."

Her mother laughed, her face alight with happiness. "I'll be sure to tell him."

After the door closed, Abby had half an hour to kill before her rideshare arrived. She stood at the living room window and looked beyond the nearest buildings to the slice of Central Park she could see.

It would be hard to find a view more different from the one in her memories of Royal, Texas.

She wasn't a weepy woman, but she felt alarmingly emotional. What had happened to her? Why was she drawn back to a Texas town with red dirt and no subway system? Lots of cows, but no Broadway.

The ostensible reason was her project about Soiree on the Bay. That much was true. But she wouldn't lie, even to herself. Her documentary had made room on the shelf for something, or someone, equally important. Carter Crane. Abby's feelings for him went far beyond the physical.

How could she be falling for a man who was so wrong for her?

At the airport, she boarded the jet, unable to ignore the undercurrent of excitement she felt. By dinnertime, she would be back on Carter's home turf. The hotel had even blocked the same room she had been in last week. Lila's recent text said everything was a go for the overnight campout on Appaloosa Island.

The festival dates were fast approaching. Abby had a lot to accomplish before then. Even if she wanted to, she couldn't afford to fool around with Carter all the time. She had to focus on her task.

Unfortunately, today's flight itinerary had two different connections, first Atlanta, then Dallas. By the time the plane finally landed in Royal, it was almost dinnertime.

Abby felt let down when there was no one at the airport to greet her. Which made no sense at all, because she hadn't told anyone her plans. Had she actually been hoping for a big, romantic scene where Carter met her at baggage claim and swore they could juggle all their differences?

She snorted inwardly as she waited for her luggage. There was a reason she produced documentaries instead of rom-coms. Her subjects were framed in truth, not romantic fiction. *She* controlled the outcome, not the notoriously capricious whims of fate.

By the time she made it to the hotel, her stomach grumbled loudly. She checked in, threw her things in the room, brushed her teeth, fluffed her hair and then headed out again. She didn't want room service, and she didn't want to eat in the hotel dining room alone. Not tonight.

Fortunately, there was a great pizza place down the street.

The elevator moved far too slowly. Or maybe Abby's patience was shot. That was the trouble with air travel. It took all day to make a little progress.

When she stepped into the beautifully appointed hotel lobby, the first person she saw was Carter. He was leaning against a column, dressed in dark slacks and wearing a snow-white dress shirt with the sleeves rolled up and cowboy boots.

His slow smile took the starch out of her knees.

He straightened and met her halfway. "Hey, Abs. I missed you."

And then he caught her up in his arms and kissed her so long and so hard that the clerk at the front desk clapped and cheered, as did a couple of guests.

Abby's face was on fire when she pulled away. "I missed you, too," she whispered.

"Where were you headed?"

"Dinner. I've been on planes all day, and little packets of peanuts don't cut it. I need real food."

"How 'bout I take you to one of my favorite hole-in-the-wall places? It's quirky, but the food is fantastic."

She looked into his blue eyes, seeing the genuine pleasure reflected there. His enthusiasm made her feel good. After two somewhat odd visits with her parents, she'd been adrift. Unsettled. Carter's presence was exactly what she needed.

As he helped her into his car, she sat back and sighed, feeling her bad mood and her gloomy outlook improve. The Caballero Cantina was just as Carter had described. The rough plaster walls inside were yellow and orange and decorated with colorful murals.

The hostess gave Carter a smile that was too flirty for Abby's peace of mind, but the young woman seated them at a nice table in a corner shielded from view by the high back of an adjacent booth.

Abby's mouth watered as she perused the Tex-Mex menu. At Carter's recommendation, she ordered a fajita bowl. While they waited, she ate far too many chips and queso. But hey—what was the point of visiting Texas and not indulging in the local cuisine? The meal, when it came, was incredible.

Carter laughed at her. "You like the food?"

"How come I've been here all this time, and you're just now telling me about this place?"

"I've been busy, I guess."

Her stomach clenched. "I'll admit, I was surprised to see you tonight."

"I thought we agreed to touch base when you returned."

She tilted her head and studied his bland expression, searching for any evidence that he was as calm as he looked. "Touch base? Or go all the way home?"

Carter leaned forward and wiped a tiny drip of cheese from her chin with his fingertip. His crooked smile was sexy and wicked. "I guess that's up to you."

Abby considered inviting him back to her hotel room, but something stopped her. She wanted him too much. Her feelings weren't so hard to decipher. She was falling in love with him, and she knew they were the least likely couple in Royal to make a go of things.

In a last-ditch nod to self-preservation, she forced herself to speak lightly. "I'm sure there will be some base touching. But I'm exhausted, Carter. Rain check? Please?"

His smile faded as his gaze narrowed. "Are you okay, Abs? What happened while you were gone?"

"Nothing really." Oh, heck. She might as well tell him. "I found out that my mother has a boyfriend. And they're moving in together."

He sat back and whistled. "That must have been a shock."

"You could say that. I didn't even know she was dating."

"Will you still feel comfortable living with her?" he asked.

Trust Carter to cut through to the basics of a situation. "Actually, she's moving in with *Bradley*. She wants me to keep our apartment, so she'll have a place to go back to if things don't work out."

"That's pretty cynical."

She sighed. "You'd have to know my mother. She's a pragmatist through and through."

"Should I say, *I'm sorry, Abby*?"

"That's just it. I don't know how to feel. When I was with my dad, I was making a fun little plan for the three of us to hang out in Malibu for Labor Day weekend. He was okay with it. He and my mom are cordial. But I didn't know about *Bradley*."

"You're gonna have to stop saying his name like that," he cautioned.

"I know."

Carter leaned back in his chair and ate another chip. "I have news that might cheer you up."

Thirteen

"Oh? Tell me." Abby was instantly intrigued, especially because Carter's smile was teasing. As if he was eager to spring his surprise on her.

He took a long swig of his drink, drawing out the suspense. "You mentioned camping out to get some shots on Appaloosa Island with the morning light..."

"Yes."

"Well, I called in a favor. A couple of my college buddies went in together five or six years back and bought one of those fancy-ass houses at the western end of the island. They share it between the families. I checked, and this weekend no one is using it. If you want to, you and I can go out there and spend a night or two. It's very private. Luxurious. What do you think?"

She thought about the camping gear she'd had shipped to the hotel. But when she balanced that against spending a romantic weekend with Carter, it was no contest. "I think it sounds great!" She knew what she was agreeing to, and why. This would be one last wonderful rendezvous with Carter. After this weekend, she had to go cold turkey.

"Good." He grinned. "I'll tell them we'd like to use the house."

"Should I offer to pay for it?"

"Nope. I'll send them each a case of their favorite whiskey, and they'll be good."

When the meal was over, Carter drove her back to the hotel. Already, she was second-guessing the fact that she had kept him at bay tonight. She had to get her head on straight. She wasn't really in love with him, was she?

The fact that she didn't know for sure made her jittery.

He pulled up under the hotel portico but didn't get out. "Sleep well, Abby."

She turned sideways in her seat. "Thank you for dinner. And thank you for working out the Appaloosa Island thing. That will be a whole lot better than sweating in a tent."

He ran a finger along her chin, his touch arousing her despite its innocence. "I'm hoping *I'll* get a chance to make you sweat, but that's up to you. We can hang out as friends. I don't expect sexual favors in exchange for our accommodations."

"I never thought you did." She reached across the console and kissed him softly on the lips. He went still but didn't react. "I want you, Carter, but I have a few things to figure out. Give me time."

"However long you need, Abs." He twined a strand of her hair around his finger. "I won't hurt you. I care about you, Abby."

The stark sincerity in his voice was exactly what she was afraid of… Carter *did* care about her. She knew that. And she felt the same way about him. But she didn't want to lose control of the situation. As long as she kept her expectations clear, everything would be okay.

She ignored those last five words he said, mostly because she didn't know how to respond.

The festival was fast approaching. After that, Abby would be spending a lot of time in LA working on the documentary.

When the film was done, she would likely go back to New York. And meet *Bradley*.

"What time this weekend?" she asked.

"I'll pick you up Friday at six. We can eat a picnic in the car. Amanda Battle's diner offers that kind of thing."

"Sounds perfect. What do I need to bring?"

The uniformed hotel employee kept giving them glances, as if worried they were blocking the drive. This time it was Carter who leaned toward Abby. He put a large warm hand behind her neck and coaxed her closer for a blistering kiss that made her quiver. "The house is fully furnished," he said huskily. "All you need is a toothbrush and a swimsuit. But on second thought, maybe just the toothbrush."

When he laughed softly, Abby wanted to forget all about her rules. She wanted to drag him upstairs to her bed. Instead, she exhaled and opened her door. "Good night, Carter. Sweet dreams."

He got out of the car and rested one arm on top of the door to give her one last smoldering smile. "You, too, Abs. We can compare notes later."

And then he was gone.

The mirror on one wall of the elevator showed a woman who was weary from a long day of travel, yet also flushed with excitement. Carter did that to her. He made everything a little brighter, a little more vibrant.

That night as she showered and got ready for bed, she pondered the implications of spending the weekend with him. It was a work trip, sure. But with plenty of time for fun. She told herself this was as far as she would let things go.

They hadn't even known each other a month. Surely this sexual attraction would burn itself out soon. She was a novelty to him.

Furthermore, she could think of at least a dozen reasons why the two of them could never be a real couple.

Bottom line? As much as she liked him, and was maybe even

falling for him, she was more like her mother than she realized. Carter wasn't part of the big picture. He wasn't Abby's *future*.

Carter went into town Thursday with a list of errands his ranch foreman would have been happy to tackle. But he was hoping to bump into Abby. How pathetic was that? He had resorted to acting like a middle school boy. All hormones and no sense.

He didn't see Abby at all, but he did run into Lila at the post office. She was in line in front of him. They chatted briefly, but when he exited, she was waiting for him.

"May I speak to you for a minute, Carter?" she asked.

"Of course." They took advantage of a patch of shade beneath a large tree. "What's up?"

"It's Abby," she said. "I know it's not my business, but it sounds like the two of you are getting close."

He tensed. "Once again, Royal's grapevine is operating on all cylinders."

"Don't be mad. I'm just worried about her. She doesn't know many people here, at least not on a deeper level. And after Madeline, you haven't dated much."

"Is there a point to any of this?" he asked impatiently.

"Yes, there is." She looked him square in the eye. "What's the deal with Abby? You know she's not staying. And you know you won't leave."

His jaw tightened. "Abby and I are just having fun. And yes, it hasn't escaped me that she's too much like Madeline for any kind of long-term relationship. Abby is big-city dreams, and I'm a Royal rancher. It doesn't get much more different than that."

"She's young, Carter."

"Not that much younger than you."

"Maybe not. But beneath that big-city polish, I think she's vulnerable. You could hurt her. Why take the chance?"

"You and Zach are total opposites, too," Carter pointed out, trying not to reveal his frustration. "But you're making it work."

"Because Zach decided he wanted to stay in Royal," she said.

Lila was giving voice to every reservation Carter had about Abby. "I like her," he said slowly. "A lot. And I care about her well-being. More than I've cared about any woman in a long time. I know this thing between us is temporary. But I haven't made any promises, and neither has she. You'll have to trust me on this. Abby and I know what we're doing."

The distress on Lila's face was genuine. "I hope so, Carter. You're a good man. I know you wouldn't lie to her. But sometimes we want what we can't have."

"I'll be careful," he said. "You have nothing to worry about."

Carter carried Lila's words like a stone in his shoe for the rest of that day and into Friday. Should he call off the trip to Appaloosa Island? Let Abby go camping alone as she had originally planned? His idea about the house had seemed innocent enough, but now he didn't know. Was it wrong to take what Abby had to give, knowing it could never be anything more than this moment in time?

By the time he picked her up Friday at six, his gut was in knots. Most of that tension subsided when he saw her. The smile she gave him as she slid into the passenger seat was happy and carefree.

Lila was worrying over nothing.

Abby wasted no time digging into the wicker hamper. "I'm starving," she said. "Can you eat and drive at the same time?"

"Not a problem."

He headed out of town and onto the highway that would take them south to Mustang Point. Abby handed him a ham sandwich and opened a bag of chips. "Royal is getting really excited about the festival. People were talking about it everywhere I went today."

Carter snorted. "Wait until the shops are overrun with tourists and all the garbage cans are spilling over into the streets."

She opened a can of soda and shook her head slowly. "You

really are a Scrooge, Carter Crane. New York has tons of people—tourists, too. But we get along very well."

"To each his own, I guess," he grumbled.

"Why don't we talk about something we can both agree on... books? Movies?"

The trip passed quickly. Abby seemed determined to put aside their differences. That was fine with Carter. He knew how very *unalike* they were. That was the problem.

Abby had read and reread the Harry Potter books, but also enjoyed political biographies. Carter was a Grisham fan and studied military history. They both agreed that the movie business was relying too much on blockbusters and not branching out enough.

When they finished their meal, Abby tucked the debris back in the hamper and returned it to the back seat. "I have a tiny bit of bad news," she said.

He shot her a sideways glance, seeing the apologetic look she gave him. "Oh?"

"I know you and I were planning to stay the whole weekend at your friends' house, but I got an invitation today for a black-tie reception at the Bellamy. It's a last-minute kickoff event on Saturday night for Soiree on the Bay, VIP only. They're going to hand out sample schedules, and I think one of the bands is going to play a few songs. I really need to be there."

"No problem," he said, refusing to admit he was disappointed. Having Abby naked and willing for an entire weekend had been a tantalizing prospect. "Am I invited?" he asked, tongue in cheek.

She took him seriously. "You probably are, but in any case, you're my plus-one...if you're willing."

He reached out and took her hand, lifting it to his mouth so he could kiss her fingers. "I know how important this documentary is to you. And I want to support you. So yes, I'd be happy to be your date."

"Great." Her grin was smug, as if she had talked him into

something against his will. Little did she know that he would do almost anything to make her happy. It was a sobering realization for a man who walked through life alone.

He had never wanted to depend on a woman again. Yet here he was, twining his life with hers. What was that old saying? Give a man enough rope and he'll hang himself? Carter was heading for a calamity of some sort. A dramatic end-of-the-road thing. And probably sooner than later.

By the time they caught the ferry at Mustang Point, crossed the water and then drove to the inhabited western end of the island, the sun was low in the sky. He handed his phone to Abby. "Read me the directions from that text."

The instructions were simple enough. Soon, they were pulling into the driveway of what could only be described as a seafront villa. The architectural style was Italian.

Even Carter was impressed, and he was used to the immense wealth in Royal. This was over-the-top in every way.

Carter chuckled as they carried their things inside. "You pick a bedroom, Abs. Plenty to choose from."

He followed her down a hall. "This one," she said. "Look at the view."

One entire wall of the master suite was glass. Actually, there were three similar master suites, but this one was the closest to the pool.

They stood at the huge windows and used the binoculars they found on a nightstand. Dolphins gamboled fairly close to shore, probably fishing for their dinner. Sailboats streaked across the bay. Palm trees, planted by landscapers, added drama to the sunset scene.

Unselfconsciously, as if it were the most natural thing in the world, Abby rested her head on his shoulder. "What should we do first?" she asked.

His body tightened. What he *wanted* to say was crude and self-evident to any man with a pulse. But he could wait. Maybe.

"How about a swim? And then an early bedtime? Since you have to be up before dawn."

She laughed softly. "I hope *bedtime* is a euphemism for something."

"Hell, yeah..."

They changed clothes in different bathrooms. Abby still occasionally exhibited a frustrating reticence around him. As if she were guarding some part of herself. Yet the more she held back, the more he wanted to push for more.

They met out at the pool. Abby was wearing a gold bikini that made his heart slug hard in his chest. Her long, toned legs, narrow waist and high, rounded breasts were showcased to perfection.

He cleared his throat. "Nice swimsuit, Abs."

She pulled her hair into a ponytail and secured it with an elastic band. "Thanks. I picked up a few more clothes when I was in New York. I honestly didn't know what I would need when I packed the first time."

He followed her down the shallow stairs into the pool, side by side. "What did you think Texas was going to be like?"

She shrugged as they waded deeper. "I didn't really know. Except for tales about everything being bigger in Texas." Without warning, she tweaked the front of his swim trunks. "That part turned out to be true." Laughing at his look of shock, she did a shallow dive and escaped to the deep end.

He chased her instinctively, energized by the game. But Abby was fast and nimble. Slippery, too. It was several minutes before he had her corralled against the side of the pool. He kissed her, tasting warm woman and anticipation. "You asked me to give you time, Abby. What did you mean by that? Time for what?"

"I couldn't decide what to do about you. About us."

"And now?" Her spiky eyelashes collected water droplets and let them fall, looking like tears.

Her smile was shaky. "I don't want to be serious right now.

I'm like Cinderella at the ball. My time in Royal is running out. Let's have fun this weekend, Carter. That's all."

He should be happy. No-strings sex. With a beautiful woman who made him laugh. Why did her answer disturb him? "If that's what you want."

"It is," she said.

Abby curled her arms around Carter's neck and kissed him. Like every time before, the taste of him went straight to her head. Like hard liquor. She felt the strength in his gentle hold and sensed his frustration that was perhaps even more than physical. Neither of them liked the way this was playing out, but they were both trapped.

She loved the feel of his body against hers. The differences were stark and arousing. Carter was a man in his prime, his muscles the product of hard physical labor. She was rapidly becoming addicted to his flashing grin and twinkling blue eyes.

But was she really the kind of woman who would give up everything for a man?

He seemed fond of her. And yes, they were dynamite in bed. But if she even *considered* making such a huge change in her life, it would have to be for one reason only. Love.

She shuddered in his arms, relishing the way he commanded the kiss and changed it from playful and affectionate to intense and erotic. Their bodies recognized each other. Whether it was the novelty of being with someone new and different, or a deeper connection, she and Carter were made for each other when it came to sexual chemistry.

His heavy erection pulsed at her belly. "I want you," he rasped, his chest heaving against her breasts.

They hadn't been in the pool long at all. Abby didn't care. All she wanted was Carter. "Yes," she whispered back.

They took time to play in the outdoor shower, rinsing off the chlorine and stripping off their suits. There was no one to witness the moment when Carter scooped up a naked Abby in his arms and strode back to the house.

She knew suddenly that this precious moment was her swan song with Carter. The poignant knowledge was a knife to her heart, the pain searing her composure.

It took everything she had to conceal her turmoil.

In the bedroom, Carter abandoned her only long enough to grab towels from the bathroom. He dried her carefully, lingering over her breasts, kissing her again and again. She shuddered as arousal wrapped them both in a veil of need.

Carter rifled through his suitcase for protection and joined her on the big bed. He leaned over on one elbow, curling his hand in her ponytail and holding her down. "You're mine tonight, Abby."

The slight tug at her scalp made her breath come faster. He was showing her an edge to their passion that they had only skated near before. She craved his forcefulness and would give him everything in return.

When he kissed her once more, she sank her teeth into his bottom lip. "I want to push you over the edge, cowboy. What do you think of that?"

His cheekbones flushed dark red, and his pupils dilated. "I think you talk too damn much." His lips and teeth and tongue dueled with hers, establishing dominance, but with a dollop of tenderness that promised safety in a storm.

When he entered her with a guttural groan, she felt the sting of tears. Maybe love didn't come so quickly. But who was to say? What she felt for Carter was an overwhelming tide, a thrilling rush of passion. She *loved* him. Or she was *falling* in love with him. What did semantics matter when the ending of their story was so painfully clear?

He took her long and hard and then soft and slow, drawing out the pleasure until she was wild with wanting him, her fingernails marking his powerful shoulders.

"Carter..." She cried out his name when she came, lost to reason, lost in a lover's embrace.

She felt the moment when his control snapped and he let his own passion overcome him. Holding him as tightly as she could, her body absorbed the aftershocks. Her fingers tousled his hair, and her breath mingled with his.

Gradually, their heartbeats slowed. The sweat dried on their bodies.

Carter mumbled something inaudible and reached to pull up the covers.

In seconds, they were both asleep.

Abby awoke hours later, disoriented and confused. The bedroom was strange. But awareness gradually returned, and she knew whose big warm body was entwined with hers.

It was 5:00 a.m. She slipped carefully out from under the masculine arm and leg that held her pinned to the mattress. Carter never moved.

With the flashlight on her phone, Abby found clothes in her suitcase and put them on. Cotton pants with a drawstring waist, comfortable, but thick enough to protect her legs if she had to kneel on the ground. A long-sleeve T-shirt to guard against a cool morning breeze. Canvas sneakers that had seen better days.

The whole process took less than five minutes. She decided to let Carter sleep. After all, he had to drive them back to Royal later today. They'd brought no provisions for breakfast. That was an oversight. But she kept energy bars in her camera bag for just such an occasion.

She made it all the way through the house and out to the driveway before she remembered that she needed the keys to Carter's car.

Muttering under her breath, she stowed her gear in the trunk and returned to the house, stubbing her toe on a loose brick at the edge of the driveway as she moved in the dark. When she

reached the top step, the door opened, and there he was, filling the space.

"Are you trying to ditch me, Abs?"

The slight hint of annoyance in his voice could have meant
anything.

"No," she said. "But you were dead to the world. And you
have to drive this afternoon. I'm used to being on my own."

"I'm sure you are."

Now there was no mistaking his displeasure. "Come on,"
he said. "I have the keys. I assume we're headed to the festival site?"

She exhaled. "Yes."

They didn't speak on the way across the island. Abby asked
him to stop a time or two for a quick shot. But what she needed
most, with her back to the east, was to see the sunrise bathe the
upcoming Soiree on the Bay with mystical light.

The weather was perfect. Only a few high thin clouds to add
punctuation to the story she was hoping to capture. Already,
she could hear the commentary.

Thousands of festivalgoers will soon descend on Appaloosa Island, eager to eat and drink and rock out to the
sounds of America's popular bands. But do they realize
what beauty blossoms here in the sounds of silence?

Carter interrupted her mental flight of fancy. "Where do you
want me to park?"

"Closer to the water, please. And you don't have to get out.
I'll be ranging around."

His silence lasted two breaths, then three. "I'll go with you,
Abby. I'm sure you don't need me, but it will make me feel
better."

"Fine." She grabbed her camera and set up the tripod. After
filming a loop of the stars cartwheeling across the heavens, she
focused on the ribbon of dawn at the horizon. When she was

satisfied, she put the tripod back in the trunk and shouldered the camera. "Let's go."

They walked the festival grounds for the next half hour, shooting empty stages gilded in light. Focusing on sawdust paths and eventually, beams of sunlight traveling across the water. The work was exacting and exhilarating in equal measure.

She had assumed she would feel self-conscious having Carter at her heels. But his presence was oddly comforting. She was used to being on her own, that was true. Still, he added something to her routine, something indefinable and wonderful.

By the time the sun was fully up and beginning to warm the moist air, Abby was starving. Carter still hadn't said much. He was wearing his clothes from last night as if he had dashed out of the house to catch her and not bothered with his suitcase.

"Thank you," she said stiffly. "It was nice having company."

He ruffled her hair. "You're welcome." A huge yawn seemed to take him by surprise. "Is it nap time yet?"

"I was hoping you could summon a fast-food place out of thin air. I'd kill for coffee and a bagel."

He slid into the driver's seat and turned on the AC. It was amazing how quickly the Texas heat multiplied. "I can do better than that," he said. "I asked my buddy to arrange for a few supplies in the kitchen. According to him, a local lady cooks for them and delivers whenever they request meals."

"Great setup!" Abby exclaimed. "Does this car go any faster?"

Back at the house, they found a container of homemade blueberry muffins on the counter and in the fridge, fresh-squeezed orange juice along with a sausage and egg casserole. The coffeepot soon produced a heavenly aroma.

They ate at the island, standing up.

Carter reached over to brush a crumb from her chin. "Not to be sexist," he said, "but I'm astounded how beautiful you look at this hour of the morning. You're the opposite of high-maintenance, aren't you?"

She put her hands to hair that was riotously out of control, because she had gone to bed with it wet. "I appreciate the compliment, but I'm going to need to seriously up my game before tonight. Would you mind if we headed on back to Royal?"

He stared at her even as she kept her gaze on her breakfast. "No morning *exercise*?" he drawled, his meaning impossible to misinterpret.

Her cheeks burned. What could it hurt? One last time? Of course, that's what she had told herself about last night. "Sure," she said, hoping the word was breezy and not filled with indecision. "It's still early."

He picked her up and tossed her over his shoulder, making her squeal with laughter. "What are you doing, Carter?" she said breathlessly.

His answer was succinct. "Saving time."

She thought he might suggest a shared shower. But no. Instead, he stripped her naked, undressed himself and bent her over the arm of the settee, taking her from behind.

He did pause at the last second to grab a condom, but after that, things got a little crazy. It almost seemed as if was trying to prove a point or maybe coax her into protesting.

Not a chance. She memorized every frenzied thrust, every touch of his hands on her body. Her heart was breaking, even as she climaxed sharply with his weight pressing her into the soft upholstery.

When it was over, he tugged her to her feet, cupped her neck in two hands and kissed her lazily. "Now *that's* the way to start a morning," he said.

Fourteen

Carter was sleepy on the way back to Royal. Abby had been right about that. And as soon as they left the ferry and made it over onto the highway, she was out cold, her neck bent toward the window at an awkward angle.

It was just as well. Carter needed time to think. He and Madeline had tumbled into a relationship based on sex, and that had ended in disaster. Was he doing the same thing with Abby? He honestly didn't think so. What he felt for her was different, not even in the same ballpark.

After Madeline walked out on him, he had been furious, but he had repaired his life and carried on.

If Abby left for good, he feared there would be a gaping hole in his chest, his world, his *heart*. He was in danger of loving her—or maybe he already did, but it was too soon to admit it. How could he let her go?

Could he persuade her to stay in Royal? Surely, she understood what bound him to Texas. The responsibilities he carried, the weight of his heritage and his family's expectations. But would it matter in the end?

She roused about two hours into the trip and reached instantly for one of the insulated flasks of coffee. After a long drink, she smoothed her hair and rubbed her eyes. "Sorry," she muttered. "You want me to drive now?"

"I'm fine." He squeezed her hand briefly. "Abby?" His heart pounded. "Have you thought about maybe staying in Royal longer than you first planned? You could move in with me until the festival is over and even after that. I have plenty of room to set up a studio for you."

Her silence echoed inside the car. It lasted for ten seconds. Or fifteen. Maybe an eternity. She had gone still as a bunny rabbit caught in headlights. "Well, I…"

The leaden weight of disappointment settled in his gut. "You don't have to decide right now. Just think about it."

He was glad that controlling the car gave him an excuse not to look at her.

Abby kicked off her shoes and curled her legs beneath her. She sighed. "I would love to stay longer, Carter, I really would. But as soon as the festival is over, my father has blocked off some time to help me with editing and postproduction of my documentary. And that will be in California."

He knew it was time to change the subject. "So have you settled on an angle for the film? A theme?"

Again, he experienced that unsettling lag between his seemingly benign question and her response. Abby tapped her fingers on the armrest. "I have. Dad and I looked at some of my early footage. I talked it over with him. He thinks the missing money angle could be a hard-hitting hook. Possibly even make my project more commercial."

"Abby, no. You're getting into something that could be dangerous."

"Who would hurt me, Carter?" There was a little snap in her voice.

"Money makes people do strange things. Besides, I think you're way off base. Nobody on the festival advisory board *needs* money. Billy Holmes is rich. You saw the evidence of that. The Edmond kids are each loaded, not even taking into account what they'll inherit from their father one day. I truly believe the whole missing money thing is nothing more than gossip, despite what Billy said. It's probably a few hundred bucks."

"Pull over, please," Abby said, her voice tight.

He swung the wheel immediately, steering them into a state rest area. They both got out and faced each other over the top of the car.

Abby's gaze was stormy. "You don't have any respect at all for my professional integrity, do you?"

"Of course I do, but you're—"

She made a chopping motion with her hand, cutting him off. "No. You don't. You think of this documentary as *Abby's little hobby.* I may be young, Carter, but I'm neither immature nor foolish. I have goals and dreams. Which is more than I can say for you."

His temper lit. "You don't know me. Don't pretend like you do. Sunset Acres is *my* ranch now, not my parents'. It's a huge part of who I am."

"Ah, yes. A Texas rancher. An esteemed member of the Texas Cattleman's Club. There's more to life than cattle, Carter. Maybe that's why your precious Madeline left you."

Though the flash of regret on Abby's face said she regretted her harsh words, Carter sucked in a deep breath and counted to ten. They were both exhausted, and if he read the situation correctly, they were each fighting an attraction that was bound to hurt them both. Why keep pushing?

His fists were clenched on the roof of the car. He relaxed them and stepped back. "Do you need to use the restroom?"

Abby glanced at the squatty brick building baking under the afternoon sun. "Yes. I'll make it quick."

Carter didn't move. As he waited for her to return, he tried to find a way out. But every idea he pursued mentally ended up a dead end.

Besides, he had no proof that Abby was as caught up in him as he was in her.

As she walked across the sidewalk in his direction, he studied her as a stranger would. Her graceful long legs covered the distance quickly.

When she slid into the passenger seat and closed her door, he got in, as well. Thankfully, he had left the engine running. The day was hot as hell. It might set a record.

He rested one arm on the steering wheel, tasting defeat. "I don't want to fight with you, Abs. Especially with so little time left. Maybe we should call a truce."

She half turned in her seat, her expression heartbreaking. "Yes," she said. "My father told me something recently that resonated. He said some people come into our lives for a season. I think that's you and me, Carter. As much as we I…like each other, there's no future in it."

She stumbled over the word *like*. Had there been another word on her tongue? Had Abby been considering *love*?

He turned the radio on, covering the awkwardness. The last thirty minutes of the trip felt like an eternity. At the hotel, he got out to help Abby with her bags. Although she protested, he carried the two heaviest items upstairs, waited while she unlocked the door and then dumped everything on the extra bed.

She shifted from one foot to the other. "You can skip the reception tonight. I'm fine on my own."

Her words seemed prophetic. She didn't need him. "No backsies," he said, hoping his smile was more genuine than it felt. "You invited me, and I said yes. What time should I pick you up?"

"Six thirty will work. Remember, it's black tie."

"Got it."

They stared at each other across what seemed like an acre of thick carpet. Her bed was mere steps away. He wanted her with a raw ache that didn't let up.

Abby was visibly nervous. Did she want him gone? Was that it?

"I should go," he said, hoping she would try to change his mind.

She nodded. "I'll see you at six thirty."

He carried the memory of her with him as he said a terse goodbye and made his way back downstairs. A woman of secrets, a woman of mystery. What thoughts raced behind those dark brown eyes?

He crashed hard when he got back to the ranch. The way he counted it, he'd barely managed four hours of sleep last night. Weaving on his feet, he knocked the AC down a few degrees and climbed into bed. But the hell of it was, Abby had taken up residence in that bed. He couldn't forget the taste of her skin, or the faint scent that was uniquely hers.

When he awoke, it was almost five. He scrounged in the fridge and found a couple of chicken legs and some potato salad. Standing in the kitchen wearing nothing but his boxers, he pondered his options. At the end of the party tonight, he could take Abby somewhere private. The Bellamy had lots of luxurious nooks and crannies. He could find a spot and lay out his argument.

The two of them had something. Sexual chemistry. And feelings. Strong feelings. If he admitted that to her and asked her to stay for him, for *them*, he figured there was a fifty-fifty chance Abby would agree.

Later, when he strode into the lobby of her hotel right on time, she was waiting for him. Was that by design? To keep him out of her room?

He was so caught up in analyzing her motives, it took him a few seconds to register what she was wearing.

When he did absorb the full picture, all he could do was shake his head. "Wow. You look incredible."

"Thank you," she said, her smile guarded.

Gone was the young woman who didn't mind getting dirty

in pursuit of her career. In her place was a female who would draw the eye of every man at the Bellamy tonight. Abby's beautiful, wavy dark hair fell down around her shoulders. Her dress was red. *Sin* red. Fire-engine red. If his physical response to her had a color, it would be exactly this shade of red.

The dress was made of a thin, silky fabric in several layers that shifted and moved, drawing attention to her tall, alluring body. Tiny spaghetti straps supported a bodice that plunged deeply in front.

Abby's breasts curved in that opening, suggesting lush, unapologetic femininity. The dress clung to her form, defining her narrow waist and hugging her hips. The floor-length hem swished as she moved, revealing silver stiletto sandals and toenails painted to match the dress. The only jewelry Abby wore was a pair of dangly crystal and silver earrings.

Carter struggled to find his breath. "I should have taken you to a party sooner," he said, only half kidding.

She kissed his cheek casually. "*I'm* taking you, cowboy. You're my plus-one…remember?"

"I stand corrected." Outside, he helped her into the car and carefully tucked her skirt out of the way. When he slid behind the wheel, he shot her a glance. "If you were hoping to keep a low profile while you investigate possible fraud, that dress isn't going to do it."

She shrugged, toying with the small beaded purse in her lap. "I've decided not to discuss business with you anymore. It only makes us quarrel."

His lips twitched. "Understood. We're keeping things personal." He reached for her arm and rested his thumb where a pulse beat at the back of her wrist. She seemed so fragile, and yet he knew differently. Abby Carmichael was strong and resilient.

She tugged away, folding her hands primly in her lap. "Behave, Carter. I need to focus tonight."

"Is it possible you're a little obsessed with this movie you're doing? If you'd relax, we could eat and dance and mingle. You know...fun, normal people stuff."

"Don't pick a fight with me," she said. "I'll dance with you. But I'm also going to network the heck out of this party."

Abby realized that she wasn't at all bothered by Carter's gibes. She sensed the two of them were sustaining a fake argument for no other reason than to keep from jumping each other's bones.

The man was seriously hot. As a rich, rugged rancher, he always looked sexy, but tonight in his tux, he could make a girl swoon. His aftershave alone made her dizzy.

When they entered the Bellamy and headed for the ballroom where the Soiree on the Bay event was taking place, the whole place hummed with excitement. At a long table just outside the ballroom entrance, Abby surrendered her invitation.

No one was wearing name tags. This was too fancy a party for that. Besides, almost everyone present was a resident of Royal. They all knew each other.

Abby tucked her tiny purse in Carter's jacket pocket. As they made their way around the outer edge of the room toward the hors d'oeuvres, she spotted a number of people she recognized. The charismatic Rusty Edmond held court in one corner of the room, surrounded by beautiful women. He'd been married four times, but was currently single, hence the crowd.

All of the Edmond offspring were in attendance, though none of them were in the same vicinity. Ross was with his fiancée, Charlotte. Asher was deep in conversation with a cluster of men who all held cocktails and ignored the crowd that ebbed and flowed around them. Gina flitted from group to group, talking up the festival and laughing with friends.

Billy Holmes stood off by himself, surveying the chaos with a pleased smile.

Then suddenly, there was Lila Jones wearing a lavender gown that flattered her pale complexion. She flashed a smile at Carter and Abby. "Hey, you two. I want you to meet my fiancé, Zachary. Zach, this is Abby Carmichael, who's doing the documentary, and Carter Crane owns the Sunset Acres ranch just outside of town."

After greetings were exchanged, Abby whistled inwardly. Sweet little Lila Jones had hooked up with a blond, gorgeous guy like this? Good for her.

When someone else demanded Lila's and Zach's attention, Carter leaned down and whispered in Abby's ear, "Quit drooling. He's taken."

She grinned. "I can appreciate a fine work of art."

Carter brushed a strand of hair from her cheek and gave her an intimate smile, his body close to hers in the press of the crowd. "Is he your type? Blond and hunky?"

"I think you know that's not true." She searched his gaze. But it was as opaque and unreadable as the ocean at night. What was he thinking?

A few moments later, Carter was drawn into a conversation with a trio of fellow ranchers, something about alarm over the falling price of beef.

Abby was happy to escape that discussion. She finally made it to the food table and snagged a couple of shrimp and a bacon-wrapped scallop. Though this was cattle country, there wasn't much beef on the spread—only a tray of candied beef jerky.

The room was sweltering. Her forehead was damp. She spotted Valencia Donovan on the opposite side of the floor. Abby made her way through the throng. "Hey, Valencia. How are you?"

Valencia fanned her face with a napkin. "Hot. And you?"

"The same. I realized after I left you the other day that I had one more question I wanted to ask."

"Go for it," the other woman said.

"After your proposal was approved, who has been your contact on the committee? Who will be the one to disburse the funds to you?"

"Ah, yes. That would be Asher Edmond. He's been so helpful along the way. And very encouraging about how soon I might have the money. I owe him and the committee a great deal."

Before Abby could respond, another guest snagged Valencia's attention. Abby was alone for the moment. She wished fervently that she had thought to bring her video camera. Shots of this event, even if she only used snippets, would have been helpful. But in any case, she didn't have permission, so maybe it was a moot point.

Gradually, the room filled with glitz and glamour and excited chatter. The tuxedo-clad men were foils for the fashionable female plumage. Abby had grown up in an elite cross section of New York society. Her mother's family had deep connections in the city.

But here, she didn't belong. Just as she had never completely belonged back at home. The ache in her chest made her wonder if she would ever feel comfortable anywhere. Or maybe her destiny was to be what the Greeks referred to as *planetes*, wanderers.

Carter's life was anchored by the ranch. He had a purpose, a fixed spot in the universe.

Abby was a planet, always orbiting. Never finding home.

Suddenly, a large hand landed on her shoulder. She flinched and backed away instinctively. When she spun around, Billy Holmes stared at her.

"We need to talk," he said.

Was she imagining a hint of menace in his words? "Why?" she asked.

"I don't think I stressed enough how much I want you to drop the missing money idea. As I said before, it's a family matter. We're dealing with it. The festival doesn't need any bad publicity. Back off, Abby."

Before she could respond to his extraordinary remarks, Carter was back at her side. Scowling. He glared at Billy. "I hope I didn't hear you threatening my date."

Billy shrugged. "She's been poking her nose in a lot of places. If I were you, I'd convince her to stick to sweet stories with happy endings. Nothing like a libel charge to ruin a budding filmmaker's career."

Abby was stunned. This was a very different man than the one who had entertained her at his home. "But is it true?" she asked. "Is some of the money gone?"

Carter took her by the arm and steered her away. He vibrated with fury. "My God, you can't let it go! There are a dozen people in this room who would be happy to give you something for your documentary, but you keep beating a dead horse. Billy Holmes can ruin you in this town. I think it would be best if you go back to New York until the festival starts."

Abby felt as though someone had punched her in the stomach. There was not enough oxygen to breathe. "I was just doing my job," she whispered, conscious of eyes watching them.

"No," Carter said. "You were endangering your health and your reputation. *If* there is a significant amount of money missing—and I'm not saying there is—then all hell will break loose when the truth comes out. If Billy knows who the culprit is and he's protecting someone, you need to stay far, far away from this story."

"It's not your call," she hissed, angry and hurt.

"Maybe not. But I won't stand by and let you get caught in the cross fire. Come on," he said. "The band is starting to play."

The last thing Abby wanted to do was dance with the infuriating, dictatorial Carter Crane. But short of making a scene, she had little choice.

He pulled her into his arms and held her close. The music and the other dancers swirled around them. Abby felt her heart break clean through when she laid her cheek against Carter's shoulder and finally admitted to herself that she was deeply in love with him.

His body was big and hard and warm against hers. When they moved too quickly, her skirt tangled with his legs, binding them close. She felt the steady beat of his heart, heard the ragged tenor of his breath. He smelled of orange and clove and soap.

For a moment, she debated telling him how she felt. Offering to move to Royal permanently. After all, he had broached the subject, at least on a temporary basis. A few weeks ago, such an idea would have been laughable. But that was before she met the man who made her want to put down roots. Royal might not feel like home, but Carter did.

Even when he was being an overbearing pain in the ass, she knew he was the man for her, the man she wanted. But it was so quick. Could such intense feelings be trusted?

Carter had already suffered through one broken relationship. He wouldn't be eager to rush into another. She knew he had feelings for her. Lust. Affection. But anything more? How could she take that gamble?

And what about her life and her career? Why did it always have to be the woman who made all the sacrifices? Again, she understood bleakly that she and Carter were the worst matchup imaginable.

When the band took a break, Gina Edmond spoke briefly. As did her brother and stepbrother and Billy Holmes. Rusty Edmond looked on with a proud smile, but didn't involve himself in the speeches.

At last, the formalities were over.

Despite how much she wanted to trust that what they had was worth fighting for, Abby couldn't get over the fact that Carter had said he wanted her to leave town. Which meant he couldn't be as emotionally involved as she was if he could so easily say goodbye. If she was looking for a sign, she had found one.

Her chest hurt so badly she wondered if she was having a heart attack. She reached in Carter's jacket pocket for her small clutch purse. "I'm leaving," she said brokenly. "I—I don't want to see you anymore. Goodbye, Carter."

His face went blank with shock. Before he could say anything, Rusty Edmond took him by the arm, demanding his attention. Abby used Carter's momentary distraction to flee. She was counting on the fact that it would take him a few moments to break free.

Thankfully, she found a Lyft driver waiting at the front entrance. She flagged him down, climbed in and gave the hotel address.

But she didn't cry until she was in her room with the door locked and the dead bolt turned.

Carter felt like he was living in an alternate universe. How could Abby simply disappear? They'd been having a fight, sure, but he thought their dance had smoothed over the rough patch. He loved holding her, moving to the music.

I don't want to see you anymore. Goodbye, Carter. It was only when he heard those words that the blinders had fallen. Yes, it was quick. And yes, such emotion was suspect. But dammit, he loved Abby Carmichael.

If he'd had doubts about that, the sick feeling in his gut spelled out the truth. He had held something fragile and beautiful in his grasp, but he had let it slip away.

For three hours he called her cell, and then the hotel room landline. Eventually, he resorted to storming the Miramar and banging on Abby's door. When the night manager politely asked that he leave, Carter drove to the ranch, momentarily defeated, but not deterred. He paced the floor until 3:00 a.m. After that, he finally slept.

The following morning was Sunday. There was nothing he *had* to do. Nothing but find Abby and tell her the truth. He loved her.

But as it turned out, he had missed his chance. She was gone. Checked out of the hotel. And he'd been the one to send her away. In fact, he had *told* her to go. He was an idiot.

His first instinct was to jump on a plane and follow her, but to what end?

The two of them had been dancing around an ugly truth for

days. They had no common ground. Even so, he was a stubborn son of a bitch. He was passionate about Abby, and he refused to believe that love wasn't enough...all evidence to the contrary.

Abby returned to New York with her heart and her composure in shreds. To make matters worse, her mother was already staying at *Bradley's*. When she heard that Abby was home, she offered to come back to the apartment. But Abby declined, keeping her voice light and cheerful.

Life would go on.

The worst part was, she *had* to go back to Royal to film the festival. That was nonnegotiable. Otherwise, all the work she had done already would be wasted.

For five days, she huddled in her bed, crying, staring bleakly at the ceiling. How did anyone survive this kind of heartbreak? Carter was all she thought about.

Eventually, she got angry with herself. There was more to life than sex and love. She would go back to being the same person she had always been.

She showered and dressed and went to a museum. Had lunch at her favorite café. But it didn't help much at all. She *wasn't* the same person. Carter had changed her. He had made her want things. And she didn't know what to do.

Though she stayed out most of the day, there were no answers to be found. Late in the afternoon, she wandered into Central Park and walked the paths aimlessly. It was cloudy. A front had come through, bringing cooler temperatures and a smattering of raindrops.

A few things were clear. First, she had to return to the scene of her heartbreak. Even if she managed to avoid seeing Carter, the journey would be painful.

Second, she *would* finish her documentary. Either with or without the stolen money angle, she would do her very best work, and she would be proud of it.

And last, she had to find some closure. Did that mean confessing her love and watching Carter squirm as he searched for a way to let her down easily? The prospect was depressing. Even if she offered to move to Royal, she didn't think he loved her. How could he? They had been together such a short time.

When her legs were rubbery with exhaustion, she found a bench and sat down to watch children playing kickball on a grassy slope. All around her, the world kept marching on. Even her mother had found love.

Abby sipped her iced coffee and tried to find meaning in her rather colossal personal failure. Was she supposed to learn something from this experience? And if so, what?

People passed her occasionally, following the path. One stopped. "Abby…"

That single word, uttered in a deep masculine voice…

"Carter?" She looked up at him, wondering if she was hallucinating.

When he sat down beside her, the warmth and solidity of his presence convinced her he was real. "I've been looking for you for hours," he said, his tone terse.

She refused to apologize. "You're the one who told me to leave Royal," she said. If the words were snippy, she couldn't be blamed.

He sighed mightily. "You can't possibly know how much I regret that."

The silence between them stretched painfully. Everything she wanted was at her fingertips. But she didn't know how to reach for it…didn't know how to be true to herself and avoid her parents' mistakes.

Carter looked as handsome as ever, although perhaps there were new lines on his face, new shadows in his beautiful blue eyes. She didn't want to make him unhappy. Heck, she didn't want to make herself unhappy.

Did he expect to pull a ring out of his pocket and have her fall into his arms? Or maybe she was assuming too much. He might be here for nothing more than a booty call.

Suddenly, it was more than she could bear. She sprang to her feet. "You shouldn't have come," she said. Despair roiled inside her. She'd spent almost a week trying to forget him. How dare he stir things up all over again? It wasn't fair.

Carter reached out and took her wrist, his fingers warm as they curled against her skin. "I had to come, Abby. We weren't finished."

"Oh, yes," she said. "We were." But she couldn't find the strength to pull away from him. "There's no solution, Carter." That was the hell of it. "I can't see a way forward. Unless I give up everything. And even then, it would be on the off chance that we might end up with more than a hot and crazy affair."

"Oh, Abs." He closed his eyes and bowed his head, his posture defeated. After long, confusing seconds, he straightened and made her sit down again. He angled his body, so she could see his face. "I love you, sweet woman. And yes, it's for real. I struggled as much as you did. We were both struck by lightning, weren't we? And it left us reeling. But even if it was quick, it wasn't fake. We have to get used to that idea, maybe. But I have time, if you do."

"I don't understand." She was afraid, too afraid to be crushed a second time.

Carter looked as if he had aged in a week. He was haggard, with dark circles beneath his eyes. The handsome cowboy was still there, but he was rough around the edges.

Now he took both of her hands. "I have never felt for any woman what I feel for you, Abby. It's as if we swapped hearts, and yours is beating inside me. When I first saw you that night, I thought you were beautiful and mysterious, and I wanted to know more. By the time we left the bar at the Miramar, you had already staked a claim."

"Love doesn't happen that fast," she whispered.

"Maybe it does." His smile was curiously sweet. "I'm thirty-four years old, Abby. I've made my share of mistakes. But I don't want this to be one of them. Tell me, Abs. Am I on my own here?"

For the first time, she saw the vulnerability deep in his blue-eyed gaze. She found her voice. "I love you, too, Carter. How could I not?"

But even then, her stomach clenched. Love wasn't the problem.

He folded her close against his chest. They had skated perilously close to disaster. He stroked her hair. "You're my heart. I'm sorry I hurt you. That was the last thing I wanted."

In his arms, she was safe. Secure. Loved. But still she felt shaky. There were questions. And hurdles. Did she have the courage to bet all her cards on this one man? What if she gave up everything, and the two of them didn't last? "I'll have to figure a few things out," she said. "But I'll do it."

Carter pulled away, his chiseled jaw hard. "No. This is all on me. And I've already put things in motion."

"In motion?" She frowned at him.

He shrugged. "I've spoken to my family. Told them I'm in love with you. And I've made it clear that Sunset Acres will no longer be my first priority."

She blinked, stunned. "What does that even mean?" Was he proposing a long-distance relationship?

Carter's eyes seemed to be sending her a message, but she was puzzled. "I'll still hold the reins if they want me to," he said. "But we're hiring a manager. My parents and my sister agreed once they understood my position. I'll still have to spend a few days in Royal once a month, but other than that, I'm yours. We'll travel the world, or you can show me New York. Whatever you want."

She put her hands to her cheeks. "But that ranch is you, Carter. You love it."

He shook his head slowly. His gaze locked on hers as if he was willing her to believe. "It's just some cows and dirt. *You*, Abby. It's you I love."

Tears leaked from her eyes. The enormity of what he was saying overwhelmed her. How could a man walk away from a legacy?

He reached in his pocket. First, he handed her an expensive linen handkerchief. It was too pretty to get wet, but she wiped her face anyway.

Then Carter held out a box. "I went to Harry Winston before I came to find you. That was probably a mistake. I realize that now. I should have let you choose. But I wanted to give you a ring, so you would know I'm serious. We can exchange it."

Was this really happening? In a situation that was impossible, had Carter actually found a way?

Abby flipped the lid. She stopped breathing for a full three seconds. "Oh, Carter." He had bought her an enormous, flawless emerald. The setting was extremely plain, so there was nothing to detract from the magnificence of the stone. It would have cost him a fortune, even by Royal standards.

When she didn't move, he tried to take it back. "You'd rather have a diamond, wouldn't you?"

The dismay on his face galvanized her. She smacked his hand away. When she pulled the ring from the box, a ray of sunlight peeked from behind the clouds, struck the stone and flashed emerald fire in a million directions. She stared at the stone in awe. "Put it on me, please."

Gently, Carter slid the ring onto her left hand. "Marry me, Abby. When the engagement has been long enough. When you're sure."

Her heart quivered with relief and hope and love. "I'm sure, Carter." She cupped his face in her hands. "Maybe you won't believe me, but I'm sure I want to live with you in Texas. Honestly, I do. All my life I've searched for a way to fit in. But then I met you, and I realized I had found home. It doesn't matter if I don't like cows, or I miss Broadway. When I'm with you, I have everything I want."

He shook his head slowly, his expression wary. "We'll talk

about this. Marriage is about compromise, or so I've been told. We don't have to make any hard-and-fast decisions today."

She beamed at him. "But you already have. You were ready to give up your family's legacy. That means more to me than you'll ever know." A man who would do that wanted more than sex. He wanted forever, it seemed. The knowledge made her dizzy.

Carter kissed her forehead. "I want you to be happy, Abs. That's the most important thing, I swear. And I'll prove it to you."

"I believe you." She held out her hand and let the sun play with the emerald.

He tucked her in the crook of his arm. "The doorman told me your mother had moved out. And that you were living up there in that apartment all alone. Though he wouldn't give me any clue where to find you, so I'm not exactly on good terms with him."

"George is a sweetie. I'll vouch for you."

Her new fiancé kissed her hard, making her pulse race. "Does that mean I can stay for breakfast?" he asked, his hot gaze locking with hers, making her shiver.

"Oh, yes." Her body heated, already imagining the long night ahead.

They stood in unison, each ready to get on with their new life. Carter tucked his arm around her waist. "I love you, Abby."

"I love you, too."

He pulled back for a moment. "One more thing. I think you may have been right about the festival money. I'm sorry I tried to steer you away."

"Tell me."

He stared at her, started to speak and then kissed her forehead. "Can it wait until tomorrow? We're going to have to go back. But we can hash it out together. Okay?"

"You're really going to keep me in suspense?"

He lifted her hand to his lips and kissed the back of it. "This thing with you and me is brand-new, Abby. And we're here in this romantic city. Let's take one night just for us. Dinner and a show? What do you think?"

She searched his face and knew he was right. The festival secrets would keep. Tonight was a celebration. As she went up on her tiptoes and kissed him, his arms came around her and held her tight. "I love you," she whispered. "And if you don't mind, I think I'd rather spend the evening in bed. It seems like an eternity since we were together."

His eyes blazed with happiness and sexual intent. "I won't argue with that, Abs. Take me to your apartment and have your way with me."

"I thought you'd never ask…"

* * * * *

Trapped With The Texan
Joanne Rock

Joanne Rock credits her decision to write romance after a book she picked up during a flight delay engrossed her so thoroughly that she didn't mind at all when her flight was delayed two more times. Giving her readers the chance to escape into another world has motivated her to write over eighty books for a variety of Harlequin series.

Books by Joanne Rock

Brooklyn Nights

A Nine-Month Temptation

Dynasties: Mesa Falls

The Rebel
The Rival
Rule Breaker
Heartbreaker
The Rancher
The Heir

Texas Cattleman's Club: Heir Apparent

Trapped with the Texan

Visit her Author Profile page at
millsandboon.com.au,
or joannerock.com, for more titles.

Dear Reader,

What fun we writers have cooking up these stories for you! I love writing the Texas Cattleman Club stories because the connected plotlines always provide opportunities to chat and brainstorm with writer friends. For *Trapped with the Texan*, I dreamed up a whole family full of Cortez-Williams brothers with Barbara Dunlop, and then we browsed Texas properties online to find the perfect inspiration for the Cortez-Williams Ranch. The process is kind of like seeing a movie with a good friend. It's more fun when shared!

So settle in for the high drama of another trip to Royal, Texas. There's a storm brewing in this story, and all the careful planning for an arts festival on Appaloosa Island is at risk. I'd love to hear what you think of *Trapped with the Texan*. You can find me online at joannerock.com or millsandboon.com.au!

Happy reading,

Joanne Rock

For Patricia Savery,
whose strong spirit inspires me.
Thank you for reading as long as I've been writing!

One

Earbuds in place, Valencia Donovan cranked up the volume of her music while she rocked out discreetly in the parking lot of the Texas Cattleman's Club. Seated in the driver's seat of her late-model pickup truck, she sang along to her personal playlist labeled "Game Time Hype," even though her appointment within the walls of the prestigious, members-only club was no game.

Fiery girl-power anthems weren't anything she'd normally listen to at home or while working at her ranch. But as a dedicated overachiever, Valencia appreciated the ferocity of the lyrics before she had to give an important business pitch. She might be well beyond the age of her high school basketball days when she'd first started the playlist, but she wasn't about to mess with her winning streak now. Not when she really, *really* needed an investment from Lorenzo Cortez-Williams to expand her horse rescue operation.

Closing her eyes, she pumped her fist and let the final strains of the song flow over her while she visualized her success.

Slam. Dunk.

Smiling, she turned off the music once her energy fired to

life. And yes, maybe she glanced around the parking lot just a smidge self-consciously to see if anyone noticed her antics. But she'd parked in the farthest corner of the lot. Now, tossing the earbuds aside, she slid out of the truck and locked the doors behind her. She paused long enough to check her reflection in the side mirror, smoothing down a few curls that had sprouted in the humidity.

Her pre-meeting routine might be on the corny side, but the outfit she wore was conservative enough. A navy blue sheath dress with a matching jacket and nude sling-back pumps. She wasn't a member of the TCC herself, but she knew how the other half lived. Her adoptive family had raised her to be comfortable in this world, and Valencia had shaken off the dirt of her roots a long time ago. Her unhappy early childhood did *not* define her.

Checking her watch as she entered the dark-stone-and-wood historic building, she noted that she was precisely on time for her meeting. Which would undoubtedly work in her favor. The retired rancher whom she was meeting was a septuagenarian with deep pockets and a reputation for philanthropy. She intended to dazzle him with her business plan for Donovan Horse Rescue, and solidify the final necessary funds to expand the rescue so she could develop an equine therapy component in the form of a summer camp for kids. Her charitable foundation had already been promised a portion of the funds raised by the ticket sales to Soiree on the Bay, an upcoming food, art and wine festival on Appaloosa Island.

Today's meeting could yield the rest.

"Miss Donovan?" a man's warm baritone greeted her.

Valencia glanced up from her watch to meet the intent regard of a wildly handsome man. He had dark brown hair and dark eyes framed by heavy brows. A deeply tanned complexion that she guessed was more due to heritage than the sun. And his gray pants and black shirt were tailored in such a way that she couldn't help but notice how broad-shouldered and fit he was. Valencia sighed appreciatively as she continued to drink him in. Well over six feet, this guy loomed over her, and she was *not* a petite woman. Even without the expensive-looking boots he wore, he would still be tall.

Yikes! How long had she been standing there ogling him?

Her manners returned along with a hint of dismay. Since when did a hot-looking man turn her head? Especially when she had just played her game-time hype playlist and needed all her focus?

"Yes. I'm Valencia Donovan." She gave him a polite smile while hoping her racing thoughts didn't show on her face.

Dressed as he was, he couldn't possibly work at the Texas Cattleman's Club, but she also couldn't imagine who else would greet her by name.

"Lorenzo Cortez-Williams." He extended his hand. "A pleasure to meet you."

"Oh." Confused, she clasped his palm automatically upon hearing the name. But hadn't her meeting been with a much older man? The extremely compelling rancher whose hand enveloped hers couldn't be more than thirty-five years old. "I'm sorry. I thought—"

"You were expecting someone else?" He smiled warmly while gesturing her ahead of him. "Our table is this way."

Knocked off her game, Valencia took a deep breath as he relinquished her hand. She'd been too rattled to enjoy the touch even though her palm retained a hint of his warmth. Of course, she shouldn't be enjoying skin-on-skin contact with a potential investor. Berating herself for the slipup, she shoved aside thoughts of her companion's potent sex appeal and focused on business as she followed him through the dark wood-paneled corridors into the high-ceilinged dining area. Hunting trophies and historical artifacts provided understated decor where some of the most influential residents of Royal, Texas, enjoyed a meal.

"I read your bio to prepare for the meeting," she admitted as he showed her to a quiet table in the back. "And the photo of

Lorenzo Cortez-Williams showed a man closer to my grand-father's age."

"*My* granddad, no doubt. That's the problem with inheriting the family moniker. There are two other formidable Lorenzos still bearing the same name. I'm Lorenzo the third." As he with-drew a high-backed leather chair for her at the round table, she couldn't help but notice the ring finger on his left hand remained bare. "My father is Lorenzo Junior. Gramp is the original."

"Of course." She lowered herself into the chair he indicated, even as she struggled to recall what else she'd read about the Cortez-Williams family on their charitable website. "Will either of them be joining us?"

He slid her chair into place before taking the seat across from her. A waiter arrived to greet her at the same moment, bring-ing a carafe of water and pouring two glasses while taking their drink orders. When the server left, Lorenzo leveled that piercing brown-eyed gaze her way again. His full focus on her.

"It will be just us today, Miss Donovan."

"Please call me Valencia."

"Only if you pay me the same courtesy." He lifted his glass of water and clinked it softly to hers before taking a sip. "And I have taken over my grandfather's former duties. Gramp has grown a soft heart for causes, and a few months ago we dis-covered he was on track to donate most of the family fortune."

She hid her renewed sense of dismay by taking her time spreading her napkin over her lap. Did the man seated across from her need to reel in the spending now? She wished she could go back in time and prepare for this meeting differently.

"That must have been upsetting for your family," she mur-mured, before lifting her eyes to his. "Was he aware that he was in danger of overextending? I hope his health is still sound."

Lorenzo was still regarding her steadily, his dark gaze un-nerving her a bit. If they'd been in a dimly lit bar for drinks, she would have felt a feminine thrill at whatever chased through his brown eyes. But now, with the success of her dream on the line, it was distracting.

"Gramp is in excellent health, thank you." He shuffled aside his menu. "But we thought it best if I took over the vetting process for charitable donations. You'd be surprised how many con artists are out there."

Bristling at the implication, she forced a cool smile. "I assure you, my efforts to rescue horses are very real. I can provide you with references. People who can vouch for my character."

"I'm not questioning your integrity, Valencia. But as a representative of my family, I need to exercise caution since all of those things can be faked." There was a somberness in his expression that told her he'd had firsthand experience with those kinds of people.

The knowledge soothed her a bit, even as the last of her plans for this meeting crumpled under the need for a new approach.

"I'm sorry to hear that there are folks who take advantage of your family's generosity that way, but I suppose I shouldn't be surprised." She waited while their server returned with the iced tea she'd ordered. Then, listening to the waiter reel off the lunch specials, she chose the carne asada while Lorenzo asked for his "usual." After he departed, Valencia returned to her subject with renewed determination. "So tell me, how can I convince you that Donovan Horse Rescue is legitimate? Rest assured that I am emphatic about transparency with my finances."

The spark of interest in his smoldering eyes told her that he appreciated the approach.

"For starters, just meeting you in person is helpful. I like to size up who I'm dealing with face-to-face." He took a pull from his longneck, his expression thoughtful.

"I can't argue with that. I rely on my instincts, too. What else can I tell you about the rescue?"

"I look forward to hearing all about it over lunch," he murmured, setting down the dark bottle. "But I won't be relying solely on my instincts when making my final decision. If I like what I hear today, I'll want to visit Donovan Horse Rescue in person. Tour your facility and see what I think."

"Fantastic." She welcomed the chance to have him see the ranch for himself. She was proud of what she'd built, and knew every detail of her expansion plan by heart so she could explain it to him while looking at the footprint of the anticipated new additions. "I realize it's short notice, but are you available after lunch today?"

A shiver ran through her as she awaited his response. Because, as much as she anticipated selling him on her foundation, she also felt slightly wary of having this extremely compelling rancher walking around her personal space. She had the feeling Lorenzo Cortez-Williams would leave his mark somehow.

Which meant she needed to tread warily with a man who held the future of her mission in his hands.

"Unfortunately, I have another appointment this afternoon." His words disappointed her more than they should have, making her aware that the undercurrent of sizzling attraction she felt hadn't eased since they'd sat down. "Are you free tomorrow, perhaps?"

The smoky quality of his voice made the proposition feel more personal.

"For the prospect of showing you my operation, I would gladly clear my schedule. But as it happens, I'm free all day."

She couldn't have held back her grin. Strictly because she knew the rescue was impressive and would make her case for her. *Not* because she was already looking forward to seeing him again.

The rapid tattoo of her heartbeat, however, already called her a liar.

Business and pleasure don't mix.

Lorenzo Cortez-Williams should have been the last man in Royal, Texas, who needed to repeat those words like a mantra. They'd been branded into his skin by his restaurateur fiancée, who'd targeted him for his wealth, ran up his credit cards and then disappeared from his life five years ago. *After* she'd signed his family's beef company to a cut-rate deal for her restaurants, a deal that had seared more resentment into him with each passing year until it was done.

So why did he need to pull into a local coffee shop to remind himself of the necessary separation between work and play, lest he show up at Donovan Horse Rescue too early for his appointment with Valencia Donovan? Probably because the woman attracted him like no one else ever had. Ex-fiancée included. Valencia had impressed him with more than her smarts even though her business acumen came across immediately during their meeting. There'd been a warmth of spirit about her obvious love for horses, a commitment to her mission that practically shone out of her eyes when she spoke. He'd been...captivated.

Tightening his grip on the take-out cup from the drive-through, Lorenzo steered his truck back onto the county route that would lead to Valencia's place, reminding himself that he wouldn't be seeing her again after today. He'd already taken the liberty of ordering an investigation of her and her business, a practice that he'd leaned on after discovering how many scammers had shaken money out of the family's charitable fund in the past. Not to mention the fiasco with Lindsey that had made him question his own judgment. His private investigator was discreet. Thorough. And Lorenzo now had a detailed report on Valencia that showed her in a favorable light. At only thirty years old, she'd already blazed quite an illustrious path for herself. She'd aced high school and college, accumulating awards and honors for her community involvement even as a teen, before going onto tremendous success in the corporate world during her eight-year stint with an agricultural company based in Dallas.

Valencia's early childhood was a gray area since she'd been adopted when she was young and there was little information available about her formative years. Yet considering all she'd accomplished since then, Lorenzo was prepared to move forward with her request if he liked what he saw at the rescue today.

Assuming he could look at anything but her. How many times had he thought about her intelligent brown eyes taking his measure when she first saw him? There'd been a moment before she realized that she'd be meeting with him, when her response to him had been purely feminine. She'd hidden it fast and thoroughly once she'd recognized her error, but he couldn't get that look out of his head. Last night, he'd spent far too long letting their innocuous encounter spin out into other, more provocative scenarios in his mind.

Now he turned into the gravel drive that led to her place, his oversize pickup truck dipping into an uneven patch despite the high-grade suspension. Settling his drink into the cupholder so he could keep both hands on the wheel, he noted the creek's proximity and an equipment barn that looked like it had been recently upgraded. An unassuming one-story stone house sat on a low hill overlooking the creek, but the simple landscaping and unfinished garage told him that Valencia had put her finances into the horses instead of the home.

Something he could appreciate, having been raised on a ranch himself. He parked off to one side of the driveway between the house and the barn, then took a last bracing sip of his coffee before exiting the truck.

The scent of pink briar hung in the air, the driveway partially lined with the airy flowers that closed up when you brushed against them. Lorenzo skirted a thick patch of them to head toward the house. Before he'd gone three steps, a sorrel Belgian came into view as it jumped a low hedge behind the house, carrying Valencia Donovan on its broad back at a lengthened trot.

Dressed in faded jeans and boots, she was even lovelier today. Well-worn denim hugged her thighs while a flowy pink blouse rippled in the breeze around her shoulders. A buff-colored hat kept the sun from her delicate features, long blond waves trailing down her back. She rode with ease that went beyond good horsemanship that was common enough around this part of Texas. The animal's gait was one of the toughest to sit gracefully, especially on such a huge draft horse that would have a powerful trot. Yet her hips moved with practiced grace, the rest of her body still, a feat that spoke of long hours of training and muscles attuned to the work.

Damned if that display didn't jolt him right back into wayward imaginings about the woman he'd thought of far too often since their meeting the day before.

"Good morning," she greeted him on a breathless laugh as she swung down from the mare, her cheeks flushed with color. "I hope I haven't kept you waiting. Sapphire has taken a few days to settle in here, and she was in such good spirits on our morning run that I found it hard to turn her around."

Another woman—a ranch hand, he guessed—approached to take the mare's reins from her. But Valencia took an extra moment to tip her head to the Belgian's neck and croon softly at her before handing them over. Her compassion was obvious. After Lorenzo had been taken in by a false-faced woman in the past, he liked to think he had a better radar for deceit now. Valencia's love of the horses definitely wasn't fake.

"Sapphire is one of your rescues?" he asked, forcing himself to think like an investor in her foundation and not a man wildly enamored by a woman.

He really needed to start dating more. He didn't normally get sidetracked this way.

"Yes." Valencia's gaze followed the Belgian for a long moment before turning her pretty brown eyes to him. "Her owner died a few weeks ago and the man's nephew contacted me about taking her in. Some animals have ended up here because of neglect or unsuitable living conditions, but Sapphire has been well cared for." She gestured toward a stable he'd noticed when he drove in. "Would you like to see the facilities we have so far?"

"Very much." The more they kept the focus on the rescue,

the less attention he'd pay to the woman herself. "It looks like you've recently upgraded the outbuildings."

"I have." She headed in the direction of the stable. "I saved every cent from my job in the corporate world to put toward start-up costs for the rescue. My plan began with the right facilities that could expand as we grow."

"I read your three-phase business model." He'd been more than a little impressed with the level of detail. She'd anticipated every potential expense. "You should be able to afford the adjoining parcel of land next."

She needed more space before she could move into the next phase—an immersive equine therapy camp for troubled kids. The end goal had made him all the more curious about the unknown portion of her background—her birth parents and early home life. What struggles had she faced before her adoptive parents came into the picture?

"Yes. If the ticket sales to Soiree on the Bay are as robust as we all hope they will be, I'll be able to buy the land at the end of the month." As they passed the stone house, she excused herself long enough to dash up the front steps and open the front door so a black-and-tan dog—a border collie mix was his guess—could bolt down the stairs and run ahead of them. "That's Barkis, by the way."

"Barkis?" he laughed. "A funny name for a dog when he didn't even make a sound at seeing me."

"Barkis was a package deal along with the first horse I rescued." Her smile faltered a little as she spoke. "I learned about the animals from an eleven-year-old girl living next door to them. She'd drawn a crayon sketch of the horse and the dog and walked into a gas station to post it on their community notice board while I was buying a bag of chips for a road trip."

He heard the echo of some painful memories in the story, and felt a new wave of admiration for this beautiful, caring woman who not only abhorred suffering, but who felt called to help in a deeply personal way.

"You intercepted her sign?" he guessed.

"I was still working at my job full-time, even though I'd already started the business plan. I was on the road that day to see one of our more remote equipment dealers. But when I spoke to the little girl about the animals who needed help—neglected, hungry animals she petted and consoled through a rusted barbed wire fence every day—I recognized that moment was going to be my beginning." Her voice had gone fierce during the story, but she paused now to draw a breath as they reached the stable. "She didn't know the animals' names, but privately called the dog Barkis and the horse Tuxedo. I still give her updates about them."

Valencia nodded toward the stable door as she preceded him inside. It took him a moment to regain his composure after the story, though, envisioning her dressed in her business suit and heels in some ramshackle gas station, taking the time to listen to a passionate kid with a crayon drawing.

She'd somehow ditched her job and saved the animals, no doubt earning hero status in the kid's eyes. He followed her into the stable, his gaze drawn to the sway of her hips before he remembered himself.

If Valencia Donovan was putting on an act to entice funds out of the Cortez-Williams family, it was a damned good show. But with every moment he spent in her presence, even the most cynical part of himself found it tougher to believe. Which meant he'd have to try twice as hard to stick to his guns and avoid the potent temptation that dogged him every moment he spent with Valencia.

Two

Determined to prove her ambitions for Donovan Horse Rescue were very real, Valencia took Lorenzo through each building and introduced him to every horse on her property over the next two hours. She refrained from sharing more personal stories after accidentally confiding the way she'd leaped into the rescue work that first time. After that slipup, she stuck to the scripted details that were available on the rescue's website, unwilling to give a potential investor any reason to think she led with her heart and not her brain.

She could share heart-tugging stories. Just not the details that crawled under her skin and made her care on a deep level. Those dark eyes of his saw too much already.

As they turned away from Buttercup, the last of the horses in the new stable, they left the second stable building and skirted the paddock. The sun had risen to its zenith, making her aware how much time she'd spent showing him around.

"Your operation is impressive," he observed, reaching to give Barkis a scratch around the ears since the dog was circling him, tail wagging in double time. "And the website does an effective

job of making the animals sound appealing to potential support-
ers and adopters."

Lorenzo straightened from where he'd pet the pup. He was
dressed more informally today in dark jeans and a more casual
button-down, but his boots were still hand-tooled leather, the
kind that rarely saw ranch work. And why did he have to look
even more appealing to her this way than he had over their
business lunch? Yesterday, she'd met the businessman. Today,
she was seeing the rancher, and yes, she liked that side of him.

She'd read more about his family after their lunch meeting,
and learned that Lorenzo was not only the third to bear the name,
but also the oldest of his siblings. It made her wonder how he
felt about being the heir to the family legacy.

"Thank you. I'm hoping Soiree on the Bay not only brings
added funds, but also more public visibility and traffic to the
site."

"I'm sure it will." He slowed his pace as they neared his
pickup truck, a beast of a model with a turbo-charged diesel
engine, built-in winch and all the extra features that were still
on Valencia's wish list. "But once you start your summer camp,
will you keep some horses stabled here permanently? When you
find animals who are a good fit to work with camp goers, I assume you'd want to keep them here."

Pleasantly surprised he'd given that much thought to her expansion project, she hoped that meant he was seriously considering financial support.

"Absolutely. And even though the campers would only ride
trusted mounts under the guidance of a certified instructor, I
hope the attendees could be involved with caring for the rescues." She'd been certified after working with an equine therapy center during college, and she missed it. For that matter, she
missed the atmosphere of healing and community that went hand
in hand with an equine center, much like the one her adoptive
parents had sent her to as a child. "Giving troubled kids another

creature to care for allows them to feel rewarded and accepted for simple acts of kindness."

He nodded while she spoke, as if her words had affirmed something he'd been thinking. Had she somehow revealed too much again?

"Your passion for the project is clear," he said gruffly, tipping his head toward her and making her realize how close they stood.

Her heart beat faster and she wondered if she'd been the one to venture so near to him, or if he'd been the one to trespass on the businesslike boundaries they'd silently agreed on. Swallowing a flash of nervousness, she folded her arms around herself to add a barrier between her and the dark, masculine appeal of the man in front of her.

"May I ask what drew you to this kind of work?" he prompted when she remained silent.

Normally, she had a scripted answer, but she wondered how much he already knew about her personal history. How well had he researched her and her organization? She didn't like the idea of anyone circling around the wounded parts of her past, and it bothered her all the more to think of this successful, formidable man seeing that side of her.

"Barkis wasn't incentive enough?" She raised an eyebrow, allowing her lips to quirk, and hoped he'd give her a pass on sharing anything more personal. He knew her business plan. She shouldn't have to bleed on the proposal, too.

"He's a damned fine dog," Lorenzo agreed a moment later, taking a step backward with a laugh and effectively breaking the tension of the moment.

She breathed a relieved sigh that he'd let her off the hook. Before she could reply, he continued speaking.

"Thank you for taking so much time to speak with me today, Valencia. I enjoyed the tour and wish you well with the rescue either way, but I'll speak to my family about your project and get back to you within the week."

She forced a smile, hoping she hadn't blown her chances to

sell Lorenzo on the idea of her horse rescue with her need for privacy. Already a pang of regret twisted inside her that she hadn't been more forthcoming about her past. But then again, sharing those darker details could have come across as too much.

Too *needy.*

And she had to keep those vulnerabilities hidden at all costs. Especially when her feelings were already so complicated when it came to him.

"The pleasure was all mine," she assured him, her eyes darting to his as the word *pleasure* tripped off her lips accidentally. Perhaps she'd spent too much time in close proximity to him to be second-guessing her language choices and cherry-picking what details to share with him. Valencia sighed. Why couldn't she have met with his gray-haired grandfather about the donation? Because Lorenzo the third was a temptation she did *not* need in her life right now. "I look forward to hearing from you."

With a tip of his hat, he walked away, his broad shoulders holding her gaze. For all his wealth and refined manners, Lorenzo had an ease around the ranch that had made it easy for her to talk to him today. And yes, she could admit she admired that in a man.

As he drove off, her canine woofed a goodbye. For her part, Valencia knew she'd have only herself to blame if the Cortez-Williams family wasn't ready to invest. The only good part about that? At least she wouldn't have to blush and stammer her way through any more parting words with the gorgeous rancher. Pressing a cooling hand to her still-warm cheek, she was heading back to the house for a bite to eat when the sound of tires crunching through the gravel on her driveway made her turn around again.

Her pulse quickened at the thought of Lorenzo returning, but the vehicle that rounded the bend could never be mistaken for a pickup truck. The sleek Aston Martin could belong only to an Edmond, one of Royal's wealthiest families.

And, sure enough, as the sports car drew nearer she could

see the oldest of Rusty Edmond's sons behind the wheel. The Edmond siblings, Ross, Asher and Gina, together with Ross's friend Billy Holmes, were the driving force behind Soiree on the Bay. The Edmond family also owned Appaloosa Island, the site of the festival. Normally, Asher was Valencia's contact when she had festival questions, so she was a little surprised to see Ross here today.

Even more so to see him heft a toddler from a car seat in the back of the coupe, carrying the curly-haired boy in his arms as he ambled toward her. They were an appealing pair. No matter that Lorenzo was the only man who turned her head lately, she couldn't deny that seeing handsome Ross with his chubby-cheeked son in his arms was enough to make any woman's ovaries hum.

"Hello, Ross," she called, striding closer. "And hello to this adorable young gentleman you've brought with you."

She'd heard that Ross had a child with Charlotte Jarrett, his fiancée and the executive chef of Sheen, a popular restaurant in Royal. But she hadn't met the little one before. She opened and closed her fist in a baby-wave she thought most toddlers would recognize.

"My son, Ben," he announced, the pride shining in his blue eyes as he looked down at the boy. Ben smiled shyly at Valencia before bouncing in his father's arms with toddler joy. "I was just on my way to Sheen to see Charlotte, and since we were driving past your place, I thought I should drop by to share an update on the food and wine festival."

His tone grew serious as he spoke, drawing Valencia's attention from Ben to his father's face.

"I hope everything is still on track for the event at the end of the month." Valencia had attended all the meetings of the festival advisory board. She and Charlotte were both members, along with Lila Jones, who worked for the Royal Chamber of Commerce. Rancher Brett Harston had initially been on the board, too, but he'd been booted off by Rusty for having the audacity to sweep Rusty's ex-wife Sarabeth off her feet. "I know at the last meeting, we talked about some funds that were unaccounted for—"

"It's a bigger problem than I first realized." Ross hitched Ben higher against his chest to combat the boy's wiggling. "A more significant amount of money is gone than what I initially believed."

Valencia stilled, a chill running through her in spite of the July heat. "But there's a chance it's a mistake, right? A bookkeeping error?"

Ross shook his head, but seemed to hedge answering the question directly. "I just thought you should know since you were counting on those funds for your horse rescue."

It took a moment for her to absorb the full import of his words. When she did, she felt her dreams rumble unsteadily. She'd worked so hard to make the summer camp a reality. To create the equine therapy component that would give troubled kids the chance to bond with animals the same way she once had.

"Are you saying that the ticket money is gone?" Her voice didn't sound like her own.

How could it be possible? The people involved with the festival were some of the town's most upstanding citizens. She'd enjoyed working with them to make Soiree on the Bay a reality.

"I'm saying we can't account for all of the income, and it's a significant amount." He scrubbed a free hand through his hair, looking weary. "I hope we'll get this figured out. But just in case, it's only fair that you know."

"I understand. And I—" She nodded, her movements jerky and abrupt since it still felt like someone had pulled a rug out from under her feet. "Thank you, Ross."

"Of course. I'm sorry I didn't have better news, but I'll stay in touch." He turned to leave, little Ben waving bye-bye at Valencia over his father's shoulder as he walked away. Valencia waved back at him, smiling at the boy in spite of her inner turmoil.

She'd pinned so many hopes on the ticket sales from Soiree

on the Bay. If Ross's fears were realized and she didn't receive any supporting funds for the horse rescue as promised, how could she possibly support the next phase of making the equine therapy camp a reality?

One thing was certain. She needed the help of the Cortez-Williams family—most especially its darkly cynical heir—now more than ever.

Seated on a leather couch inside the Cortez-Williams ranch office, Lorenzo cross-checked the information on his tablet screen, reviewing files from three different agencies on Donovan Horse Rescue.

Occasionally, while scrolling through the text, he'd pass a photo of Valencia—her pretty face smiling out at him from the screen—and feel a jolt of lust. Along with a surge of guilt about how thoroughly he'd had her investigated.

But he suppressed the guilt each time, more than bolstered by the reminder of Lindsey's faithlessness. If anything, he needed to exercise all the more caution when reviewing Valencia's horse rescue because of the pull of sizzling attraction he felt toward her. His ex-fiancée's treachery had forced him to be more careful with anyone who stirred the kind of response that Valencia had. Considering how much Valencia affected him, triple-checking the references was hardly overkill.

But he'd already floated the files past an overseeing committee earlier in the week, and they'd given her project a unanimous thumbs-up, so it wasn't just his say-so that would result in a donation. Impartial outsiders had been consulted, too.

"Lorenzo?" his ranch manager called from somewhere deeper in the building. "The vet arrived a few minutes ago. She's in the cow barn now."

He glanced up from his tablet, accustomed to interruptions in the office since it was a casual shared space for ranch paperwork, really just a corner of the equipment barn. On the other side of a big filing cabinet and bookshelf, there were trucks and tractors. Beyond that, a small mechanic shop for simple repairs. Mostly, the place was air-conditioned against the heat of a Texas July, with round-the-clock access to a good coffee machine and fridge full of cold drinks.

"Thanks," he called, returning his attention to his work. "I'll head over there before she finishes."

The veterinarian's visit was a routine check since the ranch didn't employ their own. Lorenzo wanted her to look at one of the horses before she left. But right now, he had no reason to delay calling Valencia any longer. He knew he'd done his due diligence where her rescue was concerned. And couldn't justify withholding funds she deserved just because he'd been fooled by a woman before.

Valencia did have a connection to a shady character in her past, but considering it was her birth father and she'd been taken away from her parents at an early age, Lorenzo could hardly hold that against her. Her school and work records were pristine. Her horse rescue mission a noble one that she pursued tirelessly.

And damn, but she'd been in his thoughts nonstop since meeting her. Not just because she was undeniably sexy. She was also warmhearted, hardworking and sharp as hell. He'd been even more drawn to her after seeing her with her animals. Her ease in riding, her passion for rescue and her obvious bond with every creature she cared for were all compelling to a man born and raised to ranch. Underneath her corporate polish, there beat the heart of a bona fide cowgirl.

Lifting his phone, he placed the call. In two rings, she answered, her voice a little breathless.

"Hello?" she huffed lightly into the speaker, the sound making him all but feel the rush of her exhale on his skin.

"Hello, Valencia. It's Lorenzo." Shutting off the tablet, he set it aside on the leather couch. Then, tipping his head back, he closed his eyes and imagined her on the other end of the call. He could indulge that desire now when she couldn't see him. "I have some news to share with you. Would you be able to meet me for dinner tomorrow?"

Strictly for business purposes, he reminded himself. After all, she deserved to celebrate the approval of funds from his family, and he wanted to be there to share that with her.

"Of course. Where should we meet?" she replied in a rush, perhaps to hide the moment's hesitation before her response. No doubt she'd picked up on the vibe of molten-hot attraction as clearly as he had. If anything, it was a relief to know she was conflicted about that, too.

"How about Sheen?" he suggested. The food and service were excellent, and he wanted to show her a good time if only just this once. "I can make reservations for seven o'clock."

He'd almost offered to pick her up, but he'd remembered himself just in time. This wasn't a date. But he refused to miss out on this last opportunity to see her. She was a vibrant, memorable woman, and if he hadn't met her on a professional basis, he would definitely pursue her.

The realization surprised him. He hadn't felt that kind of connection—a *need* to see a woman again—in five years. His dating life since Lindsey had been superficial, something he'd undertaken only for expediency's sake.

"That sounds great." Her voice was warmer now. Hopeful. "I'll look forward to it."

Disconnecting the call, Lorenzo shut down the tablet with the files full of information about Valencia Donovan, more excited about the prospect of seeing her than he should be. He didn't need the information anymore now that the decision was made to help her charity. She'd never know how thoroughly he'd investigated her, and it didn't matter anyway since it had been strictly for business purposes.

He'd never allow himself to have a liaison with anyone remotely connected to his family's business. Not after the last time he'd misjudged a woman. So after tomorrow night, he wouldn't be seeing Valencia Donovan ever again.

Three

No matter how many times Valencia told herself that dinner with Lorenzo would be purely professional, she'd still ended up changing outfits twice. Overthinking her clothes was *not* a good sign.

Hurrying up the sidewalk in front of Sheen, the popular new Royal restaurant, Valencia straightened the strap of her white crepe dress and told herself it was appropriately conservative. Even though she couldn't recall baring this much shoulder in her corporate job. She was just off her game tonight because she didn't know what to expect from the meal, and so much rode on Lorenzo's decision.

A gust of wind hastened her pace up the walkway, and she clutched the loose waves of her hair to keep them from blowing around. Before she reached the front door of the all-glass building, it swung open from within. Lorenzo stood on the threshold, dressed in a sharp dark suit with a pale blue Oxford shirt open at the collar. He looked…like a man she wished she were meeting under different circumstances. That must be why her heart rate jumped.

"Hello, Lorenzo." She smiled widely to cover the rush of nerves, still holding her hair in one hand. "It's windy all of the sudden."

"It's good to see you, Valencia." His gaze dipped over her once—briefly—yet she was so hyperaware of him, she couldn't help but notice. "You look lovely."

The words were easily spoken. Gentlemanly. That didn't stop the rush of pleasure she experienced. Forcing herself not to dwell on that, she murmured a thank-you and let go of her hair as he ushered her inside the cool interior, his hand finding the small of her back to help her navigate through the evening crowd hoping for a table.

The warmth of his palm sent tendrils of pleasure curling through her, heightening her awareness of him. She caught the barest hint of his spicy aftershave when they were forced closer together because of a group hurrying past them. Valencia inhaled deeply, trying to place the subtle blend of scents that made her want to lean closer.

Following his lead, she moved with him through the main dining area to a table in a corner. White candles on every table, tucked into hurricane lamps and surrounded by white flowers, gave the room an ethereal glow. Shades had fallen over some of the exterior walls to give the diners privacy, but the glass divider separating the kitchen remained visible. She wondered if Ross's fiancée, Charlotte, was cooking tonight. She'd heard the woman was extremely talented. The complex aromas—cooking spices and the yeasty scent of freshly baked bread—made Valencia eager to taste the fare.

"We're sitting right here, if this is okay with you?" Lorenzo moved around her to withdraw an upholstered chair for her.

"Of course. It's perfect." She took a seat, knowing this flattering attentiveness was probably the byproduct of good Texas upbringing and not anything personal. But it felt really nice. "I appreciate the chance to visit Sheen. It's all the more welcome this week after hearing the troubling news about Soiree on the Bay."

Worries about the food and arts festival—and developing a plan B for her horse rescue—had never been far from her mind since Ross's visit.

Lorenzo's expression turned grave as he took the seat across from her. "I heard rumors about missing money from the advance ticket sales, but I hoped they were just gossip. Anything involving Rusty Edmond seems to attract public speculation."

"I believe this is more serious than that." Valencia hesitated, wondering if Lorenzo might perceive her broaching the topic as a way to add pressure to solicit a donation from the Cortez-Williams family. But it was too late to backtrack now. "Ross Edmond paid me a visit the same day you toured the ranch. He wanted to warn me there might not be any funds from the ticket sales."

Scowling, Lorenzo shook his head. "It has to be an accounting error. And if it's not, there are only so many potential parties to blame considering the small group involved with the festival." He gave her a level stare. "You're on the festival advisory board, aren't you?"

She bristled, even as she told herself he wasn't accusing her of anything.

"I am. And I still can't wrap my head around any other possibility than a bookkeeping mistake," she concurred.

Lorenzo appeared thoughtful, but the sommelier's arrival at their table ended the discussion. Valencia gladly deferred to his preference for a bottle of wine. From the exchange between them, she suspected the vintage was something much better than anything she'd had before.

"We're celebrating, after all," he announced after the woman left their table, clearly shifting the tone of their conversation.

She was only too happy to focus on why he'd asked her to meet him tonight. Anticipation tingled through her, even as she tried to keep her hopes in check.

"Are we?"

"Definitely." His dark eyes glittered with mischief, almost as if he enjoyed keeping her guessing. "I shared your proposal for Donovan Horse Rescue with the committee that makes the final decision on donations from our family's business." He paused, the moment of suspense drawing out before he smiled broadly. "They unanimously voted to approve it."

Relief surged through her and a happy squeal she couldn't quite suppress bubbled up in her throat.

"Thank you." She reached for him in her excitement, covering his forearm and squeezing. "Thank you so much! You have no idea how much this means to me."

Even through the lightweight jacket he wore, she felt his muscles flex beneath her fingers. Her eyes darted to where she touched him...and she would have pulled away, except that at the same moment, he covered her fingers with his. Warmth flowed through her as she met his gaze again.

"You're welcome," he assured her, tightening his grip for a moment before relinquishing her. "Although it was your hard work that impressed the committee. It's clear you have a well-developed plan for making the rescue a success. Your commitment to the cause—and a worthy cause at that—came through in every page of your pitch."

Her throat had gone dry at the feel of his hand over hers, the memory of that brief touch still humming in her skin. Belatedly, she realized her hand lingered on his forearm and she snatched it back a little too quickly.

What was it about him that knocked her off balance?

She licked her lips and tried to regain her composure.

"Yet the proposal wouldn't have made it that far if not for your help. I really appreciate you taking the time to see the operation in person." Recalling his earlier concerns about con artists and shady requests for funds, she added, "To see for yourself that I *am* a legitimate businesswoman."

A shadow chased through his expression. Had she said something wrong? Or had he somehow read a hint of feminine interest in her eyes and retreated from that?

The sommelier returned, along with their server, giving Valencia a window of time to cool the heated impulses. She just needed to make it through this meal without touching Lorenzo again, and she would be home free. There would be no more cause to interact. No more temptation to throw caution to the wind with someone she would always feel indebted to.

Just get through dinner.

On the surface, it sounded simple. But considering the magnetic draw of the man, Valencia knew the challenge was very real.

By the time dessert was served, Lorenzo had stored away plenty of new information about his sexy and intriguing dinner companion. And learning about her this way was far more satisfying than the private investigator's report he'd read on her business.

But for all that he'd learned about Valencia, she still danced around the particulars of her childhood. Perhaps that was because they hadn't known one another long. Yet the studious way she avoided any talk of her own experience with equine therapy, despite the obvious relevance to her current path in life, heightened his curiosity about the notes in her background file. Especially those pertaining to her biological father—a convicted felon.

He recognized that he was particularly wary around women who might get close to him only for the sake of his bank account. But as much as he wanted to shut off that part of his brain that forced him to remain on guard, he couldn't help but watch for any signs that Valencia would leverage their mutual attraction for financial gain.

Now, as she speared a bite of shortbread with her dessert fork, she fixed him with a playful gaze. "You realize you've pried out all my secrets over dinner while telling me very little about yourself."

Startled that she'd noticed, he tried to force aside his reservations.

"Me? I'm an open book." He pushed back from the table, tossing his napkin on top of his empty dessert plate, his gaze dropping to her mouth. "A side effect of having four brothers is that nothing remains secret about me for long."

She blinked, brown eyes wide with surprise. "There are *five* Cortez-Williams brothers in all?"

"After me, there's Matias, Rafe, Tomas and Diego. Hellions all in their own way, while I—as the oldest and bearing my father's name—have had no choice but to rein in all hell-raising impulses." He was only partly kidding. "So it follows that I have less interesting secrets."

Her mouth curved into a sad smile. "As an only child who owes my adoptive parents everything, I empathize." She chewed thoughtfully on her lower lip for a moment before returning her gaze to him, a spark of flirtation in their dark depths. "But despite your skillful deflection, I still think you owe me at least one provocative factoid about yourself."

If this had been a date and not a business dinner, he would have slid his chair closer to hers so he could touch her while he imparted some of the wicked thoughts he'd had about her over the course of their meal.

For a long moment, he let the heat of that fantasy sizzle over him. But then, knowing he couldn't possibly respond the way he wanted, he settled for leaning forward so he could speak to her confidentially across the table.

"Between you and me? If I hadn't been destined to be a rancher, I would probably be Royal's resident auto mechanic."

Her eyebrows lifted in surprise, a genuine smile hovering around her lips now as if the news delighted her. "Really?"

"Really. I've wanted to fix cars—fix anything mechanical—since I got a toolbox under the Christmas tree when I was thirteen." He watched her expression carefully, searching for any hint of dismay at the hobby that still brought him as much satisfaction—more, if he was honest—as overseeing his family's ranch. Lindsey had laughed outright about his preferred pastime when he'd mentioned it to her, but she'd been outright appalled when she'd arrived early for a date and found him still underneath a tractor in the equipment barn, his coveralls greasy.

Valencia, on the contrary, appeared fascinated. "I envy you possessing that skill." She traced her index finger idly up the stem of her wineglass. "Although I'm not sure a hidden mechanical talent qualifies as an overly provocative secret."

His brain was still stuck on the first part of what she'd said. "Envy?"

Had he heard her correctly? That certainly wasn't the mindset of his father, who viewed the work Lorenzo enjoyed as somehow "beneath" him.

"Do you know how much money I would save if I knew the first thing about engine repair? I just traded in my old truck for a new one after I got a sky-high estimate to repair an oil leak that was supposedly so buried in the engine as to make it not worth fixing." Her brow furrowed. "And don't get me started on the equipment needed around the rescue."

He hated the idea that he might have been able to save her a significant amount of money on the truck and hadn't known about the problem. It surprised him how much he wanted to offer his help and know-how in the future. And yet, she wasn't his responsibility. Hadn't he told himself tonight would be the last time they spent together?

Besides, helping a woman financially had been his Achilles' heel with Lindsey.

While he wrestled with that notion, both of their phones went off. Not with ringtones—he'd most certainly turned his to silent—but the strong vibration of a local public safety alert.

Frowning, he reached for his phone, and noticed many of the restaurant patrons doing the same thing.

"Tornado alert." He read the words aloud, his attention shifting to the glass windows of the restaurant while murmurs of alarm traveled around him. With the linen shades blocking most of the view, he couldn't see what the weather looked like outside. "I need to get you home."

All around them patrons were collecting their things, calling for their checks. The residents of Royal took tornado warnings very seriously. Especially after a twister had touched down close enough to the Texas Cattleman's Club to do some serious damage less than ten years before.

Lorenzo reached for the leather binder containing the bill, thankful their server hovered at the ready. Only then did he notice Valencia had gone pale. Eyes fixed on the windows at the front of Sheen, she swallowed hard, with visible effort.

Concerned, he didn't hesitate to slide his chair closer to her now. He laid his palm on her shoulder. "Hey. Are you okay?"

She gave a jerky nod, but he thought he felt her trembling beneath his palm. "Fine. Just—you know. Worried about my animals. My ranch hands only work part-time. They've gone home for the night."

"I can help secure them when I take you home," he assured her, understanding her anxiety. Property damage was one thing, but harm to living creatures in your care was another. "We'll be on the road in no time."

She turned wide eyes toward him, but there was no mistaking the look of gratitude in her expression. "Are you sure? What about your ranch? Shouldn't you—"

"We have staff on-site that will ensure their safety. It's no trouble for me to give you a hand." Glimpsing the server returning with the leather folder containing his receipt, Lorenzo had a generous tip added and the bill signed in another moment. "Do you have a storm shelter at your place?"

"Yes. There's a storm cellar." Some of her color returned, and she appeared a bit calmer as they both rose to their feet. "Thank you, Lorenzo. Both for the incredible meal and the offer to pitch in. I really appreciate it."

An older couple hurried past them toward the exit, and Lorenzo hooked his arm around Valencia's waist to steady her. While there wasn't a sense of panic in the restaurant, anxiety buzzed in the air. With so many ranches in the area, many of the diners shared the same concerns as she did, and there was a flurry of activity as bills were quickly paid. Conversations grew louder as people speculated on the possibilities of the uncertain weather. One of the servers informed a table nearby that a funnel cloud had been spotted half an hour north of them. And at the hostess's stand, a woman read aloud from her phone about a series of tornado outbreaks across East Texas.

Lorenzo didn't question the need to tuck Valencia closer to his side, moving them quickly to the exit. Even if she hadn't gone pale, he would have felt responsible for her safety while they were together. But knowing that she was worried made him all the more protective.

Pushing open the door, he guided her toward the parking lot as a gust of wind swept past them, the air current strong enough to notch his concern higher. And although the sun had recently set, there was enough twilight to distinguish the greenish cast to the sky.

Not loosening his hold on her, he leaned closer to be sure she could hear him over the rush of squall. "I'd feel better if you'd let me drive you home."

She nodded. "I would, too. Thank you."

"Good. Come on." Relieved at her acquiescence, he led her to his truck. He opened the passenger door for her, helping her inside before jogging around the front to take a seat behind the wheel. "Is your storm cellar stocked?"

Before she had a chance to respond, he flipped on the headlights and pulled out of the parking lot, heading toward Valencia's place.

"It is." She'd rested her small leather clutch purse on the console between them, and she gripped it tightly now, her fingers digging into the material. "I'm actually very disciplined about emergency preparations, so I go through the provisions regularly to make sure nothing is expired and that I have everything I could possibly need."

Something struck him as a little off about her words, perhaps because they sounded so calm when her body language suggested she was extremely tense. Maybe she was trying to reassure herself with her measured words.

"That's excellent news. Hopefully, it won't come to that, but it's good to know the space is ready if we need it." He couldn't stop himself from reaching across the console to lay a hand over hers. Her skin was cold. "Now, walk me through what needs to happen with the animals. You have solid stables. I'm assuming you want the horses inside?"

He knew some owners allowed their animals to remain outdoors in case a building was directly hit, but good stables could protect them from flying debris.

"Yes. We need to get them all in stalls, then secure the doors and windows. I'm not worried about halters or name tags as every animal is microchipped. Including Barkis, who will come to the storm cellar with us." She shifted in her seat, sliding her hand out from under his to retrieve her phone from her clutch. "I should look for weather updates."

"Of course. Let me know what you find out." He hoped for encouraging news, but the fact that the weather warning wasn't just because of one twister, but potentially several, didn't bode well.

He remembered a day two years before where thirty-nine tornadoes had broken out across four Southern states. But he didn't see the need to mention that to Valencia. Glancing sidelong at her as he reached a stop sign, he could see the worry etched in her pretty face.

"So far the National Weather Service has reported three. All of them have been EF-0 so far, although one of them was almost an EF-1." She rattled off the information, clearly well versed in the measurement scale that related a tornado's intensity. "And it looks like there's possible activity around Trinity Bay, too."

The site of Appaloosa Island and Soiree on the Bay.

Recognizing a whole new layer to Valencia's fears, Lorenzo knew the best thing he could do for her—the *only* thing he could do right now—was to get her home and make sure her horses were all safe.

Then, he'd make sure *she* was safe. Even if that meant riding out the storm together.

Four

Cold rain pelted Valencia's face as she climbed a ladder to close one of the high windows that provided extra air circulation in the barn. She'd exchanged her dress and heels for jeans and work boots before returning to the stables to secure the animals, and she was grateful for the sure-footed tread of the boots now with the wind whipping hard against her rain jacket.

At least the ladder was built-in, bolted to the side of the barn to make it easier to reach the area that used to be a hayloft. The rungs were slippery, though, and she needed to keep one hand anchored while she stretched her free arm to reach the wooden shutter that banged against the building.

Just a little farther…

Woof!

Below her, Barkis stood guard, sounding as edgy and impatient to be out of the weather as she felt. Latching the window was the last thing she needed to do since Lorenzo had taken care of the newest stable. Thankfully, he'd had work clothes stashed in his truck, so he'd been able to hit the ground running as quickly as she had.

Thank God he was here.

Especially when tonight was triggering haunting memories of another long-ago twister. Everything about the weather—from the plowed-earth smell in the air to the grit-filled gusts of wind—reminded her of the worst day of her life. One spent in a bathtub while her drunken birth parents argued over who was responsible for keeping Valencia safe. Neither one of them had wanted that chore, the memory forever twining the terror of tornadoes with the gut-sickening realization that she was unloved.

Just then, the wind slammed the shutter closed for her, whacking the back of her hand in the process, but at least making it easier for her to pull the latch into the locked position. Her last job complete, she started down the ladder as the rain turned to hail.

The barrage of ice pellets against the barn sounded like gunfire. And the pings against her back hurt through the thin windbreaker. Even worse? Her foot slipped on the next-to-last rung, the awkward flail of her body almost making her lose her grip.

Strong arms caught her lower body even as she wrenched her arm, trying to hold on.

"I've got you." Lorenzo's voice sounded beside her ear through her hood. "You can let go."

Her heart pounded wildly, from fear of the storm and panic at the memories, to gratitude toward this man who didn't owe her anything yet kept helping her anyhow.

Off balance in every way, Valencia did as he suggested, relinquishing her grip on the ladder to give him her full weight. For one heart-stopping moment, she hung suspended against him, her back pressed to the solid warmth of his chest. Her butt slid down the front of his hips as he set her on her feet, a sensation that made heat flare inside her despite the storm trauma threatening to topple her.

Before she could turn and face him—and maybe confront whatever that sizzling connection meant—a piercing siren wailed in the distance. A *tornado* siren.

Fear tore through her. She knew what that meant.

A funnel cloud must have been spotted nearby. The sirens didn't go off in Royal unless there was confirmed tornado activity.

Barkis whimpered at the same time Lorenzo tucked her against him. She hadn't realized until that moment how much harder the rain-hail mix was pummeling her head and shoulders.

"We need to get in the shelter now." He led her toward the metal door she'd pointed out to him when he'd parked his pickup truck in front of her house.

The storm cellar entrance was a low mound between the house and main barn that the previous owner had surrounded with rock walls and bushes. The concrete shelter had been a strong point in favor of buying this property when Valencia had been searching for a spot that could double as a home and a horse rescue. Just knowing the large, steel-reinforced retreat was nearby had helped her sleep better, even though she'd never had to use it before.

A low rumble sounded like an incoming freight train, the noise growing higher and sharper as Lorenzo pulled open the low door. Dread ramped inside her as she looked around franticly for her dog.

Barkis didn't need to be told where to go. Her dog rushed down the carpeted steps into the dry, still air below. Valencia reached ahead and flipped on the switch for the interior lights, then followed him. She was grateful for the way the underground walls muffled the sounds of the sirens and the wailing wind, but still felt petrified at the thought of what a powerful storm could do to her horses.

To her *dream*. To her ability to help others with her precious animals that she loved more than anything on earth.

Heart in her throat, she stood immobile at the base of the shelter stairs while Lorenzo closed and locked the door behind him. He edged past her, taking in the space that consisted of two rooms with low-clearance ceilings—about six and a half feet. Fiberglass walls and storage benches wrapped the first room while a full-size bed dominated the adjoining one. There were pull-down benches in those walls, too, for when additional people needed shelter, but Valencia had added the regular bed for herself, knowing she would need every possible comfort if she ever had to use the space.

Her stomach dropped at the thought of using it now, of being trapped in here for hours.

Lorenzo's dark eyes shifted back to her. She hadn't noticed he'd already removed his jacket and boots. The cold dread weighing her down must have made her lose time, because she had no recollection of him doing either of those things.

"Valencia?" He approached her slowly. "Can I take your jacket? Help you dry off?"

Becoming aware of her behavior and how it must broadcast her unease, she tried to shake the suffocating memories off. Although she was grateful to Lorenzo for helping her secure the animals, she regretted the possibility that he might see her at her worst during the course of a storm.

"I can get it, thanks." She tugged down the sleeve of her windbreaker, water droplets sliding off the repellant fabric onto a rubber mat on the underground shelter's concrete floor. "There are towels under the first bench seat to the left."

Telling herself she was safe and that this is what she'd spent so much time preparing for, she tried to take comfort from going through a mental checklist of all they had at their disposal. Barkis padded over to the storage benches with Lorenzo, poking an interested nose inside the raised lid for a moment before moving off to sniff out a comfortable spot to lie.

"Wow." Lorenzo tugged two towels free from the bin, his gaze focused on the schematic taped to the inside of the lid where she had diagrammed the location of all her supplies. "You've got everything really organized in here."

"I—um." She knew her preparedness might appear over the top to some people. *Obsessive*, a former boyfriend had once phrased her need to be ready for any emergency situation.

"Thank you. We should turn on the radio and see if there are any reports about the storm."

The eerie sound of the howling wind, even muted as it was in the cellar, unnerved her.

"Sure." Turning to pass her one of the towels, Lorenzo narrowed his gaze. "What happened to your hand?"

Valencia glanced down to see the blood trickling along her knuckle, a small stain forming on the concrete floor from an earlier drip. The sight distracted her from the weather for a moment.

"Oh." She'd forgotten all about the injury amid her other worries, but she cradled the limb against her other arm now to try to stem the blood flow. "The barn shutter slammed onto my hand when I was trying to latch it closed. I didn't realize I got a cut."

Her voice sounded unnatural, even to her own ears. But although she told herself to snap out of it, she realized she was shaking. She could see her fingers trembling as she stared down at them.

Valencia didn't want to reveal so much weakness to the man in front of her, not when the fate of her rescue relied on him thinking she was completely competent. Yet, with the woozy sensation making her knees feel like liquid, she guessed she was moments away from an outright panic attack.

Lorenzo's concern grew in direct proportion to the increasing paleness of Valencia's skin. He didn't know if it was related to the storm, the injury or being in the more confined space underground, but the jitteriness he'd noted in her on the way back from the restaurant seemed to spiral into full-blown shock right before his eyes.

Her breathing was rapid, her pupils dilated, her skin almost ashen. Could she have sustained another injury she hadn't mentioned? A blow to the head even?

The idea made him more determined to check her over.

"Hey now." He shifted to put himself in her line of vision, even though he wasn't sure she focused on him even then. "Valencia? I'm worried about you. I'd like to take your boots off, and then we'll get your hand bandaged, okay?"

"I'm f-fine," she protested, teeth chattering on the words.

Yet she still hadn't moved from where they first entered the room, other than to remove her jacket.

He stepped toward her slowly, even though his own fears demanded he examine every inch of her to make sure she wasn't hurt more than she'd let on. But he couldn't startle her if she was already fearful and upset. He had no experience with people in shock, but he'd been with plenty of animals that'd shown those signs, so he hoped that the basic strategies still applied. Speak calmly and soothingly. Get them comfortable.

"Did you sustain any other injuries besides your hand?" he asked, wrapping the dry towel around her shoulders.

"No. At least I don't think so." Her answer was so soft, he wasn't sure he would have heard it if he hadn't been watching her mouth move at the same time.

But at least her breathing hadn't accelerated any more.

"I'm going to find the radio in a minute," he assured her as he dropped to his feet to unlace her boots. The fact that she didn't protest spoke volumes. "First, let's get you dry."

While he worked on the wet laces, the only sounds in the shelter were the moan of the wind, the pelt of hail on the metal door and Valencia's chattering teeth. Even Barkis was quiet, his big head resting on his paws on one of the benches in the next room.

Was it a good sign the dog didn't seem worried?

Easing off her boots, he set them aside. Then, he stood so he could tuck her against him and escort her deeper into the shelter. She trembled against him, her whole body shaking. But he thought her breath seemed more even than it had been a few moments ago.

"Have a seat here, okay?" He led her to the bed since it offered the most comfortable option, even though it amounted only to a utilitarian mattress on a metal frame, a clean sleeping bag for a cover. "I'm going to find the first-aid kit so we can take care of your hand. Would you feel better lying down?"

He wanted to wrap her in the flannel sleeping bag and hold her until she stopped quaking, but first he needed to figure out what had her so shook up. For now, he moved the towel to wrap her wounded hand.

"I'm s-sorry," Valencia murmured, her breath quickening again. "I think it's just the storm—" She broke off in a wheezing inhale, as if she couldn't draw enough air.

Damn it! He wished he knew what to do to help her. He left her side long enough to find a first-aid kit in the second bin. The schematic she'd drawn on a sheet of paper under the lid by the towels showed where every major item was located in the storage area, from sewing kit to pet care, flashlights to food.

The food supplies were all marked with expiration dates— every last one of them current. Water jugs lined a back wall. Fresh air circulated from vents high on the walls. Clearly Valencia had invested time and finances into a top-notch shelter. Because she was prepared, or were her efforts indicative of a deeper fear?

"Here we go." He brought the first-aid kit to the bed and sat down beside her, flipping on a small lamp clipped above the bed. "Let's get that cut cleaned up," he said aloud, compelled to narrate his actions as a way to keep her grounded in what was happening. Or, hell, maybe he needed to ground himself given how worried he was about her. He found the hydrogen peroxide and opened the bottle while he kept talking to her. "We're going to weather this storm just fine, thanks to you."

For a long moment, he didn't think she was going to respond while he cleaned the cut, letting the excess solution fall onto the white towel. But as he re-capped the bottle and searched for antibiotic ointment, she said, "I was in a bad tornado once." The words were gritty, as if her throat had gone dry. "I saw how much damage it could do if you aren't prepared."

Something in that softly uttered admission made him think

that whatever had happened then was causing a lot of her distress right now. He wanted to see her expression, but she stared down at the cut as he worked on it, her damp hair falling over her face to further hide it.

At least her pallor wasn't quite as ashen anymore. And her breathing seemed to have evened out once again. Still quick and shallow, but not as ragged.

"Well, you made sure that wouldn't happen again," he soothed as he tore open a bandage. "You've got everything we could possibly need down here. I can't think of any safer place to ride out a storm."

She remained quiet while he finished bandaging her wound, then set the kit on the floor near the now-sleeping dog. He left the light on long enough to tip her chin up so he could look her in the eyes. Her pupils were still wide, yet not as dilated as before. Overall, she seemed calmer. However, that didn't stop him from stroking a hand over her hair so he could feel her scalp beneath, to reassure himself she hadn't hit her head while they'd been preparing the horses.

"Are you sure you didn't get hurt anywhere else?" he asked, watching her face for any hint of reaction—a wince that could betray a bump or a cut.

Yet he saw only her eyelashes flutter, then fall closed. Her chest expanded with the first deep breath since they'd been inside the shelter, her breasts pressing against the heather-gray T-shirt she wore, adorned with the logo for Donovan Horse Rescue.

His body reacted to that in a wholly inappropriate way, considering she'd been on the verge of passing out just ten minutes before. But he couldn't have moved his hands away from her hair if he tried. He skimmed his fingers lower, tracing the back of her neck through the silky locks.

"I'm okay," she murmured, her eyes falling closed. "Just a little embarrassed, I guess."

"Why?" Genuinely perplexed, he ran his thumb along her

cheekbone, telling himself he did it only to encourage her gaze. "I can't imagine anything you'd need to be embarrassed about."

Her eyes opened slowly, a momentary flash of awareness making him damn near catch his breath. Part of him felt grateful that her thoughts had shifted away from her worries, but he also knew better than to act on the feelings stirring up between them now. "I have tried so hard to put my best foot forward professionally with you," she began, twisting around enough to tug a plush blue lap blanket off the shelf that served as a headboard. "Only to completely fall apart after our dinner."

Her hands were still shaking as she spread the blanket over her legs. It took all of his restraint not to capture those trembling fingers in his and hold them. Hold *her* until she stopped shaking. But he couldn't afford to muddle his concern for her with the attraction he'd been feeling ever since they met.

He fisted his hands instead.

"You didn't fall apart," he argued, not sure why she thought that. "Anyone would be rattled by a storm like this."

Remembering that he'd never retrieved the radio, he was only too glad for an excuse to stand, to stride away from the magnetic draw of her. Returning to her drawing of the supply layout, he traced the location of the device to the third bin. Flashlights, extra batteries and what might have been a satellite phone were neatly packaged near the radio with a hand crank and built-in charging station.

"It goes beyond the usual fears," she admitted as he returned to sit beside her.

"Because you were in a tornado before?" he asked softly, passing her the radio in case she wanted to turn it on for updates.

"When I was very young. Still living with my birth parents." She took the device, resting it in her lap on the blanket before glancing at him. "I was adopted when I was eight years old."

He knew this, of course, from the investigator's report. Recalled her biological father's unsavory past. But unwilling to admit how much he'd already learned about her history, he steered her back to whatever had happened during that long-ago storm. There was little about her early life in her file beyond simple dates.

"Would it help to talk about it?" His gaze wandered over her from her honey-brown eyes and long dark lashes, to the way her blond hair dried in waves. "Or should I try to distract you?"

Her pupils widened slightly at that last remark, and he wished he could see into her mind to know what she'd envisioned at that moment. Her mouth fell open briefly, before she snapped it shut again and speared to her feet.

"First, I should find some dry clothes," she said abruptly, gathering up the blanket that had slid off her lap. "I'm feeling a little steadier, but it would help to get warm." She shuffled back a step in her socks, reaching overhead to pull a simple curtain that divided the shelter's two small rooms. "I'll find some clothes and a couple of waters for us. Do you want to change? I have men's things here, too."

"No, thank you." He didn't think it would be wise to get too comfortable in this intimate setting with Valencia. "I'll turn on the radio," he offered instead, already adjusting the tuning dial for a station. "See what's happening. Maybe this will all be over soon."

Although the harsh whine of the wind continued outside, the hail had stopped pelting the metal door to their shelter.

"I hope so." She rummaged through her bins, opening and closing plastic lids to find what she needed.

A moment later, the sound of a zipper in the enclosed quarters had his head wrenching up. Through the white curtain, he could see her shadow moving as she shimmied off her jeans. He might have made a noise in response because she stopped midmotion, her head turning toward where he sat even though she couldn't possibly see him.

His throat went dry at the thought of her so close and half-dressed.

He pressed the volume button on the radio, cranking up the sound to cover the pregnant pause.

"...tornado outbreaks across all of eastern Texas, resulting in significant threats to life and property. Take shelter immediately." The message was a prerecorded standard tornado warning for their area, but that didn't make it any less terrifying.

From Valencia's side of the curtain, he heard a quiet exclamation, halfway between a sob and a wail. Cursing himself for turning the radio on, he tossed it aside and went to her, privacy be damned.

She needed him.

"Come here." He wrapped her in his arms, never dropping his eyes for a second even though she wore only a T-shirt now. "I've got you," he whispered into her ear, stroking her hair with one hand while pressing her to him with the other. "It's going to be okay."

He told himself it was true, and that he could make her believe it, too, even though she shook like a leaf now.

But a moment later, the lights in the shelter went out, leaving them in total blackness.

Five

The total darkness fell over Valencia like a smothering weight on her from all sides. As panic stole her breath, she clutched Lorenzo tighter, her fingers digging into his upper arms and silently demanding an anchor in a world gone black.

Right now, it didn't matter that she'd wanted to make a good impression on him, or that he held the future of the shelter in his hands. She knew only that her old fears would eat her alive if she couldn't find a way to battle them back. Having the lights go out when she was already shivering and half-dressed had catapulted her backward in time, ripping open wounds she'd kept long hidden.

"Valencia." He said her name with a sternness that made her think it wasn't the first time he'd spoken it. He still held her in his arms, but his whole body had gone tense.

"Yes?" She tipped her face up toward where his would be.

"I need to find the flashlights," he told her more gently, his fingers rubbing along her back through her T-shirt. "Let's get you settled with a blanket, then I'll retrieve a lantern from the bin."

"Okay. Sounds good," she agreed, even though she couldn't seem to ease her grip on his arms. Her fingers were still vise-locked on him, her nose buried in the soft flannel of the work shirt he'd changed into before he'd helped secure the horses. She breathed in his scent, pine and musk, and told herself to let go.

To no avail.

He waited a moment, probably giving her time to move away. When she didn't, he stroked a hand over her hair, his lips lowering so that he spoke close to her ear.

"Want me to go with you? Help you find the bed?" he asked, his words a raspy rumble that stirred something inside her.

Something that wasn't fear.

"Yes. Please." Her voice was small and soft. Tentative. The vulnerable parts she showed him now were a far cry from the strong face she normally presented to the world.

But she couldn't afford to care what he thought about her. Not when she could fall apart in a million tiny pieces if her old demons gained a toehold in her thoughts.

She'd been alone in the bathtub when the roof ripped off the house. The screech of the metal peeling away from the rafters mingled with the sound of her mother's screams.

Swallowing hard, she tried to tamp down rapidly encroaching memories as Lorenzo shuffled her sideways in the direction of the bed. Ignoring the angry thrash of the wind against the exterior door, she focused on the sounds within the storm cellar. The steady thrum of the rancher's heartbeat under her ear. The soft thunk of his leg meeting the resistance of the utilitarian metal frame a moment before he lowered her to the mattress. From near their feet, Barkis made a snuffling noise in his slumber.

"Here you go." He drew the fleece lap blanket around her, his denim-covered knee brushing her bare thigh as he shifted.

Once more, sizzling awareness stirred within her, offering a welcome distraction from rational thought and memories. And as the bright, clear flame of heated attraction flickered over the shadowy fears, scattering them, her breath caught. Held.

The inconvenient response almost made her regret that the power had gone out before she could finish changing into dry clothes, her clean T-shirt barely covering her hips. She hadn't had time to pull on a dry pair of sweats. Then again, if not for the hot flare of lust roaring inside her, she would be shaking from the chill of the past.

"Will you stay by me?" she asked, willing to sacrifice her pride for a chance to keep her anxiety at bay. "Just…wait a few minutes to get the flashlights?"

Beside her, she felt him tense as his body went still. He'd let go of her to wrap the blanket around her, but afterward his right arm had returned to the small of her back, where his palm rested, steady and strong.

"Of course," he answered after a long moment, then huffed out a slow breath between his teeth. "Are you sure you don't want to talk about whatever happened in the last tornado?"

She gave an involuntary shudder. "No. Distraction would help more."

His fingers flexed against her spine, the heat of his hand permeating the fleece.

"Valencia." Her name sounded like a warning and a plea at the same time.

Although maybe she heard those things only because she felt equal parts danger and desire herself. Just then, something heavy crashed into the metal door at the top of the stairs. A big tree limb, maybe. Or a part of the house?

The *roof*?

Her gut roiled.

"Please?" She clutched the blanket around her like a cape, wishing she could crawl into his lap and stay there until the tornado ran its course.

Instead, she pressed closer to him, hip to hip, her thigh squeezing against his.

He made a ragged sound of protest, but at the same time, he

encircled her shoulders with his arm, tugging her nearer. For a moment, he rested his cheek against the top of her head.

"Maybe you could suggest an appropriate distraction," he urged, the words sounding like he gritted them out. "Because my thoughts are all running in the wrong direction."

Her heart picked up speed. Was *she* the wrong direction? She hoped he understood she wasn't trying to seduce him. She was scared, damn it!

"Let's play two truths and a lie," she suggested, desperate for anything to lighten the tension for them both while still keeping him next to her. She *needed* him by her. "You can tell me two true things about you and one false, then I'll guess which is which."

"Two truths and a lie," he repeated slowly. Musingly?

She wished she could see his face to help her guess what he was thinking. Did he take her request seriously? Or did he find her frivolous?

"A game will help distract us." She hoped. "Besides, it helps to listen to your voice. It reminds me I'm not alone."

Without her conscious permission, her fingertips landed on the flat, hard plane of his pectoral muscle. She smoothed her hand over it, absorbing his warmth, savoring his strength. Feeling him, breathing him in, set this tornado apart from her past. Because having Lorenzo here with her, in *this* moment, gave her a physical reminder that she wasn't scared and alone while her world cracked apart.

Maybe he heard some of the residual fears in her voice because he relaxed a fraction, some of the tension easing from him.

"Right. Two truths and a lie." In the pause while he was thinking, a lightning crack vibrated through the storm cellar, making her jump. Lorenzo's lips went to her hair, pressing a comforting kiss there before he spoke again. "I play guitar in my free time. I hold the record for fastest calf roping among my brothers. I once shot the principal of my middle school with a BB gun."

In spite of everything, she couldn't help a surprised laugh.

"Please say you didn't hit your principal with a BB gun. Although that's so specific, I feel like it has to be true."

She focused all her attention on the man beside her. His warmth. The scent of the outdoors on his work shirt. The flexing muscle in the arm wrapped around her. Right or wrong, his presence felt like a lifeline while the wind raged outside.

"I can't give you clues," he chided, his tone gently teasing. "You have to guess the lie."

"Okay. The lie is that you play guitar."

"Wrong. We should have made stakes for this game. What do I get if I win?" His voice was husky and low, rumbling between them in the dark.

"You can play guitar?" she asked, intrigued.

"My whole family is musical. Diego is the most talented, and he's a guitarist for a local band attracting some regional attention recently." Brotherly pride tinged his voice.

"That's so cool." She imagined Lorenzo playing guitar, his long fingers skillfully moving over the strings. "Do you ever all play together?"

"Sometimes on the holidays a bunch of us will break out instruments. But more often than not, we pass around a guitar and everyone takes a turn."

Having grown up an only child—both with her birth family and later with her adoptive parents—Valencia loved the idea of sharing a talent with siblings. "An invitation to your house at Christmas must be highly sought after."

She could almost hear the music in her ears. The mingled voices of five brothers. How lucky they were to have one another.

He chuckled. "I don't know about that. But we keep each other entertained." Pausing, he lowered his voice before speaking again. "So what do I win?"

A pleasurable shiver stole through her. Was he flirting with her? Or was she hearing suggestive intimacy just because she felt attracted to him? She knew he wasn't the kind of man who would flirt casually just to distract her.

Her pulse jumped.

But she knew better than to put too much stock in the awareness pinging through her, so she rerouted the conversation.

"I'm not sure we can declare a winner until I hear more about the BB gun incident." Her voice betrayed her breathlessness. She licked her lips and tried again. "Is that the lie?"

Outside the wind redoubled, making her edge back on the bed, inserting more space between her and the door.

But just as her old fears threatened to swallow her up again, Lorenzo moved with her, keeping her cradled against his side. His warm strength anchoring her. *Tempting* her.

"Wrong again, Valencia." His voice was a sexy vibration in her ear that put all her focus back on him and the way he made her feel. "We'll have to double the stakes since I've fooled you twice."

Her skin tingled at the idea of him claiming a prize from her in this dark, intimate hideaway. Just when she thought nothing could distract her from the storm, the heated image seared the edges of her fears.

The promise of forgetting was too tantalizing to ignore. Maybe that's how she was able to scrounge up the boldness to meet his challenge head-on. To walk toward the attraction instead of away from it.

"Never let it be said I didn't honor my debts," she murmured softly, her breathing shallow and quick. "Name your price."

Lorenzo knew better than to mix romance and business.

And yet.

These were *extraordinary* circumstances.

Valencia was a strong, independent woman who'd worked hard and sacrificed to build a rescue that would save animals, yet she'd shown him a decidedly vulnerable side when she'd admitted she was frightened and in need of distraction. Was it so wrong to offer her that when she shook against him every time the wind rattled the door? To scavenge a few moments of pleasure together when they could walk out of here to a gravely different world in the morning?

He didn't want to take advantage of her. Far from it. He wanted to shelter her in his arms. Offer her whatever escape he could. The attraction had been there from the moment they'd met.

Would it hurt to call on it now, just for a little while, to help them ride out the storm?

"What if I claimed a kiss?" He told himself that talking about it didn't mean it would happen.

Even just *mentioning* the idea was a better distraction than any game they might play—the possibility it enticed. He sat so close to her he could feel her interest as sharply as his own, the darkness heightening his other senses.

Valencia's soft gasp of surprise was too close to his ear for him to miss. Her back arched a fraction underneath his palm, as if she swayed toward him already.

"Just one?" Her breathless words held a note of expectation. Her hand shifted, landing briefly on his chest, then darting away again, as if she wasn't sure she should commit to the touch. "I thought we were going to double the stakes."

Ah, damn. He hadn't expected her to embrace the idea so fully, but here she was, calling him on his bluff.

Heat rippled through him at her bold words, the sultry promise behind them making him forget everything but pressing his mouth to hers. How could he have known that talking about a kiss would push them closer to the precipice over the hot attraction that bubbled between them?

Every heartbeat sent a hot surge of want through his veins, until the kisses were a foregone conclusion. He would make sure she never forgot them.

"That we are," he promised huskily, angling toward her in the dark, his free hand moving to her bare knee so he could brush light circles along her skin. "But I need you to agree to one before I take a second."

A small hum of pleasure vibrated up her throat, calling an answering growl from his. He had to taste her. *Now.*

"Valencia." He tightened his hold on her knee, his voice growing demanding as his need ratcheted higher. "Do you forfeit your lips to me?"

He felt her quick nod before she spoke. "Yes. That is—" The words cracked on a dry note. "Please."

With considerable effort, he made himself move slowly. He needed this to last, wanted this distraction to spin out for as long as possible. Not just to keep her from thinking about the storm, but because he craved a thorough taste that would leave her hungry for more. Already he knew one kiss wouldn't *ever* be enough for him.

Removing his hand from her knee, he lifted it to her face, brushing her shoulder on the way before landing on her jaw. He skimmed back and forth, tracing the gentle curve from her ear to her chin before laying his thumb over the plush softness of her mouth.

Her breath warmed the digit. He felt her inhale. Then the soft, shaky exhale.

Hunger for her surged, a primal need commanding he lay her down. Cover her. Distract them both in the best way possible.

Instead, he lowered his lips to hers, kissing her with a gentleness made possible only by ruthless restraint. Valencia sighed into him, her breasts pressing against his chest, the tight points of her nipples making him ache to undress her so he could taste her there, too. Shutting down the instinct, he refocused on the soft slide of her mouth over his, needing this kiss to last. He let her get used to him before teasing apart her lips with his tongue.

Then, things got out of control.

Valencia's needy moan went right through him, compelling him to give her more. To answer that primitive need. He sifted through her silky hair to cup the back of her head, holding her where he wanted her while he explored every inch of her mouth. He learned what kisses made her shiver and which ones made her whimper. The rose-and-vanilla scent of her skin teased his nose, beckoning him to sniff out more of it. To find the source of the fragrance.

She arched harder against him, her curves molding to his body. Reminding him she wore only a T-shirt over her panties, the lights having gone out before she could finish putting on dry clothes. That mental visual slammed him, nearly taking him down for the count. He waged a desperate internal battle with his hands not to touch more of her, not to test the softness of her skin where her hips curved or where her thighs shifted restlessly.

She'd agreed only to a kiss, he reminded himself. He would honor that, damn it. But as his restraint stretched thin, nearing the breaking point, he recognized he had to end the embrace before things went further.

Except before he could pull away, she twined her arms around his neck, hauling him down to the mattress with her.

He landed on top of her, barely getting an arm out in time to prevent all his weight from crushing her. Still, his hips pinned hers, his thigh sliding between her legs.

Desire scorched over him, dragging a guttural groan from his throat. The sound mingled with her sigh of satisfaction. And somehow, hearing the way she responded to that friction of their bodies, threatened to incinerate all his good intentions. She felt so good against him, her body fitting to his perfectly. Visions of sinking inside her weren't helping him to get a handle on this situation.

If anything, every second they spent with their torsos pressed intimately together only made it tougher to pull away. One more minute and he would release her. He *had* to, damn it.

Thump!

The entire storm cellar vibrated as if an earthquake hit it, the bed rumbling beneath them.

Lorenzo broke the kiss, body tensing.

"What is that?" Valencia's fingers clenched tighter around his arms, her voice shaking.

Even as she spoke, the rumbling had ceased. The wind still howled, a constant angry shriek, but the vibrating had stopped.

He dragged in long, ragged breaths, trying to recover himself. His blood still ran hot, but he was almost grateful to the storm for reminding him he couldn't take things further. And how messed up was that thinking? The tornado could be wreaking destruction out there.

That thought finally helped cool him off.

Get a grip.

"Maybe a tree fell outside," he guessed, doing his best to speak calmly. He didn't want her to panic. "I should find the lantern and turn on the radio. It would help to hear a report on where the storm is moving."

He didn't mention that he needed to see her face, too. Without the visual cues of her expression, her skin color and her eyes, Lorenzo couldn't be sure how she fared. If she was on the verge of another panic attack, he needed to know.

And he needed to be in command of himself, too.

Because although he hadn't wanted to end their lip-lock because of potential danger from a tornado, it was fortunate things hadn't gone any further between them. The kiss might have been his idea, but he hadn't meant for it to get so out of hand. She tested the limits of his control unlike any other woman, no matter what he'd told himself about pulling away from her.

Lorenzo shot to his feet, needing to put some space between them. To focus on keeping her safe. He had a responsibility to this woman, especially when he knew that she'd been petrified of the storm. He might be able to justify their teasing around the attraction to distract her, but taking things beyond a kiss would have been wrong. Unethical.

"Okay. Good idea about the lantern." A rustling noise told him she was already sitting up on the mattress while he felt his way around the storage bins.

Fur brushed his right arm as he felt Barkis join him, the dog's quiet panting a comfort as turmoil raged outside.

"I've got it." Lorenzo leaned back on his heels, then switched on a powerful flashlight.

The bright white beam gave him a glimpse of her standing beside the bed as she slid on a pair of navy blue sweatpants, her pale thigh disappearing under the knit cotton. He stifled a groan, returning the light to the bins. He found bottled water and poured one container into a dog dish for Barkis, then brought two others over to the bed to sit beside a now fully dressed Valencia.

His shaky restraint thanked her for putting clothes on, even as his baser thoughts lingered over the sight of her bare thigh.

Luckily for him, she seemed as intent as him on putting the kiss behind them, all of her attention now focused on the radio she'd pulled into her lap. Flicking on the power, she adjusted the tuner until they could hear the stock tornado warning again. Then, she spun the dial until she found a regional weather report listing towns that had already reported significant damage from the storm.

While they listened, Barkis lapped at his water, and the two of them drank from their bottles in the relative quiet. The wind had eased outside. At the moment, it was less of a shriek and more of a sustained moan.

Lorenzo remained on his feet while he chugged down his water, knowing the temptation Valencia presented just being next to him. Her sweet, floral scent clung lightly to his clothes, or maybe it was on his skin. He didn't dare inhale more deeply to find out. Her fragrance was like an aphrodisiac.

"Should we look outside yet?" she asked, her cheeks a little flushed as she glanced up at him.

Her lips swollen from his kiss.

He swallowed hard at the visual. The sight made him want to kiss her again. To haul her against him and finish what they'd started. But he knew that couldn't happen. He'd allowed himself the pleasure of touching her only because she'd asked him to distract her, the request revealing a vulnerability that wouldn't allow him to refuse.

Right. As if he hadn't been *dying* for more of her.

"No, it's best to stay here for a while longer. We could be in the eye of the storm." He strode toward the stairs that led to the overhead door and stood still to listen.

A moment later, Valencia spoke again, her head bent over her cell phone. "My phone is still charged, but I'm not surprised there's no signal. Even on a clear day it's hard to get a connection down here."

Her comment reminded him how thoroughly prepared she'd been for a storm. "You don't need a cell signal to access outside information when the radio is working to give updates. The original tornado warning said there could be storm activity through midnight. It's not even eleven o'clock yet."

She shook her head, setting aside her device. "I can't believe that when it already feels like we've been down here forever." Her brown gaze darted to his, her already pink cheeks flushing deeper. "I mean, the first half hour we were in here was terrifying."

But the last half hour passed in a haze of heat and hunger, the time flying past while they kissed. She didn't need to articulate it for him to know they were both thinking it.

Remembering.

"Are you okay?" he asked in the heavy silence. "You were really rattled when we first came down here. I was worried about you."

Her fingers traced the outline of the emergency radio, a French manicure unspoiled by their rush to secure the horses.

"Bad memories settled on me like a toxic cloud. I couldn't seem to see outside of them, the past and the present tangling up because of the storm." She took a sip from her water bottle before re-capping it. "I hadn't realized how triggering a tornado would be."

He wondered what had happened during the other storm. The one that haunted her. But he knew this wasn't the time to ask about it. Not when the second wave of the storm could still bring more destruction down on their heads.

"But you're feeling more steady now?" he asked instead. They might have another hour or more of storm to weather, and he'd prefer to understand her fears more before that happened.

"Thanks to you." A smile curved her lips for a moment as she met his gaze again. "I appreciate—" Her teeth sank into the plump fullness of her lower lip. "That is, I know you were distracting me because I asked you to. And it did help."

His heart slugged hard in his chest, his blood heating with the need to pull her against him again.

Damn it. He'd never survive being stranded here with her if he couldn't rein himself in.

Giving her a clipped nod, Lorenzo stalked back toward the stairs.

"If the wind doesn't pick up again in another ten minutes, I'll try the door," he assured her.

Because getting sucked into a tornado might be the only thing that would keep him from tasting her again.

Six

The next hour ticked by slowly for Valencia, waiting for news that the tornado had passed.

Her fears had calmed since the game she'd played with Lorenzo. Then, her fears had receded even more when they'd kissed. The memory of those smoldering embraces taunted her even now as she stroked Barkis's furry head and listened to the latest updates on the weather.

Many Texas and Oklahoma communities had been threatened—from Royal all the way to Appaloosa Island.

Valencia wished Lorenzo sat beside her now while they listened to the reports, but he'd pulled away after their kiss, making her wonder if he regretted what happened between them. He'd paced the small shelter for a few minutes when they'd started hearing the news. Then, he'd made himself at home on one of the storage bins that converted to a bench, leaving plenty of distance between them since she'd never left the comfort of the flannel-lined sleeping bag on the bed.

Now, Lorenzo entertained himself with a three-dimensional maze that had been a gift from the tornado shelter company when she'd upgraded some of the features in the storm cellar. The intricate marble maze lit up, helping her to see him tilting the small box to the right and left, the motion moving the marble through the obstacles. They'd turned a lantern on the lowest setting to illuminate the shelter, but they were both sitting just outside the pool of yellow light it threw. Lorenzo's strong features and dark eyes were visible, but shadowed.

"The news from Appaloosa Island sounds serious," Valencia remarked softly, more to herself than to the man who seemed determined to put thoughts of their kiss behind him.

No doubt he shared all her same reasons for resisting intimacy, considering they were doing business together. She understood why that was a bad idea.

She just wished his withdrawal hadn't been so complete that he needed to sit as far from her as possible while the storm continued outside. Things had certainly quieted down, but until they heard an all clear for the area, Valencia wouldn't be able to stop imagining the worst-case scenario.

"The take-cover warnings are standard procedure when the threat level is high." The maze box went still in his hands as he spoke. "But that doesn't mean they've been hit."

"I know." She nodded, trying to focus on Barkis's trusting face as she stroked his silky ears. "It just feels like one thing after another keeps thwarting the art and music festival. Somehow, even after the news of the missing money, I keep holding out hope that it will all come together."

Lorenzo set aside the maze. "With good reason. Usually, everything the Edmond family touches turns to gold. I'm sure this will be no different."

She sifted through his comment, wondering what it was about the handsome rancher's words that suggested he held some hidden resentment.

"You're not a fan of the Edmond family?"

"I like them well enough," he mused, as if considering the question for the first time. "I don't know Gina at all, but I consider Ross and Asher to be good men. Rusty, on the other hand—"

He hesitated, making Valencia wonder if there was a history between Lorenzo and the Edmond family's oft-divorced patriarch. But then he continued with a careless shrug.

"I have no beef with him. I'm just surprised that the head of such a wealthy family doesn't support more good causes. If not for Billy Holmes's influence, Soiree on the Bay wouldn't have even come together. I don't care that Rusty is considered cantankerous and unapproachable. But not doing more with his wealth is a strike against him in my book." Standing, Lorenzo walked closer, but his focus was on the radio, not her. "I think they're about to talk about Royal."

Her thoughts of Rusty Edmond evaporated at the prospect of news about the tornado. Although she did tuck away one piece of insight from the discussion. Clearly Lorenzo saw supporting charitable works as part of his community duty, something that only raised her opinion of him.

Another reason to regret they hadn't met under different circumstances. If her horse rescue hadn't been dependent on the Cortez-Williams family's goodwill, Valencia would already be thinking about ways to repeat that toe-curling kiss.

Lorenzo turned up the volume on the radio as the broadcast shifted to their county. They'd bounced back and forth between the weather service and local news for the last hour, hoping to keep current.

"...Local tornado warnings have been lifted," the announcer informed them. "But we've received reports of significant tornado damage from all over the county, so use extreme caution when exiting your home or driving on roads in the area. Be prepared for power outages, downed electric lines and fallen trees. And the National Weather Service has confirmed at least five tornadoes ripped through the area—"

Valencia didn't hear the rest of the broadcast. She felt almost dizzy with the news that *multiple* tornadoes had struck. A panicked buzzing started in her ears, not just because of the past, but also very firmly in the present, demanding she check on her horses now that the immediate danger had passed.

"I need to get outside," she blurted, shooting to her feet. She rushed toward the door, where Lorenzo had hung their coats to dry. "I've got to make sure the horses are safe."

To his credit, he was a step behind her.

Heart hammering, she shoved on her boots at the same time that she reached for her windbreaker. Meanwhile, Lorenzo snapped off the radio and retrieved two powerful flashlights.

"Take this," he demanded, passing her one of them. "The exterior lights won't be on unless you have a backup generator for the barn."

"It wouldn't come on automatically, but I do have one I can wheel out there later." Assuming she could still access it in her garage.

There was no telling how much damage they might find when they opened the door of the storm cellar. The last tornado that swept through Royal had ripped the roof off the Texas Cattleman's Club and brought the town to a halt.

Some of her worry must have shown on her face because Lorenzo rubbed a soothing hand along her back.

"Try to relax. The calmer you are, the calmer your animals will be." His steady voice rumbled in her ears and hummed along her senses.

The practical advice helped her to breathe through the churn of anxiety, giving her the best possible motivation to stay focused.

"Thank you. I know you're right," she murmured, grateful all over again he'd been with her throughout this ordeal. She didn't even want to contemplate how terrified she would have been in the storm shelter by herself, without Lorenzo's patient, soothing presence to keep her grounded.

"Let me go ahead of you, okay?" He edged past her to mount

the steps to the door. "That way I can clear a path if there's any fallen debris."

After her silent nod, she waited while he lifted the latch, hugging herself tight. At her feet, Barkis whimpered softly, wagging his tail as he gazed up at her.

A moment later, the plowed-earth scent of the storm filtered through the metal door as Lorenzo pushed it open. Moonlight shone weakly through a few leftover clouds, suffusing the night with a glow that seemed almost bright compared with the dimness of the shelter. A few wet leaves blew down the steps, covered with gritty mud.

Heart pounding, she tried to peer around Lorenzo's broad shoulders to assess the damage. And although she held the flashlight with one hand, her other had gripped the hem of his jacket at some point, her fingers seeking to touch any part of him for comfort. How had she gotten so close to this man so quickly?

With an effort, she unclasped her hand to relinquish her hold while she waited for his verdict.

"Well? Can you see the barn?" she asked as he stepped over the threshold into the night.

Valencia held her breath, her airway constricted tight. The moment seemed to draw out forever, her fear swelling, threatening to swallow her whole.

Then at last he turned back around, giving her a short nod over his shoulder.

"I see it. And from this side it looks unharmed." It was probably a good thing that he offered her a hand to help her the rest of the way out of the shelter, because her relief was so swift it was almost dizzying.

Thank God.

Scrambling out the door, she almost ran across the muddy yard to reach the barn, a horse's soft whinny the sweetest greeting she'd ever heard. These animals were her whole world now, and she wouldn't let anything—or anyone—distract her from her mission to build a safe haven for them.

* * *

As a lifetime rancher, Lorenzo appreciated animals and respected people who did the same. So of all the things he found appealing about Valencia, it shouldn't have been a surprise that her transparent love and deep affection for the horses in her care topped the list.

He'd helped her settle down two nervous stallions and an old mare, turning them out to the smaller of two pastures after he'd secured a few places where the fence had been damaged. But seeing her coax one of her newest skittish rescues out of a stall, soothing the mustang's fears with soft, crooning words, had made some invisible band tighten around his chest.

Even now, drying his face and hands on a gray guest towel after he'd accepted her offer to wash up before heading home, he felt the tug toward her. His admiration for her was all the stronger after seeing her comfort that mare when he knew that no one had comforted her in whatever long-ago tornado she'd weathered.

Her resilience humbled him. Her appeal winding around him like a lover's touch. Tempting. Teasing.

Emerging from the downstairs bathroom inside her minimalist ranch home, Lorenzo told himself he should bid Valencia goodbye and head home. It was past one in the morning, after all, and he'd already walked a knife's edge of wanting her after that kiss in the storm shelter. He had no restraint left, so he needed to put some distance between them until the world settled.

Decision made, he found her in the farmhouse-style kitchen, seated at a table on the wide-plank floors. The white cabinets and natural wood accents were free of clutter and decor, though a few worn cookbooks rested on a shelf over one counter. Under the glow of an industrial-style pendant light, her honey-blond hair had a warm luster as she bent over another small weather radio.

The announcer's voice became more distinct as he approached.

"…an E2 tornado, but significant wind damage has been reported on the southern side of Royal."

"Everything okay?" he asked when she didn't look up from the radio. His hand itched to touch her, to rest between her shoulder blades where he suspected she'd be tense.

Not that he'd be able to stop touching her there if he had that opportunity. He remembered all too well how she felt against him. The need to claim her lips again vibrated through him like a physical imperative.

"Yes." She shot to her feet as if nervous. "Just listening to the damage reports. Apparently County Route Twelve is washed out."

"Route Twelve?" The road between his place and hers.

Of course.

She nodded, nibbling her lower lip. "I'm sure you want to get home and check on your place, but you're more than welcome to stay here. It's late anyway. Maybe the road will be cleared in the morning."

His heart pounded a slow, warning thud as she stared back at him with concerned brown eyes.

He wasn't supposed to have feelings like this for her. But the time they'd spent together had been intense, escalating their relationship to something deeper. Still, he tried to hold back the need to ravish her.

"They're calling it an E2? Already?"

"Yes. So not as bad as it might have been, but it touched down less than a mile from here, so—" She exhaled a long breath, but it didn't fully hide the way her lower lip trembled.

Relief at the near miss washed over him, all but taking his knees out when he thought about how close a twister had been to demolishing this place she'd worked so hard to build.

"We were so damned lucky." He couldn't help but open his arms to her.

She didn't hesitate. Valencia threw herself into him, her arms locking around his waist as she buried her head against his chest.

"I know." Her whisper was hoarse with emotion in the otherwise silent kitchen. "I've been sitting here going over and over it in my head. If it had been a direct hit, the horses would have—" She choked on the words and lifted her head, her brown eyes red-rimmed with unshed tears. "I should have left them outside where they could have run free to safety."

"No. You can't think like that." He framed her face in his hands, needing to impart the truth of the words. "They could have been hurt that way, too, caught up in mangled fences or hit by lightning, hail, flying debris. You know that. Your barn is strong, and they're fine."

Nodding tightly, she blinked away the tears, letting only one roll down her cheek. He thumbed it away, wishing he could swipe aside her old fears as easily.

"Thank you. I know you're right. I should be fine now that it's over, but I just feel so—" She seemed to search his gaze, as if looking to see if he felt it, too.

The relief. The adrenaline rush of getting through something life-threatening.

Lorenzo couldn't have said what she saw in his eyes. But he felt the moment that the relief morphed into desire. Heat roared through him, demanding an outlet. Or maybe it was a simple need to celebrate being alive. Whatever it was, he had zero chance of containing the need to kiss her again.

To lick and taste her. Claim her. Revel in the fact that they'd made it through the storm.

Their mouths fused together, heads tilting for better access, tongues tangling. The sounds she made—soft, hungry sighs— only added fuel to the fire inside him, driving him higher. Her palms splayed along his back, skimming and rubbing, as if she couldn't feel enough of him.

He lifted her against him, and she responded by curling her leg around his middle, climbing up his body until her ankles wound around his waist. Groaning at the feel of her lush curves against him, he cupped her ass in both hands, squeezing, directing her hips right where he needed her.

Cotton and denim didn't begin to dull the heated throb where her sex met his. And between the greedy way she kissed him and the way her thighs clamped around him, like she'd never let him go, Lorenzo guessed she wanted him every bit as badly as he craved her.

Still, he broke the kiss to be certain. He tipped his forehead to hers, raking in a breath.

"I need to be sure you want this—"

"*Please.* Yes. My bedroom is in the back of the house." She tipped her head in the direction she meant, and his boots were already charging over the wide-plank floors to find it.

He toed open a whitewashed door into a bedroom, visible only by dull moonlight slanting through plantation shutters above the king-size bed. The room had few furnishings save the cast-iron bedstead, and he headed toward it, spinning around so he could sit on the edge of the gray-duvet-covered mattress, keeping Valencia on his lap.

He skimmed his hands under her shirt and then stopped himself. "Do you have condoms? Mine are in the truck."

She helped him by tugging her shirt up and off, giving him a mouthwatering view of perfect breasts molded by a black satin bra, two tiny bows at the straps unnecessary decorations for so much beauty. "Lucky for us, yes."

Leaning to one side, she towed a wicker basket out from under the bed where an unopened box lay on top of a psychology textbook, a pair of fluffy socks and a bright pink case shaped like it probably held a sex toy.

A guess that seemed all the more probable by how fast she shoved the basket back under the bed. The thought only made him doubly determined to please her, the urge to satisfy her hammering through him with every pound of his pulse.

"You're so gorgeous." He raked the straps of the bra off her shoulders, then ran his tongue along the two swells above the black satin cups. "I've wanted to touch you all night. Since dinner. Hell, before dinner."

Her back arched, bringing her breasts even closer to his mouth at the same time it pressed the V of her thighs against the rock-hard length of his erection. He didn't know which stole his breath faster, but the need to have her naked grew exponentially.

"Touch all you want," she urged him, her nails raking over his chest, scoring him right through the cotton T-shirt. "But I want to feel all of you, too."

She tunneled under his shirt and dragged it up and over his head. He used the moment to unhook her bra, releasing the soft weight of her into his palms. He lifted one mound to his mouth to tease over the dark nipple, circling and suckling until she whimpered. Then he moved to the other side to repeat the treatment.

She forgot about touching him for a long moment, her hands catching at his hair instead, holding him in place, showing him what she liked. Knowledge he would not waste.

Never stopping his worship of her breasts, he flicked open the button on her jeans and lowered the zipper enough to slide his hand inside, fingers sliding down the satin panties along one side. Dipping beneath the silky fabric to find her wet and ready for him.

She cried out at his touch, as if that one stroke was enough to bring her close to the edge. Releasing one of her nipples, he gazed up into her face, taking in her closed eyes, her head thrown back. Experimentally, he stroked her there again, savoring all her sweetness, and her fingers clenched his shoulders tighter.

He had a hundred things he longed to do to her, myriad ways he wanted to touch her and bring her to the pinnacle of pleasure. But he also yearned to do whatever she craved. What would make her feel best. So he watched, and stroked.

"You feel so good here." He palmed one breast with his free hand and licked over the nipple on the other. "I could touch you all night just like this."

"Don't stop." She breathed the words quietly, her nails digging into him deeper. "It's been so long for me, and—"

She broke off on a gasp as he slid two fingers inside her. Immediately, he felt her pulse around him, her body squeezing him tightly. He pressed deeper inside her, needing to feel every spasm, wanting to coax as much as she had to give him.

Lorenzo had never seen anything so beautiful as her riding his fingers, her soft cries filling the room as she found her pleasure.

The need to be inside her redoubled, filling his chest with a possessive fire so primal his hands shook with the effort to be gentle as he undressed her the rest of the way. But Valencia was having none of that. She about tore his jeans off, raking his boxers with them until they tangled in his boots and he had to help her free him.

"Please, please, *please*." She murmured it like a chant, her silky long hair sliding over his body as she moved around him, undressing him. "Hurry."

Knowing that she needed him, too, cut the chains on his hunger. When they were both naked, he hauled her into the middle of her bed, his eyes roaming over her beautiful body while he tore open the box of condoms and rolled one onto place.

All for me.

The fierce need rode him hard, demanding more of her.

"Did that feel good?" He breathed the question into her ear as he stretched over her, making room for himself between her thighs.

"So good," she gasped, her hips lifting to meet his.

"There's more where that came from," he promised as he nudged his way inside her, her tight heat stealing his breath. "We're only just getting started."

Seven

This. Man.

Valencia stared up at him in her darkened room, wondering if he had any idea how much he turned her inside out. Her feelings for him had exploded in a hundred directions during the storm, leaving her utterly raw. She had no barriers now, all her nerve endings exposed to his skillful touch. His hypnotic words.

We're only just getting started.

She wasn't sure she'd escape this night with her heart intact.

For now, she could only cling to his strong shoulders to try to anchor herself as he filled her. Stretched her. Made her see stars behind her closed eyelids. It wasn't until he kissed her mouth—slowly, tenderly—that she realized she'd been holding her breath.

"You okay?" he asked, stroking her face.

Her eyes flew open as she realized he'd been holding back for her sake, giving her time to accommodate him.

A piece of her heart definitely chipped away at the thoughtful look in his chocolate-brown eyes.

"More," she demanded, writhing against him, wanting him to take as much pleasure as he'd already given.

Her word worked like a magic spell, setting his hips in motion and launching her into a higher plane of heat. The delicious friction built inside her, as if she hadn't just orgasmed all over his hand.

He seemed to sense that she was close all over again because he rolled her on top of him, his dark gaze missing nothing as he reached between them to stroke her.

"Oh." Her thighs clenched him, sensation rocking her core.

No one had ever propelled her body to heights like this before. Then again, had anyone ever tried? She stared down into his eyes as he worked that tight bundle of nerves exactly the way she needed. And she flew apart.

Absolutely *imploded*. Her release squeezed him over and over, her feminine muscles fluttering wildly.

Only then did he shift her to her back again, driving home between her thighs, again and again until he found his peak. He strained against her, his body tensing in a way that showed off every single muscle, delineating each masculine ridge and hollow. The sight affected her. The whole night had wrecked her, but seeing him find pleasure in her body made her want to curl against him and never let him go.

It was just as well that his eyes were closed at that moment because she guessed everything she was feeling would have been visible in her expression. She tried to tuck in all those feelings as he panted through the last of his release, his body slumping to one side while he kept the bulk of his weight off her.

He couldn't know that she would have welcomed it. Would have savored being pressed deeper into her mattress underneath him. So she tamped down the rush of tenderness that overcame her and turned her head to the side in time to see him settle beside her on the pillow.

She couldn't look away.

For long moments, they simply breathed each other in, and she wondered if he felt like his world was off its axis or if that was just her. But then he blinked, a slow closing of his eyes.

When he reopened them, there was a distance there that hadn't been in place before. A guarded look that told her he planned on keeping the boundaries between them.

A moment later, he smoothed a strand of hair off her face, a sweet gesture she might have misinterpreted if she hadn't been watching him carefully. She'd seen the moment that he'd mentally pulled away from letting this night have any deeper meaning.

Valencia wasn't just being paranoid. She could feel him already retreating from her. From her point of view, the night had brought a monumental shift in her relationship with this man. But she understood Lorenzo saw her as a business associate first and foremost.

What had just happened between them didn't change that.

Maybe he was already regretting it even now. As he pulled the blankets over them and tucked her against him, he didn't reveal any other tangible sign of his retreat from her. But the heated touches of earlier had turned to cold comfort now, no matter how close they lay together when they finally fell asleep.

Valencia's fears about Lorenzo were confirmed when she woke up alone at daybreak.

She glanced over at him now—shortly after noon—as she sat beside him in the Cortez-Williams family's private helicopter. They were on their way to Appaloosa Island to assess the damage from a separate tornado that had ripped through the festival site the night before.

He'd already been on his cell phone arranging for the short helicopter flight while seated at her kitchen table when she'd emerged for breakfast that morning. And even though everything in Lorenzo's demeanor had told her he was resurrecting the old professional boundaries between them, he had still invited her to come along with him.

How could she refuse the offer when the future of her rescue was so entwined with the fate of Soiree on the Bay? So she'd agreed, and the roads in Royal had been cleared enough for them to drive over to the Cortez-Williams place where Lorenzo kept the family helicopter.

Now, the pilot of the small aircraft circled Appaloosa Island, giving them an overhead view of the destruction from the storm. In the middle of the blue waters of Trinity Bay, the island seemed to float like a shipwreck. Downed trees lay in every direction, the upturned roots exposing big gashes in the earth. Roofing tiles were scattered like confetti over the ground, while mangled fencing jutted from random dirt piles. And one of the temporary buildings erected for the festival was demolished on one side.

"Oh, no," Valencia murmured, peering out the window as the chopper neared the ground. "How will we ever clean this up in time for the festival to open at the end of the month?"

She was meeting members of the advisory committee here today. Would any of them have a clue how to proceed in the face of so much damage?

For that matter, did they even have enough of a budget to make repairs? The money woes hadn't disappeared.

Lorenzo swore softly. "I can't imagine how they'll ever clear it all. Although that looks like a truck from Bowden Construction down there giving it a valiant start."

He tapped the window to show her where he was looking, his strong arm reaching over her. A shiver went through her at his nearness, memories of their night together never far from her thoughts since she'd awoken alone. But she couldn't afford to think about that when Lorenzo had not acknowledged what had happened in any way, almost as if those sweltering stolen moments didn't exist. So she forced herself to find the oversize pickup for Jack Bowden's construction company.

"Maybe that's a good sign," Valencia tried to assure herself, even though hope felt like a scarce commodity today.

Between Lorenzo's defection, the rumors about the vanishing festival funds and seeing the festival grounds in ruins, Valencia felt everything she'd worked so hard for slipping away.

"It has to be." He unfastened his seat restraint as soon as the helicopter touched down on a rough patch of torn-up grass, the loud *whap, whap* of the rotor blade sounding even louder as the door opened for their exit. "There are a lot of good people backing Soiree on the Bay. They'll make it come together."

Valencia hurried to unbuckle from her seat as Lorenzo offered her a hand out of the aircraft. Flashbacks of his hot, searing touch shivered through her as she braced herself for the feel of his skin on hers.

"You know as well as I do their money has gone missing," she reminded him, needing to contradict him to keep herself from relishing the warmth of his fingers around hers. She couldn't help that his touch, and his proximity, were still deeply arousing to her, even though he'd decided to resurrect all the boundaries of professionalism between them.

"I do. But the Edmond family isn't the only sponsor of the event. My brother Rafe has invested heavily in Soiree on the Bay." Lorenzo released her hand as soon they were out of range of the chopper blades.

"Rafe. He's the one after Matias?" She tried to recall what he'd told her about the five Cortez-Williams brothers, a conversation they'd had at Sheen last night before all hell had broken loose.

So much had happened since then. Her whole life had been turned upside down along with Appaloosa Island.

"That's right. Rafe owns RCW Steakhouse."

Once again, she didn't miss the note of pride in his voice at the mention of his brother's accomplishments. But any response she might have made was halted as Lorenzo gestured toward a small group of people gathered under one of the giant live oaks still standing near a demolished stage. A man and a woman stood close together, arms looped around each other, while two other women peered down at a shared tablet, heads almost touching.

Festival advisory board member Lila Jones was one of the women, and Valencia thought the other lady who held the tablet worked with Lila at the Royal Chamber of Commerce. The couple was Brett Harston and Sarabeth Edmond, one of Rusty's exes. Brett had been an advisory board member until the Edmond family patriarch booted Brett off for seeing Sarabeth. Valencia had enjoyed getting to know them over the last few months planning the Soiree, and at the sight of her business associates, she tried to swallow the ache of hopelessness she'd been battling all morning.

Greetings were exchanged all around. Lorenzo already knew Brett from the Texas Cattleman's Club, but he hadn't met Lila before. Lila's new assistant, Megan, said a quick hello before excusing herself to take a call. Lila, with her intensely blue eyes and long, dark hair, had recently become a social media star thanks to a romance with a notable online influencer, Zach Benning.

The brunette's pretty smile was nowhere to be seen today, however. She appeared as gutted as Valencia felt inside.

"Has anyone spoken to Jack Bowden?" Lorenzo asked, his dark eyes moving slowly over the damaged festival preparations. "We could see from the air that one of his construction crew's trucks is already on-site."

Lila nodded as she tucked her tablet under her arm. "We saw him a few minutes ago. He said he's assessed the destruction and is sure he can repair the stage and the buildings in time for the festival."

Valencia's breath caught. Hope flared.

"That's good news, right?" she asked, peering around at the other faces, wondering why they weren't more excited to hear it.

"It would be," Lila admitted, flipping her long ponytail over her shoulder. "Except that when he called Edmond Ranch with an estimate for the cost of repairs, he was told there is no money."

No money? And more important, *why not?*

Speechless, Valencia could only shake her head. She refused to speculate about the Edmond family in front of Sarabeth, unwilling to make Gina and Ross's mother uncomfortable. But what on earth was going on?

Sarabeth cleared her throat, a few strands of shoulder-length blond hair blowing over her cheek as she spoke. "I called Ross to ask him about the missing funds, but he told me the same thing I'm sure he's told all of you." Her gaze darted to Brett and then back to the group. "A great deal of money is missing from the account with the funds from the ticket sales. Ross says they're still trying to track it, but his meeting with the bank was delayed by the tornado."

Lila made a soothing comment about the delay being unavoidable, but Valencia couldn't suppress the heat of anger building inside her. The accounting for something like the festival wouldn't be elaborate. If money was missing and a reasonable explanation hadn't been found yet, that meant something underhanded was going on.

She didn't want to think the worst of anyone, but what other reason could there be? Ross Edmond was a smart man. If he couldn't find a paper trail, there was no hope of recovering what they'd lost. The money was gone.

And so were her dreams for the rescue.

A knot twisted inside her chest, raw and chafing.

"Excuse me," she murmured, overcome with so much frustration she didn't know where to put it all.

Turning her back on the group, she walked away from Lorenzo and her friends on the advisory board, needing to collect herself. She strode quickly toward the water, the beach not too far from any location on Appaloosa Island.

She wished she'd brought Barkis with her. The solid presence and unconditional love of her dog would help unfasten the tangle of emotions tightening inside her. Picking up her pace, she'd almost reached the water's edge when a voice from behind her left shoulder raked over her senses.

"Talk to me, Valencia. How can I help?" A strong masculine hand wrapped around her elbow, stopping her short with the gentlest of tugs.

Blinking back her surprise, she spun on her heel to face Lorenzo, all of the hurt and anger from the storm bearing down on her. And now, seeing his face when she was reeling from the news that the money for the Soiree on the Bay festival really was gone, she couldn't help but remember how he'd tried to shut her out this morning.

"How can you help?" she repeated coolly, folding her arms around herself as she stopped at the edge of the beach where the surf rolled to the tips of her toes. "Are you sure you want to? You've made it clear you're only interested in a business relationship, so there's no need for you to get tangled up in my personal disappointments."

She gazed out over the waves, powerless to rein in her words when she was exhausted from the emotional roller coaster she'd been on over the last twenty-four hours. Reliving the fears from her childhood—and having Lorenzo there to witness them—had taken more out of her than she'd realized. She felt like she didn't have the strength to hold herself together any longer.

"That's not fair." He came shoulder to shoulder with her where she stood, but he made no move to touch her. "I'm here, aren't I?"

Valencia shivered at the distance between them. He might be only inches away from her, but it was telling that he didn't lay a finger on her after everything they'd experienced together the night before.

That hurt.

"Not for me, you're not."

Lorenzo dragged in deep breaths of the air blowing in off Trinity Bay, reminding himself he hadn't done anything to deserve Valencia's anger today.

She'd been through a lot, and he understood her frustration at the possibility of not being able to grow her horse rescue the way she'd dreamed now that the arts festival might be a bust.

But he truly had flown out to Appaloosa Island mostly for her sake. He'd wanted to do something nice for her after pulling away from her following their night together. He had hoped seeing the festival site for herself would alleviate some of her worries. Instead, it had only confirmed them.

That wasn't his fault, though.

"I realize this is a disappointment for you." He turned toward her, taking in the delicate contours of her face as she stared out over the water, her honey-brown eyes focused on some distant point. "This is a setback, but you'll find another way to support the rescue. You've accomplished so much already."

Pursing her lips, Valencia darted her gaze briefly toward him, then back to the glittering expanse of blue water. "Have you ever known what it's like to struggle? To be denied something you've worked so hard for?"

He ground his teeth together, ignoring a question that wasn't relevant. "The Soiree could still happen. The Edmond family might still pull this off."

She nodded slowly before turning thoughtful eyes on him. "It could. But neither of us believes that anymore."

Lorenzo couldn't argue with her. Hell, he didn't want to. He hated that their time together had been tainted. First by his recognition that he'd broken his own cardinal rule not to get involved with someone he did business with, and then later by the unraveling of Valencia's plans for the ticket sale money from Soiree on the Bay.

"Today definitely didn't turn out the way we'd hoped," he acknowledged, not sure how else to comfort her.

Still, the weight of regret seemed to anchor his feet in place on the beach beside her.

"Maybe we should cut our losses." She looked him in the eye, squaring her shoulders to his. "I can get a ride home with Lila or one of the other board members."

He blinked in the face of her...*dismissal*?

"I don't mind waiting for you to finish up—" he began, but she was already shaking her head.

"I know that. You're too much of a gentleman to leave me

stranded." She gave him a gentle smile, and he remembered how they'd touched and held each other in that dark shelter. Her lips had been so soft beneath his. But she definitely wasn't remembering their shared kisses now. "What I mean is, I'll be okay on my own, Lorenzo. You can go now, and you certainly don't need to feel badly about it."

A knowing glint in her brown eyes told him they weren't just talking about the helicopter ride.

Somehow that got under his skin. That she would suggest he didn't need to feel guilty about sleeping with her and then walking away. He wanted to deny that he had done any such thing, because of course he'd prefer to see her again. To take her to his bed over and over.

But unless she planned to refuse the support of the Cortez-Williams family for her horse rescue, he couldn't continue to see her since they had business dealings. And he'd never ask her to renounce that support so that she could be with him.

Regret burned hotter. Deeper.

Yet he wouldn't compromise what was right.

"Are you sure you'll be okay?" he asked finally, hating to end their time together like this.

"I'll be fine." She gave a clipped nod. "Bye, Lorenzo. And thank you, for everything."

It was wrong to walk away without another kiss. Without another touch. But that's exactly what he did. Leaving Valencia and the beach behind, he headed toward the family's helicopter still parked in open grassland near the staging area.

The only positive thing about ending their liaison now was that at least Valencia would never know how thoroughly he'd investigated her personal life as part of awarding her the grant money. She wouldn't like knowing that he'd glimpsed some of her secrets before they'd ever met.

With the hole burning in his chest at her impending absence, however, Lorenzo wondered if it would have been worth her learning the truth for a chance to be with her again.

Eight

Safety goggles sealed to her face, Valencia lined up the laser guide on her table saw, then lowered the blade. Sawdust flew as the metal teeth seared through another board to repair her paddock fence, the scent of new lumber swelling in the muggy July heat. She'd kept the big barn doors open to begin her project that morning, wanting the fresh air to keep the dust at a minimum, but now that the sun had risen to its peak, she was ready to call it a day.

Her shoulders ached from hunching over the boards while she worked, and she stretched as she straightened. A full day had passed since she'd visited the Appaloosa Island and things had unraveled fast with Lorenzo. She'd tried to focus on tornado cleanup around her property so as not to spend too much time thinking about their falling-out and what it might mean for the rescue. Backbreaking labor was good for wearing her out so thoroughly she couldn't be too stressed.

Except today, as she added the last cut plank to a pile in her truck bed for a round of fence repairs later, she couldn't hide her head in the sand anymore. She needed to call Asher Edmond and see what was happening with the festival. To find out if her chance of receiving any money from the Soiree on the Bay ticket sales was gone, or if there was still some hope that the event would come together.

For all Valencia knew, her disagreement with Lorenzo—and sleeping with him before that—had pulled her rescue off the list of the Cortez-Williams family's approved charities. Which could mean her horses might not receive a single cent in donation from either of the groups that had once seemed so promising.

That would be painful enough in itself. But Valencia couldn't deny another persistent ache since her argument with Lorenzo. She missed him. She'd thought about him countless times since her return home from Appaloosa Island without him. Now that he'd spent time in her world—meeting all her horses, helping her to care for them before and after the tornado—she had memories of him here. She could look out over her paddock and picture him coaxing in her most stubborn and moody old mare when the storm had been brewing. Inside the stable, she remembered how he'd laughed when one of the docile draft horses had nuzzled his shirt pocket, hoping for a treat.

And in her bedroom alone the night before, she'd remembered how it felt to have Lorenzo there with her, too. He'd worked his way into her life so quickly she hadn't had time to consider how much it might hurt if things didn't work out between them. But there was no "them" and it was foolish of her to think otherwise.

Peeling off her leather work gloves in exasperation, Valencia rested a hip on the tailgate, then pulled her phone from the back pocket of her jeans.

The sound of cicadas filled the air, an audible reminder of the summer heat even as she stood under the shade of a bald cypress tree. She pressed the contact button next to Asher Edmond's name on her screen. One ring later, the call went to voice mail, the same way it had done for days. Disconnecting, Valencia ground her teeth in frustration and moved down her contacts list to try Asher's stepsister, Gina Edmond. At twenty-six years old, Gina was four years younger than Valencia, but they'd moved in enough common social circles over the years that they were friends.

The call rang twice before Gina answered.

"Hello?" The young woman's voice sounded hoarse with emotion.

Valencia stilled, her senses all focused on the call.

"Gina? It's Valencia. Is everything okay?" She straightened from where she'd been leaning against the tailgate.

"Oh, my God, no. Things are not okay at all." Her friend's voice broke, her pitch high and breathless.

"What's wrong?" Valencia's stomach knotted, foreboding stirring. "Should I come over? Do you need someone to be with you?"

She'd never been to Gina's home, but the woman sounded too upset to be alone.

"No. That's okay. It's just that—" She paused, as if sucking in a deep breath. "Asher has been arrested. On embezzlement charges linked to Soiree on the Bay. I just can't believe this is happening."

"Asher?" Valencia shook her head, certain Gina must have said the wrong thing. The wrong name.

Asher Edmond was a good man. Rusty had adopted him when he married Asher's mother, Stephanie Davidson. Rusty had since divorced her, but Asher remained an integral part of the Edmond family.

"Yes. Asher. And I can't believe it, either. How could he do such a thing?" There was a note of despair in Gina's voice, and Valencia's gut churned in sympathy.

She glanced around at the projects she had in progress around the rescue today, but told herself it could all wait if Gina needed a friend.

"He might not have," she said carefully, hoping the words brought comfort and not false expectations. "Just because the police arrested him doesn't mean he did it."

"I know you're right, but they must have had convincing evidence to arrest him in the first place." Gina sniffled once, then again before continuing. "I'm so sorry to unload all this on you. You didn't call to hear about my problems."

"Don't be sorry. It's no wonder you're upset. And I only called because I've wondered how things are going with the festival," she admitted, scraping some damp hair from the back of her neck. "Gina, it's no trouble to come over if you need a friend. I want to be there for you—"

"No. I'll be all right. I appreciate the offer, though." She spoke with a bit more composure, her voice softer now. "I should probably talk with Ross and figure out what this means for the festival. Maybe there's a chance it will still happen if—"

Valencia hung on to her words. Yes, for her friend, but also because the future of the rescue and the equine therapy camp were riding on the festival. "If what?"

"I was going to say maybe the festival will happen if the police have traced the money from the ticket sales, but I guess a part of me doesn't want that to be true because it would mean Asher really *is* guilty," she admitted.

Valencia's heart ached for what Gina must be going through. Of course she would worry about her brother. And the scandal of having an Edmond arrested was going to hurt the whole family. She understood the shame of that better than anyone knew. Because while her adoptive parents were wonderful people, Valencia had never felt free of the taint of her biological relations, especially her father with his long history of fraud, forgery and identity theft. Logically, she knew that shouldn't reflect on her, but that didn't stop her from sometimes feeling like an imposter in the privileged world she inhabited now.

"Please know you can call me anytime," she told her. "If you need anything…"

"Thank you." Gina sniffed again. "I appreciate that more than you know. Bye, Valencia."

The call ended and she slumped back against her truck fender.

The day had gone from bad to worse in a hurry, but with her horses counting on her, she couldn't waste a day for a pity party.

Returning her phone to her pocket, she tried not to think about Lorenzo or what he thought of the latest developments with Soiree on the Bay. Instead, she slid behind the wheel of her truck to drive the perimeter of her fence so she could patch the broken areas.

Too bad there wasn't a patch job for her aching heart.

Two days after Asher Edmond's arrest, Lorenzo took the ferry back to Appaloosa Island. He'd had family ranch business in Houston, so he'd taken the helicopter to Mustang Point, splitting the difference between Appaloosa Island and the city. Now that he'd finished his business, he wanted to see if any preparations were happening toward the festival. Just because he was curious, of course.

Not because he wouldn't stop thinking about Valencia.

A breeze blew in off Trinity Bay as the ferry moved through the water. Lorenzo tipped his face into a light spray kicking up, remembering the way the rain had pelted them the night of the tornado before he'd taken shelter with Valencia. So much had happened in such a short time. Learning more about her fears and her hard work, seeing her commitment to her horse rescue with his own eyes. Then, later, he'd lost himself in her arms, tasting and touching every delectable inch of her beautiful body.

Memories of the time in her bed had filled his dreams every night since. Again and again he undressed her, peeling away the layers that kept her from him. Again and again, he heard her soft whimpers in his ear, then woke up aching.

Alone.

Logically, he knew he'd done the right thing in walking away. He'd been burned before by crossing the boundaries between romance and business, and he refused to take that risk ever again. For her sake as well as his own. But knowing he'd made the only possible choice didn't stop the churn of regrets where she was concerned about what might have been. And it sure as hell didn't prevent him from missing her.

It would be one thing if all he missed was the sizzling intimacy. But he also wondered how she was faring with repairs at her rescue. How she was dealing with the news of Asher Edmond's arrest. He couldn't remember the last time a woman had so thoroughly preoccupied him. Maybe because no one else ever had.

When the ferry reached Appaloosa Island, Lorenzo stepped onto the pier along with a couple dozen other people. He didn't know what he'd expected to see once they docked, but it definitely wasn't the mayhem unfolding in front of his eyes.

A group of network news vans were parked on the grass outside the festival headquarters—a small public building requisitioned by the Soiree on the Bay coordinators to oversee preparations. And, to add to the pandemonium, protestors crowded the parking area near the beach. They were carrying signs that read I Demand a Refund and I Paid for a Soiree Scam, and there were also a few photos of Asher Edmond with the caption Swindler on the Bay.

The atmosphere was raucous, with reporters standing at various points in the crowd to obtain video footage while others broadcast live updates. Between the shouting demands of the unruly protest groups and the private island's lack of public facilities to maintain the visitors on the eastern undeveloped side, it seemed like a disaster waiting to happen. While there was a resort on the western side with some amenities, a business catering to tourists surely wouldn't want to host the unhappy protestors if they could help it.

"Lorenzo?"

A familiar voice called to him from a group of people standing off to one side of the protestors.

Searching the faces, Lorenzo spotted his brother breaking off from the group and heading toward him.

"Rafe." He clapped his sibling on the shoulder. "I'm surprised to see you here."

Dressed in black jeans and boots, Rafe wore a silver-gray button-down. His years in the restaurant business had given him a more cosmopolitan air than the rest of the Cortez-Williams brothers. But he didn't have any of his usual genial charm around him today. He looked downright grave.

"I don't know why I keep showing up here, either," Rafe admitted, his dark gaze roaming the unhappy protestors. "I invested heavily in the festival and I keep hoping that this nightmare will end. That it will all be a mistake, and they'll find the missing money—"

He broke off, shaking his head in disgust. Before Lorenzo could speak, Rafe turned toward him, continuing, "*Missing money.* Who am I kidding? It's a poor turn of phrase for funds that were clearly stolen."

The venom in his voice was unlike anything Lorenzo had ever heard from his younger brother before. Concerned, he lowered his voice before asking, "How much did you invest?"

"Too much," Rafe spat out. "Not enough to ruin me personally, but enough to bankrupt the business."

Lorenzo swore. "You know I'll help—"

Rafe was already shaking his head. "And you know I'd never ask. Thanks just the same."

For a moment, both men were quiet. Lorenzo understood his brother's pride. No doubt, he'd feel the same way if their positions were reversed. But that still didn't stop him from wanting to offer any assistance he could.

Rafe rocked back on his heels and said, "It's unbelievable how fast things soured. Or were we just that naive to trust the Edmond family?"

"I still can't see Asher doing something like this," Lorenzo muttered, his gaze going to the cutouts of Asher's face on the signs the protestors were waving around.

"I always liked the guy."

"Me, too," Rafe acknowledged. "But sometimes people only show you what they want you to see."

Lorenzo couldn't deny the truth of the words.

They spoke for a few more minutes before his brother left to see if he could find Ross Edmond. Lorenzo hoped Ross would have answers for his brother, but wasn't holding his breath. Seeing the Soiree on the Bay festival fall apart was hurting a lot of people. Not quite ready to make the ferry trip back to the mainland, he headed toward the beach to take a walk. The sun was setting, turning the water a shade of greenish blue while the sky was streaked with violet.

Normally, he didn't take the time to appreciate that kind of thing. But back home, he knew he'd have only thoughts of Valencia waiting for him. So he headed away from the crowds toward the quieter part of the beach to clear his head for a little while. There were a few cabanas dotting the sand along the tree line, but for the most part, the view was unspoiled here. Maybe if he walked far enough he'd leave behind the raised voices of the protestors, too.

Too bad he couldn't outrun his regrets while he was at it.

Cursing his attempt to vanquish his own demons, Lorenzo stopped. He had responsibilities back home in Royal. A ranch to run. Family that counted on him. He shouldn't be wasting time at the site of a doomed festival that was bringing his brother financial trouble. Lorenzo turned on his heel to head back to the ferry when he spotted a female figure he recognized well.

Tall and willowy, the woman stood at the edge of the water, a pair of sandals in one hand while her fair hair blew behind her. A pink pencil skirt hugged her curves while the sheer sleeves of a filmy white blouse skimmed her shoulders.

His breath caught. Held. And it was almost as if she could feel his attention on her because at the same moment the woman turned to face him, her pretty features lit by the setting sun.

"Lorenzo." She said it almost as if she wasn't surprised to see him, but he knew that couldn't be the case.

Maybe it simply felt inevitable to run into each other again.

"Hello, Valencia." He stalked toward her, boots silent in the soft sand.

She straightened as he came toward her, shoulders tensing.

The fact that he made her anxious was one more thing he'd regret. He'd never intended that. Now, he weighed his approach while the water lapped softly at the beach.

"Last time we were here, I was so sure the festival wouldn't happen," she observed, keeping her attention on the water where streaks of purple light glowed on the waves. "But I guess I couldn't help hoping I was wrong."

He didn't like the self-deprecating note in her voice. Hated that her hard work on the rescue wasn't going to be rewarded with the festival donations she deserved.

"We all had every reason to hope the festival would still take place." He'd encouraged her to think positively, in fact.

Did she hold that against him?

"You have to admit things look bleaker today." Turning toward him, she ran a weary hand through her loose hair. "I'm not sure who is worse, the protestors or the reporters."

His gaze tracked the movement of her fingers even as he imagined the stroke of those silky strands through his own hands. "You can't blame folks for trying to hold the Edmond family accountable."

"I don't." She shook her head and heaved a sigh as a small wave washed over her toes. She stared down at her feet disappearing into the sand as the water receded. "But their presence is a sign of how much things are falling apart. If the festival was happening, the Edmond family would have coordinated some kind of response to the protests. A PR person would be talking to the crowds and the news, spinning a narrative."

"Right." He understood her point. "The lack of response speaks for itself."

Echoes of their argument returned to his ears as they stood in silence for a long moment. She'd accused him of never having known struggle. While he didn't think that had been fair, he also recognized that she'd been dealing with a lot. Yet he wasn't certain he knew how to navigate that conversation now any better than he had been before.

So, for the moment, he sidestepped it for a topic where he could be more proactive. Make some kind of impact instead of feeling so damn helpless.

"How are you doing with cleanup at the rescue?" he asked instead.

He'd missed her voice. Her intelligence. Her passion for her work. He wanted to keep her talking. To extend this unexpected time together.

"I just finished the fence repairs today," she answered, never missing a beat. Maybe she was as eager to avoid the topic of their argument as he'd been. "The horses romped around like new colts once they had access to the big field again. They were ready to run."

"I'll bet." He grinned at the image, understanding well how it felt to throw off restraints put on by the world. "I'm sure the restoration work has been keeping you busy." He knew firsthand how many hours could disappear into efforts like that without dedicated ranch hands to help. "You'll be ready to play like a new colt, too, when you have a day away from fence repair."

She laughed, lifting one foot to drag a toe through the wet sand, the pattern she made disappearing when another wave lapped against the shore. "Maybe I will be."

The music of her laugh still whispering through his head, he had the overwhelming urge to ask her to spend that day of relaxing with him, but that negated every guideline he'd put in place for mixing business and pleasure. He'd backed off for good reason. But reason never spoke as loud as attraction and desire when it came to Valencia.

"How were things at your place after the tornado?" she asked, turning her light brown eyes on him.

She was so lovely. Her high cheekbones and easy smile. Her

athletic strength honed day in and day out with physical labor. The bright banner of fair hair.

Realizing he'd been staring, he cleared his throat.

"Not bad, all things considered. The animal areas didn't receive much damage, but an old windmill looked worse for wear." He backed up a step to keep his boots away the surf and Valencia followed him up the sand.

"Do you still use it?" She stopped as they neared the tree line, her face in shadow as she turned to face him again.

"We have a few new turbines set up for irrigation and generating power, so the old mill from my great-great-grandfather's time is more nostalgic than anything." He'd devoted a day to reattaching a broken sail, then found himself ordering other parts to keep the machinery in working order. "It sits in a picturesque spot along the river near the original cabin. The cabin is in disrepair, but I'd like to maintain the windmill."

"Good. Nothing says 'welcome to the country' like a weathered barn and a fantail windmill. I like spotting them on road trips." She bent to slide on her sandals.

Was she getting ready to leave?

Lorenzo couldn't deny that it had been good to see her again.

What if there was a way to maintain their friendship without letting the attraction take over? Shouldn't he at least explore the possibility?

"Valencia." He reached for her, just to put a hand on her arm and encourage her attention.

But as his fingertips slid over the silky material of her thin blouse along her forearm, he was swamped by the need to feel more of her. Her skin was cool beneath the fabric, and he ached to touch it without a barrier.

Her gaze fixed on his. Awareness of her filled his senses, drawing him in, pulling him closer...

"I should probably go," she murmured, though she didn't pull away. "It's a long drive back to Royal. I rode over with Lila and Zach, and I'm sure they'll be ready to leave soon."

Lorenzo forced himself to release her. Still, he couldn't help but make a case for what he wanted to happen next.

"My helicopter is in Mustang Point. Fly home with me and you can be in Royal in a third of the time."

In the silence that followed, he could hear the protestors' voices in the distance. He really wanted to make sure Valencia got home safely.

"I'm not sure that's a good idea after—" She shook her head impatiently. "That is, I don't want to blur the boundaries that I know are important to you. To me, too."

"A ride home won't blur any boundaries," he promised, recognizing that she deserved better from him than how abruptly he'd pulled away before. "Besides, I owe you a return trip after the way we parted company last time."

He'd regretted that, even though Valencia had been the one to suggest they go home separately.

She nibbled her lip for a moment, making his pulse stutter with the memory of how her lips had felt on his. But then she wrapped her arms around herself as she peered up at him.

"Just a return trip?"

"One return trip only," he agreed, trying to ignore the swell of victory over winning her over. "I can even have the pilot put the chopper down near the rescue if you want to be delivered to your doorstep."

"I don't think my horses would forgive me for that. But if you don't mind me tagging along with you as far as your ranch, I'd be glad for the ride."

The fresh rush of pleasure he felt at her acceptance nearly stole his breath.

But could he trust her in a way he'd never been able to trust his former fiancée? He dismissed the question since it couldn't come to that anyway. For tonight, he'd simply escort her home and enjoy her company.

"Good. Should we get on the ferry?" He offered her his arm.

She rested her hand there as she nodded. "Okay. I'll text Lila to let her know I'm going with you. As a newly engaged couple, she and Zach will probably be just as glad for the time alone."

Wincing at her choice of words, Lorenzo found it a challenge not to crave "alone time" with the woman who'd starred in his dreams every night since the tornado—the same woman who walked beside him now, her arm trustingly wound through his.

One way or another, he would make good on his promise to deliver her back to Royal without taking another taste of her lips.

Nine

Valencia gazed through the helicopter window to the ground below, the lights of Royal piercing the night. The flight was long enough for conversing through the headset microphones—but she'd been glad to keep the exchanges limited and focused instead on the sights along the way.

A lit-up baseball diamond where a local game was in progress. A summer festival on a town square. A drive-in movie theater. They'd spotted a few places with tornado damage, but overall, the destruction had been minimal outside of Appaloosa Island.

Better to stick to small talk about the sights than to let herself think about how it felt to have him beside her again after their disagreement and the ensuing days apart. Seeing him on the beach at Appaloosa Island had been like a moment straight out of a fantasy. She'd been musing about him and suddenly, he was *right there*.

Now, seated in such close proximity that his knee brushed her bare one, she struggled to keep her expression neutral while seized with the urge to lean into his big, strong presence. To tip her head against his shoulder and close her eyes long enough to forget how her dreams for the equine therapy camp were vanishing more every day.

And based on how strong the urge grew, Valencia knew she should head back home for the night as soon as the helicopter touched down. She couldn't risk falling back into Lorenzo's arms, no matter how enticing that might be.

"We're home," he announced a moment later, the low rumble of his voice through the headset stirring memories of the night they were stormbound together, his deep baritone a comfort in the dark. "There's the Cortez-Williams ranch."

He pointed to a spot out the window, and she looked out to see two well-lit gated entrances on either side of a palatial main home. While the surrounding ranch acreage remained mostly in darkness, the security lights along the driveways illuminated the main house, a pool and separate cottage. With stone walls, deep wooden porches and aluminum roofs, the buildings were a blend of modern farmhouse and Spanish influences. A large horse barn and paddock were visible near the house, although she guessed there were more stables for such a large working ranch, but they might not be lighted at night.

"What a beautiful home," she murmured as the helicopter descended in a nearby field. "And I envy those stables."

Lorenzo's laugh came through the headset. "Why am I not surprised you'd appreciate the horse lodgings more than anything else?"

She smiled, warmed to think he knew her so well. Perhaps she shouldn't feel pleased about that, when sleeping together had probably ruined her chance of securing the donation she'd counted on for Donovan Horse Rescue. But she'd striven her whole life to be viewed on her own merits. It was a relief to think Lorenzo recognized what was most important to her.

"I have spent a lot of time reviewing stable plans this year," she admitted. "If there's any chance that one day I'll have camp goers entering my horse barns to work with the animals, I want to be sure they're spacious and high-functioning."

"Would you like to see them?" he asked as the aircraft landed, pulling off his headset. "A quick tour before I drive you home?"

The invitation in his dark eyes wasn't what drew her in. If anything, it made her warier of spending time together since she knew how vulnerable she felt where this man was concerned.

But she really couldn't turn down his offer to show her the stables. Not when she'd poured so much thought and time into crafting her plans for the next phase of building at the horse rescue. She didn't have many opportunities to walk through facilities like his.

"If you don't mind showing me," she said as she pulled off her headset and unbuckled her seat belt. "I'd be glad to see them and dream about the future."

A few moments later, Valencia strolled through the field beside Lorenzo, the helicopter rotor slowing behind them.

"Will you be okay in those shoes?" he asked, his palm grazing the small of her back to guide her toward the path to the stables. "I didn't think about that, but you're not dressed for the barns."

How could a touch so subtle give her so many shivers?

"I had a meeting with the festival advisory board," she explained, her words a little breathless thanks to his nearness. "So it gave me an excuse to break out some of my old wardrobe from my days in the corporate world. But at least the sandals are flat. I'll be fine."

He shot her a sideways glance. "Do you ever miss that work? Your lifestyle must have done a one-eighty."

Now that the helicopter had shut down, the night seemed all the more quiet. The soft cadence of crickets mingled with the rustle of the leaves in a mild breeze. Enticing. Romantic.

Risky.

"It did, but I was ready for the change. I'd rather spend the days on horseback in jeans than chasing the next big account in a designer skirt." She slowed as they reached the sliding double doors in front of the tall, cream-colored stone barn. Sighing appreciatively, she skimmed a hand along the pale rocks, tracing her fingers through the mortar seams. "This is really beautiful. I would have loved to do my stables in stonework. Especially having just been through a tornado."

The dark thoughts of worst-case scenarios had circled her head for days afterward. Stone buildings were safest. If only she could build such sturdy walls around her emotions.

He paused in front of the doors and then turned to face her. Shadows faded, the concern in his expression easily visible now that they'd neared the security lights that illuminated the roads between buildings.

"The workmanship on your new stable is excellent," he reminded her gently. "I thought that the first day you showed me around. And it did weather the storm with almost no damage."

She appreciated his reassurance, knowing it was well intended.

"You're right. Although there's always room for improvement." She attempted a smile, recognizing he couldn't possibly know the extent of her personal fears after the tornado she'd been in with her birth parents. Besides, it wasn't a good idea to revisit her more recent memory of a tornado since Lorenzo figured so prominently in it. "Let's see the rest."

She was grateful when he slid open the heavy door on the right, admitting them into the dimness. He hit a switch on the wall to turn on the lights along the center aisle, leaving off the fixtures over the individual stalls. There was a swell of horse greetings at their arrival, surely more subdued than usual given the hour. A couple of whinnies. Some stomping of feet and tossing of heads. And one long snort.

Lorenzo walked to the closest stall first, greeting an alert-looking black paint with a pat on the neck. But Valencia's main attention was fixed on the wide aisle and immaculate stalls, the familiar scent of fresh hay and leather tack permeating the place even though the building housed ten animals. There were empty stalls on either end of the barn, with movable partitions to make larger stalls for foaling. A spacious tack room in the back beckoned, but she was tempted to say hello to all of the animals first.

"I am all the more impressed with your stables now that I've seen the inside," she announced, extending a hand to a pretty strawberry roan quarter horse peering over its stall door at her. "But how am I going to focus on the building when you have all these beauties in here?"

Encouraged by the animal's greeting as it nudged a nose under her palm, Valencia stroked a hand over the glossy coat.

"You're really good with horses," he observed quietly, his voice sounding closer than he'd been a moment ago.

Glancing over her shoulder, she saw him pause a few feet away, watching her. Awareness stirred, tingling through her bloodstream and dancing along her nerve endings. She hoped it didn't show as she swallowed back the feelings.

"They saved me," she told him simply, confessing a truth she didn't trust to many people. But she realized she wanted him to know this about her. She trusted him with that piece of herself. "I felt more heard and understood talking to a horse for the first time than I ever had by anyone before then."

When he remained silent, she rushed to speak, to smooth over the awkwardness of the admission.

"It might sound strange to someone who doesn't know horses. But you do." Her gaze flicked to his face briefly before she tipped her forehead to the roan's cheek. "I was overwhelmed by how easily a horse can offer trust. How simple and straightforward it could be to form a bond with a big, powerful animal."

She knew her explanation might stir more questions than answers, but she really wasn't ready to share more than that about how painful her early childhood had been. For her, it was enough that she'd worked past those memories to live a life on her own terms. Trust, however, was still hard to come by.

"They trust you, too," Lorenzo observed simply, moving to the next stall to soothe a gray Arabian that head-butted his door.

"It's easy to see how they gravitate to your calm demeanor. We used to offer boarding services on the ranch, and I can remember nervous owners visiting their mounts, agitated about every little thing, and convinced their horses were high-strung. But those same animals would be relaxed as can be as soon as the whirlwind of nervous energy was out of the stable."

Grateful to him for keeping the conversation light despite what she'd shared, Valencia laughed appreciatively.

"Funny how that works." She had observed the same phenomenon herself. And now that she thought about it, maybe that was some of what drew her to this man walking through the stable with her.

She'd recognized his ease with the animals when he'd visited her rescue. She'd gravitated toward it then.

Even after all that had passed between them, she couldn't deny the pull of that quality in him. Was it weird that she trusted what a horse thought of a man?

Get it together, Valencia.

Of course it was weird.

But she wasn't relying solely on the equine endorsement. She liked him, too. The fact that a temperamental Arabian was nuzzling his hair affectionately was just icing on the proverbial cake.

"I should go." She hadn't meant to blurt the words, but a sort of panic seized her as she acknowledged how much she still wanted Lorenzo. It wouldn't be wise to give in to that combustible attraction again when it had already come back to bite her after the tornado. "That is, I'm sure you have things to do and you've already been kind enough to give me this much of your time. I should just—" ger gaze locked onto his dark eyes "—go."

It wasn't a graceful exit. But when the alternative might be plastering herself against his chest and whispering all the secret longings of her heart, she figured it was better to make the awkward retreat.

She hastened outside into the moonlit night, her heart pounding as she heard his step behind her a second before his hand slid around her wrist.

"Valencia." He held her only a moment before letting go. Just enough to claim her attention. "Please wait."

Lorenzo watched Valencia as she hesitated, her feminine figure silhouetted in the full moon sitting low on the horizon. He wasn't ready to let her go.

He'd known the magnetic pull between them wasn't finished, but the electric current that sparked from just the brush of his hand over her arm underscored how quickly the attraction could ignite.

"This—" She gestured back and forth between them. "Whatever is happening between us isn't wise. You know it as well as I do."

Of course he knew. He'd been fighting the urge to kiss her every second they'd spent together almost from that first meeting.

"That doesn't make it any easier to walk away." Even now, he battled the need to sift his fingers through her hair and cradle the back of her head so he could taste her. Slowly.

Thoroughly.

Not just because he wanted her. But because of a connection that kept flourishing every time they were together.

Her words from inside the barn kept chasing around his head. *They saved me.*

Valencia had trusted him with that much of her past, a piece that he guessed she'd rarely shown to anyone. She'd allowed him a glimpse beyond the polished, successful woman she'd become to the vulnerable girl born into a family that clearly hadn't deserved her.

I felt more heard and understood talking to a horse than I ever had by anyone before then.

With those heartfelt words, she'd made him regret every time he'd suspected her of unscrupulous motives for fundraising on behalf of the rescue. The knowledge of her father's criminal history weighed on him since it had been obtained by a paid investigation into her past, cheating him of having her confide in him on her own terms.

More important, he'd robbed Valencia of the trust she'd deserved from the start. Instead, he'd been one more person in her life to let her down. She didn't even know how fully he'd failed her yet, a thought that felt like lead in his gut. Especially since he now knew that she was *nothing* like his ex-fiancée, and he'd let his prejudices color all of his decisions with Valencia because of them.

Pacing, she wrapped her arms around herself, her body language defensive. "Sometimes it's better to walk away than to keep making the same mistakes."

He hated that he'd inspired the wariness.

"Is that we're doing?" Maybe he should have just let her go, but he really wanted to know. "Making mistakes?"

In the distance, a coyote howled, stirring answering calls in the night. The sound echoed every lonely, hungry impulse inside him.

"You must have thought so, Lorenzo, given how fast you retreated the day after the tornado."

He ground his teeth against the exasperation of how wrong he'd been. But she deserved to know he regretted his actions, whether or not it made any difference to her now. So he forced his jaw to unclench and met her gaze.

"No. I never thought it was a mistake—"

She raised an eyebrow. "Do you mean to tell me it was a coincidence that you dodged morning-after awkwardness by being glued to your phone when I woke up alone that day?"

Even when he was the target of her cool anger, he couldn't deny a flash of admiration for the way she called him out for his role in what had happened. He owed her an explanation.

"I will admit I worried about sacrificing our professional relationship when we'd just come to terms for how my family's charitable program could benefit the rescue." He'd resorted to work instead of confronting the gray area of his relationship with Valencia. "And you have to admit we'd been on an emotional roller coaster the night before. Was it any wonder if I was still reeling a bit?"

Her expression softened a fraction. She swayed toward him.

"I may have been reeling a little, too," she admitted, blinking fast. "The tornado was a lot to process."

The note of fragility in her voice brought him closer. He couldn't help the urge to protect her, even if that meant he needed to keep her safe from any distress he might cause.

"I should have talked to you about what happened. And I regret how I handled that. But believe me, not for a minute did I regret being with you." He'd thought of little else since then. He missed seeing her. Talking to her. Kissing her.

Hell, he just missed *her*.

And having her here beside him now, seeing the favorable way she looked over his ranch and his horses, filled him with a sense of rightness. Like she belonged here.

For a long moment, she remained quiet. Thinking. Her gaze roamed over the main ranch house and some of the outbuildings while she seemed to ruminate over what he'd said. When at last her focus returned to him, her look was still guarded.

"Then don't keep me in suspense," she said finally, tilting her chin up at him. "What would you have said if you had the chance to go back and talk to me about our night together?"

His lips quirked for the briefest instant, registering some amusement that she wanted an accounting. But just as quickly, he acknowledged that this might be his one and only chance for a do-over, and he'd better not mess it up.

Dragging in a breath, he dug deep for the right words. Scratch that. He couldn't worry about the best phrasing. He owed her the truth.

"I would have told you that the night we shared was the most memorable one I'd ever spent with any woman. Period."

She made a small gasp, but pressed her lips tight around the sound as if trying to hide it.

He let the truth of that statement sit with her for a moment, allowing her to hear and see how deeply it resonated for him. Then, he continued.

"Considering the short time we've known one another, that realization rattled the hell out of me—then and now—but it has to mean something."

She gave a wordless shake of the head, so subtle he wondered if she realized she was doing it.

Only because of that, he finally permitted himself to touch her. Just enough to capture her chin. Tilt her face up to his.

"You disagree?" he asked, running a fingertip under her jaw. Noting the way her lips parted at just that simple caress. "Our time together didn't mean anything?"

"We can't allow it to." Her words were a quiet whisper, but there was a thread of desperation in it, almost as if she'd made the same argument to herself a few times. "My work is too important for me—and to future generations of troubled kids who need the kind of help I can offer—and I can't afford to choose a personal relationship over a professional connection that could be the difference maker in getting an equine therapy camp off the ground."

Disappointment stabbed him. How could he argue with her passionate commitment to a good cause?

He forced his fingers away from the temptation of her skin, his hands falling to his sides.

"I respect whatever you want, but you don't have to choose between them."

Her breath hitched. He could hear it through the sound of the crickets breaking into multipart harmonies in the live oaks sheltering the driveway.

"What do you mean?" she asked.

"I mean the donation is beyond my control now. The office of my family's charitable giving has already approved the funds. I couldn't revoke that even if I wanted to. But I assure you, I don't."

It shocked him to see the relief go through her in a visible wave. Had she been stressed about that this whole week?

He cursed himself all over again for not clearing things up better with her after their night together. But before he could apologize for not making that perfectly apparent, Valencia wound her arms around his neck.

The feel of her suddenly in his arms chased away everything else. Reason. Logic. Boundaries.

There was only the trace of roses and vanilla from her skin. The soft weight of her breasts pressed to his chest. The hypnotic pull of her dark eyes as she stared up at him in the moonlight.

"Are you saying that if I kiss you tonight, there's no chance I'm going to blur any boundaries?" Her fingernails clenched at his shoulders, a gentle scrape that stirred him like nothing else.

"Zero." He articulated the word clearly even though his breath rushed in and out of his lung like a bellows.

Her lips pursed. She gave a nod—all business—like they'd just concluded an important negotiation.

Then, fingers tunneling through his hair, she pulled his head down to hers and kissed him like she didn't plan on coming up for air for a long, long time.

Ten

Valencia had restrained herself as long as humanly possible.

But then she'd gone and spent too long under the influence of a hypnotic full moon listening to Lorenzo methodically break through all her boundaries. Who could resist a man who said things like: *The night we shared was the most memorable one I'd ever spent with any woman. Period.*

Her knees had been a little wobbly ever since, the desire for him so strong she couldn't draw a breath without anticipating the way he would taste. Then, once he'd insisted there were no boundaries to blur anymore—no way what they were doing would affect the status of the rescue with his family's foundation—how could she hold back?

Especially when she so rarely let herself act on an impulse, afraid of somehow revealing her unsavory roots.

Tonight, she was shoving all that aside to embrace the way Lorenzo made her feel fully alive and present to the moment.

Wanted.

Breaking the kiss to peer up at him through half-closed lids, Valencia hauled in gulps of air to try to catch her breath.

His voice rumbled low and warm against her ear. "I'm hoping that means you want to come inside the house with me."

"Yes. Please."

Pivoting on his heel, he took her hand and drew her toward the massive two-story house that wrapped, L-shaped, around a pool and cottage. Except he didn't pause by the back entrance of the main home. Instead, his boots charged unerringly across the stone path toward the smaller, separate residence on the opposite end of the pool.

"You live *here*?" she asked, taking in the more modest building that was about the size of her own home, whereas the main house had to be close to ten thousand square feet.

"I do." He led her onto the covered porch and unlocked the front door while she vaguely noted gray-painted rocking chairs and a wooden map of Texas that served as wall art between black-shuttered windows.

"Then who lives in the main house?" She hoped it wasn't a nosy question, but since Lorenzo ran the Cortez-Williams ranch, it seemed only natural he'd live in the dwelling clearly built for the owner.

"My parents." He didn't seem to mind her question, holding the door wide for her while she stepped into the cool interior of a Spanish Colonial–style home, the terra-cotta floors and exposed beam ceiling visible by the glow of a wrought iron pendant lamp that hung in the foyer. "They raised six kids there, and my brothers still come home most weekends for barbecues. For as long as my mother enjoys the extra space, I want her to be comfortable there. She makes better use of it than I would."

She followed him through the living area, where leather couches were surrounded by low wood bookshelves filled with old volumes. Her eyes drifted to a silver-framed photo on the mantel that must be his whole family standing near an outdoor fireplace. Flanked on both sides by dark-haired sons, an older couple stood in the center.

"How lucky for you all to get along so well that you can live in close proximity like that," she observed.

Abruptly, Lorenzo stopped in front of her and turned, his hands finding her waist. This close to her, she was reminded how much bigger he was. Taller. Wider. Stronger.

"Thank you. But I'm hoping that's the last we talk about my family tonight." His fathomless gaze locked on hers as the heat of his palms stroked lower, settling on her hips. "Or anything that's not you and me."

"Oh." She made a shaky exhale, the sound emerging like a half-stifled moan as anticipation stirred. "Good idea."

Heart hammering, she canted closer, ready for more.

Heat flared in his eyes. His chest expanded with a breath, making that strong wall of muscle brush lightly against her breasts. Her skin tingled everywhere.

"Come with me." His eyes smoky with need, he took hold of her hand, pulling her toward the hallway to the left. Leading her through the first arched door, then closing it behind them, Lorenzo sealed them in a big master suite dominated by a king-size bed draped in all-white linens.

A moment later, his mouth claimed hers again. The intensity of his kiss made her realize how much he'd been holding back before. Because now, he didn't just taste and explore. He *devoured* her.

Backing her up against the door, he pinned her in place with his powerful body, a welcome weight she'd longed to feel every day they'd been apart. She tipped her head against the unforgiving oak, submitting to his hunger, letting it stoke hers.

Heat raced all over her body, like a small blaze following a path of accelerant, every place it touched turning to an inferno. His hands molded to her body, tracing her curves through her clothes before tunneling under her skirt to grip the backs of her thighs. Lifting her.

She twined her arms around his neck and locked her heels behind his waist as he walked her toward the bed. Every step rocked his hips against hers. The hard ridge in his jeans pressed between her thighs with such friction that it made her see stars behind her eyelids.

When he settled her on the edge of the bed, he relinquished her to unfasten the buttons of his shirt. She tried to do the same, but the visual of the bronzed muscles he exposed along his abs kept distracting her as he worked. Finally, after he yanked his shirt off, he knelt between her thighs to finish unfastening the buttons on her blouse.

They both watched his progress, their foreheads bent together, breath mingling.

She pressed her knees against his sides, the fiery warmth of his skin tantalizing her. In another moment, he had her last fastening undone, and he skimmed the top off until she sat on his bed in a skimpy lace bra and the wrinkled pink skirt already rucked up her legs. She felt entirely wanton, craving every delectable sensation he could wring from her body.

"I've been dreaming of this. Of you." He sketched a finger down one strap of her bra, then traced the lace edge of the cups. "Having you here in my bed."

"I've dreamed about you, too," she admitted, unable to stifle the impulse to arch her back in offering. "Every night."

He tugged down the lace with his finger, exposing a nipple already tightened to an aching point. When he bent his head to flick his tongue over the tip, she gripped his shoulders and held him there, needing more.

"Lorenzo." His name was a plea on her lips.

His only answer was to shift to the other breast, repeating the same exquisite kiss there. She speared her fingers into his thick, dark hair, keeping him close. Only then did his hands shift to her thighs, traveling slowly up from her knees.

Higher.

She rocked her hips, craving the pressure and friction of him at the juncture of her thighs. But his hands continued their maddening crawl, his splayed fingers caressing every inch of her on their way up her legs.

When he reached the band of white lace at last, she thought she might come out of her skin. He leaned back to look at her, his dark eyes scanning her body until his gaze positively smoldered. She thought she might combust.

Instead, she skimmed her palms along his shoulders and contented herself with soaking up the feel of him. His warmth. His strength. His potent masculinity. She stroked two fingers up his corded neck, delighting in the heavy swallow beneath the skin. Did she affect him as much as he affected her?

She couldn't possibly if he could afford to take so much time teasing along the sensitive flesh of her inner thighs that her legs began to tremble. Maybe he felt the quivers of her muscles because a moment later, his hand was inside her panties and his tongue was in her mouth.

A moan tore through her, but he captured it, their lips sealed together. His touch was sure. Steady. As if he knew exactly how to drive her higher, his fingers playing over her slick folds. For a fleeting instant, she wondered how he'd learned her body so well the last time they were together, but then all her thoughts scattered as tension knotted inside her. Tighter. *Hotter.*

Pleasure built to a fever pitch, the sensations so delicious she could only hold still for the onslaught. Then, all at once, her release broke over like a rogue wave. Her feminine muscles clenched hard while a gasp tore from her throat. She clung to him, arms wrapped around his neck and clutching him to her. He felt like the center of her whole world for those long moments as she came, his hand anchoring her in the rough sea of her pleasure.

Oh. My.

Rattled and still buzzing with the aftershocks, she wasn't ready to let go of his neck, but he gently pried her arms free, pausing to drop a kiss on her lips before he stood to undress.

Their eyes met briefly as she watched him, then her gaze

dipped to his rigid erection, the sight reminding her how much she wanted to please him in return. That put her into motion again, shimmying out of her lacy underwear before she slid off the bed to kneel in front of him.

He'd never seen anything so sexy.

Still flushed pink from her orgasm, her lips swollen from his kiss, Valencia blinked up at him from her spot on the floor. He wanted to make her feel good. To make this night about her after the way he'd pulled back from her the last time.

But when he reached for her, thinking he would lay her back on the bed and come inside her, he found his fingers sifting through her silky hair instead. Petting. Stroking.

Savoring.

And heaven help him, her tongue peeped out of her mouth then, running around the rim of her lips as if to ease him into her, and he was lost. His control shredded. Instead of lifting her up, he drew her nearer. The soft moan she made was something he knew he'd replay over and over again forever, the note of anticipation in it as difficult to miss as her distended nipples.

Or her lust-dazed dark eyes.

So when her lips parted around him, he sank inside her sweetness, his brain blanking to anything but her plush mouth and the tentative fingers holding him steady. Desire scorched over him, burning up everything except for this red-hot connection. Her head bobbed, knees inching closer, one hand splayed on his thigh to steady herself, and he'd never experienced anything hotter.

Too soon, he teetered so close to the edge he didn't know how much longer he could hold back. And he *had* to finish between her legs. Needed to feel her there after he'd given her an orgasm. And yeah, maybe he wanted to make sure she felt him there, too.

"Come here." Somehow, he found the willpower to lean over her and lift her to her feet. "I have to be inside you. *Now.*"

She gave a wordless nod, looping her arms around his neck to drag him down to the bed with her so he stretched out over her. Honey-brown eyes locked on his, she arched up, grazing her hips to his.

He was so far gone he nearly sank into her at the blatant invitation. But he didn't even have a condom on. And damn, he'd never been so wound up that he'd been in danger of forgetting. Heart thudding, he pulled away to retrieve a condom from the nightstand drawer.

Lids at half-mast, she watched him tear open the wrapper and roll the protection into place. Her one foot teased up and down his leg while she waited, almost as if she craved contact with him every moment. Or maybe that was what he wished, and he was projecting it onto her. Because damn, he never wanted to stop touching her.

When he was ready, he put one knee on the bed, his arms bracketing her shoulders. She shivered beneath him, a sensual little undulation of her body that made him long to discover every single thing that affected her that way.

Cupping her chin, he kissed her until they were both panting.

"Are you still ready for me?" He remembered how she'd felt coming apart around his fingers.

"So ready." She gave a fast nod. "Hurry."

With that encouragement, he slid a hand around her hip, holding her in place. Then, tipping his forehead to hers, he sank inside her inch by incredible inch, until they were fused together. Their satisfied groans twined together in the still room.

Damn.

His heart pounded like it wanted to burst out of his chest, and he'd only just gotten inside her. She disarmed all of his restraints, stripping him bare.

He wanted to think about something else, any possible distraction, to make this time with her last longer. But he'd been hungering for her for days on end. Having her in his bed now, real and honest, sweet and sexy at the same time, was too much. Besides, she deserved for him to be right there with her every moment of this extraordinary encounter. He couldn't pretend that being with her was anything less than earth-shattering.

Because this woman was rocking his whole world.

"You feel so good," she chanted softly, her fingers flexing against his chest. "So, so good."

Valencia rolled her hips and locked her ankles around his waist, as if letting him go wasn't even an option.

Something about that act—the possessiveness of it—shoved him even closer to the ledge. Heat shot up his spine, his release hovering. He reached between them to touch her, to tease the tight bud of her sex, wanting to take her over the edge with him.

Her breath caught. Her teeth clamped down on her lip.

Then she shuddered. Hard. She squeezed all around him, the spasms pulsing.

A shout tore from his throat as he came, his hips pumping into her as the release shook him to the core. The heat of it raked through him for long moments until he was all but light-headed from it. He slumped to her side, trying to regain his breath.

Failing.

He closed his eyes for a long moment, willing himself to recover. No easy feat when being with her was the best feeling he'd ever experienced. Hands down.

As his skin began to cool and they gently disentangled themselves, he tried not to think about *why* being with her affected him that way. Wasn't ready to look beyond the physical when he'd only just patched things up with her after the way he'd failed her the first time.

For now, he could focus on the physical, couldn't he? Especially since that's all she appeared to want from him.

This time, he'd hold her. Talk to her. Let her know he wasn't checking out on her just because their passions had been spent.

He dragged a pillow closer to tuck it under her head, then hauled a light blanket up from the foot of the bed to cover them. Afterward, he lay down beside her again while the wrought iron ceiling fan spun slowly overhead, stirring the air.

He combed through her hair with his fingers while he made himself comfortable next to her. "So I think we proved in no uncertain terms that our first time together was *not* a fluke."

The corners of her mouth kicked up and a sound suspiciously close to a giggle tripped from her. "You sound almost disappointed. Were you *hoping* the first time was a fluke?"

It amazed him that making this beautiful woman laugh could feel even more rewarding than making her come. Another sign that merely enjoying the physical side of this relationship might not be as simple as it sounded.

"Hell no. If anything, I couldn't wait for a chance to test the theory." He traced the delicate arch of her eyebrow. "But the question is, now that we know the chemistry isn't going away, how do we handle that?"

The question was one he'd been posing to himself, of course. But he hadn't meant to share it with her. Certainly not tonight, anyhow.

A tiny furrow appeared between her brows as she seemed to consider. "I don't know. But at least we don't have to worry about having business dealings anymore. You said that wasn't a concern now that the horse rescue has been approved by the foundation."

He smoothed the small indent between her brows, regretting that he'd made it appear.

"It's not a concern," he assured her. Then, realizing he'd never shared anything about his former fiancée with Valencia, he wondered if knowing about the other woman would help explain his actions. He didn't want to give her any more reasons to worry about his family's support of her rescue. She deserved to rest easy about that. "I may have been overzealous about distinguishing between my business and personal lives after my ex-fiancée convinced me to give her restaurant company a substantial discount on my family's meat for five years."

The story still embarrassed him. But Valencia seemed to key in on different details than what upset him.

"You were engaged?" She went still.

"Unfortunately." The bitterness was still there, but for the first time in a long time, he felt a bit...*less* resentful. Was it because of Valencia? "She targeted me for my wealth, and I failed to see it until she'd run up my credit cards and disappeared."

"What a horrible woman." The indignation in her voice surprised him as she levered herself up onto one elbow. "No wonder you have a difficult time trusting."

Valencia's dark eyes flashed with anger, and he couldn't deny a surge of tenderness for someone who would be so defensive of him.

Would she feel the same if she understood his inability to trust was what had driven him to investigate Valencia's past? No doubt she would consider it a violation of her privacy. Guilt swelled.

"I just figured it was a better practice to keep my private life far from work," he explained, his hand settling on her hip through the blanket. "And it served me well enough until I met you."

Her eyes narrowed as she caught his hand in hers, threading their fingers together. A playful gleam lit her gaze.

"Are you suggesting I messed up your plans?" Her voice was warm and teasing.

The blanket shifted lower on her breasts, and he wanted her all over again. Not just because she was way sexier than any fantasy. Because she was kind and good.

His voice thickened when he spoke again. "I'm saying you are worth breaking the rules for, Valencia. Meeting you made me realize I'd be foolish to pass up the chance to know you just because of some worn-out commitment to keeping my personal life separate from work."

Her breathing quickened, her chest rising and falling faster. Her dark eyes softened.

Damn but he needed her once more. This time, he'd take as

long as he wanted to make her feel good. To show her that he wasn't playing around.

So he covered her body with his, and showed her everything he wasn't ready to put into words.

Eleven

Stealing out of Lorenzo's bed in the middle of the night, Valencia scooped up a black T-shirt off the floor. He'd offered it to her to sleep in…and then had promptly pulled it back off to make love again. Falling almost to the middle of her thigh, the fabric was impossibly soft and smelled like clean laundry with a hint of the pine and musk scent that usually accompanied him.

She lowered her nose to her shoulder to breathe in the scent of the fabric again as she peeked back at his big, sleeping form in the moonlight slanting in through the blinds. So strong and male, the muscles of his shoulders and arms apparent even when he was at rest. And as much as she'd like to be sleeping now, too—especially since he'd worn her out in the most delicious of ways—she'd awoken feeling a little antsy. Restless.

Quietly, she slipped out the door of the master suite and into the living room. She felt too anxious to remain indoors, but she hesitated to exit the front door, where she might be visible to anyone looking out of the main house. It might be four in the morning, but still she knew her relationship with Lorenzo wasn't to the point where they were ready to share it with friends and family.

Were they?

The question told her exactly what had her too revved up to sleep. Her relationship with Lorenzo had gone hurtling forward tonight, but she wasn't sure what she wanted that to mean. Worse, she wasn't sure what *he* wanted from it, either. But the night had been too amazing to do anything other than simply enjoy the connection. To revisit all the comfort and pleasure he'd given her the night of the tornado.

And he was right, the chemistry had been no fluke.

Spying a back door off the kitchen, Valencia padded toward it in her bare feet. Then, pushing it open, she stepped outside onto a private patio where a wicker couch with deep cushions faced a cold fire pit. No one would see her out here since there were only fields and four rail fences in the distance—or at least as far as she could see in the moonlight.

Dropping into the cushion with a sigh, she had just tipped her head back to stargaze when the door to the house opened again.

"Valencia?"

The sound of his voice shimmied through her, all of her senses going on high alert just from his nearness. It wasn't fair how much he affected her.

"I'm out here." She lifted a hand to make it easier for him to see her in the dark. "Sorry if I woke you."

He was already closing the distance between them. And she felt her heart rate quicken, her defenses falling fast.

"That's okay. I'm a light sleeper." He dropped into the cushion beside her, dressed in a pair of gray cotton gym shorts and a white T-shirt. "Everything all right?"

His hand landed on her knee since she had her legs tucked up underneath her. She shivered in spite of the warm night, remembering the ways he'd touched her and how quickly she'd unraveled.

She was falling for him.

The realization hit her all at once. Not just because of his mesmerizing touch. But because of the concern in his eyes right now as he looked at her.

"I'm fine," she said a shade too brightly, not sure what to do with this new knowledge. "Just a little trouble sleeping."

His gaze wandered over her for a moment before he seemed to accept this answer. Reaching toward her, he drew her against him so she could lay her head on his chest.

"Talk to me," he ordered softly, arranging her hair so she could settle comfortably against him. "Tell me whatever's going through that pretty head of yours."

She smiled. Did he have any idea how lovely it felt to have her cheek rest on his warm chest? To feel the rumble of his voice beneath her ear as he spoke? Breathing in his delicious pine-and-musk scent, she nuzzled closer.

His invitation to confide in him touched her deeply. Gave her courage. He'd told her something of his past earlier. Perhaps it was time for her to share more of herself if she wanted any chance of building a real relationship with him. And with a fresh wave of tenderness welling inside her, she couldn't deny that was exactly what she hoped for.

"You know how much I want to launch the equine therapy camp," she began slowly, tracing circles along his chest with her fingertip as a cooling night breeze stirred her hair. "But I haven't fully explained why."

"In the barn tonight, you mentioned something about horses saving you." He continued to smooth his palm over her hair, a comforting gesture.

"My adoptive parents put me in an equine therapy camp when I first came to live with them. A counselor recommended it for me because I'd been...neglected. Earlier in life." She still stumbled over saying she'd been *abused*, finding the word personally triggering. It felt at odds with her determination never to see herself as a victim, but she knew that was a very personal hang-up.

If she'd learned one thing in her personal journey, it was

that no two people reacted to trauma the same way. The things that had worked for her, and had been healing for her, wouldn't necessarily help someone else. But it was important to respect each path and let people find the tools that worked best for their emotional recovery.

"I'm so sorry, Valencia." His fingers never quit stroking. "When you said that you'd felt understood by a horse, I wondered what that meant about your family."

"They were awful people." She was grateful that most of her memories had grown dim with the passing years, but there were still some that remained as jagged as ever. "My mother didn't have a nurturing bone in her body, and she seemed to think it was a game to taunt my father when he was angry. Which was most of the time."

Echoes of old fights, ugly screaming accusations, could still give her nightmares. Not often, thank goodness. But the past seemed like a dark stain in her mind that would never fully fade.

Lorenzo went motionless now. Tense.

"You don't have to tell me. Especially if it upsets you." His voice sounded strangled.

She closed her eyes for a long moment, examining her feelings. But she felt close to him. Safe in his arms. And she wanted to share something after he'd confided in her about his unhappy engagement.

When she opened her eyes again, she murmured, "It's okay. I want to tell you."

Sinking into the comfort of the darkness and the steady slug of his heartbeat beneath her ear, she continued, "They were a volatile couple, young and poor. My mother was a teenage runaway when she met my father. In a *bus station*. That was where he taught her how to panhandle to distract people so he could pick their pockets. My earliest memory is of being in my birth mother's arms while we—while *she*—ran from the cops."

Counseling had taught Valencia how to separate herself from the actions of her parents. But no amount of therapy had taken

away the sudden awful gut clench she felt to this day upon seeing uniformed police officers. Or the guilt that went hand in
hand with the reaction.

Lorenzo's hand slid to her shoulder and gave a gentle squeeze.
"Valencia—"

"Just let me get through this, okay?" she pleaded, wanting
to have the basics shared so she didn't have to revisit the memory. "The last time I spent with them was in a tornado. Locked
in a bathroom while they fought over who should have to stay
with me. Neither of them wanted to." The snippets she recalled
from that argument were the most vivid of her childhood. "But
the angry words stopped when the tornado ripped most of the
house away."

Lorenzo's arms wrapped around her. He murmured some
quiet words of comfort against her hair.

"They were both injured, I think." The aftermath was hazy
for her, the timeline less linear. "I remember my mother saying she was going to find help afterward, and for me to stay
there—in the bathtub. But she didn't come back. Rescue work-
ers found me two days later and that's how I ended up in foster
care briefly until I was adopted."

She didn't dwell on those two days alone. The period spent
in the eerily quiet remnants of their small mobile home was
frightening, but at least the time seemed to pass quickly. Perhaps because she'd been in shock and numb to everything. She
wouldn't have been able to leave the old cast-iron tub even if
she'd wanted to since debris had fallen over it, trapping her there.

For a moment, they remained in silence. The night sky had
lightened by degrees while they spoke, a pinkish-gold glow
warming the horizon.

"My God," he said finally, huffing out a rough exhale. "No
wonder you were terrified in the storm last week. I can't imagine how traumatizing that must have been after what you went
through."

His words soothed her. Yet, beneath her ear, his pulse sped

faster. Was he troubled about what she'd confided? She tried not to be defensive, but she was all too aware of how many people judged her for her parents' sins.

She straightened from where she'd been curled against him, looking into his dark eyes for the first time since she'd began her story. His gaze darted away from hers.

"It wasn't as bad as it could have been," she assured him, not wanting to linger on that aspect since the tornado was in the past, and her horses were all safe. "Having you with me really helped."

"I'm glad I could be there with you." He sounded sincere enough, but something about his demeanor seemed...off.

Was he contemplating another retreat?

That didn't seem quite right considering he'd sought her out to talk to her.

"The storm anxiety doesn't happen very often," she admitted. "So it's less problematic for me on a day-to-day basis. More often, I struggle with feeling tainted by my father's criminal past—"

"But I remember when that massive twister hit Era," he said quickly, steering her back to the storm. Almost as if he wanted to avoid talking about her father. "The damage was catastrophic."

Surprised he recalled that, she started to nod.

Then, a thought occurred to her. She froze.

"Did I mention I lived in Era?" The small town north of Fort Worth wasn't well-known.

A shadow crossed his eyes. His whole face changed as his mouth worked silently for a moment.

A cold knot tightened in her gut. She'd missed something in this exchange and her brain slammed into high gear to pinpoint it.

"No. But it was the biggest—" He began to speak, but at the same time, her mind filled in the blanks about how he'd identified where she'd lived as a child.

Disbelief warred with a deep sense of betrayal.

"You knew all of that already?" The question was rhetorical, so she didn't wait for an answer. "How?"

"Please." He straightened on the patio sofa, shifting so he faced her. "I wasn't aware of most of it—"

"How. Did. You. Know?" She spit each word like a bullet, anger roaring to life that he would mince words with her when she had a question that required an immediate answer.

He jammed his fingers in his hair and tugged on the strands, his agitation clear. But when he answered her, he met her gaze again.

"A private investigation." He seemed to allow that a moment to sink in before he continued. "I told you that I am thorough when I vet potential charities for donations from the ranch's foundation."

His words chilled her.

He'd had her investigated? Without ever mentioning it, despite all the time they'd spent together?

Anger simmered.

What the hell had it revealed? She was uncomfortable enough with her past without having it typed up in a report for Lorenzo's personal review. Something he should have told her already, damn it.

"You never mentioned a personal investigation was part of the process." Standing, she needed to pace away some of this frustrated energy. It angered her to realize she was barefoot and wearing his T-shirt.

She'd slept with the man who had her investigated and never bothered to mention a thing about it.

"I should have told you." At least he had the courtesy to acknowledge it. Too bad the confession came too late to make a difference.

Her chest burned with the realization of how foolish she'd been. How she'd thought they were getting close. In reality, all that had happened was that she'd embarrassed herself in front of this man. She'd laid herself—her heart—bare.

"Yes. You should have. Especially before I poured out my personal stories for you, thinking I was—" She blinked away the sudden liquid heat in her eyes, horrified when two fat tears rolled down her cheeks.

She turned to swipe them furiously away.

"Thinking what?" he asked softly from behind her.

"You don't get to ask questions." She turned on him, pointing an agitated finger. "You already paid to have your questions answered."

"It's been hard for me to trust." His quiet admission, the reminder of the way his ex-fiancée had treated him, softened her heart.

Until she remembered the way he'd let her prattle on about her past without telling her he already knew it. A fresh surge of anger made her recognize she'd been wrong about him.

He wasn't the man she'd believed him to be. Only now that he'd broken her trust did she realize how much she'd placed in him. How much fragile hope she'd already built up in her mind about a relationship. A future.

"I understand why you'd want to protect yourself against false women." She almost wavered when she saw the flash of desolation in his eyes. "But I've done nothing to betray you. Who is going to protect me from false men who can't be honest?"

Whatever raw, unshuttered emotion she'd thought she saw in his gaze died a moment later. She'd probably misread him. Again.

His jaw flexed, his stony silence speaking volumes. Pain and disillusionment cracked her apart that he had no words to reassure her. Nothing else to say.

Mustering as much dignity as she could manage while wearing only his T-shirt, she drew in a deep breath as she turned toward the house. "I'm going to call a car—"

"I can take you home, Valencia." He moved to follow her, his long strides eating up the distance between them, his voice full of frustration.

Well, she was *more* than frustrated. She was crushed. Heartbroken. And so very angry.

"No. Thank you." She was close to breaking, her emotions in turmoil. She didn't want to be anywhere near the man responsible for the deep ache in her chest. "I can't be with you right now."

Maybe never.

Pivoting away from him, she hurried inside the house to find her phone and get dressed. Whatever she and Lorenzo had shared, it was over now.

Twelve

Ten days later, Lorenzo plowed down a dirt road in a shortcut toward Elegance Ranch, taking every pothole so hard it challenged even the top-notch suspension of his truck. But there just weren't enough potholes in Texas to help him get over the pain of losing Valencia.

He'd known that she'd meant it when she said she needed to be alone. But he'd still tried to contact her. Four times, damn it. He still wanted to frame an apology in a way that would make her understand why he'd hadn't been more up-front with her.

But when ten days had passed without her taking his calls, he knew she wasn't interested in hearing from him. Maybe the feelings that had taken root in him hadn't been reciprocated. Because he missed Valencia more than he'd ever dreamed it would be possible to miss someone who'd been in his life for such a short time. And that stung so much worse than he'd expected. Far more than even when Lindsey had tried to wipe him out of every last cent.

Now, he tried to channel the hurt of losing her—the anger at *himself* for losing her—into something more productive. Like finding out how the Edmond family was going to make it up to the people whose lives they'd ruined with the sham music and arts festival that never got off the ground. He steered the truck off the back road onto the finely paved private road that would take him to the Edmond family compound.

Soon, he parked his pickup truck in front of the security gates at Elegance Ranch, then let the engine idle while he pressed the intercom button and waited. He'd tried contacting Ross or Rusty, but they never returned his calls. It seemed the world was ignoring him these days.

Impatient with the lack of response, Lorenzo stabbed the button again, waiting for an attendant or someone from the main house to answer him.

"Hello?" A woman's voice finally answered. Unfortunately, it didn't sound like Gina Edmond's voice.

"It's Lorenzo Cortez-Williams. I'm here to see Ross," he said evenly, willing to play nice to obtain an audience.

"Ross isn't here, sir," the woman replied. "The whole family is away."

"Away?" Irritation laced his voice. The July heat wafting in through his open window only added to it. "What about Rusty? Or Gina?"

"I'm sorry, sir, there's no one here today but staff. If you'd like to leave a message—"

"How about Billy Holmes? He's not family." Lorenzo recalled Ross's college friend Billy Holmes was one of the organizers of Soiree on the Bay, and the guy had been living in a guest cottage on the ranch property for the past two years.

"I'm sorry, sir," the woman repeated more firmly. "No one is allowed on the premises when the family is away."

Refusing to bother staffers who'd surely fielded flak from the media already, Lorenzo thanked the woman and put the truck in Reverse. Driving away from Elegance Ranch, he headed toward the Texas Cattleman's Club, too keyed up to return home, where thoughts of Valencia bombarded him around every corner.

His house was crammed full of memories of her from their last night together. He'd hardly slept in the days that followed their breakup, finally changing bedrooms so he didn't keep seeing her hair spread over his pillow, or recall her smile as she pulled on his old T-shirt before lying down with him for the night.

Hands fisting around the steering wheel, he was grateful to pull into the lot for the Texas Cattleman's Club a few minutes later, needing something to distract him from the way he'd failed her. She was nothing like his former fiancée, but his prejudices had allowed him to paint her with the same brush, seeing dishonesty that wasn't there. And now it seemed there was no repairing the damage he'd done with his lack of trust.

With a nod to an older rancher exiting the stone building beside his wife, Lorenzo stepped inside the cool interior of the historic clubhouse. He could count on one hand the number of times he'd shown up here by himself, using it only as a meeting place for business. But going home alone right now wasn't an option.

"Can I get you a table, sir?" the young hostess asked, reviewing her electronic tablet.

"Yes. It's just me today—" he began when his gaze shifted to the bar behind her.

Where Billy Holmes sat alone at the far end, tipping a glass to his lips.

Unbelievable. He'd looked all over town for any of the Edmond family, and here was Billy Holmes, dressed in an impeccable blue suit and hiding in plain sight at the Texas Cattleman's Club. Perhaps, because the club was private, it was one of the few places in town where media didn't have access.

Still, it ticked Lorenzo off to see the guy having a drink in the middle of the day, casual as you please, when his failed festival had hurt so many people. News broadcasts for the past week had focused on a series of vendors who'd invested heavily in Soiree on the Bay and wouldn't recoup their losses. Just thinking about it made his blood boil. And, of course, it upset him more than he could say that Valencia would be struggling to make her dream of an equine therapy camp happen. Not to mention that Rafe could still lose his restaurant...

Lorenzo turned back to the hostess.

"Actually, no table for me." He slid her a tip just the same since he recalled the woman was a college student. "I'm going to have a seat at the bar."

He strode through the cool interior, passing a few tables that included people he knew. He nodded to the other ranchers politely, but kept his eye on his quarry.

"Billy." Lorenzo greeted the man as he took a seat nearby, leaving one bar stool free between them.

As he glanced up from his now-empty glass, Billy moved a bit slowly, and Lorenzo guessed he'd been drinking for a while.

"Lorenzo." He nodded cordially, then flagged down the bartender, signaling for another drink.

Grinding his teeth together to hold back the accusations he wanted to let fly, Lorenzo waited until he'd ordered a drink for himself—bourbon, neat—then pivoted hard to face Billy.

"You have a lot of nerve coming around here today, leisurely drinking when the Edmond family has ruined the lives of so many people." His anger ran hot. And yes, it felt good to have an outlet for his own defeat with Valencia. For screwing up something really special.

"Is that right?" Billy Holmes was well-known for his charm. Rumor had it that he'd sidled into Rusty Edmond's world almost immediately when Ross brought his friend home from college. Apparently Billy had the cantankerous billionaire's ear better than Rusty's own kids did.

Either way, there was little evidence of that charm now.

"One hundred percent," Lorenzo continued. "Do you just not give a damn about the victims of this festival scheme?"

"I do, actually." He went silent when the bartender returned with their drinks, setting the glasses on the bar in front of each of them. When the guy left, Billy lifted his bourbon but didn't take a sip. "I'm as much of a victim as anyone. No one knows how much I've lost."

The dark bitterness behind the words was unmistakable. But that didn't stop Lorenzo's jaw from dropping at the guy's audacity.

"Excuse me?"

Billy continued, almost as if he hadn't heard the question, "I should have suspected that Asher was up to no good," he muttered, swiping condensation off his glass. "I always sensed a rivalry between Asher and Ross. That Asher felt Rusty favored his biological son over his stepson. Don't you think?"

"I never noticed anything," Lorenzo argued, wondering where this was going.

Clearly, Billy didn't take any ownership for the crisis. And maybe he didn't deserve any. But it seemed wrong of the festival organizers to just disappear when so many people had lost money to the farce of Soiree on the Bay.

"I guess blood is thicker than water," Billy continued, sloshing some of his drink over the edge of his glass before it reached his lips. "Biology is destiny, right?"

"I've got to call BS on that," Lorenzo disagreed, not comfortable with the idea that Ross Edmond had received preferential treatment over Asher. It just wasn't true from what he'd witnessed over the years. "Just look at how close Rusty is to you, and you're not his son."

Billy went still. Then nodded slowly. "An astute observation. Maybe Asher was as jealous of me as he was of Ross. Perhaps that's why he took down the festival."

Lorenzo thought that was missing the point, but arguing with a guy who was already a few drinks in was probably a waste of his time. Still, he couldn't help asking, "What do you think the Edmond family will do to make it up to people who've lost so much because of this?"

Obviously, no one was going to give Rafe his money back or

Valencia the donation she'd been promised, but he wondered if they'd at least thought about a plan.

"I have a good feeling that in the end, everyone will get what they deserve." Billy lifted his glass in a toast to that, but Lorenzo had no cause to drink to it.

He didn't believe that was true, for one thing. And for another, it only ticked him off more that Billy didn't seem to take the festival failure seriously. Shaking his head, he stood, ready to leave.

But the sight of Valencia crossing the dining room, deep in conversation with Lila Jones, stopped him dead in his tracks.

Damn, but she looked so lovely she stole the air right out of his lungs. She wore a black pencil skirt and pale gray blouse with full, feminine sleeves. Her hair was loose around her shoulders, reminding him of how she'd looked on the beach at Appaloosa Island when she'd held her sandals in one hand, dipping her toes in the sand.

He could have sworn time suspended for a minute as he watched her in animated conversation with Lila. He felt a physical ache so strong it rooted him to the spot. Still, she must have felt his stare somehow because she glanced over her shoulder just then, turning back to look behind her before leaving the club.

Their eyes met. Held. He could have sworn he saw an ache in her gaze that echoed his own.

And a moment later, she was gone.

The crushing weight of knowing she didn't want to see him felt like more than he could stand. Beside him, Billy whistled low. Lorenzo turned, realizing the guy had observed the exchange somehow.

"Is she someone special to you?" Billy asked, rattling the ice cubes in a now-empty glass.

Lorenzo didn't need to think twice about that one. Because something inside him had shifted this week. And seeing Valencia just now only confirmed what he'd suspected for the past several days.

He was in love with Valencia.

"Yes. She is special." He regretted that he hadn't realized it sooner, but it couldn't be too late. "And she's one of many people suffering because of that damned festival."

Slamming his glass onto the bar, he stalked away from Billy, fueled by a new determination to see Valencia again. To convince her to hear him out. He noticed that Lila Jones had lingered behind Valencia, who'd already departed.

Hastening his pace, he intercepted Lila just as she left the hostess's stand.

"Lila," he called out before he joined her near the door. "Do you have a minute?"

"Well, hello, Lorenzo." The brunette's gaze went to the window overlooking the parking area where they could both see Valencia closing the door of her pickup. Her attention then returned to him. "Sure. What's up?"

"How are things going with the festival? Have you heard from the Edmond family?"

She adjusted her purse strap on her shoulder. "Unfortunately, no. I think they're just waiting for things to blow over."

"Which they won't." He wondered how Valencia was doing, but knew he had no right to ask. "The festival was supposed to be in two days. Have you heard how any of the performers are responding to the canceled event? How they're handling things?"

He'd read online that many fans were unhappy that they wouldn't be seeing the popular musicians they'd paid to hear live. There was a lot of backlash on the bands, who couldn't help that there was nowhere for them to perform.

"A couple of them have decided to do some local shows as a way to connect with fans. Two of them will be performing at the Silver Saddle on Saturday when the festival was supposed to begin."

"Really?" His gaze tracked the progress of Valencia's truck as she backed out of her parking spot, powerless to keep his eyes off her.

"For what it's worth, I think Valencia will be there."

His head whipped back to the woman beside him. Lila's lips curved in a small smile. Ah, he had an ally after all. A good thing, since he needed all the help he could get.

"I have been trying to find a way to talk to her," he said carefully, unwilling to intrude on a friendship in a way that might further risk Valencia's trust, but he was grateful for any other hint this gracious lady cared to drop. "I owe her an apology."

Lila tapped her chin thoughtfully for a moment, then she leaned closer, her long dark hair slithering off her shoulder as she spoke.

"She's been busy trying to find accommodations for some new rescues. The tornado left a rancher without a barn near Mustang Point. It's been in the news, and she's been working to coordinate a way to get them all here."

While Lorenzo hated the idea of Valencia being upset or stressed, he couldn't deny that this news gave him an opportunity to help her. And he needed something constructive to do. Even if she never spoke to him again, his heart belonged to her. He wanted the best for her.

"You've given me an excellent idea for an apology." If she threw it in his face, then so be it. He still owed her the words. "I can't thank you enough."

Straightening, Lila winked at him. "Good luck, Lorenzo. Maybe I'll see you Saturday?"

Filled with new purpose mixed with wary hope, he nodded. "Count on it."

He might not be able to replace the funds Valencia had lost to the missing ticket money from Soiree on the Bay. But he knew how to transport and board horses. He had the equipment, the manpower and the means.

Now, he just hoped Valencia would hear him out. Because he couldn't escape the feeling that this was his last chance to win back the woman of his dreams.

* * *

"I'm sorry, I don't understand." Valencia sighed with exasperation into her cell phone as she slid off Sapphire's back and led the Belgian to the paddock by her reins. She needed to cut their morning ride short in order to take this call from a farm in Mustang Point. The spread had been hit hard in the recent tornadoes and she'd been trying to help them by taking in some of their displaced animals. "Did you say your horses are *gone*?"

She'd been running Sapphire at a full canter when she'd taken the call, so she was a bit out of breath now. Maybe she'd misheard? Poor Sapphire could have run for another hour, but Valencia really did need to return to work.

For three days, she'd been calling all her local resources to see who could accept those five horses left stranded by the same tornado that had ripped through Appaloosa Island. The animals were beautiful. Well cared for. Well mannered.

But the farmer who'd been keeping them had lost everything. Including his favorite mount—a young gelding quarter horse. He'd been so distressed that it was hard for him to think about rebuilding for the remaining animals in his care. Valencia empathized. And she wanted to take the animals because she suspected they could be great fits for the therapy camp. Plus, they would be somewhat local in case the farmer changed his mind once he was done grieving.

So it made no sense that the farmer's daughter was telling her the horses had already been taken care of. How could that be? What had happened to them? Were they safe?

"A man came yesterday with two big horse trailers," the younger woman explained, and in the background Valencia could hear her shuffling papers. "I have the paperwork here, somewhere, but it was a rancher my father knew from the Texas Cattleman's Club. And we were so grateful because we have nothing here to feed the horses. Even the hay was ruined."

"I know about the hay," she reminded her, putting the cell phone on speaker, then clipping the device to her belt before tugging off Sapphire's bridle once they reached the paddock. "That's why I've been in a hurry to get everything coordinated. I was planning to get the first of the horses myself this afternoon."

"Well, your friend saved you a trip. The man who loaded them up said he was holding them for Donovan Horse Rescue."

Her *friend*?

Valencia stopped her trek toward the tack room, where she'd been headed to hang the bridle.

"He's holding them for me? Did you get his name?" It must have been someone she'd called in the last few days. Although no one had said they were prepared to take on the boarding, even if they'd been willing to help her with the transportation.

And actually, no one had agreed to that, either. She was perplexed.

"It was a long name. Lorenzo something. He was really, really good-looking."

Valencia dropped the bridle. It couldn't possibly be him! Surely the woman misheard.

Valencia breathed through the tension, the grief, knotting in her chest. She was probably just missing him so much—even though he'd hurt her, damn it—that she was hearing his name when no one had said it.

"Lorenzo?" she repeated softly, still liking the way it flowed from her lips.

Still missing saying it aloud since she'd refused to speak to him. She hadn't even told anyone that he'd broken her heart. Although Lila might have guessed over their lunch the day before.

"Yes, that's right. I have it on the paperwork he left with us," the farmer's daughter continued. "He said he was going to stable them for you until you were ready to house them. I think he lives near you. He was from Royal."

The air whooshed right out of her lungs. Lorenzo. Somehow managing to be a part of her life even when he wasn't present.

Bending to retrieve the bridle, Valencia didn't know what to make of the news. Was it a good sign? Had he wanted to do something kind for her? Or was he simply using it as a way to speak to her because she'd refused to answer his calls?

Either way, it was kind. Tremendously so. He'd always been so supportive of her passion for rescue and equine therapy. He deserved a thanks for his thoughtfulness. And she intended to do so.

Right after she figured out how he'd managed to find out——

Lila.

Valencia sagged back against the tack room wall, her legs shaky at the thought of facing Lorenzo. She'd told Lila about the horse dilemma over lunch yesterday, and then she'd seen Lorenzo on her way out. He must have stopped to speak to the woman. It hadn't taken him long to act. She couldn't deny that she was touched.

"I'll have to talk to him, then," Valencia managed finally, straightening from the wall and draping the bridle over the proper hook. "I'll be sure to let you know how they're doing once I've got them settled," she promised. "Call anytime if your father changes his mind."

The woman's gratitude echoed after Valencia disconnected. She clutched the phone to her chest as she stepped back outside under the shade of the live oak. Barkis trotted over to greet her, nosing her hand for a pet.

What did Lorenzo's gesture mean?

So many nights she'd lain awake in her bed, her eyes gritty from crying, asking herself if she'd done the right thing walking away from Lorenzo. Yes, he'd hurt her by not telling her about the background check. But it wasn't that she minded his looking into her personal background. From a business perspective, she understood, and would have gladly welcomed it for the sake of securing the donation from the Cortez-Williams family.

It was that he hadn't told her about it once they'd started to get intimate. To trust him not only with her body, but with an emotional piece of her past... Only to find out he'd known all along and hadn't mentioned it—that had been what hurt. Still, would it sting so much if she hadn't begun to care for him deeply?

Her phone buzzed against her hand, while she mulled that over. Even with her screen brightness turned all the way up, she had to shade her eyes to see the incoming text message.

From Lorenzo.

I'll be at the Silver Saddle tomorrow at 4 p.m. I really need to talk to you.

Her breath caught as she read the words. And she knew from the way her heart skipped a beat that she couldn't possibly refuse. She needed—no, she *ached*—to see him.

And for the first time in nearly two weeks, a tendril of hope sprouted inside her.

Thirteen

Had he scared off Valencia for good with that text message?

Heart hammering double time in his chest, Lorenzo searched the crowd for her from a private table inside The Silver Saddle bar and tapas restaurant, a Royal hotspot inside the luxurious Bellamy resort property. The place was filling rapidly for the promised entertainment, a popular band that had been booked for Soiree on the Bay. For now, a deejay spun upbeat country music from a booth by the dance floor, but the instruments for the band were in place on a nearby stage. A few couples were already two-stepping, and the volume from nearby conversations picked up as the crowd grew.

In the ten minutes since he'd sat down, Lorenzo had already spotted Abby Carmichael, the documentary filmmaker who'd been following the festival debacle. Lila Jones sat at the bar with Zach Benning, the social media influencer whose online platforms had attracted a lot of interest in the festival. Lorenzo wondered how the implosion of the event affected him, but the guy seemed fully focused on Lila right now, his arm wrapped possessively around her.

The sight shot a pang through Lorenzo, making him miss Valencia even more. Would she really skip this event altogether just because he'd let her know he would be there? He sighed. But the bigger question was... Had he finally found the woman meant for him, his *soul mate*, only to lose her? And if he had, he knew he had only himself to blame.

He waved away his server, not ready to order anything yet. His stomach was in knots anyway. As the male waiter hustled off to another table, Lorenzo finally caught sight of the woman he'd been waiting for as she entered the bar. His breath hitched.

Hope burned with a reminder of just how high the stakes were. Had his gesture with moving the horses been enough to win her back? Or was she simply here to issue an obligatory thank-you? Each long-legged step brought her closer to giving him his heart's desire...or dashing his hopes for a future with this incredible woman.

Dressed in a simple blue wrap dress that hugged her feminine curves, Valencia smiled and waved to friends as she wove her way through the packed bar. Part of him longed to go to her so he could clear her path, but he knew he didn't have the right to escort her.

Something he hoped like hell would change after he had the chance to speak to her. For now, he contented himself with watching her, acknowledging the overwhelming pleasure of seeing her again. Then, when her honey-brown eyes found his, awakening memories of how it had felt to be the center of attention, he shot to his feet to wait for her.

Nerves jumping, he thought his heart might break right through his chest with the way it knocked around inside him.

"Valencia. I'm glad you're here." He held a chair for her as she neared the table. "Won't you have a seat?"

He couldn't read her gaze, her face revealing nothing except for the high color in her cheeks. Was she agitated? He hoped this meeting didn't cause her any stress or unhappiness, but it was too much to hope that the rush of pink in her skin could be from the same awareness that never failed to stir inside him whenever she was near.

"Thank you," she said softly, brushing past him to accept the seat, leaving a hint of rose-and-vanilla fragrance in the air as she lowered herself into the high-backed leather chair tucked into the private corner.

Grateful to have her here, to know she was granting him this audience after how he'd hurt her, he did his best to situate her comfortably before taking the seat opposite her. With their backs to the wall, they could have a good view of the room, but right now, he had eyes only for her.

"Thank you for joining me," he began, his heart in his throat as he thought about all that was riding on this conversation.

Before he could begin, however, a woman hurried over to their table. She was dressed in black pants and a white blouse, simple clothes similar to the attire of the staff, but Lorenzo knew she wasn't their server. Besides, her handbag was tucked under her arm as she edged around a tray of drinks balanced on a high table nearby.

"Excuse me." The woman held up a finger as if to indicate she needed only a moment. "I'm so sorry to interrupt you, but I'm trying to set up some appointments with people about the festival debacle." Reaching in her bag, she withdrew a white business card and laid it on the table between them. "Lani Li, private investigator."

Lorenzo exchanged looks with Valencia, wondering what she thought of the intrusion. But his companion's expression was difficult to read as she reached for the card and read it over.

"Who hired you?" Valencia asked the newcomer as she looked up from the card and passed it to Lorenzo.

The woman—mid- to late-twenties, he guessed—scooped her long, sleek ponytail off her shoulder and shoved it impatiently behind her back.

"I'm not at liberty to say. But I assure you, my client is prepared to get to the bottom of who is responsible for the failed event." Lani crouched closer so she could lower her voice, as if she didn't want anyone to overhear.

Interesting.

"Besides Asher Edmond?" Lorenzo asked, curious to learn if someone else had suspicions about a bigger cover-up at work. Something about Asher's arrest made him uneasy.

"I plan to review all of the evidence from start to finish," she returned, sidestepping what he knew had been a loaded question. "I'm making no assumptions. I'm only interested in learning the truth." She turned her gaze toward Valencia. "I've been hoping to speak with you, Ms. Donovan, as I know you were on the advisory board. Would you be willing to talk to me about your experience with the festival? I'd be glad to come to you to make it easy."

Valencia didn't hesitate. "Please call me Valencia. And assuming you are who you say you are, I would be happy to speak to you. I can be reached at Donovan Horse Rescue anytime. I think we can both agree that this isn't the right time or place for further discussion."

The private investigator nodded. "Fair enough. I'll be in touch, Valencia. And thank you."

Lorenzo echoed the thanks over the woman leaving as he watched her bustling away, withdrawing another business card from her bag as she made a beeline for Lila Jones. Then his focus returned to the beautiful woman across from him.

A woman who deserved so much more from him than he'd given her.

Valencia slid a finger under the tiny horseshoe pendant she wore on a gold chain at her neck, then slid the charm back and forth while she studied him across the table.

"So? You must know I'm curious why you wanted to see me."

The suspense was killing her.

She'd been a few minutes late to this meeting with Lorenzo because she'd been nervous and unsure how to proceed. Should she ask him about the horses he'd transported on her behalf? *Thank* him?

As grateful as she felt about what he'd done, she wanted to hear him out first. She needed to know how he felt about what had happened between them. Did he take any ownership for it, or understand how his actions had hurt her? She was nervous about the outcome of this conversation, fearing it could be the last time they spoke. Fear...anxiety...and yes, love, welled inside her.

As she searched his dark eyes for answers, the rest of the noisy bar fell away for her.

Until a server appeared.

Thankfully, Lorenzo seemed as eager to be done with their drink order as she was, and the waiter disappeared a moment later.

"Valencia." His voice was a warm rumble across their table as he met her gaze once more. "You asked me why I wanted to see you," he began, his expression earnest. "And the truth is I've never stopped wanting to see you. I've missed being with you every single day—every hour—that we've been apart."

His admission made her tingly inside. She couldn't deny it. But she could hardly confess to missing him, too, if he didn't understand why she'd left in the first place. The nervousness she'd felt going into this meeting was still there.

He continued, however, laying both hands on the polished tabletop as he spoke. "But I know you deserve better than someone who is anything less than fully honest with you. I had a responsibility to tell you about the private investigation before we got involved romantically, and I failed you. I'm so incredibly sorry for letting you down like that."

She appreciated his directness, and some of her anxiety eased a fraction. She forced herself to let go of her horseshoe good-luck charm.

"I know things escalated quickly between us with the tornado," she acknowledged, recognizing that her uncomfortable past had been part of the reason she'd taken comfort in his arms that first night. "But even if you'd told me after the storm, I would have been more understanding."

It wouldn't have hurt so very much.

Nearby, the musicians started to play. The gentle twang of a country love song filled the bar, the crowd quieting a fraction to enjoy the strains of the fiddle.

Lorenzo's face was solemn. Sad, perhaps. "I have no excuse, and, again, I'm sorry. I allowed my experience with Lindsey to taint my feelings so much I've had a hard time trusting anyone, much less my own judgment."

Even his words sounded pained. Could the ache he felt over their split be as agonizing as her own? She leaned over the table a bit at the private nature of their conversation. Also, maybe because she found it almost impossible to resist the magnetic pull that she'd felt toward him from their very first meeting.

"I know how past hurts can color your choices," she admitted, wanting to share a conclusion she'd reached in the last two lonely weeks without him. "I've spent a long time trying to shed the taint of my birth family. But I'm not them, and I'm tired of trying to be the best at all times just to set myself apart from them. It's exhausting."

His brows furrowed with what looked like concern. "You're a good person with a warm, giving heart. A charitable nature. Anyone who can't recognize that doesn't deserve your time."

The passionate inflection behind the words touched her. And stirred a hope that Lorenzo's feelings for her hadn't faded.

She wanted to hear more, but she spied the server heading toward them with their drinks and wondered if she'd ever have Lorenzo to herself for more than five minutes at a time.

"Would you like to dance?" he asked, extending his hand to her as he pushed away from the table.

He was dressed in a dark suit with a white shirt left unbuttoned at his neck, though his expensive leather boots still marked him as a Texas rancher. An extraordinarily compelling one, at that.

Valencia nodded. "It might be our only chance to speak privately here." She placed her palm in his and allowed him to draw her to her feet, her blood rushing in her ears at the feel of his skin warming hers.

His touch brought back so many memories.

For now, she followed him onto the dance floor, her breath catching when he stopped to pull her into his arms.

With one hand settled on the small of her back, the other wrapped around hers, he led her to the spot farthest from any other dancers while the music wrapped around her.

"I deeply regret hurting you, Valencia." Lorenzo's gruffly spoken words picked up right where he'd left off earlier. "I knew as soon as you left my house that night that I owed you an apology. And I don't blame you for not wanting to hear it. But I can't rest until you know how sorry I am. I hope you can accept my apology."

She saw the sincerity in his eyes. Felt his concern for her in a hundred little ways, from how he looked at her like she was the only woman in the room to the way he hadn't pressed her into meeting with him.

And he hadn't once brought up the kindness he'd done her by securing the horses she'd been anguished about rescuing all week.

"I forgive you." She stroked her hand lightly along his shoulder where it rested on his tailored suit. The warmth of his body beneath it sent a shiver of awareness through her that he must feel.

His hand flexed on the small of her back, a slight clenching of his fingers. But he didn't pull her closer.

"You do?" he rasped.

"Yes. Of course I do." She felt sure of it to the depths of her being. Sure of *him*. "I was so hurt that night. Not just by what you'd done, but also that you barely seemed to acknowledge it. But I've searched my heart, and I know you're a better man than that. A mistake is just that—a mistake."

A long breath shuddered through him as he wrapped his arms

around her fully. Tightly. She felt his relief at her answer, and knowing how tense he'd been about this conversation soothed any last fragments of frayed pride she might have been feeling.

The song ended and another began as he held her. They were out of the way of dance traffic, however, and no one seemed to mind that they clung together to one side of the floor. ▪

"You're an amazing woman, Valencia Donovan." Lorenzo's words were for her ears alone, spoken into her hair as they swayed together to the new duet sung over the strains of a steel guitar. "I would give anything for a second chance to show you how much I care for you."

The tender feelings she had for him swelled stronger as her new hopes took root. She couldn't imagine any place she'd rather be than right here in his strong arms, his heart pounding so hard that she felt it against her breast.

"Like transporting five beautiful horses all the way from Mustang Point?" she asked, reaching up to stroke his jaw.

"No. I'd give far, far more than that."

Her lips lifted in a half smile as her hand dropped back to his shoulder. "Well, the horses were a wonderful place to start. Thank you so much."

"It was my pleasure to do something for you, but I hope it was only the beginning." He speared a hand through her hair to cradle the back of her head, then tipped her face up to his.

Electricity seemed to crackle through her, zinging its way to all her nerve endings until she hummed with it.

"A beginning?" Her tongue darted out to moisten her lips gone suddenly dry. She probably gazed up at him like a woman under a spell, but she couldn't find it in her to care about anything other than this man in front of her right now.

Her feet stopped moving.

All her attention solely on Lorenzo.

"Yes." There was a fierceness in his voice. A new determination. "It took my head a while to catch up with my heart,

Valencia, but I know now that I love you. And I'm going to do everything I can to prove to you how much."

The intensity of his gaze made her knees go weak.

Happiness soared inside her so high she felt light-headed. Although his mouth now hovered so close to hers that the promise of a kiss might have contributed to that light-headed feeling.

"Then take me home," she whispered, her breath coming fast as her emotions threatened to spill over for the whole world to see. "Because I love you, too, Lorenzo. And I think we need to start showing each other how much."

His lips claimed hers as if he wanted to taste the words for himself. Seal them between them. And she wanted that, too, because she could have lost herself in that kiss for hours. Days.

A lifetime.

"We're going to do that," he assured her when he broke away, breathing heavily. "Because I'm going to love every minute of showing each other how we feel. But I want you to know that you don't have to prove a thing to me. You're a woman of your word, and I will never question that again."

He stroked a fingertip over her still-quivering lip. Around them, the song ended, and the other couples applauded for the band. But Valencia could think only about her new beginning, and the man who loved her.

So she didn't mind, not even a little bit, when he swept her off her feet and into his arms where anyone in the Silver Saddle bar could see them. Happy laughter bubbled out of her as she wound her arms around his neck, delighting in the romantic gesture from this ruggedly handsome, pragmatic man who would never give his heart lightly.

They earned a few wolf whistles, and she thought that Lorenzo got a couple of slaps on the back on his way out of the crowded bar. But Valencia had eyes only for the man who held her, the rancher whose strong arms would shelter her through any storm.

* * * * *

How To Catch A Bad Boy
Cat Schield

Cat Schield is an award-winning author of contemporary romances for Harlequin. She likes her heroines spunky and her heroes swoonworthy. While her jet-setting characters live all over the globe, Cat makes her home in Minnesota with her daughter, two opinionated Burmese cats and a goofy Doberman. When she's not writing or walking dogs, she's searching for the perfect cocktail or traveling to visit friends and family. Contact her at catschield.com.

Books by Cat Schield

Sweet Tea and Scandal

Upstairs Downstairs Baby
Substitute Seduction
Revenge with Bene its
Seductive Secrets
Seduction, Southern Style

Texas Cattleman's Club: Heir Apparent

How to Catch a Bad Boy

Visit her Author Profile page at
millsandboon.com.au,
or catschield.com, for more titles!

Dear Reader,

Every time I get to participate in a Texas Cattleman's Club series, it's so exciting. This book was no exception. I have never had as much fun writing a bad-boy story as I did with *How to Catch a Bad Boy*. Former professional polo player Asher Davidson Edmond may be many things—irresponsible, egotistical, sexy as sin—but he's no thief. Unfortunately, with all the evidence pointing to his guilt, he needs someone to believe in him. Too bad the one woman who could help him is the one he let get away five years earlier.

I love writing a strong woman of color, and Lani Li is a badass private investigator with something to prove and a padlock on her heart when it comes to her former lover. Too bad Asher's as sexy and charming as ever. These two were complete opposites of each other, and making them have to work together to figure out the mystery of the missing money was such fun.

I hope you enjoy this enemies-to-lovers bad-boy reunion romance.

Happy reading!

Cat Schield

To Bri and Ella.
Thanks for all your support so
I could get this book written.

One

Asher Davidson Edmond lay on the jail cell's hard bunk, arm thrown over his eyes to block out the gray concrete walls and dingy ceiling. How the hell had he gotten here? Correction: he knew how. A police escort in the back of a cruiser. As to the chain of events that had landed him in this mess, he'd been completely blindsided.

Despite some of the risky behavior he'd demonstrated in his thirty-one years, he'd never imagined landing behind bars because of something he hadn't done. And he definitely *hadn't* been embezzling funds from the festival. He might've bent or even broken a law or two in his youth, but that had been petty stuff. Stealing for his own gain was the last thing he'd do.

"Hey, rich boy."

The mocking voice belonged to the blocky, muscular cop who'd escorted him back to his dank, windowless cell after his arraignment. Asher's molars ground together at the man's taunt. Apparently, he'd gone to high school with Deputy Vesta's younger sister and hadn't treated the girl too well. He had to take Vesta's word for it because he didn't remember those teenage years all that well. Something about laughing at her when she'd asked him to prom... Not one of his finest moments, obviously.

"Yeah?" Asher responded, not bothering to move. Quashing his jittery emotions, he packed as much sardonic boredom as he could into the single word, all too aware that he wasn't doing himself any favors by acting like a jerk. Still, nothing would change Vesta's rock-solid perceptions of him, and after years of coping with his adopted father's nonstop disapproval, he reflexively retreated into behaving like a sullen, entitled prick.

"You've got a visitor."

Hope exploded in Asher's chest.

Had Ross and Gina changed their mind about his guilt after failing to support him at yesterday's bail hearing? While his siblings' abandonment had aroused panic and uncertainty, Asher had known better than to expect his adopted father to show. Nor did he expect Rusty Edmond had come to see him now, unless to drive home his acute regret for adopting his second wife's son.

Asher had his own complaints on that score. Why had Rusty bothered with a legal connection when he'd never truly embraced Asher as one of his own? Or maybe he had—the man demonstrated little affection toward either of his biological children and between criticizing Ross's abilities and dismissing Gina's talents, none of the Edmond offspring had a great relationship with him.

That hadn't stopped Asher from spending his teen years fighting an uphill battle to win Rusty's affection though. And when all his efforts had failed, Asher had begun acting out. If he couldn't win his stepfather's approval, then he figured he would become truly worthy of Rusty's disdain.

Yet as difficult as his relationship with his stepfather was, Asher's connection with his stepsiblings was as close as if they were blood relations. Ross had been twelve and Gina ten when fifteen-year-old Asher had come to live with them. He'd enjoyed playing big brother to the pair and the trio had bonded immediately. Even though Rusty had only been married to his mother for three years, they'd been formative ones for all three kids and they'd remained tight even after Rusty and Stephanie divorced and Asher headed off to college.

Which was why the silence from the Edmond siblings was so ominous. Since his arraignment, he'd consoled himself by speculating that Rusty—intent on teaching his adopted son a lesson—had barred Ross and Gina from showing up in court. But as the hours stretched out and he'd not heard from either of his siblings, Asher started to worry that they believed he was guilty and had turned their backs on him.

Unrelenting panic swelled in his chest. At the arraignment he'd learned the charges against him were worse than he'd been led to believe. It wasn't just the theft of the funds—that could've been handled locally—but the money had disappeared from the banks, sent by wire transfer and that meant the feds were involved. Even if he'd wanted to, Rusty couldn't use this as a teachable moment for his adopted son and make the charges go away.

Asher was in *deep.*

With his bank accounts frozen thanks to the embezzlement charges, he hadn't been able to post his own bail. Naturally he'd hoped that his family would believe that he'd never do anything like what he'd been accused of and help him out. But as the hours passed, his despair had grown. Only now it appeared as if he'd been worried for nothing. One or both of them had decided to help him out.

"You've got five minutes," Deputy Vesta said, his tone brisk.

Asher sat up and blinked in the sudden brightness. As his eyes adjusted, he focused on the person standing on the other side of the bars. The individual was neither his tall, lanky brother nor his stylish sister, but a petite woman in figure-hugging jeans and high-heeled boots, her long black hair slicked back into a neat, low ponytail. Probably another fed come to pick at him about the missing funds.

But then she stepped closer and he glimpsed her features.

"Lani Li?"

He could barely breathe as recognition landed a sharp jab to his gut. Then he rallied and pushed to his feet, fighting to remain upright as his emotions executed a wild swing between delight and confusion at her appearance. Had she heard about his plight and come rushing to help him? His heart hoped so. It thumped hard against his ribs as he processed his outstanding luck.

However his euphoria dissipated as he noticed the glower in her mink-brown eyes. Spots of color flared in her cheeks, marring the uniform perfection of her pale skin. She'd compressed her luscious lips into a flat line that broadcast her disdain and the only thing keeping her arched brows from touching was the bottomless vertical indent between them. To say she looked less than pleased to see him was an understatement, but putting aside his desperate need for rescue, her arrival flooded his mind with vivid, racy memories.

Until she spoke…

"Asher." Her tone was all business.

"What a surprise," he murmured, advancing toward her, drawn like a bee to a flower.

Her scent hit him before he wrapped his hands around the bars and leaned in. She smelled like warm vanilla and spicy cinnamon, all lush sweetness and mouthwatering delectability. He remembered burying his nose in her hair and drawing her unique perfume into his lungs. How she'd tasted like sweat and sunshine as they'd made love beside a raging river, crushing pine needles beneath their straining bodies and releasing the astringent scent. The simple act of breathing her in now slowed his heart rate and soothed his restless nature.

"What's it been?" he continued blithely. "Five years?"

She gave a curt nod. "About that."

"Long time."

"Yep." Lani narrowed her eyes and scanned him from the top of his close-cropped brown hair to the toes of his brown Berluti loafers. "You look like hell."

"Well," he drawled with a lazy shrug while his brain scrambled to process that she was standing there. "I have been locked up in here for a day and a half, so..."

While finishing the sentence, he trailed his gaze over her, following the buttons of the white button-down shirt she wore beneath a practical navy blazer, over the swell of firm breasts and the flat plains of a taut abdomen to the waistband of the dark denim. He knew that body. He *adored* that body. Curves in all the right places. Honed muscle beneath silky soft skin. He'd spent long hours guiding his lips and hands over every inch, learning what made her shiver, moan and whimper.

"You look really great," he drawled, recalling that time he'd nipped the firm mound of her perfect butt and made her squeak in surprise. "So, what brings you by?" Asher posed the question lazily, chatting her up as if they'd bumped into each other at a barbecue rather than a jail cell. One corner of his mouth kicked up as he delivered a smoky look her way.

"I've gotta say, you're the last person I expected to see here."

"I'm on a case," she told him.

"I'm intrigued. Care to tell me about it?"

"I'm investigating the theft of the festival funds."

"Who do you think did it?" he asked.

She cocked her head and shot him an incredulous look. "You."

"So, you're on the Asher-is-a-thief train." He nodded, unsurprised by her answer. "I thought you might believe I was innocent."

With a long-suffering sigh, she swept aside her blazer and set her hand on her hip. The gesture exposed an empty holster clipped to her belt. He stared at the telltale harness as lust blindsided him. The thrill wasn't entirely sexual. Since he was a kid, Asher had lived for the next great adventure and had spent most of his twenties chasing anything exciting or dangerous. The thought of Lani packing heat turned him on in so many ways. His skin tingled and the tips of his fingers began to buzz with the need to touch her.

"Looks like you became a special agent after all," he said, his gaze drifting up her torso, pausing momentarily to revisit the enticing curve of her breasts before making contact with her hostile glare. "What are you? FBI? ATF? DEA?"

Her sooty eyelashes flickered. "I'm a private investigator."

"You don't say." This intrigued him.

Lani had been on the cusp of attending graduate school when they met five years earlier and planned to study criminal justice. She'd graduated college with a degree in sociology and a passion to make the world a better place. Despising injustice, she'd decided a career in federal law enforcement would offer her the best chance to make a difference.

"Well," he continued, "get me out of here and you can do all the private investigating you want."

Even before her eyes flared in outrage, Asher regretted flirting with her. She was the only person who'd come to see him and he was treating her like some random chick he'd met at a bar instead of the dazzling prize he'd foolishly let slip through his fingers.

Her full lips, bare of lipstick, puckered as she let an exasperated breath escape. As if they'd last kissed yesterday instead of five years ago, he recalled how her lip balm had tasted like strawberries. How her long silky hair had tickled the back of his hands as he'd drawn her close. From their first kiss to their final heartbreaking embrace, he hadn't been able to get enough of her.

"You're still the same frat boy, aren't you?" Her words splashed icy water on his libido.

"I'm not."

The nickname stung the way it had five years earlier. They'd met while she'd been employed as a waitress on Appaloosa Island in Trinity Bay off the coast of Texas. He'd been lazing around before what had turned out to be his final season playing professional polo. Intrigued as much by her brilliant wit as her killer body and gorgeous face, every time he ate at the resort's restaurant, he'd made sure to be seated in her section.

To his chagrin, nothing about him had charmed her. Unimpressed with the giant tips he'd left her, she'd sized him up as idle and aimless and dubbed him "frat boy" even though he'd left college behind half a decade earlier.

"These days I'm the vice president of operations in charge of The Edmond Organization's Bakken business." He puffed out his chest, wondering if he could impress upon her that he was serious and successful, someone who had a plan and stuck to it instead of roaming around the world chasing one polo season after another.

Although his practiced tone was one of pompous confidence, it didn't reflect his true feelings. In fact he hated the endless dull details demanding his attention and made the barest effort to manage his team. He'd been with the company for a little over nearly two years, bullied into taking the position because Rusty was tired of subsidizing Asher's "unproductive lifestyle" and threatened to cut off all support unless Asher did something to earn the money.

"Yet you're barely ever in the office," she said, her skeptical expression indicating she'd already heard an earful about him.

"I've been busy with the Soiree on the Bay festival." An exaggeration. He'd had little to do with the practical aspects of organizing the luxury food, art and wine extravaganza.

"Yes," she murmured dryly, "that seems to have led to your current state of incarceration."

As much as Asher wanted to argue, what could he say? The steel bars blocking him from freedom said it all. Nor could he point to anything he'd done since they'd parted ways that would meet with her stringent standards. She was one of the most focused and task-oriented people he'd ever met. From the beginning she made it perfectly clear that his lack of ambition frustrated her. In every way that mattered, they were opposites. Yet he was drawn to her by an undeniable hunger that proved as distracting as it was intoxicating.

While it might have been her striking looks that first attracted him to her, what inflamed his pursuit in the face of one rejection after another was her courage, unflinching strength of character and no-nonsense outlook.

And he loved a challenge.

Her aloofness fired his determination to discover the woman hiding behind her prickly exterior. Yet as satisfying as the chase had been, catching her had surpassed his wildest dreams. Nor had his attention shifted to his next conquest after getting her into bed. She'd proved to be more exhilarating than any woman he'd ever known. And through the course of their whirlwind affair, she'd had a profound effect on him.

During those blissful summer months, he'd become someone...*different*. Someone who stopped joyriding through life and started to question his purpose. Someone who considered another's hopes and desires might be just as important as his own.

Yet it couldn't last. They were heading down two completely different paths. She was off to graduate school in the fall, destined to make something of herself. Faced with losing her, he'd relapsed into the aimless, restless, the unreliable "frat boy" she'd christened him. And often in the intervening years, he'd wondered what would've happened if he'd been a better man.

Lina raised a slim black eyebrow and shook her head. "Do you have any idea how much trouble you're in?"

Her stony demeanor brought him back to the predicament facing him. "I'm starting to," he grumbled, his panic surging once more. If he could only get her on his side... "It's all a huge misunderstanding."

"Is it?" she countered. "The evidence against you is pretty damning. Millions are missing from the festival accounts and all the withdrawals appear to be in your name."

"I swear I didn't steal a single cent."

For days Asher had been denying any knowledge of where the money had disappeared to. No one believed him. Not his family. Nor the authorities. He appeared responsible, so everyone believed he was guilty.

"I've talked to the investigators," Lani went on as if she hadn't heard Asher protest his innocence. "There were payments made to a tech firm, a music company, a luxury jet charter enterprise. Many of the transfers seemed as if they could be legitimate, but the companies don't exist and money was siphoned out of the accounts as soon as it was put in."

This was more information than he'd previously heard. Fake corporations with real bank accounts. That sort of thing took calculation and finesse. And if anything pointed to Asher's innocence, it was that his planning skills were subpar, just ask his team at The Edmond Organization.

While he'd been mulling his shortcomings, Lani's gaze rested heavily on his face, her expression grave and expectant. "No one has any idea where the money is now."

"Me included." Heat flared in his face as frustration bubbled up inside him. It was one thing for the Edmonds to believe his guilt, but he needed Lani's help if he was going to get out of this mess. "I didn't take any of it."

Unfazed by his continued denials, she continued to assess him with cool detachment. "There's a condo in the Maldives with your name on it."

"It isn't mine." Anger flared. Where was all this damning evidence coming from? With the money trail leading directly to him, was it any wonder no one believed his innocence? "I don't even know where the Maldives is."

"It's an island off the coast of India." She paused and studied him through narrowed eyes. "More importantly, there's no extradition treaty with the US."

"Meaning I intended to take the money and run."

He barely restrained a wince at her obvious disgust. *Damn.* As hard as it had been to glimpse the betrayal and disappointment on his family's faces as he'd been escorted out of the Edmond headquarters in handcuffs, the scorn rolling off Lani cut even deeper. He'd never admit it, but once upon a time he'd wanted to be her hero. Obviously his need for her admiration hadn't dimmed.

"I'm telling you that I didn't steal any of the festival's funds and I didn't buy a condo in the Maldives." Asher gave his head a vigorous shake. "I didn't do this. Why won't anyone believe me?"

Lani glared at Asher, unable to believe that five minutes ago, as she'd walked through the door leading to these jail cells, she'd been besieged by an attack of butterflies—*butterflies!*—at the thought of seeing him again. She braced her will against the pull of his striking good looks, broad shoulders and overwhelming masculine appeal and cursed the part of her that revisited the bliss of his hard body surging into hers and the peaceful aftermath snuggled against his big warm chest. The double-barreled shot of mind-blowing sex and tender romance had torn her defenses apart.

She'd spent the last five years putting her walls back up. Yet when it came to Asher Edmond, she always underestimated his charisma. Her throat clenched. She remained as woefully susceptible to him as ever. At least she hadn't let on how her heart had leaped at her first glimpse of him. Or given any hint of how she'd rushed from a client meeting with the famous musician Kingston Blue, to this jail cell in Royal, Texas, breathless and giddy and all too aware that this new case would bring her into close proximity with Asher once again. Last time she'd almost ruined her life because of him. She must *not* be led astray again.

Recognizing that she was grinding her teeth, Lani unlocked her jaw with an effort. "If you didn't do it, then who did?"

"I have no idea."

His denials didn't surprise her. Given the serious charges facing him, Asher would be a fool to admit wrongdoing. At least not until his lawyer had plea-bargained his sentence down for cooperating with the investigation.

"It would be good for you if the money was returned." A

pause. "I could help with that." Kingston Blue wanted answers. She intended to get them.

"If you think I have a clue where the missing funds have gone, then you're going to be disappointed."

"When it comes to you," she retorted without considering her words, "I'm used to being disappointed."

For a second he looked stricken and Lani wished she'd guarded her tongue.

"What I mean is…" Rummaging through the ashes of their brief romantic fling to dig up all the old hurts and disappointments was not the way to get him to trust her. "Look, I'm here to do a job. I'm not here as your friend. We had a lot of fun that summer, but let's not pretend that we ever intended on seeing each other again once we parted ways."

Asher winced. "I'm sorry for how things ended between us."

Lani scoured his expression to determine if he truly felt remorse or if he was merely spouting more of his pretty words. *Fool me once…*

"Don't give it another thought." She pressed her lips into a grim line. The man already thought too much of himself. Why give him an inkling that their breakup had bothered her at all? "I haven't."

That summer everyone had warned her about him. She should've listened, should've followed her initial gut instincts and steered clear. Especially after her parents voiced their disapproval of their relationship when Lani had started reconsidering whether she should head to graduate school as planned or take a gap year and spend the time with Asher. She'd been such an idiot to think he'd been at all serious about her.

"I know I was a bit of a tool back then," Asher said as if she hadn't brushed off their fling as inconsequential. "But those days are behind me. I'm not that guy anymore."

His reputation said otherwise. He had an active love life, playing as fast and loose with women's hearts as he had with the festival's bank accounts. Every social media post featuring him should be captioned #*heartbreaker.*

"Forgive me if I have a hard time believing that given that you're behind bars at the moment."

"Like I said, I'm innocent." A muscle ticked in his jaw. "I was set up."

Don't be taken in by his earnest denials. Lani steeled herself against the agony in his intense brown eyes, but couldn't quell the sudden frantic pounding of her pulse. His silver tongue had drawn her in all those years ago and she'd almost given up her dreams to be with him. She just couldn't allow a lapse in judgment to happen again.

"Do you have any evidence of being framed? Or a theory who might be involved?" When she spied the way his chiseled lips thinned in frustration, Lani nodded. "That's what I thought."

For a long moment they stared at each other and Lani couldn't decide if she wanted him to be innocent or guilty. For his sake, the part of her that had once loved him hoped that he had been set up, but the heartbroken portion needed him to be a bad guy. Since they'd parted, she'd been telling herself that she was better off without him. Misery loomed if she stopped believing that.

"I guess that's it then. Your mind is made up. There's nothing more I can say to convince you." He looked so despondent that Lani's heart contracted in sympathy. "Well, it's been really great catching up with you. Good luck with the investigation."

Crap. Well, she'd done an outstanding job of alienating him before learning anything. "If you're innocent, you could use... help." She couldn't bring herself to say *my help.* Sucking in a steadying breath, she tried again. "My client wants me to find the money..."

"Did my father hire you?" Asher looked hopeful. "He was very impressed by you back when we dated. In fact, his only criticism was why a woman with your brains and ambition would waste your time with me."

"My client would prefer to remain anonymous."

Which wasn't true. Kingston Blue had given her no such instructions, but she was here to get information, not give it out.

The musician had agreed to perform at Soiree on the Bay and, like many people, he was out a lot of money thanks to Asher's embezzlement. Kingston Blue had deep pockets and wasn't in any desperate financial straits, unlike many of the vendors and attendees of the aborted festival, but he was a savvy businessman who didn't take lightly to being swindled. He'd met the entire Edmond clan and was quite convinced that there was more to the story than Asher Edmond acting alone to defraud all the people who'd put money into the festival.

Lani had been surprised when a high-profile client like Kingston Blue had contacted her about the case, but it became clear right away that the singer had done his homework and knew all about her connection to Asher Edmond. Kingston also knew that their fling hadn't ended amiably, at least not on Lani's part.

Professional ethics prompted her to warn Kingston that her prejudice against Asher might affect her work, but the musician believed her familiarity with the family made her the perfect person to investigate them and find the money. After the first obvious leads had panned out, progress had stalled on discovering the bulk of the missing funds. The feds had stopped investigating other suspects once all the evidence solidly pointed at Asher.

Despite her misgivings, in the end, the outrageous retainer Kingston offered was too tempting to resist. Plus, a check in the win column would open the door to other prominent clients. This case was the gateway to turn her fledgling business into the most sought-after investigative firm in Dallas.

But first she had to find the money Asher had stolen and for that she needed his cooperation.

"Sure. Okay. I understand." Asher raked his fingers through his short dark hair. "But when you see my dad, tell him I've learned my lesson. It would be great if he could bail me out now."

Lani saw no reason to correct Asher's assumption that his

father had hired her. If he believed that Rusty wanted him to cooperate with her investigation, all the better.

"Let me go see what I can find out about that," she said, suddenly eager to escape.

Asher stared at her intently, his gaze growing ever more piercing as the seconds ticked by. Heat flared beneath her skin at the intensity of his stare. His look wasn't sexual in nature, yet she'd always been so aware of his body and keyed into his moods. She saw now how longing and relief mingled in his expression as he believed, perhaps for the first time since his arrest, that someone might be willing to stand in his corner and believe in him.

"Thanks."

"Don't thank me." She needed to find the money. He was her ticket to do that. "I'm on a case. I think you can help me with it. That's all. Don't read anything more into it."

"Sure. Whatever you say." His even, white teeth flashed in a relieved grin as she turned to go. "And, Lani..."

She hated the way her heart spasmed as she headed for the exit. The powerful lure of their shared history was a stronger temptation than she'd expected. But she couldn't let herself be ensnared by her longing for him. He'd been bad for her back then, and he'd be even worse for her now.

"Yeah?" Standing before the door, waiting for the buzz that would indicate it was unlocked, she made the mistake of glancing Asher's way.

A smile of genuine delight lit up his brown eyes and softened his lips into sensual curves. "Seeing you again is the best thing that's happened to me in a long, long time."

The buzz sounded. Without uttering another word, Lani yanked open the door with far more force than necessary and left. She collected her phone and keys from the deputy guarding the cells, and then she was run-walking through the police station and stepping out into the blistering hot August afternoon. She didn't stop moving until she'd reached her SUV in the parking lot. Breath coming in ragged gasps, she bent forward and set her hands on her knees while the blood pounded in her ears.

As her pulse slowed, she unlocked her vehicle and slid behind the wheel. She couldn't do this. Pulling out her phone, she began to scroll through her contacts in search of Kingston Blue's name. To hell with the money or the boost to her reputation this case offered, working in close contact with Asher was going to mess with her emotions again.

"Lani," Kingston's smooth deep voice soothed her ragged nerves. "I didn't expect to hear from you so soon. Did you meet with Asher Edmond?"

"Yes." She searched for a way to extract herself from the case without damaging her credibility. "He claims he's innocent."

"Do you think he is?"

Did she? "The evidence suggests he's guilty."

"But you know the guy. What's your take?"

"It's all a little too obvious." Lani didn't realize this fact had been bothering her until right now. "Asher isn't stupid or naive. How could he possibly think he could get away with it?"

"So, you agree that there's something more going on."

"Maybe. I don't make assumptions this early in a case."

"Fair enough." Despite Kingston's neutral tone, his inflection reflected disappointment. "So what's your next step?"

"Well, having Asher behind bars makes getting information from him about the festival bank accounts nearly impossible, and since the feds froze his assets and his family isn't stepping forward to help, it doesn't look like he can make bail."

"If I put up the money to get him out, I'm counting on you to make sure he doesn't run. That means he's your responsibility twenty-four/seven."

"That's…"

Impossible. Outrageous. Too much to expect from her.

She couldn't handle that much contact with Asher. There had to be another way. Yet even as she scrambled for a logical excuse to give Kingston, she knew there was only one answer.

"Doable."

"Great, then get me the details so we can get his bail paid and let's hope our boy can lead you to the missing money."

Two

Confronted with spending another miserable night cooling his heels in jail, Asher set aside his dinner of a roast beef sandwich, snack-size bag of potato chips and fruit cup. No doubt refusing the simple fare would be perceived as snobbishness, but in truth, the acid churning in his stomach left him unsure if he could keep anything down.

"Your bail's been posted," Deputy Vesta said in clipped tones as he unlocked the door to his cell.

Asher lacked the energy to hide his overwhelming relief as he pushed to his feet and approached the opening. "Was it my dad?"

Even though Lani hadn't confirmed that Rusty had hired her, he was leaning into the hope that his father had come around to believing his adopted son was innocent.

Vesta scowled in disgust. "Do I look like I care?"

No doubt the deputy—along with most of the town—believed he deserved to remain permanently behind bars and was disappointed at this turn of events. Suspecting further questions would irritate Vesta further, Asher kept his mouth shut. Per the terms of his release, he was fitted with a court-mandated ankle monitor and instructed about the rules surrounding his release.

After collecting his belongings, he stood in the police station lobby while the public defender assigned to his case talked on the phone. Asher peered through the glass front door into the golden sunshine of early evening, wondering who had paid his bail and when they would show up to give him a ride back home.

His spirits rose as he spied his sister approaching the police station entrance. Gina was looking at her phone as she pushed through the door and didn't see him until he greeted her.

"Gina, hey," Asher called. He stepped forward to intercept her, his arms open wide. "It's great that you're here. I'd almost given up on anyone coming to pick me up."

"You're out?" Gina stopped dead, and then actually backed up several steps and cast her eyes around frantically as if desperate for someone to rescue her. "How?"

"You paid my bail...?" Asher trailed off at her headshake. "Well, *someone* did. Maybe it was Ross?" Doubts began to close in when she continued to look panicked and confused. "Or dad. I think he hired an investigator to help find the missing money."

Asher trailed off as his sister's knuckles whitened on the hand that clutched her purse strap. The strain she'd been under these last few weeks was fully evident in her ashen skin and the tick at the corner of one dry red-rimmed eye.

"Dad didn't post your bail. He still believes you're guilty." A pause. "Everyone does."

Disappointment filled him as she emphasized *everyone*. "Then why are you here?"

"The detectives have more questions for me." She dodged his gaze. "I don't know how much more I can tell them. I didn't put through any payments. You did."

"Damn it, Gina, you know me!" Asher tempered his tone when she flinched, and finished, "How can you think I had anything to do with it?"

"What else am I to think?" Her eyes flashed. "You authorized all the financial transactions that went missing."

"I didn't make those payments. I swear everything I did was legitimate."

"Obviously not, or the money wouldn't have vanished." She paused for a second, before adding with low vehemence, "Can't you just admit what you did and take responsibility?"

Asher recalled how the public defender had presented what would happen if he admitted what he'd done and returned the money or kept pleading his innocence and took his chances in court. Guilty or not, he was screwed.

"I'm not going to admit to something I didn't do."

Gina's expression closed down. Her next words demonstrated that she didn't have the tiniest amount of sympathy for him. "You don't seem to realize that the entire family is suffering because of what happened with the festival. Our family name is ruined. And there's talk that we could be kicked out of the Cattleman's Club because of this."

Her words gutted him. Asher stood rooted to the spot as she dodged around him and headed toward the reception desk. In a daze, he made for the exit, forgetting that he was no longer free to move around at will until he reached the sidewalk and became aware of the electronic monitor's unfamiliar weight rubbing against his ankle.

He was on house arrest until his trial. Whenever that was. While this situation was better than being stuck in jail, he still chaffed at the restrictions. Of course, he could venture out in Lani's company. As long as she notified the officials of their movements, he could accompany her on excursions. He had only to persuade her he could help her investigation.

Bolstered by determination, Asher glanced around, unsure how he was supposed to get back to Elegance Ranch to begin his court-ordered confinement. No doubt his car remained at The Edmond Organization. He doubted anyone had thought to remove it from the parking lot. Should he head there to pick it up? How much trouble would he be in if he didn't go straight home?

Asher started to pull his phone out of his pocket only to remember that it had been seized as evidence. How was he supposed to arrange a ride home without it? He could probably go inside and borrow a phone to call someone, but then remembered how Gina had acted toward him. What if everyone said no? He was a pariah now. No one would want to touch him with a ten-foot pole.

Cursing under his breath, he stood on the sidewalk and struggled to recall a moment when he'd felt more helpless. He'd been in plenty of dicey situations where he'd survived thanks to skill and/or good luck. His current predicament was unique and terrifying because he had no clue how to fix what was happening to him.

He couldn't run or charm his way out of the situation. This was a problem he had to face head-on. Usually when disquieting emotions erupted, he'd turn his attention to something pleasant. Naturally Lani's image popped into his head, and as he recalled their conversation earlier that day, the frantic thrumming of his nerves eased.

Almost as if his powerful need had summoned her, a black SUV pulled up to the curb and the passenger-side window rolled down. The woman behind the wheel turned her head in his direction. Her eyes, hidden behind aviator sunglasses, Lani regarded him for a heartbeat, assessing him. A moment later, she issued a two-word command.

"Get in."

Asher didn't hesitate. He needed help and Lani had appeared as if in answer to his prayer. Grinning at this uptick in his fortune, he opened the door and got in.

"Thanks for—"

"Save it."

Her grim expression declared just how untrustworthy he'd become in her eyes. Yet for some reason this didn't set him back the way it should. As dark as things had become in the last few days, Lani was here. She'd come to his rescue. No matter what she said, deep down, some part of her believed he wasn't capable of stealing millions of dollars.

"How did you know I was out of jail?"

"Because I'm the one who paid your bail. I need access to you in order to do my job and that's impossible with you behind bars."

Not the rousing endorsement of his innocence he was hoping for, but he was thrilled to have her on his team even if his freedom was nothing more than a means to an end for her.

"Thanks," he repeated. Not wanting to irritate her further, he quelled the urge to say more.

She took her foot off the brake and the car rolled forward. Lani drove with the same focus she applied to everything. As if by sheer force of will, she could control what happened next. Yet Asher perceived several hairline cracks in her confidence. His former lover gripped the steering wheel like it was the gunnel of a pitching boat while her attention remained locked on the road ahead of them as if expecting sinkholes to open up out of nowhere.

"My car is at The Edmond Organization," he said, noticing that she was headed in the opposite direction. "If you want to drop me off."

"It's not there."

"What do you mean it's not there?"

"Your car has been seized by investigators. They are going over it now."

Asher's skin prickled. "Why?"

"They're looking for evidence."

"In my car?" he demanded.

"Your car. Your devices. Your home and office."

As if spending the night in jail and being shunned by his family hadn't been stressful enough, it appeared as if nothing in his life was going to escape unscathed by this mess.

He squashed his disappointment and lapsed into resigned silence as they headed out of town in the direction of Elegance Ranch, the Edmond family estate. The thought of being stuck in his apartment over the barn for the uncertain future gave Asher the chills. He hated being tied down... It was part of the reason his job at Edmond Oil frustrated him. There was no thrill or exhilaration being tied to a desk.

And that was why he'd jumped at the chance to be involved with the festival. It was a much-needed break from his routine. If only the whole thing hadn't failed so spectacularly. Maybe it would've turned out if he'd kept a better eye on everything. Not that he could've predicted the tornado that destroyed the place. But if he'd paid more attention to what was going on, maybe he wouldn't have been caught flat-footed with millions of dollars missing and all signs pointing straight at him like a ring of laser sights aimed at his head and heart.

"I want to hire you," Asher declared abruptly, turning his head to stare at her elegant profile. "To prove I'm innocent," he clarified, determined to do or say whatever it took to get her on his side.

"I already have a client."

He refused to be deterred. "You can work for both of us at the same time."

"You can't afford me," she reminded him with a hint of a smirk. "Your assets are frozen."

"I have ways of generating cash."

Her dark eyebrows rose above her sunglasses. "You've found someone else to steal from?"

He ignored the flippant jab. "I have twelve horses I'm training as polo mounts. They aren't all ready to go, but selling a couple of them would pay your fees."

Lani shook her head. "It's not just about the money. It would be a conflict of interest to work for you while I've been hired to investigate the theft and find the money."

"The way I see it, he hired you to get to the truth." Asher kept a close eye on her reaction to his reasoning. "I know I didn't steal the money. So, if I hire you for the same reason, then you don't have to be worried about any conflicts of interest."

She rolled her gaze his direction before returning her attention to the highway. "My intention is to find out what's going on. I'm not going to stop until I get to the bottom of what happened to the money."

"Good. Then we're on the same side."

"We're *not*." His assumption had obviously set a spark to her temper. "Just to be completely clear, I believe you had the means and the opportunity to steal that money. I'm really good at what I do. I will find out what happened and where the money went. And when I do, I'll know who's guilty and who's not."

Asher pressed his point. "That's fine with me because I swear to you that I didn't take the money."

"Gaslighting won't work on me." She paused and took in his confused expression. "Gaslighting. Where you keep saying something over and over in the hopes that I'll eventually believe that it's reality."

"If I'm repeating the same thing over and over, it's because I'm telling the truth."

"Let's just agree to disagree," she said, echoing something he'd said to her before they parted ways five years earlier.

It hadn't been the words as much as his dismissive tone as he'd delivered the cliché. Afterward she spent a lot of time thinking about how that abrupt breakup made her feel. What bothered her at the time was how he hadn't taken her concerns seriously. She'd not felt heard. Her feelings had been swept aside as if they hadn't matter. As if *she* hadn't mattered to him.

And that, in a nutshell, was what had been wrong with their relationship the whole time. It hadn't just been a summer fling for her. She hadn't had enough experience with men to be able to lock her heart in a box and engage in some truly phenomenal sex as if it were some sort of trendy new aerobic exercise.

Maybe if he hadn't been her first, she would've been more emotionally sophisticated. More capable of keeping their relationship in perspective. Of realizing that no matter how special he treated her in an effort to get her into bed, it was all just a means to an end. She'd been little more than a distraction that summer, a fact that had become clear when he'd never contacted her again.

Neither one of them spoke until Asher gave her the key code to unlock the gate.

"Are you still in the apartment above the stables?" she asked, angling toward the driveway that led past the main house.

"I prefer the horses to Rusty's company."

Lani shored up her resolve as a smile ghosted across his lips. The last thing she needed was to get sucked in by Asher's attempt to manipulate her emotions. He needed her on his side, a friendly ear to fill with his tales of woe. Well, she wasn't going to fall for his tactics. She wasn't on his side. And nothing he said or did was going to change that.

She parked the SUV behind the stables and while Asher slid out of the vehicle, Lani reached for the duffel bag she'd stashed in the back. He glanced at it as she joined him at the base of the stairs that led to the two-bedroom apartment above the barn.

"What's in the bag?"

A little tingle of excitement danced across her skin. "I'm planning on staying here while I get to the bottom of what's going on."

"Staying here?" he echoed, his expression softening with interest. "With *me*?"

Oh, no. She recognized that look. Her pulse jumped at the implications. Whatever assumptions he was making, she needed to shut him down ASAP.

"This isn't a booty call," she declared, wincing at her raspy tone. "You have two bedrooms. I'm planning on using the one you don't sleep in."

"You're welcome to, of course," he murmured, watching her

from beneath heavy lids, a smoky glow kindling in his gaze. "But are you sure you'll be comfortable alone here with me?"

Oh, she'd definitely be uncomfortable sharing four walls with him, but with the future of her business riding on this investigation, she intended to keep things professional between her and Asher.

Don't worry about my comfort, frat boy. Worry about the mountain of evidence against you. It's what she should've shot back. But that's not what came out.

"I have no intention of sleeping with you ever again." Even as the declaration escaped her, Lani knew she'd overreacted.

"Okay." He drew the word out while peering at her expression. "It seems to me that you had no intention of sleeping with me five years ago, but look how great that turned out."

Lani noted the heat surging through her veins at his smugness and registered annoyance and impatience. Not desire. Not yearning. She was angry at him for reminding her of something she couldn't forget.

"I didn't know what I was doing back then."

"Maybe not at first," he agreed, misinterpreting her response. While she sputtered in mortified dismay, one side of his mouth kicked up into a wicked grin. "But you sure got the hang of things. And if I remember correctly, you even managed to teach me a thing or two."

Cheeks flaming, Lani silently cursed. From the moment she'd agreed to take this gig, she'd warned herself to remain focused on the case and not rehash how their summer romance had played out.

"Why don't we concentrate on the present," she suggested in a desperate rush, once again questioning her wisdom in taking on this assignment.

He gave a lazy one-shoulder shrug. "You're the one bringing up our past."

She set her foot onto the stairs and stomped up the stairs ahead of him. Why hadn't she argued more vigorously against

Kingston Blue's insistence that she was a perfect investigator to take on the mystery of the missing millions? Every time she tried to follow her instincts when it came to this man, the best way forward was always murky.

Reaching the landing at the top, she shifted to one side and waited for Asher to enter the unlock code, but he merely turned the knob and pushed open the door.

"After you," he gestured with exaggerated gallantry.

Lani stared at the door. "You don't lock it?"

"What's the point? There's fencing all around the property and a gate at the entrance. Who should I worry about getting inside? Ross? Gina? Rusty?"

"They're not the only people who live here. What about Ross's college friend?"

"Billy Holmes?" Asher chuckled. "The guesthouse where he's staying is way nicer than this. Besides, he doesn't seem the type to show up uninvited."

"But there are parties on the property. And staff. How many people have access to your apartment?"

"I never thought about it." He made a shooing gesture to urge her inside. "And anyway, I don't keep anything of value for someone to steal."

"That watch you're wearing isn't cheap."

He glanced down at the Breitling on his wrist and from his surprised expression, he obviously didn't register the ten-thousand-dollar accessory as being anything out of the ordinary. Lani didn't know whether to laugh or hit him. Five years ago, dating him had opened up a whole new world for her. She'd grown up in a comfortable middle-class home and never lacked for anything, but once she'd been drawn into Asher's circle, she'd gotten a firsthand glimpse into all the finest things money could buy.

Not that this had anything to do with why she'd gone out with him that first time. In fact his determination to buy her affection with huge tips had reinforced her resistance to his pursuit.

Still, dating him had swept her into a fairy tale and she'd enjoyed being a princess for a little while.

"Holy sh—"

Asher's shock roused Lani from her musings. The apartment was torn apart—every cabinet in the kitchen was open, plates, cups, pans and silverware all over the countertops and floor. The couch cushions had been pulled apart and the small desk near one of the windows had been ransacked.

"What did they think I was hiding?"

His shoulders sagged as he rubbed his face. Sympathy whiplashed through Lani before she could steel herself against it. To her dismay, the profound defeat gripping Asher did little to distract from his sex appeal. In fact she was seized by an overwhelming urge to slide her arms around his broad shoulders and revisit the intense physical connection she'd only known with one man. *This* man.

Lani ground her teeth and slapped some sense into her emotions. She might no longer be in love with him, but his ability to burrow beneath her skin was alive and well.

"This is definitely worse than I expected," she murmured, bemused by the devastation. "Why don't you go grab a shower while I clean up."

After tossing her duffel bag into the empty bedroom, Lani put in earbuds and set to work putting the kitchen back together. Given that the theft had happened electronically, they could've been looking for a thumb drive and something that small could be anywhere. She swept scattered pasta and cereal into the trash and loaded the dishes and drinkware back into the cabinets. Sorting the silverware into the drawers took some time and as she worked, Lani couldn't help but wonder if the investigators had left the mess as a warning to Asher or if they'd had a limited amount of time to complete a thorough search.

She didn't notice Asher had returned until a light tap on her shoulder caused her to whirl around. He was standing right there, inches away, smelling of soap and minty toothpaste. Her brain went off-kilter as she stared at his lips, moving as they formed words she couldn't hear because…

He plucked her left earbud free and before she could make a grab for it, he'd fitted it into his ear. One eyebrow shot up as he listened to the song.

"I thought you only listened to Lowercase when you were worried about something."

His question was the yummy center of a raspberry-filled donut. Her mouth watered as if the sugary-sweetness flowed across her taste buds. How was it possible that he'd remembered her obscure taste in music after all this time?

"It helps me think." Lowercase was a music genre built around unheard ambient sounds.

"What are you thinking about?"

Lani held her hand out for the earbud, not wanting him to read anything into tonight's musical choice. His fingertips grazed her palm as he dropped the one he'd taken back into her keeping. Weathering the zing of pleasure at the contact, she popped both earbuds back into their case and slid it into her jacket pocket.

"This case. My next steps."

"You always have a plan, don't you?" He sounded resigned.

"It beats running around without direction, hoping something will develop."

"If you plan for everything, nothing will surprise you." He spun her around and tugged the elastic band down her ponytail, freeing her long hair. "I've really missed this," he murmured, threading his fingers through the dark curtain, fanning it over her shoulders. Several strands spilled over her cheeks, tickling her skin. "Your hair is like satin. I've never known anything like it."

She stood transfixed as he gathered her hair together and then proceeded to separate the strands into three sections. The gentle pull as he began braiding launched her into the past. The first time he'd done this for her she'd been surprised by his skill. He'd explained that while a polo horse's mane was shaved to keep it from interfering with the reins, the tails were braided and taped up for competition.

"There you go," he murmured, securing the bottom of the braid and giving an affectionate little tug the way he always did. "Ready for bed."

With her skin awash in goose bumps, Lani turned to face him. They were standing so close. As he leaned into her space, she gathered soft folds of his T-shirt, clutching the material between trembling fingers, needing something to ground her.

Cupping the back of her neck, he lowered his forehead until it was touching hers. "Thank you."

These weren't the words she'd been expecting him to say and frustration spiked.

"Asher." His name whispered out of her in protest, in longing. "Please stop thanking me."

"I can't," he murmured. "You're the only one who's helping me."

"I'm on a case. That's all there is to it." Yet even as she restated her purpose, her spine arched ever so slightly to bring her torso into contact with his. After an instant of contact, her breasts grazing his chest, she retreated.

This was madness. She had to stop this. To back away. But with his breath caressing her heated skin, she couldn't move. All it would take for their lips to come together was the slightest shift from either of them.

Temptation gnawed at her common sense. Her whole body ached with longing. She hadn't been celibate in the years since they'd parted, but no man awakened her hunger like Asher. It wasn't fair that his body could drive her wild with pleasure when his temperament clashed with everything she believed in.

Tingles shot down her spine as the tips of his fingers caressed her nape, moved along the side of her neck. Lani nerves sang. Desire moved through her like a ghost, terrifying her. How long had they been standing here like this? Seconds? Minutes? Time blurred when Asher touched her.

Kissing him would set a bad precedent. Her professionalism was a press of lips away from being thrown out the window. On the other hand, her job was to find the festival funds. A kiss hinted that her belief in his guilt was fading. Pretending to be on his side could convince him to trust her. What happened after she figured out where Asher had hidden the money was a problem for the future.

"Lani." The low throb in his voice intensified the ache blooming between her thighs.

"Yes?"

As he grazed his knuckles along her jaw, her lips parted in anticipation and her breath rushed out in agitated puffs as every nerve in her body went on full alert. He set his thumb beneath her chin, a promise of what came next. Craving a barely-there brush of her lips against his, she rose on tiptoe just the tiniest bit. She'd lost control of her purpose. But instead of a kiss that curled her toes and inspired her to dance in the moonlight, he planted his lips against her forehead.

"See you in the morning."

Lani reeled back a step and cleared her throat, blathering out the first thing that popped into her mind. "Sure. I'll be here when you get up."

"Sleep well."

Before he walked away, his dark eyes searched hers, and a small perceptive smile tugged at the corners of his lips. If her skin weren't already on fire, she was certain she'd be flushing scarlet beneath his knowing look. She'd thought to play him and instead he'd expertly turned the tables on her. Lani sighed. She'd been a fool to suppose a single kiss would propel Ash to confess his guilt and spill his guts. She was playing with fire letting the old chemistry between them ignite once more. Yet the tactic could still work if she could manage to act the part without getting sucked in.

Five years ago she'd been slow to trust Asher, but eventually his persistence and irresistible sex appeal had worn her down.

Once her hormones had seized the wheel, they'd driven her heart straight into a solid brick wall of misery.

This time, while she might be too wise to tumble head over heels for his effortless charm and handsome face, if she kept missing signs and misinterpreting signals, she could be in way too deep before she knew what hit her.

Despite not having slept at all in the jail cell the night before, Asher lay in the middle of his king-size bed, hands tucked beneath his head, ankles crossed, eyes tracing shadows on the ceiling. He'd retreated to his bedroom a couple hours ago, but adrenaline still surged through his veins, keeping him awake.

Lani Li was here. In his home. Sleeping ten strides from where he lay. The thrill of it kept his exhaustion at bay. He pictured her curled on her side, long braid coiled around her throat, her thick straight lashes a dark smudge against her ivory cheeks.

Not one thing about her had changed in the last five years. She continued to be the most intense, uptight, no-nonsense female he'd ever met. Except in bed where uptight and no-nonsense had given away to curious and naughty.

He'd been her first. The shock that delivered to his system had cemented her as the most memorable woman he'd ever had in his bed.

His lips still tingled from the silken heat of her skin when he'd kissed her forehead. They'd both been on the verge of moving too fast, of losing themselves in the fierce chemistry between them. Last time she'd been an innocent and he'd won her by awakening her sensual appetites. And then he'd lost her because he'd failed to treat her heart with the same care.

Asher hadn't realized how much he'd missed her until she'd appeared in front of his jail cell. Probably because after they'd ended things, he'd gone out of his way to purge her from his system.

With his thoughts filled with Lani, he finally fell asleep and woke with her foremost in his mind late the next morning. From the position of the light, he could tell it was mid to late morning. Reaching toward the nightstand for his phone, he remembered the police still had it. Cursing, he sat up and noticed the scent of coffee mingling with bacon. His stomach growled, reminding him that he'd skipped dinner the night before.

Pulling on worn jeans and a black polo shirt, he shuffled into the open-concept kitchen and living room and spied Lani at the kitchen island, typing away on her laptop.

"You made breakfast," he murmured unnecessarily, checking out the pan on the stove. "Have you already eaten?"

She didn't look up from her computer. "Hours ago."

"I didn't sleep at all the night before." He clamped down on further excuses and poured a cup of coffee, topping hers off in the process. After doctoring his cup, he pushed the sugar and creamer in her direction.

The eggs were freshly cooked and exactly as he liked them. His heart bumped against his ribs as he surveyed the scrambled eggs with fried onions and cheddar cheese melted through. He finished them off in record time and stood watching her work, gnawing on the final piece of thick-cut bacon.

"Stop staring at me," Lani muttered, picking up the coffee cup near her elbow and sipping the strong brew.

"Why?" He ran hot water over the pan and dishes before sliding them into the dishwasher. "You're the most interesting thing around."

"You can stop right there. I'm not susceptible to flattery."

"The fact that you felt the need to tell me that makes me think otherwise." He sent his gaze trailing over her features. She was even more beautiful than she'd been five years earlier. "And I'm not trying to flatter you. It's the truth. You fascinated me from the moment I first laid eyes on you."

"Don't confuse what happened between us five years ago to what's going on between us today. You are a *job*. Nothing more. I bailed you out because I need you to tell me where you stashed the money."

He was pondering how long she would stick around before his inability to provide the information she needed would cause her to give up on him…again…when she let out an impatient huff.

"Shouldn't you be doing something productive right now?" She jerked her head, indicating the apartment's front door.

He had horses he could exercise, but they would keep for a little while longer.

"I thought you needed my help with your case."

"Not right this second."

Coming around to her side of the island, he leaned his forearm on the cool countertop and peered at her laptop screen. Their shoulders bumped and he hid a grin as she shifted away. Obviously his presence bothered her. He could work with that.

"You are always so single-minded. At first, I thought that was just a cute personality quirk until I got to know you better. Then I realized how incredibly sexy your intense focus could be."

He'd barely finished speaking when she slapped the laptop closed and slid off the barstool.

"To be clear," she said, sliding the computer into a protective sleeve, "I am not here because I have any interest in starting up anything with you again. Let's just keep things between us professional."

"I don't see why I should have to do that. It's not as if I'm a client or anything."

"I'm investigating you," she reminded him.

"You're looking for the missing festival funds and trying to discover the real story. That puts us on the same side. Nothing wrong with hooking up with a fellow truth-seeker, is there?"

"Hooking up…?" Outrage crackled in her voice. "Don't even get me started on how wrong it is."

"You used to find me irresistible."

"You had your moments." She slipped into the same blazer she'd worn the day before and slung a tote bag over her shoulder, signaling her plans to leave. "Your situation was completely different back then."

Meaning that he might have been a *frat boy* but, as far as she knew, he hadn't been a criminal. Was his appearance of guilt all that stood between them? Would she relent once it became clear he hadn't stolen any money? Or should he get her back into his bed so she'd be motivated to clear him? Either way he would win. Cleared of all wrongdoing and Lani as his lover once more.

The whole thing seemed so simple until he remembered the strong evidence mounted against him. Just because he hadn't stolen from the festival, didn't mean he wouldn't go to jail for the theft. So far, his denials hadn't convinced anyone of his innocence. Nor should he expect to be taken at his word. Buying that damning house in his name in the Maldives had been clever. Somebody was setting him up. But who? Was it possible that someone had stolen his identity? He recalled Lani's reaction to his unlocked door. Maybe it wasn't far-fetched. But how did he go about proving something like that? No doubt she had the resources to follow the money. But how did he steer her to look for whoever had framed him when she was so convinced he was the bad guy?

"Where are you off to?" he asked.

"I have to meet a new client."

Asher loathed the idea of being left all alone with his problems. "Can I come along?" Even as he offered her his most-winning smile, he felt like a puppy begging to go for a car ride.

"No."

He strode into the kitchen and selected the largest knife in the drawer. Lani watched him through narrowed eyes as he set his foot on the counter and slid his finger beneath the strap that kept the electronic monitor on his ankle.

"What do you think you're doing?" Lani's voice rang with annoyance.

"I suffer from separation anxiety," he declared, carrying the dog metaphor beyond the absurd. "There's no telling what I'll get up to if you leave me alone here."

"Don't be ridiculous," she snapped, but her eyes remained glued to the knife. "You are perfectly fine on your own."

"Normally." He tested the edge of the blade with his thumb. A line of red appeared. Damn, it was sharper than he'd expected. "But I'm under a great deal of stress at the moment and I might do something completely rash without someone to keep an eye on me. Like maybe remove this monitor." He paused. "How much is my bail?"

"A hundred thousand." She ground out the number between clenched teeth.

"That's a lot. And you're responsible for me, right?"

Her nostrils flared as she sucked in a sharp breath. "Asher."

"Let me come along and I swear I won't be any trouble."

"Your middle name is trouble," she muttered. "Fine. I'll call and let the people monitoring you know that we're heading to Dallas."

"I'll put on some shoes."

Ten minutes later they were speeding toward Dallas with Lani behind the wheel and Asher studying her profile. She was trying to appear impassive, but her tight lips betrayed her inner turmoil.

"So, how come you're a private investigator?" he said, breaking the stony silence between them. "What happened to becoming a fed?"

"I got in." Her knuckles turned white as she clutched the steering wheel. "But in the course of my training, the amount of gender discrimination I encountered was more than I could stand. The good ol' boy network is alive and well at the FBI. Eighty percent of the trainees discharged prior to graduation are women and that's mostly because the people in charge dismiss mistakes made by male trainees as isolated incidents and declare them to be retrainable at a disproportionately higher rate than their female trainee counterparts."

"I'm sorry," he murmured, hearing the pain she was trying to mask with a clinical recitation of facts. "I know that was important to you."

So important that she'd chosen to pursue the dream over him.

"Tell me more about your firm,"

"I started it two years ago after finishing up with my master's degree. I worked with an investigator for a year before striking out on my own."

"You must be doing pretty well."

A shadow passed over her face before she mustered an off-handed shrug. "I'm doing okay."

But not as well as she'd like to be doing. Asher tapped his fingers on his thigh. His restless nature intensified when he was stressed or bored. Usually being around Lani calmed him, but he'd picked up on her tension and found himself uneasily pondering why she hadn't pursued law enforcement the way she'd intended.

"What sort of investigations do you do?"

"I've made a name for myself as a financial investigator. Divorces. Fraud. Embezzlement." Her gaze twitched his direction at the last word.

"You carry a gun," Asher pointed out. "Is there a lot of violence in financial investigations? I would've figured it would be done by being in an enclosed room with a computer."

"I do what needs to be done. I have a technical guy that does contract work for me, a cyber specialist who can get all sorts of information."

"Legally?"

A muscle jumped in her jaw. "If you're asking whether he can dig into everything you do online, then the answer is yes. There aren't too many secrets that escape Donovan."

"So, he's looking into me." He paused, giving her room to answer, but when she remained silent, he continued, "When you find out that I'm an open book with no secrets at all, will you trust me then?"

"*Trust* is a word I don't use lightly when it comes to you."

"But if you don't find anything," he persisted, "you'll have to believe me when I tell you I had nothing to do with the missing money."

"Or you're just real clever."

Asher gave a wry snort. "Well, at long last I have something to crow about. Lani Li just called me clever."

She shot him a look. "You make it sound like I think you're stupid. That's never been the case. What I think you are is underachieving."

He winced at her blunt, if mostly accurate, declaration. As a teenager, when he'd failed to win his adoptive father's approval, frustration had led to resentment. The things Asher had a passion for, activities he excelled at—polo, extreme sports, playing the stock market—were never going to impress Rusty.

Yet deep down he still clung to the hope that one day the impossible old man would be proud of his adopted son. It was part of what had prompted Asher to switch gears and take a job he hated with The Edmond Organization. But as the months went by and Rusty was as indifferent as ever, Asher realized he'd made a mistake.

Maybe if his dad had lived and Asher could've had a father who loved him unconditionally, he might have had a solid foundation to build something out of his life. Often he'd wished for a positive paternal figure who'd listen to him and offered advice based on what he enjoyed doing. Instead, Rusty had ignored or criticized him in turns. With support, he might've been able to focus on what he loved. To fully commit instead of fighting against other people's expectations and always falling short.

"You're right about that," Asher said, not letting his angst slip into his tone. "Ask anyone in the family. I'm the quintessential underachiever."

"You don't seem thrilled to be working at The Edmond Organization," she said. "So, why are you doing it?"

"Rusty got tired of supporting me and decided to give me the choice of working for the company or being cut off." At least that's what everyone assumed was going on because that was part of the bargain he'd made with Rusty.

"Let me get this straight." She took her eyes off the road and speared him with a dubious look. "You gave up polo and came to work for the company in order to keep your lifestyle intact?"

"Seems like the obvious choice, don't you think?"

She didn't react to his flippant tone. "Obvious, maybe, but you don't seem happy."

"Since when are you an expert on what makes me happy?" he shot back, still pained by her blunt opinion of him all those years earlier.

What made the sting so much sharper is that she hadn't been wrong. He'd loved playing polo, but he hadn't played up to his abilities. He hadn't had to with Rusty's money backing him.

"I'm not," she said, her voice somewhat softening with regret. "I'm sorry I said that. I don't know you at all and have no business making assumptions."

"No, I'm sorry." He rubbed his chest where a tight knot had formed. Damn. "It's just that I never imagined our reunion happening because I was accused of embezzlement and that you'd believe I was guilty."

"Wait." She frowned in confusion. "You imagined that we'd have a reunion?"

"Sure."

"Unbelievable," she muttered, tossing an indignant look his way. "Then why haven't I heard from you in five years?"

Three

Lani breathed slowly in and out through her nose, struggling against the anguish that had just blindsided her. Damn it. Why had she asked that ridiculous question? Now the infuriating man would think it bothered her that they'd never reconnected.

"I don't have a good answer," Asher admitted, sounding more subdued than he had a moment earlier.

"Of course you don't."

Why couldn't she stop being surprised when he disappointed her? After all, she'd traveled to Royal to investigate him for embezzling millions of dollars.

"Did you want me to?"

"I…" Had she?

Lani's heart began to race. Once upon a time she'd prided herself on being straightforward and honest with people. Experience had taught her that this tactic didn't always produce the results she desired. Bottom line? She learned to mislead people in her pursuit of the truth or justice for her clients.

Kingston Blue had chosen her because of her past romantic connection with Asher. Was it wrong to take advantage of that to get him to trust her? If she appeared to believe he was inno-cent, maybe he'd drop his defenses and slip up.

"Well?" he prompted.

"It would've been nice to hear from you," she admitted, keep-ing her tone from revealing her inner conflict.

"Really?" He practically vibrated with curiosity. "The way things ended, I thought you'd be happy never to hear from me again."

"Yes…well." She couldn't give in immediately or he'd be suspicious. He had to work for it.

"You were pretty mad the last time we talked," he reminded her.

"You told me a long-distance thing between us would never work after I told you I thought I was falling in love you, and then when I asked how you felt about me, you said you liked me, but didn't think it was that serious between us." Acutely aware of Asher's gaze on her, Lani stared straight ahead and resisted the urge to glance his way. She focused on calm thoughts to reduce the heat scorching her cheeks as she revisited the humiliating scene. "And then you said it wasn't your intention to upset me."

"See, I was right. You are still mad at me."

"For pulling that typical guy crap and turning the whole dis-agreement back on me? You bet I am!" Her temper flared. "As if I was being unreasonable because I wanted to keep things going."

"Even though it would never have worked?"

Lani released a frustrated breath. "We could've at least tried." But agreeing to attempt a long-distance relationship would mean he had feelings for her and that had obviously not been the case.

"What can I do to make it up to you?"

He could tell her where the money went. "Not a damned thing."

"I don't believe that."

"Really. I don't want you to make anything up to me. We went our separate ways five years ago and it was for the best. In fact,

I should thank you. Dragging things out in an effort to make it work and then failing would've been a lot harder in the end."

"Lani…"

She gave her head a vigorous shake to keep him from saying something that would make her wonder…was there a way they could find their way to each other this time?

"Let's just keep the past where it belongs and focus on keeping things professional between us."

To her relief, Asher lapsed into silence and focused his attention on the landscape speeding past them. Lani let out an inaudible sigh.

Why was she surprised to be no closer to figuring out what made him tick than she had been all those years ago? Back then, little had seemed to bother him. The only thing that seemed to get under his skin was the way his adoptive father treated him with such indifference and even when she'd asked him about it, Asher had shrugged it off as Rusty's issue, not his.

Asher was an expert at putting up a good front, never admitting anything was wrong, never asking for help. His reluctance to dwell on anything that made him uncomfortable had made it hard for them to develop the sort of intimate connection Lani craved. Not that this stopped her from falling deeper under his spell with each day that passed. And yet, despite his unwillingness to share how his father's death had affected him, she sensed that the loss left him unsure how to let people in.

Maybe if he'd opened up to her, shown that he needed her, she might not have given up on him so easily. But she couldn't figure out where she fit in his life and in the end she'd let him go.

Which had relieved her parents to no end. They'd been afraid she'd put off her education to run around the world with some rich, entitled polo player, thus ruining her life. While staying on the path she'd laid out for herself had been sensible, her decision wasn't without regret. Especially after her dreams of a career in the FBI had abruptly ended. Add in her struggles to build her business, and she sometimes wondered if she could've been happy following Asher from Argentina to England and all over the US.

One thing was for sure, she never imagined he'd take a position at the family organization. She knew he must have hated being tied down and yet didn't Rusty's threat to cut him off if he quit feed perfectly into a motive for Asher to steal the money? The amount that had gone missing would've funded his polo playing for many years. Or had he planned to roam the globe in search of thrilling adventures?

Yet Asher made it sound like he was relying on the Edmond family fortune when she'd noticed that he'd moved up the ranks and started doing really well as a professional polo player. His Twitter feed reflected numerous endorsements and photo shoots he'd done, capitalizing on his good looks. He'd engaged in a fair amount of philanthropic work, as well. So why was he promoting the impression that he'd been barely getting by without Rusty's money?

"Tell me something about the client you're meeting," Asher prompted, pulling Lani from her thoughts.

For a moment she thought of refusing, but talking about her work beat brooding over this man. "She came to me because her husband is cheating on her and she wants to make sure she has a clear financial picture to take to her divorce lawyer."

"I don't know why men do that."

"Do what?" she quizzed, shooting a sidelong glance his way. "Get married, cheat or hide money?"

"Get married and then cheat." Was he thinking about Rusty who'd been married four times—once for three years to Asher's mother—and was currently single and definitely mingling? "What's the point of agreeing to love someone 'til death do you part only to change your mind a few years later?"

"Is that why you never got married?" she found herself asking.

"I never got married because playing professional polo kept me from settling down with the right woman."

Was he talking in generalities or had his heart been claimed before or since they'd been together? The question raised all the insecurities she'd experienced that summer. The vividness of her reaction was like standing next to a warning siren when it went off. Her muscles twitched in response, sending a pulse of adrenaline through her.

"You seem to have settled down now, so why haven't you reached out?"

"Who says I haven't?"

"Is she in a relationship or married?"

"Neither. But she doesn't really trust that I'm not the same man she once knew."

Lani wasn't sure how to answer him. Nor could she figure out why she was pouring lemon juice on an old cut that had never fully healed. At least she knew why he hadn't wanted to try a long-distance relationship with her. Obviously he'd never gotten over the woman he'd once loved.

"You should get in touch with her. She might surprise you."

"She might," Asher murmured, his expression pensive.

With the mood between them growing incredibly awkward, Lani was thrilled that her office was only five minutes away. She pulled into the underground parking garage and slipped into her dedicated spot. Now that she and Asher had arrived, Lani was quite sure that agreeing to let him tag along had been the wrong decision.

"There's a café and lounge on the first floor where you can wait," she said, snagging her laptop out of the back seat and slipping from the SUV. "My meeting shouldn't take too long."

"Do you mind if I come along? I'd like to see your office."

"It would be better if you didn't."

Asher pointed to his ankle monitor. "Separation anxiety, remember?"

Since Lani couldn't trust him to refrain from doing something that might blow back on her, she had no choice but to agree. And she couldn't ignore that she wanted to show off a little. The spot she'd chosen for her firm was north of downtown Dallas in a glass-enclosed building with great views. Her office was on the eighth floor. She shared a spacious waiting area with a lawyer and an accountant and had done work for both of them in the year since she'd moved in.

"This is me," she declared unnecessarily a few minutes later, unlocking the door to the dual-office suite and making her way down the hall.

Entering her airy workspace with its glass walls and north-facing windows, she circled her desk and woke up her computer to check if any email had come in during the drive from Royal.

Asher glanced around the space, noting the light spilling in the floor-to-ceiling windows. The room was spacious enough to accommodate a table with four chairs, her desk and a pair of guest chairs.

"Who works there?"

Lani looked up. His attention had shifted toward the empty workspace they'd passed. "No one at the moment." Seeing his curiosity hadn't been satisfied, she sighed. "When I leased the space, I'd hoped to expand. Add an associate. I still plan to. It's just that I don't have enough business at the moment." Hopefully that would change once she completed this job for Kingston Blue. "So, now that you've seen my office..." She hoped he'd take the hint and leave her to await her client in peace. "Like I said, there's a café downstairs. Or you can sit in the waiting room."

"Why not there?" He indicated the empty office. "No one's using it."

Before Lani could argue, a woman appeared in the open doorway from the waiting room. Shooting Asher a withering glare, Lani smoothed her face and stepped forward to greet the newcomer.

"Hello, I'm Lani Li."

"Mika Sorenson."

Sensing that he'd already pushed his luck too far with Lani, Asher waited until the women were seated before he popped into Lani's office.

"Can I get you anything?" he offered. "Water? Coffee? Soda?" He'd spied a small interior room with a copier, storage and a beverage cooler.

"Nothing for me." Mika gave him an appreciative smile. "Thank you."

"Ms. Li?" The way her eyes flashed, Asher could tell he'd gone too far.

"I'm fine." Her teeth were firmly clenched as she added, "Thank you."

With a smirk Lani's client did not see, Asher ducked out of the room and headed straight into the empty workspace. Because the building was going for a sophisticated modern aesthetic with industrial vibes, glass walls divided this office from the larger one where Lani sat. Asher settled back in the office chair with his back to Lani, and strained to hear the conversation. The women spoke in subdued voices, making it impossible to discern more than a word here or there. Asher had resigned himself to the fact that he wasn't going to learn anything, and was about to head down to the café when a tall man wearing an expensive suit and a stormy expression strode into the office.

When the man's furious gaze locked on Mika Sorenson in Lani's office and his fingers curled into fists, Asher was on his feet and standing in the man's path before the guy had taken more than two steps.

"Can I help you?" Asher demanded in a tone that said he had no intention of being the least bit cooperative.

"That's my wife."

"Okay."

Before Asher could say more, Sorenson's red face contorted in rage and he made as if to charge into Lani's office and take his bad temper out on both women. He set his hand on the man's shoulder, determined to get the guy out of there, but Sorenson was completely focused on his wife.

"You stupid bitch," the man yelled, pushing his weight against Asher in an effort to power past him. "Who the hell do you think you are hiring a private investigator to spy on me?"

The situation was deteriorating fast and Asher had to get the guy out of there. He caught the man's arm in a tight grip. "Let's go."

Although Asher and Sorenson were the same height, the other man lacked Asher's strength. But what Sorenson lacked in muscle, he made up for in outrage.

"Who the hell are you? Let go of me."

"You need to leave," Asher said.

"The hell I do. I'm not going anywhere without my wife."

Asher didn't need to look over his shoulder to know that Mika Sorenson was afraid. And that Lani was not. Years of playing polo had given him the ability to widen his senses and track the ever-changing dynamic of a game where eight players, each riding a thousand-pound horse and swinging a three-foot mallet, all raced after a fist-sized ball. He knew Lani was going to get in the middle of this scuffle and that she might get hurt. Sorenson needed to go before that happened.

"Call security," Asher advised Lani, his gaze never leaving the other man.

Sorenson didn't seem to hear. "Get out of my way."

Keeping his tone mild, Asher responded, "I can't do that."

When the man's fist came toward his face, Asher leaned out of the way. Off balance from the wild swing, Sorenson wasn't at all ready when his opponent snagged his foot and used his own momentum to send him toppling to the floor. Asher winced when Sorenson's head bounced off the hardwood flooring. Convinced Sorenson wasn't about to jump up and go for round two, Asher glanced toward Lani.

Her eyes had gone wide as they bounced from him to the man on the ground. Already adrenaline surged through his veins from the altercation, but seeing the unbridled hunger in Lani's mink-brown gaze, his whole body went up in flames.

"Security," he rasped, wanting nothing more than to take her in his arms and claim the passion parting her soft lips. "You can thank me later." The declaration was both a warning and a promise. Unlike the previous night, there would be no chaste kiss on her forehead. He intended to accept her gratitude in spades.

In the end, with some sense knocked into him, Sorenson left on his own, escorted to the elevator by Asher. When he returned to Lani's office, a white-faced Mika Sorenson was making an appointment with a divorce attorney and Lani was arranging a safe place for her client to temporarily stay.

Lani was standing at her office window, staring out at the storm blowing out of the west when Asher returned from walking Mika to her car in the parking garage. Lightning flashed and the building rumbled as thunder rolled over them. Asher crossed to stand beside her, noting that her tension was as charged as the atmosphere outside.

"Thank you," she muttered, sounding not one bit convincing.

"Oh, you're going to have to do better than that."

She turned toward him, eyes fierce, arms crossed. "Fine. Thank you very much."

Asher snaked his left arm around her waist and brought her up against him hard. "Better," he coaxed, his tone lifting on the latter syllable.

"I don't know what more you want."

"Oh, I think you do." Dragging his knuckles over her flushed cheek, he lowered his head until his lips hung a whisper above hers. "I want you to say it."

"Say what?" The mutinous line of her mouth wavered even as her muscles softened, bringing her pliant curves into sizzling contact with his hard planes.

"Say that you were glad I was here to take care of you and your client today. How having me around was a good thing."

"I could've handled him just fine." She let loose a shocked

gasp as he slid his palm up her spine, wrapped his fingers around her ponytail and gave it a sharp tug. "But I'm glad you were here so I didn't have to."

"Better."

The uneven cadence of her breath matched his as he covered her mouth with his in a deep kiss meant to remind her how they'd once burned up the nights. Electricity danced down his spine as his stomach somersaulted. Rain battered the window beside them. And lightning flashed once more, this time behind his eyes as her tongue darted forward to tangle with his. Her sultry moan filled his ears while her warm skin scented the air with roses and jasmine. She lifted her fingertips to his face and ran them over his stubbly cheek. He loved when she touched him like this.

This made sense. Her lips. Kissing her. Feeling once again like some part of him was complete. Why did it only happen when she was in his arms? Everything inside him quieted, making room for this amazing explosion of fulfillment and joy.

Lani angled her head, taking him deeper into her mouth, breathing him in as her fingers tunneled through his hair, nails digging into his scalp. Her lashes were a butterfly kiss against his skin as she pulled him closer, pressing her breasts into his chest and sliding her knee up his thigh as if by wrapping herself around him, they could meld and become one.

Asher lowered his hand to her hip and was seconds away from cupping her butt and lifting her off her feet when an annoying buzzing sound began. Lani noticed it too and rolled her head back, disengaging from the kiss.

"Ignore it." Issuing the command, he fanned his fingers over her lower back to keep his iron-hard erection firmly pressed into her slowly rocking hips. "Stay just like this," he murmured, in awe of her power over him.

"We shouldn't be…" She twisted free of him, her chest heaving as if she'd finished a mile-long sprint. Scrambling to where her phone was still buzzing madly on her desk, she raked a trembling hand over the tendrils that had escaped her neat ponytail. "Yes?"

Asher leaned back against the cool glass window and shuddered while another boom of thunder rolled through the building. Or was that just the reverberation of his pounding heart? He couldn't catch his breath. The shock of that kiss. Lani's ardent response. How lust had transformed her into living flame... It was all so *exhilarating.* He'd forgotten how intoxicatingly blissful kissing her could be.

He loved her complexities. Straightforward and practical in her role as an investigator and her pursuit of her career goals. Recklessly passionate when it came to her heart. She'd trusted him when she shouldn't have and doubted him when he'd been most honest with her.

While she settled behind the desk and started typing on her keyboard, he let his gaze roam over her lips. She was gnawing on the lower one and he had to look away as sweat prickled his skin.

"Is everything okay?" he asked as she concluded her call.

She'd sat back, narrowed eyes glued to the computer screen. In the space of ten minutes, she'd cooled to focused professionalism. Meanwhile his defenses were down and his anticipation was sky-high.

"Everything's fine." She did a slow blink and seemed to return from whatever deep dive her brain had done. "Are you ready to go back to Royal?"

"I thought maybe while we're in Dallas we could have dinner." Somewhere romantic and far away from the accusing eyes in Royal so he could lavish his charm on her and see if he could soften her attitude toward him.

She glanced at her phone. "We really need to get back. I already have dinner plans."

"Here in Dallas?" A spike of jealousy caused his voice to harden. Until this moment he hadn't considered that she might be involved with someone. But if she was, would she have kissed him like that?

"No," she said. "In Royal."

"Something having to do with the investigation?" With their passionate embrace sparking his baser instincts, Asher was feeling possessive and didn't come off nearly as nonchalant as he'd hoped.

"At the moment the investigation is my main focus."

A non-answer. And from the look on her face, all she was planning to give.

Four

Lani's dinner engagement with Rusty Edmond had stirred a fair amount of interest amongst the members of the Texas Cattleman's Club. Given his family's connection to the Soiree on the Bay debacle, she'd been a little surprised that the oil tycoon wanted to meet in such a public venue. She'd thought he'd prefer to keep a low profile and share a quiet meal somewhere discreet. Instead, as the hostess led her to a table in the middle of the TCC's large dining room, Lani realized that she would be a headliner performing on the center stage.

Great.

It made sense that a man like Rusty Edmond wouldn't be chased away by some negative gossip about his family. No doubt he'd ruffled a lot of feathers while amassing his enormous fortune. What did he care if people whispered about him behind his back?

"Ms. Li." Rusty stood as she approached, his cordial smile not reaching the winter gray of his assessing gaze.

"Mr. Edmond," she countered, wondering if he remembered he'd invited her to call him Rusty the last time they'd met.

The nickname struck her as a blatant attempt to make the man approachable. It was ridiculous. Russell Edmond Sr. was an intimating man by nature. One of the richest oilmen in Texas, he had a mercurial temperament and a roving eye when it came to women.

"Call me Rusty," he rumbled in warm tones, his eyes taking in her measure, lingering a little too long on her breasts for Lani's comfort. Which made her doubly glad she'd resisted the impulse to wear something more flattering. He stuck out his hand as she drew within reach. "May I call you Lani?"

"Of course." As her hand was swallowed in his grip, she was struck by the man's imposing physical presence, as well as the aggressive potency of his personality. "Thank you for agreeing to meet me."

"I understand you bailed my son out of jail."

Okay, so they were diving right in. "I've been hired to investigate where the missing money has gone." *And who took it.*

"Have you asked Asher?" Rusty's expression gave her no clue to whether this was a serious question or if the man was being droll.

"Yes. He claims he didn't steal the money." Lani paused for a beat, waiting for the older man's reaction. "I'm not sure he gains anything by taking it."

Rusty snorted. "He gains millions of dollars."

"Yes, but the theft was so obviously done by him. Why hadn't he fled before the funds were discovered to be missing? He used part of the money to buy a house in the Maldives. Surely he had to know that would make him the prime suspect."

The waitress stopped by their table and took Lani's drink order. Rusty already had a mostly-empty crystal tumbler sitting in front of him and ordered another whiskey.

"So, you think Asher is innocent." A statement, not a question. "Even though he purchased a house in the Maldives."

"I'm not sure that he did. And he's not the only one with access to the festival accounts who needed money. You disinherited Ross."

Lani paid careful attention to how Rusty reacted to her pointing a finger at his biological son, unsurprised by the man's cold glare. The oil tycoon had cut off Ross several months ago after finding out he'd slept with an employee and fathered a son with her. The tension between Ross and Rusty had eased somewhat in recent weeks, but it was completely possible that Ross might've started skimming the festival funds after such a dramatic reversal in his fortune.

"My son isn't a thief."

Which son? Lani's heart clenched in sympathy for Asher.

"I'm just pointing out that Ross had means, motive and opportunity. And he could've misdirected the investigation so that all the evidence points to Asher."

"Are you trying to say that Asher was set up?"

"It's a possibility."

Skepticism rolled off Rusty. "You two dated a while back." His lips twisted into disdain. "Are you sure this isn't personal for you?"

Despite preparing to be asked this question, Lani's cheeks heated. The incendiary kiss she and Asher had shared earlier made any denial she might make now a big fat lie.

"I was hired to find the missing money. If the federal investigators believe Asher is guilty, they won't be following any other leads." Lani's gaze clashed with Rusty's wintery one. "If neither Asher nor Ross are guilty, do you have any idea who else might have stolen the funds?"

"I don't." Nor did Rusty Edmond look happy about that. He was a man of decisive action. It must be difficult for him to sit by and let the situation play out. He finished his drink as the waitress set the new tumbler before him and swept away the empty glass. "I recommend the rib eye."

Lani didn't order the eighteen-ounce bone-in steak. Instead she chose a center-cut filet mignon that melted in her mouth.

Five years ago Asher had brought her here for dinner. That night she'd been a starry-eyed girl unaccustomed to such lavish service and exquisite cuisine. Watching Rusty attack his own dinner with relish, Lani wondered if any of the Edmond family could survive without their cushy safety net of wealth and privilege.

Although her dinner companion kept turning the conversation away from any further talk of the failed festival or the tornado that had devastated Appaloosa Island the month before, Lani repeatedly circled back. From the way Rusty spoke about Ross, Gina and especially Asher, his pessimistic opinion of them predated any mishandling of Soiree on the Bay. Lani was utterly depressed by the time he waved away the waitress's attempts to list off the daily dessert specials.

She was gathering breath to thank the oil mogul for his time when someone approached their table. Lani recognized Ross's friend Billy Holmes from her preliminary research into everyone connected to the festival. The man's chiseled cheekbones, dark hair and assessing blue eyes combined into a face of arresting handsomeness. Maybe his long nose was a shade too narrow, the cant of his mouth a bit self-indulgent. But as he sized her up in turn, she sensed he knew how to work a room.

Rusty lit up as he and Billy exchanged greetings, startling Lani. She'd heard that Billy had Rusty's ear when his own children couldn't get his attention. Seeing the way the man oozed charm, she understood why Rusty liked him. And apparently so did many of the women. Lani spied four at nearby tables that gazed at Billy with a range of fondness and hunger.

As much as she'd have loved to stick around and ponder this fascinating rapport between the patriarch and his son's good friend, Lani realized her audience with Rusty Edmond had come to an end. Murmuring thanks for the meal, she headed for the exit, eager to share her thoughts with Asher.

But when she arrived back at the ranch, she discovered he wasn't in his apartment. Before panic seized hold, she decided to check the barn. Sure enough, she found him in a grooming stall running a brush over a gray gelding.

"How'd dinner with my father go?" he asked, his voice cool.

Lani winced. She should've known better than to keep quiet about her meeting with Rusty. No doubt her evasiveness had fortified the barriers between them. Maybe subconsciously that had been her plan. Their kiss had shaken her confidence. How could she do her job if emotion disrupted reason? Would she overlook something because she wanted him to be innocent? Worse, what if she found out he was guilty and couldn't bring herself to send him to jail?

"It went okay."

She picked up a brush and went to work on the opposite side of the horse, running the soft bristles over his shoulder and down his front leg.

"Is he the one who hired you to figure out where the money went?" He'd asked the question before and she'd refused to answer. Silence reigned between them for several uncomfortable seconds. "You don't want to talk about it."

"Not really."

As much as Lani wanted to tell Asher that she'd been hired by Kingston Blue, thinking his father had hired her was keeping Asher off balance and she needed whatever advantage she could get if she was going to find the money.

If he was actually responsible for the theft.

While they worked without further conversation, Lani couldn't stop her gaze from chasing the strong lines of Asher's cheekbones and the delectable curve of his lower lip. She shivered as that afternoon's kiss replayed in her mind. The same raw masculinity that had tantalized her five years ago was no less potent, nor had her susceptibility to it dimmed. He'd grown harder in the intervening years. Less indulged rich boy and more a man who wasn't happy with how his life was going.

It's what made him even more interesting. She'd prepared herself to resist his meaningless flirtation and dodge his sexual banter. The melancholy beneath his glib sophistication was more pronounced than ever. He hid it well, but most people probably didn't bother looking past his easy charm and playful humor. She'd trained herself to see into those in-between moments and easily detected the dissatisfaction that plagued him.

"I thought tomorrow I'd head to Appaloosa Island," she said, the idea having come to her on the drive back to the ranch. "I haven't seen the festival site."

"Neither have I."

"I'm surprised," she said. "Didn't you go check on the damage after the tornado hit?"

"No."

"Would you like to come along?"

She was surprised when he didn't answer right away. He'd always been restless and up for anything.

"I guess I'd better take advantage of my freedom for as long as I can."

Asher wasn't feeling particularly chatty during the three-hour car ride to Mustang Point, an elite waterside community with a large marina in Trinity Bay. Because Appaloosa Island was only accessible by helicopter and boat—a ferry crossed to the island daily—the Edmond family kept several boats for their own use.

The investigators had returned his car and Asher had insisted he drive. The luxury sedan was far more comfortable for a road trip than Lani's utilitarian SUV. Plus, with him behind the wheel, she could spend the trip working on her laptop. If she noticed his reserve, she gave no sign. Which, of course, only fueled his frustration.

Being investigated by his ex-lover was bad enough. That his father had been the one to hire her cut deep. And how could he talk to her about how betrayed he felt without plunging deep into the complex emotional crap that defined his relationship with Rusty?

Maybe he should just go ahead and tell her what was really going on. Why he'd quit polo and gone to work for The Edmond Organization. More than any time before, he wanted her to know the man he truly was. For her to choose to have faith in him. To recognize that not only was he innocent of stealing the festival funds, but that he would never in a million years stoop to something so low.

And what if he told her everything and it didn't change her perception? He sensed that it was habit for her to regard him with a jaundiced eye. As with his adoptive father, she found it easier to write him off. To her, he would remain "frat boy" and his pride rejected having to prove that he was no longer that guy.

They had lunch at the marina restaurant before heading to the dock. The forty-foot boat that Asher had been staying on when he first met Lani had been replaced by a sixty-foot model that handled like a dream. He keyed in the code to unlock the double-glass doors and swept his arm in a grand gesture for her to precede him inside. Far from looking pleased by his gallantry, she shot him a repressive frown before entering the comfortable cabin with panoramic views from the wraparound windows.

The sleek open space held a lounge area with a comfortable sectional couch and a large well-appointed kitchen with tons of countertop space for food prep and an eat-in banquette.

"Are you thirsty?" he asked, determined to play the part of a good host. "The boat is fully stocked with everything you could ever want."

Her eyebrow arched at that. "I'll take a sparkling water if you have it."

"I know we do." Practically everything Gina drank had to have bubbles. "We also have that jalapeño vodka you like so well. I make sure the boat is stocked with it. You know, just in case…"

Her lips parted as if she wanted to ask, *In case of what?* But she settled for shaking her head in disapproval before continuing to survey the elegant surroundings.

"This looks new," she murmured as he pulled out glasses, filling them with ice and a slice of lime.

Still annoyed that she'd had dinner with his father the night before and refused to tell him why or what they'd discussed, he shot back, "Is that your way of asking me if I used the festival funds to buy a new boat?"

"You need to take this more seriously." She regarded him steadily as he poured sparkling water over the ice. "You're in big trouble and flippant remarks like that are not making my job any easier."

He coped with stress by making light of things. *Never let them see you sweat.* No one knew the amount of anger, insecurity or frustration he'd bottled up over the years. But he'd learned that if you play the part of someone unbothered by problems, then those difficulties have less of a chance of wearing you down.

"I didn't steal the funds and the boat doesn't belong to me." Summoning a weary half smile, Asher held the glass out to her. "But you already know that." For several seconds the only sound in the space was the happy explosions of a hundred tiny bubbles. "I'm not the villain here."

He could probably say it a million times and she'd never believe him until the truth came out, proving his innocence. What he wouldn't give for someone, anyone—but *especially* her—to believe he wasn't a thieving asshole.

His patience was rewarded when she stepped forward to accept it and their fingers grazed, sending an electric current of longing through him. Lust flared, compelling and dangerous. If he took her in his arms and kissed her the way he wanted to, they would be naked and on the floor in minutes.

But passion was easy. It was the moments in between that made a relationship grow and flourish. Or fail miserably. Whatever came, he wanted a shot with Lani.

Reacting to his volatile mood, she sipped her water in silence.

"I mean," he continued mercilessly, "if I were to steal millions of dollars, I wouldn't spend it on a boat or a house in the Maldives. I'd choose someplace more interesting than some remote island to buy real estate."

Lani studied him. "I don't get you."

"I assure you, I am quite simple to understand."

"Maybe once." She spun away from him, gliding toward the open glass doors that led to the semi-circular couch off the back of the boat. "I'm not sure I believe that anymore."

Asher trailed after her. "What's changing your mind? Am I wearing you down with my incessant claims of innocence?"

Suddenly he saw the clever trap he'd made for himself. Although it was in his best interest to convince her that he hadn't stolen the money, as soon as he stopped being a suspect, she'd be off chasing new leads. And he wasn't ready to let her walk out of his life just yet.

"Never mind." She rubbed her temple. "I must be tired. I don't know what I'm saying anymore." Still, she gave him a long searching look before speaking again. "Should we be going?"

"Don't you want a tour of the yacht first?"

"It's a boat. I'm sure I can find my way around if I need to."

"There's two state rooms," he narrated as if she hadn't already shut him down. "You can have your pick, although I have to say the views from the one in the stern are much better."

She looked surprised, and then worried. "This is a day trip. Out and back. We're not staying here overnight."

"I thought it'd be fun." His smile was all innocence. "For old times' sake."

Bright color burned in her cheeks at his words even as outrage made her eyes snap in irritation. Her spine stiffened as she seemed to gather breath to deliver whatever scathing rebuttal she hoped would shut him down. His remark hadn't been the least bit suggestive, but she certainly took it that way. *Interesting.* Obviously she was remembering how things had been between them all those years before.

"Is there a problem?" He continued before she could argue.

"I mean we're living in close quarters at the ranch. It's not different if you're alone with me here, is it?"

"Of course not," she shot back. "I just thought we'd head to the festival site and then go back to Royal. I wasn't planning on making a night of it."

"It was a long drive. Let's just spend the night and head back tomorrow."

"I didn't pack for an overnight stay," she reminded him.

"Not to worry, Gina always keeps an assortment of clothes on board. I'm sure she wouldn't mind if you borrowed something."

"I guess we can spend the night." She gave in with a grimace, looking less sure of herself by the minute.

"Great." Asher didn't put too much energy into his voice, not wanting her to realize how delighted he was to have won this standoff. "I'll start the engine and then cast off the lines."

"I've got it."

Five years earlier they'd spent a lot of time together on the previous yacht and she was familiar with the routine. Still, Asher was surprised when she headed for the mooring lines and began removing each one from the cleats. He'd been out on a variety of boats with a lot of women, but none of them lifted a finger to help. They believed their contribution was to parade around in bikinis, providing eye candy. While he wasn't opposed to beautiful, scantily clad women, he'd always appreciated Lani's helpfulness. Just another way she stood out in his mind.

To his surprise, she came up to the bridge as he reversed the yacht out of the slip. One level above the lounge, the fly bridge came equipped with top-of-the-line electronics and offered impressive views. Asher registered disappointment as Lani settled into the spacious seating area to his left. Seriously, what had he expected? She wasn't about to come snuggle beside him the way she used to back in the day. Forcibly tamping down his emotions, he navigated out of the marina and pointed the sixty-foot yacht into the bay.

The distance from the marina to the festival site on Appaloosa Island was a quick fifteen-minute trip. They'd chosen to locate the event on the undeveloped side of the island, far from the resort where Asher and Lani had met for the first time and away from the expensive homes that lined the waterfront.

Despite his initial excitement over the festival, after the preliminary idea generation and brainstorming sessions, he'd left the organizing to others and focused on the vendors. He'd been involved in several charity events during his years of playing polo and endorsements were a big part of that. Plus, his family had rejected many of the suggestions he'd made about the location and vision for the festival, leaving him feeling less and less connected to the nuts-and-bolts aspect of organizing the event. When he'd stopped attending board meetings, no doubt his family had chalked it up to yet another time that Asher failed to follow through on something. But he had a hard time sticking with anything when his heart wasn't in it.

As the boat neared the festival grounds, his gaze swept over the ruin of what had been the hopes and dreams of so many. His stomach gave a sickening wrench. No wonder everyone hated him.

Five

As the boat idled past the festival site's devastation, Lani kept her attention fixed on Asher's face. Convinced she'd glimpse something that would establish he'd been guilty all along, her righteous triumph faded as his shock and horror never wavered. The torment in his eyes as he gazed over buildings wrecked by the tornado made her throat tighten.

The dock had been spared, but Asher made no attempt to head that way. Instead he moved parallel to shore and pushed a button on the control panel. A muffled thunk reached her ears and then the floor beneath her feet began to vibrate as the anchor chain emptied from the hold.

"What are you doing?" she asked, shivering at the grim set of his expression.

"Anchoring," came his clipped answer.

When they'd first met, she'd viewed Asher as a charming libertine, engaged in an unending pursuit of entertainment. And watching him now as he skillfully maneuvered the giant yacht, she was reminded of how in the early days of getting to know him, his easy confidence with everything he did had won her over. She was a woman whose self-reliance had been encouraged by her parents. And was used to doing things for herself. So, sitting back and relying on someone else for a change had been a unique and thrilling experience and one she still struggled with.

"There's no way we can tie up to that dock." His attention appeared fixed on the process of making sure the anchor latched onto the floor of the bay, but a frown appeared as he shot glances toward the island. "Even if I trusted that the storm hadn't damaged the dock, it wasn't built for boats this size. What happened to the one that could accommodate twenty or more yachts?"

The answer was so obvious that Lani just stared at Asher in bemusement. She couldn't process how genuinely baffled he looked. Her instincts told her he was utterly mystified, but how was that possible? He would've been involved with the festival organization from the start. Didn't he know what had been going on here?

"Or did they manage to build it and it was destroyed by the tornado?" He continued to voice his troubled thoughts out loud.

At moments like these, moments like when he lavished his attention on his string of polo horses, dedicating himself to their health and welfare, she questioned if he was as irresponsible as he seemed.

"As far as I know, this was the only dock that was ever built," Lani said, her voice gentler than she'd meant it to be.

Once he seemed satisfied that the anchor was secure, he shut off the motor and remained where he was, staring at the shore. "So many people were counting on the festival," he murmured. "We'd promised to fund Valencia Donovan's horse rescue charity with a portion of the proceeds from the festival ticket sales. She was going to expand her property and start an equine therapy program. And I know Rafe Cortez-Williams took out a second mortgage on his restaurant to invest in the festival." He screwed his eyes shut and rubbed his face. "With all the losses they're facing, it's selfish of me to think only about my problems. But

someone set me up. Someone close to me. I feel so betrayed."
The anguish in his voice tore at her.

"I'm sorry this is happening to you," she said, the words coming before she'd considered them.

Asher's dismay was getting to her. And that couldn't be allowed to happen. Feeling sorry for him was the wrong way to go. This was his fault, after all. *He* caused this problem when he stole the money. Which meant he didn't deserve her sympathy or support. He'd done a terrible thing and ruined countless lives.

Yet if this were true, why did she keep falling for his denials? If she was so convinced of his guilt, shouldn't she be able to see right through his excuses? Granted, it had been ages since she'd last seen him, but why would he have done something so obvious? He had to know he was going to get caught. Asher might be reckless, but he wasn't an idiot. What was his endgame? She recalled his reaction when she told him about the house in the Maldives. He'd genuinely looked clueless as to where that was.

"Come on."

"How are we going to get over there?" She looked at the thirty or so feet of open water between the boat and the dock.

"We could swim."

"I don't have a suit."

"I'm sure one of Gina's bikinis would fit you."

His gaze drifted down her body, a slow, lazy leer that made her skin pebble at the thought of his hands trailing over her flesh. Despite the afternoon's humidity, she shivered. It wasn't fair that the man could turn her on with a mere look. But the heat moving into her cheeks wasn't fired by irritation. It kindled as she recalled other afternoons when they'd swum together off these waters while golden sunlight sparkled on the blue surface. And she'd never forget that one night when they'd gone skinny-dipping, clad in nothing but moonlight. Asher had licked the cool salty water droplets off her naked breasts as he'd dipped his fingers into the slippery heat between her legs. The memory of that encounter hit her like a freight train and Lani's hands began to shake.

Coming here had been a bad idea. She'd brought him to the island to face reality. To show him the damage he'd caused. Instead, he'd reacted in a way that made him seem more victim than villain. She'd lost control of the situation and the only person learning a lesson here was her.

He was dangerous. To the people around him who he'd stolen from, and to her own peace of mind. She'd spent years telling herself that she'd been a fool to be taken in by Asher Edmond. Time and distance had allowed her to believe that she'd never be misled by him again. Yet here she was lost in the past, remembering only the good times and doubting what she knew to be true. That Asher had a knack for telling people what they wanted to hear and making them believe he was a better man than he actually was. Or was that just her wounded heart talking?

"Isn't there some sort of a dinghy we can take over to the island? I don't feel like swimming."

Asher regarded her silently for a moment. The lush sweep of his lashes shadowed his brown eyes, making his expression hard to read. Lani tried not to think about how much she loved that soft fringe tickling her skin or how the raspy glide of his stubble over the sensitive area where her shoulder and neck connected had driven her mad with desire. She'd been so weak back then, so susceptible to every sensation Asher visited upon her inexperienced body. Was it any wonder she'd fallen head over heels for him when he given her such pleasure? When every grace of his fingertips or the heat of his gaze could set off a maelstrom of unquenchable yearning.

"The dinghy it is," he said, his matter-of-fact tone at odds with the questing weight of his gaze.

When he turned away toward the ladder that descended from the fly deck to the main level, Lani sagged. Only as he disappeared below did she realize she'd been using all her strength to withstand the pull of longing he evoked.

Asher used a crane mounted on the bow to lower the dinghy into the water. As he worked, the wind caught the edges of his unbuttoned shirt and spread it wide. Lani ogled his lean, muscular torso, all too aware that the familiar surroundings were triggering long-buried emotions. Fighting to quell her rioting hormones, she joined Asher at the back of the boat where a swim platform extended off the stern. He'd maneuvered the small inflatable there and tied it to the structure.

"Give me your hand," he said. "The dinghy is a little unsteady."

She waved him off. "I've got this."

"You know," he began, his tone tight and impatient, "you could let me take care of you."

To her dismay, Lani's skin flushed. The first time they'd made love Asher had calmed her nerves by whispering, *Let me care of you.* And then he proceeded to do just that. She'd had a half-dozen orgasms that night, mind-blowing explosions of pleasure that he'd given her. Afterward, she'd been grateful to have been initiated into the physical act of love with that level of expertise. Unfortunately starting off with such an outstanding lover had its downside. Since then, numerous disappointing sexual experiences had followed with men who were not Asher.

Lani stiffened her spine, refusing to let him get to her again. How could she claim to be a professional if spending two days with her ex-lover turned her into a pile of needy mush?

Determined to avoid touching him again and risk revisiting the longing for still more physical contact, Lani ignored Asher's hand, choosing to board the dinghy unassisted. What began as an inelegant clamber onto the inflatable's unstable surface ended in a scene out of a rom-com when the wobbly craft shifted as she stood with one foot in it and one on the swim platform. The next thing Lani knew, she was off balance and pitching sideways. Her shoulder hit the edge of the structure. Pain shot through her as cold water closed over her head. Shock held her in its grasp for several immobilizing seconds before the need for air awakened in her lungs. Lani swept her arms out and down, wincing as the movement sent a sharp twinge through her bruised shoulder.

She surfaced, gasping and splashing, only to be hauled unceremoniously out of the water by big strong hands. Her butt settled onto the swim platform with a thump. She blinked water from her eyes and became aware that Asher cupped her head with one hand while the fingers of his other whisked drops from her cheeks.

"Are you okay?" His deep voice held an unexpected hint of panic that warmed her faster than the hot August sun.

The urge to cry rose up in her so fast that she gasped in dismay. She hated that Asher's concern for her made her feel weak and fragile. She was a street-smart private investigator, prepared for any and all emergencies. Not some silly female who needed a man to take care of her. Yet damned if she didn't appreciate being rescued by Asher. Even if it was his fault in the first place that she'd fallen in.

Scowling, she pushed Asher's hands away. "Leave me alone. I'm fine."

He opened his mouth as if to argue, but then the corners of his eyes crinkled as mirth replaced worry. He pressed his lips together as his shoulders began to shake with suppressed laughter. Lani glared at him in rapidly escalating indignation as she sat in her sopping wet clothes, overcome by embarrassment.

"It isn't funny," she snapped, shoving her palm into his shoulder, taking her discomfort out on him. "And it was all your fault that I fell in."

"Not true. If you'd let me help you into the boat, none of this would've happened." His amusement dimmed. Beneath bold dark eyebrows, his gaze became somber and intense. "Too bad you're always so determined to reject assistance."

"You say that like it's a bad thing that I rely on myself."

"It's not a bad thing to rely on yourself, but when you can't let yourself count on anyone else, then it stops being something positive."

Stung, she jumped on offense. "I don't think you're the best person to give advice on how I should act."

His face wore a mask of bland indifference. "You're probably right." He held out his hand. "Want to try again?"

"You go. I'm going to dry off."

With a brief shrug, he nimbly stepped into the dinghy and untied it. Lani huddled in her wet clothes and shivered, watching as Asher started the outboard and steered the inflatable toward the island.

Asher roamed the festival site for an hour, barely able to process how the whole damned thing had gone so wrong. Even without the tornado damage, the missing funds meant a lot of people had been ruined. If not for the storm, it wouldn't have come out that no payment had been made to the insurance company that was supposed to protect them against such a tragedy. Yet even before the winds had ripped apart buildings and uprooted trees, the festival had been sabotaged. How could things have gotten so bad?

And who in the hell had set him up for stealing the money?

It had to be someone close to him, or someone actively involved in the festival organization. He just couldn't imagine anyone he knew doing something so nefarious. Or who might have been opportunistic enough to embezzle. Obviously Lani was an expert at these sorts of investigations, but with her gaze focused directly on him, how hard would she look at anyone else?

In a grim mood, Asher returned to the boat. Lani was nowhere to be found so he headed into the lounge, poured himself two fingers of whiskey and shot back the alcohol. As the spirits seared his chest, warming his whole body, he closed his eyes and reviewed the day's events.

Lani so clearly believed he was the villain. And frankly, after looking at everything that had been done and scrutinizing the financials, he was starting to see why everyone thought he'd stolen the money. Nor did his current situation inspire anyone to give him the benefit of the doubt. He was living at his father's estate, working in a job that had been handed to him because of his connection to Rusty. He had little that he hadn't been given. It didn't cast him in the most flattering light. One thing was for sure, his current predicament was a major wake-up call. He'd given Rusty two years at The Edmond Organization. Time to make a new plan and dive into his future.

That is, if he *had* a future. The way things were going, it was looking pretty likely that he'd have many years behind bars to ponder the errors of his ways and figure out a better way to go forward.

He didn't realize his eyes remained closed until he felt a stirring in the air and realized he was no longer alone in the lounge. Pushing out a steadying breath, he got his expression back under control and opened his eyes.

Lani stepped into the kitchen and leaned against the cabinet near the sink with her arms crossed. She wore a pair of tropical-print wide-leg pants with a shoulder-baring crop top in royal blue. Her bare toenails peeked from beneath the flowing hem. Although the resort wear suited Lani, it also stripped away the professional veneer that made her so attractive to him.

She was a woman of substance, someone he valued for her authenticity, her intelligence and her drive. In so many ways they were complete opposites. She was focused and organized. While he tended to careen through life, moving from one experience to another.

"Are you planning on getting drunk?" she asked, glancing pointedly at the tumbler in his hand.

"Don't you think I deserve to?" Since he was still standing by the bar, he poured himself another shot of whiskey and then began to accumulate the ingredients for Lani's spicy margarita. "Feel like joining me? There's an icemaker there." He indicated the stainless-steel door beside the beverage cooler. "And you'll find limes and fresh jalapeños in the fridge beside it. I'm afraid you'll have to do with off-the-shelf sweet-and-sour mix, but in that cabinet you'll find chili salt."

"This isn't a party," Lani said, crossing her arms over her chest and refusing to move. "We're here on business."

"And you've never met a client over drinks?" Like the night before when she'd dined with his father at the Texas Cattleman's Club.

"You're not a client. And I don't think you should be drinking."

"Too late." He toasted her with his glass, downed the whiskey and lifted the bottle once more.

She was right to say he shouldn't be drinking. The alcohol wouldn't help defuse the tension in his gut put there by what he'd seen on the island. Nor could it dim his urgent pleasure at having her back in his life even under these terrible circumstances. As for diminishing the temptation to cross the room, wrap his arms around her and slide his lips onto the strong pulse in her throat...

"Lani." He lowered his chin and blinked slowly as warmth raced through his veins. She was so beautiful. He'd missed the way she crossed her arms and glared at him. Or how she looked so sleepy and sweet in the mornings. The corners of his mouth curled up in a slow grin. "Do you remember how we loved to picnic on the boat, make love all night and then have breakfast in bed the next morning?"

"Stop it right now." She leveled her finger at him. "I'm not doing this with you. We are not going to sleep together."

Her lips said no, but her eyes weren't quite as convincing.

"Because you don't want to?" he taunted. "Or because it would be unprofessional?"

"Both."

"I don't believe you." He spoke each syllable with deliberate care so she wouldn't miss his point.

"I don't care what you believe." She glowered at him a little too aggressively. "It's the truth."

Wondering what it would take to get her back on his side, Asher raked his hand through his hair. Once upon a time he'd been able to convince her to take a chance on him by capitalizing on the sizzling sexual energy that exploded between them whenever they touched. Yet while hormones had raged during those sultry summer months they spent together, he'd gotten the impression that he was some sort of curiosity to her. The good girl wanted to walk on the wild side just once before settling down to a career steeped in rules and regulations.

"Is it the truth?" he demanded, tired of her denials. "Or is that what you tell yourself at night when sleeping all alone in your bed?"

These words were not at all what he wanted to say to her, but with frustration and longing a tangled knot inside his gut, hollow charm lost out to desperate honesty.

"You're so sure I'm sleeping alone?" She was so obviously bluffing that he almost smiled.

"Yes," he said, chest tightening as she scowled at him. "Am I wrong? Have you found somebody that gets you?" Because he hoped she wouldn't settle for anything less.

Needing something to do, Asher moved into the kitchen. He ignored her obvious show of maintaining a safe distance from him as he opened the refrigerator and pulled out the produce he'd mentioned earlier. Finding a cutting board and a sharp knife, he gestured for her to join him. Then he began fixing a spicy margarita just the way she liked it.

"Someone who gets me." She gave a rough laugh as she rinsed the jalapeño, before picking up the knife. "Don't act as if you give a damn about my love life."

Asher's mouth went dry. He took a step in her direction and lowered his voice. "Of course I give a damn. I want you to be happy—"

"Don't." She whirled on him with a twelve-inch blade extended in his direction. He gulped. The stainless steel glinted wickedly in her hand. Her stormy eyes practically begged him to say more. "Don't pretend that you care. I'm not going to fall for you ever again."

Fall for you.

Five years earlier he hadn't understood what he was doing when he'd relentlessly pursued her. At first she'd been a challenge. Resisting him at every turn. Refusing to give him a chance. Reluctant to let him in. And even when he'd broken through her well-fortified defenses, she'd kept the key to her heart well hidden.

Until the lazy summer days began to grow short and he realized he didn't want to lose her. He'd invited her to come to Argentina for the polo season and she'd told him that she loved him, but that she couldn't give up on grad school. He'd been terrified by the gift she'd offered him and clueless how to keep their good thing going now that the summer fling had turned into a serious romance.

"I did care about you," he countered, shaken by the mistake he'd made all those years ago when he'd chosen his freedom over her love.

"Oh, please. I watched you hit on women for a week before you even noticed me."

She looked plenty put out that she hadn't been his first choice. Except that wasn't the case at all. From the moment he had spotted her waiting on adjacent tables, he'd been mesmerized. He just hadn't been ready for the emotions that had slammed into him. Lust he could handle. Longing had caught him by surprise.

"What do you want to hear? That you were unlike any other woman I'd ever met and I didn't know how to handle that?"

"I'm only interested in what's real," she declared, slicing the lime with malevolent force.

"That is the truth." But he could see from her ramrod-straight spine that nothing he could say would convince her.

"Just be straight with me." She set the knife down and shot him a hard look. "Tell me where you put the money. That's the only truth I'm interested in hearing."

Six

"Where are we off to today?" Asher asked the morning day after their impromptu visit to Appaloosa Island.

If she'd hoped that compelling him to confront the damage to the island would provoke his confession about the missing funds, she'd been completely wrong. While he'd seemed disturbed by all he'd seen, he hadn't confessed or behaved in a way that confirmed his guilt.

Lani scanned his handsome face, fighting the sheer enjoyment of his gorgeous smile and ready energy. Yet even as she fell into the trap of wanting to do whatever made him happy, she recognized that he could be putting on an act.

She searched for evasion in his lively brown eyes, but saw only genuine curiosity and good-natured enthusiasm. It sucked that she no longer trusted her own judgment. Five years ago, his ability to twist her emotions and make her lose control of her sensibilities had almost been her ruin. Fortunately, she'd woken up just in time. While turning down his invitation to go with him to Argentina had been the hardest decision she'd ever made, no good would've come from giving up her carefully crafted plans.

And Lani was convinced that even if she'd followed Asher Edmond into an uncertain future, they never would've lasted. So what if her days weren't as bright and shining without him in it. Look at how he'd ended up. Eventually he would've dragged her down with him.

"*I'm* going to visit Abby Carmichael," she said, emphasizing the first-person singular pronoun. Letting him help with this investigation was a really bad idea.

"Abby… Carmichael. The name is familiar."

"She was filming a documentary on the festival."

"Oh, sure, she interviewed all of us." Asher arched his eyebrows. "What's your interest in her?"

"She has footage of what was going on with the festival."

"What do you think you'll find on it?" His lips twisted into a sardonic quirk. "Video of me sneaking off with bags of money and burying them in the sand somewhere?"

Although he spoke in a light, mocking tone, Lani recognized his dark humor masked concern. Her time training to be an FBI agent hadn't been a waste. In those moments when she could put her emotional response to him aside, she saw his anxiety clearly.

"That would be really helpful," she responded, arching her eyebrows at him. "Especially if they are marked with big dollar signs, indicating that the bags are full of cash."

As her not-so-witty repartee made him relax, Lani sighed in weary frustration with herself. She came out of her thoughts and caught Asher regarding her intently. It was in moments like these when she glimpsed his somber watchfulness that she knew there was more to this man than he let people see.

"Can I come along?" he asked. "Maybe a third set of eyes could be helpful."

Against her better judgment, Lani found herself nodding. "Sure, why not."

Why did she keep pandering to his needs? What was she *thinking*? That if they could work the investigation together, then maybe they'd have some sort of shot in the future?

He wasn't good for her. Once she got him out of this situation, she'd probably never hear from him again. The thought made her heart clench. Five years ago she'd foolishly believed if she told him that school was important to her, then he would agree to try the long-distance thing. She'd hoped that maybe by the time she graduated, he would've settled down and their differences would've stopped being an issue.

But clearly fate had other things in store for them both.

"Thanks." He looked as if he wanted to say more, but then just gave her a smile that didn't quite reach his eyes.

Before she acted on her need to reassure him, Lani grabbed her jacket and headed for the apartment door. Before she could reach it, Asher was there, gazing down at her with his most-earnest expression. The heady scent of his cologne encircled her, causing an uptick in her pulse.

"I really mean it," he said, fingertips skimming her arm. The light contact aroused a flood of longing, but if it showed on her face, he didn't appear to notice. "It means the world to me that you are giving me the benefit of the doubt."

I'm not...

She might've been able to resist if he'd swept her into a passionate embrace and kissed her with wild abandon. Bracing against his onslaught of sensual persuasion was her first instinct. Instead, her steely resolve was being chipped away by his fleeting touches, the unexpected flashes of sincerity, his apparent gratitude that she was going to bat for him because she believed in his innocence. Guilt swept through her. Did he recognize how little she trusted him? Or did he think his tactics were working?

"Asher..."

Before she could figure out what she planned on telling him, he dropped the sweetest, lightest, most-affectionate kiss on her lips. The gentle pressure came and went so fast it was like being kissed by a butterfly, but she doubted her whole body would've lit up from a glancing brush of gossamer wings.

"It's enough that you're letting me come along." He swallowed her fingers in his warm, strong hand and drew her out the door. "You don't need to warn me that I'm still suspect number one. It's just nice to have some control over my fate."

A warning trembled on her lips. He had no control whatsoever. But his optimistic expression overwhelmed her caution. Why crush his hopes when there was nothing concrete to do the stomping?

Instead she gave his fingers a quick squeeze and said, "Let's go."

The day before she'd made this appointment to meet with Abby Carmichael at Carter Crane's ranch. Two months earlier the filmmaker had arrived to capture background on the town, the Edmond family and many of those participating in the Soiree on the Bay festival.

Lani had heard that the couple was an opposites-attract pair who'd met and fallen in love in the midst of the festival development. Abby was a city girl. Carter a rancher. Lani couldn't help but compare the couple's romantic destiny to what had happened between her and Asher. While Abby had moved to Royal, letting romance upended her world, Lani had sacrificed her personal life in favor of her career. She was eager to see how Abby was faring in the aftermath of her decision.

The woman who answered the door had long straight dark hair, inquisitive brown eyes, and a beautiful light brown complexion. A cropped white T-shirt and skinny jeans showed off her lean body and her smile was positively gleeful as her gaze landed on Asher.

"I don't suppose I could get you to sit for another interview."

Lani stiffened protectively. She'd forgotten that word around town was that Abby intended to change the focus of her documentary to an exposé on the failed festival and the scandalous missing funds.

"Maybe after I'm exonerated," Asher replied with a suave

grin that made Lani's toes curl even though she wasn't on the receiving end of his attention.

"You don't think he's guilty?" Abby's eyes went wide as her gaze bounced between Asher and Lani.

"I'm investigating the missing festival funds," she said, irritation firing as she reminded the filmmaker of the reason they were here.

She knew better than to let her personal feelings for Asher get in the way of doing her job. No matter how bad the case looked against him, she had blurred the lines between doing the job Kingston Blue had hired her for and saving her former lover from jail. That the two missions might be on a parallel course would only work for her as long as Asher was innocent.

"May we see the footage?" Lani prompted.

"Of course," Abby demurred, leading them toward a large workstation with several monitors, keyboards and other computer equipment. "I pulled footage from the various visits to the island with the organizers of the event. I also have interviews with everyone involved." Her gaze flicked to Asher. "Any idea what you're looking for?"

The massive volume of video the documentarian had recorded was overwhelming. But helpful.

"Let's start with the footage from the visits to the island."

Abby began scrolling through various files, clicking on several in search of what she was looking for. "There are a lot of people involved. Between the Edmond family, the construction crew, marketers, food vendors. The list goes on and on..."

With the embezzlement evidence pointing directly at Asher, the investigators had stopped searching for other suspects and begun building a case against him. No one else would be looking at what Abby had recorded.

To Lani's mind, the people who were closest to the Edmond family were at the top of her list of suspects. Specifically Ross Edmond. Despite Asher's assurance that his brother couldn't have stolen the money, and then taken the extra step of framing Asher, Lani intended on taking a good look at him.

"That's odd," Asher murmured.

Lani braced herself for whatever had caught his eye. She'd worried that even if there was nothing of interest in what Abby had filmed, Asher would create some sort of distraction that would lead her down a divergent tunnel. His specialty was deflection and the man had a knack for getting inside her head. Who knew what crazy theory she would be chasing next if he got his way.

But it was Abby, and not Lani, that took the bait. "What's odd?"

"I wasn't along on this particular visit to the festival site." He turned to Abby. "Can you run this back about ten minutes?"

"Sure."

"Look." The footage that had caught Asher's attention was a shot of Rusty and Ross walking the grounds, looking relaxed in each other's company. From the state of the building going on and the lack of a rift between the father and son, the footage must've been shot several months earlier.

"What are we looking for?" Abby asked eagerly and Lani was happy to let her lead.

Asher hesitated before answering, his focus locked on the monitor. "That." He pointed to a corner of the screen where Billy Holmes appeared. Although at first his expression appeared innocuous, on closer viewing, his charming veneer had slipped, replaced by a cold glare.

"He's staring at Ross and Rusty like they've done something to annoy him," Asher said, sounding triumphant. "Which is strange because I've never ever seen him looking anything but absolutely pleased with himself."

Wow. Interesting indeed.

"Well, he certainly isn't looking so happy there." Asher sounded intrigued. "How much more footage is there of this day?"

While Abby and Asher leaned forward, scanning the images on the monitor, Lani pondered this new development. Was this a significant lead or just a red herring?

"You know, when I interviewed Billy around the time that this was shot, he let it slip that some money was unaccounted for from the accounts." Abby turned in her chair and faced Asher. "He said the oddest thing. He called it a family matter and then said that *we're* handling it." She emphasized the inclusive pronoun. "He acted very protective of Ross. At the time I just thought it was because they were such good friends." Abby's gaze strayed back to the monitor and a dent appeared between her eyebrows.

Lani had never considered Billy as a suspect because he hadn't had access to the festival accounts. But she remembered Kingston Blue's theory that Ross was involved. Could they be in on it together?

If so, why did it upset Billy that Ross and Rusty seemed to be getting along?

They spent another hour reviewing footage, but nothing else jumped out. Nevertheless Lani asked Abby for copies of whatever she had featuring the Edmond family and Billy, including the individual interviews with the Edmonds.

Following the meeting with Abby Carmichael, Lani was in a thoughtful mood as they headed back to Elegance Ranch. Asher was wondering if he was being too optimistic to think that he was starting to see cracks forming in the thick wall of doubt Lani had constructed to keep him at bay.

"Weird about the way Billy was glaring at Ross and Rusty," he muttered as his curiosity grew too overwhelming to bear in silence. "What do you suppose that means?"

She took one hand off the steering wheel and rubbed her temple as if trying to alleviate pain. "I don't know."

But by watching her, seeing the telltale tightening of her lips and a slight indent between her brows, she obviously *did* know, and whatever was bothering her had caused some sort of shift in perception. Hope blared in him like a car alarm. Could she be coming around to believing that he hadn't stolen the money?

"I had no idea Billy was the one spreading word of missing funds," Asher said, continuing to chew on one of the many disturbing things he'd discovered today. "I mean, what did he think he was doing? He had to know the news would hurt our family."

"Explain to me again about Billy's relationship with Ross and how he came to be living in one of the guesthouses on the estate."

"He and Ross were good buds in college," Asher told her. "He showed up in Royal a couple years ago. As to why he's living in the guesthouse…" He thought back. "Rusty took to him right away." He made no effort to hide the bitterness in his voice. "I guess all it takes to get on Rusty's good side is to kiss his ass twenty-four/seven. Billy's an expert at that."

"You don't like him."

Asher had a ready answer. "Do I sound like a jerk if I admit that it bugs me that this guy comes out of nowhere and gets my dad to like him when I've spent my whole life waiting for Rusty to acknowledge me for doing a good job at anything?"

"I think you are justified to want Rusty's attention. He's the only father you've ever known. It makes sense that you want him to be proud of you."

Venting about being slighted by his father left Asher feel like he'd been kicked in the gut. Sharing that hadn't been easy and he appreciated Lani's empathic response. They didn't talk until she stopped the SUV behind the barn.

Asher turned to her as something electric and powerful sizzled in the air between them. "Are you heading back to Dallas right away or can you stay for dinner?"

The festival case wasn't the only one she was working. Lani was helping several clients.

"I have time for dinner."

Five words that flooded him with excitement. "Great."

She preceded him up the stairs to his apartment and keyed in the code. At her urging, he'd started locking his door. Until she came along, he hadn't considered that his stuff or his person could be in danger and her insistence on security was adorable. He didn't want her to think he wasn't taking her seriously, but the truth was, the only thing of value worth locking up was his heart and the more time he spent with her, the less confident he was at being able to keep it safe.

"Pour me a shot of whiskey," she said, setting down her laptop and slipping her blazer off her shoulders. "I'll be right back."

Asher did as she asked and then began hunting in his refrigerator for what he could use to put together a meal. He had steak and pasta. She liked Gorgonzola cheese. Would she remember the recipe they'd made on the boat that summer?

It wasn't until ten minutes passed that he noticed the water running in the bathroom. She was in the shower, probably thinking through what they'd learned that day. While he waited for her to reemerge, he sipped at his whiskey and stared in the direction of the guesthouse where Billy Holmes stayed.

"Is this mine?"

The sound of her voice broke Asher out of his thoughts. He turned around and the sight of her made the room tilt.

He blinked.

She wore a large blue button-down shirt that had definitely come out of his closet and nothing else. The sight of her pale bare legs and unbound silky black hair made his chest seize. As he stared at her in astonishment, she tipped the crystal tumbler and tossed back the entire contents. He watched her throat as she swallowed the whiskey and savored the widening of her eyes at the impact of the fiery liquid.

Asher wasn't sure if the intensity of his gaze or the liquor put color in her cheeks, but two bright patches appeared over her cheekbones.

"I hope you don't mind but I borrowed one of your shirts," she said. "I jumped into the shower before remembering that I didn't have any clean clothes. I tossed my things in the washer. They'll be clean and dry by the time we're done with dinner."

She was *naked* underneath his shirt? Damn it. Now he was the one with fire raging in his veins.

"I'm afraid I can't have you wearing my clothes," he joked, somehow managing to maintain a humorous demeanor despite the hunger clawing at him. "Take it off."

He definitely succeeded in surprising her because her lips parted in a soft *O*. It took him a second to realize she didn't intend to complain. Instead her eyebrows rose boldly in answer to his challenge.

She set her hands on her hips. "Did you miss the part where I have nothing else to wear?"

"Don't you think it's rude to take things without asking permission?" he countered, advancing in her direction.

A smile played around her lips, sizzling sweet as she methodically backpedaled toward the hall that led to the bedrooms. His gaze followed the trail of her hand as she slipped one button after another free, baring more creamy skin with each step. She was taunting him, daring him to catch her before she reached the guest bedroom. But he could move faster. That is, until his shirt smacked him in the face, blinding him just long enough for her to disappear.

Instinct took over. He tossed the shirt aside and charged after her. Three enormous strides and he closed in on her. Snatching her around the waist, he lifted her off her feet, intending to haul her into his bedroom. He had to find a bed. *Now*. While her passions were all lit up. Before her brain kicked in.

But the instant her naked body careened against his, he found the first solid surface available and set her back against the wall beside the door leading to the master bedroom.

Sliding one hand under her round butt cheek, he sank his fingers into her soft flesh and lifted her. She latched her arms around his shoulders, encircled his waist with her thighs and flicked her tongue into the sensitive skin beneath. His shoulder muscles bunched as a tsunami of arousal pounded through him.

"I need you to take me right here." She purred the demand against his skin, nipping his neck for emphasis, knowing it would drive him crazy. "Right now."

"Hell, yeah."

Her mouth bashed into his, lips parting, tongue searching. He dove straight into the hungry assault, sucking, kissing, erasing their years spent apart. Her skin grew slick as the tempest burned hot between them. He pulled back, determined to shift them to the bed in his room, but her thighs tightened around him.

"Here and now, frat boy," she taunted, rocking her hips and grinding against his arousal, making him moan.

He lost the will to argue with her. If she wanted it hard and fast up against the wall, he would give it to her. Later he could spend lazy hours chasing her curves with his fingers and lips, but for now he thought he'd die if he couldn't bury himself in her hot tight heat.

Sliding his hand over her rib cage, he cupped her breast, grazing her tight nipple with his thumb. Her breath grew ragged as he leaned forward, kissing her soft skin where shoulder met neck and trailing his tongue into the hollow of her collarbone. She ground against him, her muscles flexing in a familiar rhythm. He longed to be moving with her, *in* her. She was an addiction he'd never recovered from.

He reached down to unfasten the button holding his jeans closed and slid down the zipper. Her fervent arousal called to him as his dick sprang free. She gyrated wildly, bringing her slick heat into contact with his erection. He was an instant away from plunging into her when the need for protection struck him.

What was he doing? He'd dreamed about a moment like this for nearly five years. Why was he rushing? With her thighs clamped around his body, he spun them both and moved toward the bed. Before they went any further, he needed to get as naked as she was and to make sure she was safe.

She seemed to understand what drove him because as soon as her back touched the mattress, she sat up and began to tear at his shirt. While she stripped it off, he strained toward the nightstand drawer. To his relief, his fingers located a condom on the first try. Skimming off his jeans and boxers, he tore open the wrapper and sheathed himself.

Then he was on her, lips seeking hers, legs tangling, fingers splayed over her lower back to bring their naked skin together. Her lips were designed for his kisses. He'd memorized every curve until all he had to do was close his eyes and let his imagination run riot.

He nuzzled his lips into her neck as she pushed her bare breasts against his chest. A delicate mewling sound came from her throat as he eased his hand over the gorgeous curve of the nearest one and scraped his fingertips over her tight nipple. His mind was already fast-forwarding to how she would writhe as his mouth closed over the sensitive peak, feeling it turn into a hard pebble as he applied suction. With her slender leg trapped between his, she clung to him, purring with delight as he turned his attention to the other breast.

Her hands moved lazily over his shoulders, palms drifted up his neck before she tunneled her fingers into his hair. He trailed his fingers along her abdomen, letting the tips tickle over her belly in a way that made her squirm. Her thighs parted to let him glide along the crease that hid her sex. He dipped into her slippery wetness, lightly stroked her until she cried out, and then withdrew to circle her clit. Her body quaked as he toyed and teased before retreating. Lost in her pleasure, she trembled and bucked her hips, chanting his name. With each second he grew impossibly harder, but refused to stop what he was doing until she came for him.

"That feels *incredible*," she murmured, her chest heaving. "I'm so close…"

As if that triggered her, Lani threw her head back and howled. She climaxed in a rush. Her muscles tensing. Nails biting into his shoulders. He rubbed himself against her hip, caught up in her pleasure. The explosion that ripped through her was almost strong enough to take him with her.

He wanted to laugh at the sheer perfection of it, of her, but he needed her to experience even more. He slid his finger into her and pressed the heel of his palm against her clit. Legs spread wide, she thrashed her head from side to side, drove her mound hard against him and cried out for more.

Oh. Hell. Yes! This is what he'd missed. His senses magnified each harsh rasp of her ragged breath, the scent of her musk mingling with the delicious earthiness of her spicy perfume. Asher smiled as their tongues danced, the taste of whiskey invigorating his nerve endings. And the way her thighs clamped around him as she strained toward another orgasm, her smoky gaze locked with his, set him on fire.

Settling between her thighs in the welcoming cradle that had always felt like coming home, he waited for her to wrap her arms around his neck before pulling his head down to hers. He had to focus hard on not slamming into her. Despite her obvious burning need to meet her body with his, he wanted to remind himself of the texture of her skin, get his mouth on her breasts and glide his fingers over her tantalizing curves.

"Asher." His name was an urgent plea.

"Easy," he coaxed. "Let me take care of you."

"I love it when you say that," she whispered fiercely.

Her nails scraped down his spine and sank into his butt muscles. A curse escaped his lips when she barely paused before reaching between them. She latched her fingers onto his aching erection and drew him into contact with her hot, wet arousal.

"Now, Asher. I need you *now.*"

He needed her, as well. More than needed. He'd craved this for five long years. Having her beneath him on his bed was a dream come true. The moment deserved as much smoldering all-in passion as he could produce. But the heat between them had a mind of its own and all too soon the head of his shaft was pressed against her tight entrance while she panted inarticulate words of encouragement between breaths. Heavenly voices sang in his head as he thrust into her searing heat. He groaned at the firm clasp of her inner muscles around him and lost himself in the homecoming that was Lani Li.

With the magic of the moment consuming his soul, he began to move inside her. Fanning his fingers and gathering her butt in his palm, he began a slow withdrawal, culminating with a teasing hesitation to drive up anticipation. He waited for her to open her eyes and meet his. She always did this. Every time.

When her lashes lifted, baring her mink-brown gaze, her pure, unapologetic joy was the sexiest thing he'd ever seen. He dusted a kiss across her forehead, before he lowered his chin and grazed her lips with his.

"I've missed this," he whispered. "You have no idea how much."

Her tremulous sigh tickled his jaw. "So have I."

What she did to him was unique and one-of-a-kind. He was on fire and she was the gasoline that turned him into a raging inferno. They moaned together as he plunged into her once again, rejoicing as she took all of him. Stroke after stoke, he dove deep, thrusting smoothly while hoarse, hungry cries emanated from her throat.

Shudders slammed through him as desire wrestled for control of his muscles. He struggled to stay present and hold off, fighting to withstand the orgasm bent on claiming him. He needed her to come a second time. He moved harder, changed the angle of his deepening thrusts and watched her strain for her release, her rocking hips driving him mad.

She must've known what he wanted for her because she lifted her head and sank her white teeth into his earlobe. The painful nip sent lightning streaking straight to his groin and shattered his willpower.

"More," she commanded, meeting every one of his nearly frantic thrusts with equally reckless abandon.

This wasn't the Lani Li he knew from these last few weeks. This was a return to the wild, wanton woman he'd known that smoking hot, oh-so-memorable summer. Sex with her had ruined him for anyone else. No one matched her curiosity or her focus. She'd investigated his body and discovered all his pleasure spots with the same level of curiosity she'd shown while attacking the embezzlement case.

Pleasure drove him on. The air around them seemed to waver from the heat pouring off their bodies. He struggled for breath that wasn't there. Still, he persisted. The pounding rhythm of her pants pushing him harder. She thrashed her head from side to side, long hair tangling on her sweaty shoulders. Her legs tightened around him, the strength of the vise letting him know she was close.

Her back arched, head rolling back, baring her throat. "Come with me." The guttural order spilled from her parted lips.

She possessed just enough air to call his name before her muscles went taut, the rhythmic pulse of her release triggering his own. He wanted to hold off, to push her harder, give her more, but her power over him was too potent. There would be plenty of time later to take her past the fiery edge of satisfaction. Right now it was more important for them to be together in this momentous rejoining of body and soul.

He'd love to say he let himself go, but the truth was she grabbed hold of him and yanked him hard into a bone-jarring, roaring avalanche of satisfaction and unending joy. *She* did this to him. She made him crazy and so incredibly happy.

He collapsed into her arms and caught sight of her blissful smile before he entwined their sated bodies. As their skin cooled in the aftermath, Asher stroked back the hair from her face and let his lips drift over her damp shoulder. He hooked the comforter over both of them and grinned as she snuggled her nose into his throat.

When it was just the two of them like this, he could imagine everything would be okay. He'd just stay focused on that for tonight and enjoy that for a little while his life made sense again.

Seven

With her favorite Lowercase album pouring from Asher's Bluetooth speakers, Lani pushed back from her laptop and rubbed her tired, dry eyes. Over the past week, one lead after another had dried up, including any connection between Ross and the missing funds. Faced with a plethora of dead ends, she'd become aware of a growing panic. Was Asher guilty? Lani hoped not. She wouldn't have renewed their physical relationship if she didn't question the validity of the evidence stacked against him. At least she hoped not. She would hate it if she on the verge of making a colossal mistake.

Between long hours at her computer and late nights in bed with Asher, making up for lost time, she'd been lost in a bubble of work and sex. And Lani couldn't remember the last time she'd been this happy.

"Come on," Asher coaxed, his hands sweeping her long hair away from her neck so he could glide his lips over her skin. "You've done enough work for one day. I think you should take a break."

"What kind of a break did you have in mind?" She glanced up at him, anticipation making her breathless.

"I have twelve polo ponies in training and they need exercise. Wanna help?"

Lani blinked at him, adjusting to this unexpected development. "Help how?"

"How long has it been since you've been on a horse?"

"A while."

When they first met, he'd been intrigued that she'd been a barrel racer when she was young. He'd persuaded her to take him to visit her parents' hobby farm. Introducing him to her horse had gone a lot smoother than meeting her parents. Once they found out he was a professional polo player, they'd definitely not approved and campaigned for her to break things off.

Maybe part of her recognized that she and Asher were too different to work, but she'd waved away their concern, telling her parents that it was just a summer fling and ignoring their exchanged looks that said they believed otherwise.

"What's *a while*?"

Although her folks hadn't sold her horse, she'd been too invested in starting up her investigation firm to take time for recreation. "A year."

"That's too long. Why don't you throw on your boots and I'll saddle Royal Flush for you. She's the best I have and she'll take care of you."

"I guess I could use a break," she said and went to change her footwear.

When she entered the barn, Lani found he had pulled out two horses and was in the process of saddling one of them. She sidled up to the closest one and extended one of the carrots she'd brought as a treat.

"This is Cactus," Asher said, reaching beneath his horse's belly to snag the end of the girth and buckle it into place. "And Royal Flush."

"Hello, beautiful." She scratched the chestnut's shoulder and felt her lean into the caress. Her own horse always seemed to have an itch at this exact same spot. It made her smile.

Asher slid the halter off the bay and plucked the bridle off his shoulder. He threw the reins over the horse's head and poised the bit against the mare's long yellow teeth.

"You're using a gag bit," Lani murmured, recognizing the three-part bit with two joints. "When I raced, I used something similar because Reggie tended not to bend around the barrels and the gag bit really helped with that."

"The gag bit in polo came into popularity in Argentina because the players there were always looking for ways to improve their game. And they found that this style of bit made the horses more linear and less lateral."

"Do you miss it?" Her question caused Asher to still for a moment.

"Do I miss galloping down the field with seven other guys' mallets whizzing past my head as we pursue a little white ball?" His mocking grin flashed, knocking the breath from her body. "Hell ya, I miss it."

"So why aren't you still doing it?"

"Do you think you can manage an English saddle? Or should I put a Western one on Royal Flush?"

The difference between an English and Western saddle was pretty significant. A Western saddle had a deep secure seat with a substantial horn atop a pommel at the front and a high cantle behind. Weighing upward of twenty-five pounds, the design enabled cowboys to stay firmly seated while on bucking broncos and chasing down erratically moving cattle.

English saddles, on the other hand, were flatter and less bulky by comparison and required the rider to work to stay balanced atop their mount. That being said, because of the reduced weight, it was the saddle of choice for jumpers and polo enthusiasts.

Lani could see the dare in Asher's gaze and knew he was trying to divert her attention from the question she'd asked. Still, she gave her options serious consideration. She'd ridden English before, but never while running full tilt across a polo field or while trying to hit a ball with a mallet.

"I think if I plan to stay on, I'd better take the Western saddle."

Ten minutes later they were leading the horses out of the barn and toward a large fenced field. She'd mistaken it for a turnout before this. Instead the groomed grass indicated that this was Asher's training ground. Out of habit she tested the girth before fitting her foot into the stirrup, making sure it remained snug around Royal Flush's belly.

"You don't trust I can saddle a horse?" he teased, swinging up on the bay with no effort whatsoever.

Lani's muscles protested this unaccustomed exercise and she grunted at the effort it took to swing her leg over the Thoroughbred's back. Seating herself with an ungainly thump, she shot a glance Asher's way, hoping he hadn't seen her struggle. While Royal Flush stood still despite her awkward landing, Asher had his hands full keeping his own mount in place.

"Reggie loved to hold his breath when I saddled him and I always had to double check the girth after I walked him around a bit."

While Royal Flush stood perfectly still, waiting for Lani to cue her, Cactus was full of impatient energy as she sidestepped and backed up.

"She's new," Asher explained, his calm handling of the antsy equine demonstrating a level of patience and skill that was having a dangerous effect on her hormones. He didn't saw on the reins in an effort to control the horse, but sat quietly letting his legs and seat tell the horse what to do. "I adopted her from Donovan Horse Rescue. She's a former racehorse, purchased by an inexperienced rider and badly neglected before Valencia Donovan got her. I guess she was skin and bones. Valencia thinks she might've been abused. But she's fast and loves to run—it's the slowing and turning that we have to work on."

"How come you have so many horses? I thought a string was two or three."

"That's typical for a hobbyist. Three to four is common for a more serious player and if you're professional, a string can be up to ten."

"Are you training these horses because you're considering going back on the professional circuit again?"

"No, these days I play to give these guys experience. It's hobbyist-level action, but I can't give it up entirely. I enjoy the training far too much." He urged his mount forward and used his head to indicate she should come along.

"So once they're trained, then what?"

"I'll sell. I have several people coming to look at horses over the next week or so."

She could hear the ache in his voice. This wasn't something he was doing lightly.

"Why?"

He gave her question a negligent shrug. "Since it doesn't seem as if my family's going to help me and I'm going to be facing some pretty stiff legal bills, I thought I should generate some cash."

They rode in silence for several minutes while Lani processed Asher's pain.

"Are you ready?" he asked, stroking the bay's sweaty neck. The mare had worked herself into a lather before they'd walked to the end and back.

"Ready?" Lani echoed, unsure what he had in mind.

A second later he and Cactus shot away at a gallop. Lani felt Royal Flush gather herself to follow and keyed the mare. As the ground whizzed by, she realized how much she'd missed this. Losing the battle to contain her excitement, a whoop ripped free. All too soon she had to slow the horse as the far fence loomed.

As she drew back on the reins, the chestnut slowed to a smooth canter. Lani's heart was thundering in her ears and she was sure she was grinning like an idiot from the amusement on Asher's face.

"How did that feel?" he asked, sidestepping his mount over to the fence where a couple of mallets sat propped against the railing.

Lani was breathing hard from the exertion. "She's really fast."

"Argentinian born and bred. They take their polo ponies seriously down there. I bought her as a two-year-old and trained her. She's the best I've ever owned."

And yet he was selling her because his family refused to help him out. Once again Lani had to withstand the urge to comfort him. Still, she hoped the mare went to a good home.

"Let's see how you do with one of these." He handed her a mallet, his wicked grin on full display. "Head weight on that one is six ounces, which is on the lighter end. You should be able to handle it without problems."

As Lani swung the mallet to get the feel of it, she braced herself against the challenge in Asher's expression. Five years earlier, after discovering a mutual love of climbing, white-water rafting and mountain biking, they'd pushed each other to do all sorts of crazy stunts. Afterward, hyped up on adrenaline and endorphins, they'd fallen upon each other in ravenous desire.

Feeling a familiar tingle between her thighs, Lani shifted in the saddle, but this only pressed her sensitive areas against the leather's firm surface, intensifying the ache there. A breeze blew across her hot skin, and she savored the cooling caress. Damn it! The man could get her hot and bothered just by being in the same vicinity.

She was glad when Asher started demonstrating the finer arts of polo. Riding a horse while holding the mallet was challenging enough. Successfully connecting the mallet with the ball absorbed all her focus and energy. They played for an hour and with each minute that passed Lani's appreciation for Asher's talent grew.

"I won't be able walk tomorrow," she groaned, the overworked muscles of her inner thighs protesting as she mounted the stairs to his apartment.

"You just need a hot bath and a massage." His eyes kindled. "I can help with both."

Lani emerged from the bedroom, dressed for work, jeans, boots, white button-down shirt and black leather jacket. Asher sat at the breakfast bar, a mug of coffee within easy reach as he texted. She wondered if his sister had responded to any of his messages. He'd reached out to her once a day since being released.

In the seconds before he noticed her arrival, she snatched the opportunity to regard him. Worn jeans hugged his lower half while a blue polo shirt molded to the muscles of his shoulders and chest. The faint scent of hay and horse hung in the air. He sat perched on a barstool, the heel of his left boot caught on the lower rung. He looked ready to spring into action. All this inactivity was clearly driving him crazy. He hummed like a live wire, his energy zapping and sizzling with the need to go and do.

She didn't know if she made a sound or if he was just so tuned in to her presence that he became aware he was no longer alone in the room. His eyes lifted from the phone screen and darted her way. The impact of his gaze raised goose bumps on her arms. A familiar breathless state came over her. This was bad. She never should've started up things with him again, but he was irresistible and she was powerless against her own longing.

"Have you heard back from Gina?" she asked, needing a distraction from her thoughts.

"Yeah." His neutral tone gave away none of his feelings. "She knows if anyone can find the money it will be you." His gaze roved ever so slowly over her outfit. "Looks like you're dressed for business. I guess we're not going to spend the morning in bed."

"You're the one who got up."

Her response was a little too tart. But honest all the same.

Because deep down she was disappointed that he'd left her in bed to go tend to his horses. It had always been that way with her. She'd been so starved for his attention that any distraction left her feeling bereft and insecure.

"I didn't realize…" He set down his phone, held out his hand, a silent command to come to him and one she lacked the strength to ignore.

All too aware that a week earlier she might have flung up some sort of defense against him, Lani let herself be drawn toward him, nearly purring as his long fingers stroked her cheek and tangled in her hair. Her whole body swooned with pleasure as he hooked her hip with his other hand and drew her between his thighs. His lips grazed the sensitive skin below her ear and she shivered. Damn the man for being so good at this.

"You didn't realize what?"

There was a catch in her voice as she asked the question. He couldn't fail to hear it, couldn't fail to understand what caused it. When he touched her, she became someone else. Someone who forgot who she was, forgot right or wrong, up or down. There was just his touch anchoring her to him, helping her make sense of the emotional maelstrom inside her. All she needed was this man. His deep passionate kisses. His body possessing hers. The rest of the world didn't exist when he was kissing her.

"I didn't realize how much you miss me." He curved his hand over her butt and pulled her pelvis against the growing hardness behind his zipper. "When I'm not around."

Although it was true, confronting this chink in her armor was a puff of icy air against her hot skin. She stopped clinging to his impressive biceps and shoved against his chest. Not hard, nor with any vigor, but with enough pressure to part them, allowing her to take a half step back.

"I have a meeting in half an hour that I need to get to," she said, refusing to notice the smug light in his eye.

"May I come?"

Lani tugged her jacket straight, all too aware of the unfulfilled ache in her breasts and the clammy texture of her over-heated skin. "Not a good idea."

"Because it's about the investigation?"

Plucking an elastic tie off her wrist, she fastened her hair into a low ponytail. "That *is* why I'm here."

"I hope that isn't the only reason why you are here."

He had her there. She'd already determined that he had no intention of skipping town. And the electronic bracelet around his ankle would allow the cops to track him down in a heartbeat if he ventured beyond the estate without her. She really didn't need to babysit him. In the beginning she'd stuck around to get inside his head. She could entertain the theory that he'd been set up and go back to her apartment in Dallas.

Yet the thought of being parted from him awoke a sharp pang of reluctance. She wasn't ready to move on from the long passionate nights in his arms. Or to ponder what might happen in the days to come.

"I really have to go," she said, uncomfortable with the direction her thoughts had gone.

"Who are you meeting?"

"Zach Benning."

The social media influencer had come to Royal to promote the festival and fallen in love with Lila Jones, Royal's Chamber of Commerce representative.

"I'd heard he's living in Royal now. Moved in with Lila Jones." Asher's gaze sharpened as it rested on her. "Gave up his entire life in LA just to be with her."

Lani found herself bristling at his thoughtful tone. What point was he trying to make? That she should've given up her plans for a master's degree five years earlier and trailed after him like some lovesick idiot? For how long? He'd offered her nothing she could count on. Made no promises. He had no plan for what they would do in Royal. She was a girl who needed a set of achievable goals to move her forward. Playing things by ear was *not* in her comfort zone.

"Yes, well…" She glanced toward the kitchen, dodging his assessing gaze. "I'd love a cup of coffee, but there's no time. I don't suppose you have a to-go mug?"

"I always have a to-go mug," he said, his lips lifting into a sardonic quirk. He was no stranger to their differences, but rather than ignore them, he was more likely to lean into the problems created between them. "I'd really like it if you'd let me go along. Where are you meeting him?"

As he spoke, he went into the kitchen, pulled out a travel mug. Once he poured in the coffee and doctored it the way she liked, he handed it to her. Appreciation threatened as she took the mug. Damn him for being so good to her.

Against her better judgment, Lani felt herself softening toward his entreaty. Why not bring him along? He'd already proven a handy guy to have around and by sleeping with him she'd crossed a professional line. Plus, if she really believed that he wasn't responsible for taking the money, then maybe having his perspective would prove useful. Oh, hell. She was making excuses. Before this case she'd always worked alone and liked it. Relying on anyone besides herself meant she couldn't control the outcome.

"At the Royal Diner." She wondered if the public location would deter Asher.

He wasn't exactly anyone's favorite Edmond right now. A lot of people had suffered in town because of the failure of the festival. Keeping a low profile was a better way for him to go; but one thing about Asher, he never seemed to take the safest route.

"Will you wait while I change? I just need to get out of these barn clothes."

With a reluctant sigh, she nodded. "I'll call the monitoring company and let them know you're coming with me."

He winked at her before departing for the bedroom. Lani's insides turned to mush as her gaze locked on his tight rear end. A sigh whispered out of her before she realized what she was doing. *Stop!* Sure, the man had a body to die for and a knack for getting beneath her skin with his cocky smiles and heated glances, but she shouldn't indulge in his candy-coated yummi-ness during the day. She was a professional with a job to do. She needed to stay focused on that.

Before she'd finished her phone call, Asher had reappeared in clean denim and a light gray button-down shirt with the collar open to reveal the strong column of his throat. Her gaze locked on his tan skin as she remembered nibbling her way along it the night before and the heady sounds of his groans. She'd been so entranced by the sounds he'd made that she'd continued ex-ploring him with her lips, teeth and tongue far into the night. A familiar flutter of excitement awakened deep in her belly as she picked up her laptop case.

"Let's get going," she said tersely, hating the husky note in her voice and the heavy pulse of longing that made her want to tear off his shirt and taste him once more.

"After you," he murmured, a wry smile softening his hard masculine features into irresistible boyish charm.

Did he know what she was thinking? She was known for her poker face, but he had a knack for reading her emotions. As they walked down the stairs toward the barn, she surrepti-tiously touched the back of her hand against her cheek. Was she warmer than normal? Did a hot pink flush betray the heat ris-ing in her? How could she remain professional when her body betrayed her at every turn?

"Do you want me to drive?" he asked as their feet crunched along the gravel path, leading from the back of the barn to a series of turnout paddocks. Asher gestured to their cars, sit-ting side-by-side.

"No, I will."

"Okay." He sounded disappointed.

Lani shot him an impatient glance. "What?"

"I thought maybe after last night…" The previous evening they'd discussed her need to be in charge all the time.

"When it comes to my case, what I say goes."

"Yes, boss." He coupled his snarky comeback with a long-suffering sigh.

"I'm not your boss."

His raised eyebrows said she was sure acting like one.

"You like being in control. It seems like having a minion would suit you." He shot her a wicked grin before heading toward the passenger side of her SUV.

He was right. She wanted staff. More investigators meant she could take on more clients, but she needed more cases to be able to afford to hire anyone. When she'd started her investigative business, she hadn't taken into consideration how important contacts would be. Which was why solving this case for Kingston Blue was so critical. Finding the missing festival funds and bringing the embezzler to justice would boost her reputation.

Which was why it made no sense that with so much riding on this case, she was sleeping with the one man who everyone thought was guilty.

"If driving is that important to you," she snapped, deflecting her self-reproach onto him, "then be my guest."

"Thanks."

This single word, spoken with gratitude and delight, further inflamed her heated emotions. All he was trying to do was be helpful. He wanted to participate in clearing his name and she continued to behave like a prickly pear cactus. It wasn't his fault that she'd made the mistake of crossing the professional line. She could've been stronger. Punishing him for her transgression wasn't fair.

Stewing, Lani slid into the passenger seat of his luxury sedan and tried not to enjoy the way she sank into the butter-soft leather.

"So how come you're meeting with Zach?" Asher asked as they sped through the estate gates and turned onto the highway. "Do you think he could be guilty?"

"I'm talking to everyone involved with the festival. And no,

I don't think he's guilty. For one thing, he has a lot of money already."

"Yes, but he makes that money as a social media influencer. Something he's put on hold since moving to Royal. Maybe it was embezzling funds from the festival that gave him the ability to leave his life as an influencer behind."

Lani wasn't sure if she was more surprised by the fact that Asher had obviously been doing some research of his own regarding the festival's participants or the theories he'd developed for why Zach might be a suspect. She'd never given him credit for being capable of such serious, deliberate thought. And that certainly wasn't fair. Yet had he ever indicated that his thoughts were full of anything other than where the next party or exhilarating adventure was?

She winced. How often had she noticed that there was more to Asher than met the eye and then dismissed it as ridiculous? Had it been fair to look no deeper than his gorgeous appearance and his party-boy antics and assume that was all he had to offer? Five years earlier he'd given her a taste of his luxury lifestyle and she'd assumed because he hadn't earned his money that she was better than him.

Is that why she'd determined from the start that it would be a summer fling and nothing more? Because she didn't believe he wasn't capable of or interested in being more than that? She'd avoided discussing serious matters with him. Was that to keep from dwelling on his shallowness or dodge getting too attached? When she'd confessed her love to him, what had she expected would happen between them? Despite toying with the idea of not going on to grad school, the thought of altering her meticulous plans for the future had unnerved her.

Or had she done him a disservice? He hadn't seemed to mind their casual interaction. Lani thought about those true crime books sitting on his shelf. Had getting to know her that summer sparked a passion for unsolved murders? He'd asked a lot of questions about her process and thrown himself into helping her find the missing money. Would he be as interested if he hadn't been charged with the crime?

How come you haven't taken on any associates?

Was that just idle curiosity or was there something more behind the question?

Lani glanced at his profile and wondered what it would be like to partner with someone. To have another person to talk to about cases. To brainstorm ideas. To interact with clients.

No. She'd be crazy to even consider letting Asher get anywhere near her business. She was doing just fine on her own. She'd be doing better after the successful conclusion of this case. After that, she'd go her way and Asher would go his. It was what had happened before. It would happen this time too.

Eight

A merry bell sounded as Asher pulled open Royal Diner's front door. Both a welcome and a warning, the tinkle seemed louder than usual because the classic diner-style restaurant was only half-full. Asher braced as his shocking appearance stirred the atmosphere. For the last week or so he'd actually forgotten about his increased notoriety around town. But now, as the whispers began, Asher ground his molars. He wasn't used to so much negativity directed his way.

Twenty feet of black-and-white-checkerboard tile separated them from the red vinyl booth where Zach Benning sat. A dozen pairs of unfriendly eyes watched his progress as Asher followed Lani past the counter service area. Curiosity and contempt battered him, but he acted oblivious to the commotion he was causing.

Asher focused his attention on the guy they'd come to meet. His gray designer T-shirt gave him an LA vibe. Coupled with his expensive haircut, Zach looked every inch a city boy.

"Hi, Zach, thanks for meeting me." Lani glanced Asher's way before amending, "Meeting with *us*."

"Sure." Zach's eyebrows sank below the rim of his sunglasses as Asher slid into the red vinyl booth beside Lani. "You're out?" This he directed at Asher.

"On bail." Lani spoke up before Asher could explain and her quick explanation left him feeling defensive.

Retreating into sardonic humor, he stuck out his leg and showed off the edge of the ankle monitor. "I'm on a short leash."

This seemed to mollify the other man because after scrutinizing the device, he gave a short, satisfied nod, dismissing Asher as a threat. After that, Zach focused his full attention on Lani and the volume rose on his charisma as he pointed a lopsided smile in her direction. Asher bristled as Lani relaxed beside him.

The two men were close in age and similar in nature, each preferring a freewheeling lifestyle of parties, women and luxury. But where Asher was cavalier about his image, Zach had cultivated his particular bad-boy style into a huge social media following that had made him a multi-millionaire.

Familiar with Lani's weakness for pleasure-seeking reprobates, Asher slung an arm across the back of the booth behind her shoulders and twisted his upper body so he could easily watch the pair interact.

"As I mentioned on the phone, I'm looking into the money that's gone missing from the festival."

Zach's gaze flicked toward Asher and the corners of his lips flattened in derision. "Shouldn't you be asking this guy?" He kicked his thumb in Asher's direction.

"I didn't take the money," Asher growled, letting his annoyance get the better of him. "I'm trying to figure out who did."

"You're trying to figure out...?" Zach looked from Asher to Lani. "I thought you were the one doing the investigating."

Lani gave Asher's thigh a hard nudge with her knee in warning and leaned forward, resting her forearms on the table. "I'm exploring the possibility that someone set Asher up."

While it wasn't a resounding declaration of confidence in his innocence, the tight knot of irritation eased in his chest. Most days he vacillated between relief that she was finally looking into alternate theories of the theft and worry that, without any evidence pointing to another's guilt, her logical mind would return to the most obvious theory that he was responsible.

"Somebody?" Zach echoed. "Like who?"

"Various people." She paused. "I'm talking to anyone who had a connection to the festival—"

"Wait one second," Zach interrupted vehemently, leaning forward. "I had nothing to do with the actual operations and—"

Lani threw up her hands in a pacifying gesture. "Not you, of course." She softened her expression, but didn't actually smile.

"If you're going after Lila, I've got nothing more to say."

"No. No. It's nothing like that," Lani assured him.

Lila Jones was a member of the festival's advisory board in addition to working for the Royal Chamber of Commerce. A hardworking, serious-minded woman, rather forgettable in Asher's book, she'd engaged Zach to promote the festival through social media. Apparently seeing potential where no one else had, Zach had sprinkled some sort of fairy godmother dust on her and turned Lila into an Instagram sensation. The pair had become romantically involved and Lila had been seen around town sporting an enormous diamond on her left hand.

Although normally Asher paid little attention to the love lives of those around him, he was beginning to see a pattern of couples finding each other thanks to the ill-fated festival. He glanced Lani's way. Would that same magic work for them?

"But you were around many who were involved," Lani continued, "and I wanted to hear your impressions."

"I don't know how I can help you." Zach's tension eased marginally. "Early on I showed up, did a photo shoot—not anywhere near the actual site of the festival because of all the construction for the stages and restaurants. I didn't meet all that many people."

Lani offered an encouraging smile. "I'll bet you know more than you realize."

"It was all pretty chaotic. Really disorganized." Zach looked thoughtful. "Wait. Now that I think back, I did catch wind of how materials weren't showing up because bills weren't getting paid. Money problems were delaying everything." Once again Zach glanced toward the guy who everybody thought was the guilty party.

Asher's gut tightened. He could almost hear Lani's brain whirring as she processed what Zach had to say. Okay, so obviously something fishy had been going on with the money all along. And yeah, he should've paid more attention, but the day-to-day details of the project had really not been his cup of tea.

"Besides the funding, did anything else strike you as unusual or wrong?"

"Not really." But Zach grew thoughtful. "Well, maybe this one thing. I kept seeing a guy that I thought I knew from back in LA."

Beside him, Lani stiffened, but her voice sounded nonchalant, almost blasé as she asked, "What guy?"

"Your brother's friend," Zach directed this remark to Asher. "I can't remember the name he introduced himself as, but I remember running into him several times in LA. The names didn't match. But I *swear* it was the same guy."

Ross's friend? Asher thought back to everyone who'd been to the island. When they were pitching it to various vendors and people they knew, they'd brought hordes of people to check out the site and hear the pitch. That had been the fun part... Entertaining the investors, painting a picture of the exclusive event, the delicious food, fantastic wine, the famous headliners like Kingston Blue set to perform, with all the proceeds going to charity.

Turns out he'd done too good a sell. In fact he'd oversold the festival. *Literally.*

The festival had suffered from neglect on the part of the principal players. Ross had been focused on his reunion with Charlotte and getting to know his two-year-old son, Ben. His attention was further disrupted by the major blowup this had caused with Rusty. Being disinherited can sure distract a guy. Sort of like being falsely accused of embezzlement.

Gina had been preoccupied with her mother's return to Royal after a nineteen-year absence and the family drama that had ensued.

That left Asher. His talents involved persuading people to trust him and painting their investors a picture of how awesome the festival was going to be. Initially he'd brought in a lot of the funds that had then gone missing.

"Which friend is that?" Lani asked, returning Asher's attention to the conversation. "Can you describe him?"

"Tall guy. Dark hair. Blue eyes. He seemed as if he knew the family really well. And he spent a lot of time sucking up to your dad."

It sounded like Billy Holmes. Ross's friend from college. He'd been a major player in the festival organization and always seemed to be around.

"You said you couldn't remember his name," Lani began, but before she could go much further into the questioning, Zach snapped his fingers and cut her off.

"Howard Bond," he declared. "No wait, not Howard Bond…"

While Zach scrunched up his face and racked his memory, Asher struggled to keep from shouting at the guy to get on with it. What the hell was going on? Who was Howard Bond? And what did any of this have to do with the embezzled money?

"Bond Howard," Zach announced, looking pleased. "That's it. I remember meeting the guy at a pool party thrown by an executive producer at Universal. I usually meet a lot of people at these events, but he stuck out in my mind as being a first-class dick."

"Why was that?" Lani asked, her flat tone hinting at only casual interest while Asher's heart thumped like a pile driver at the unexpected direction this interview was going.

"The party was loud and I didn't catch his name at first so he repeated it. He's all like, *it's Bond, as in James Bond.*" Zach intoned this like an exaggerated imitation of Sean Connery. "I thought to myself, that's crazy because who names their kid Bond? More likely he was called Howard and his last name is Bond so because it was LA, and everybody changes their name, he switched it to Bond Howard, which is much cooler."

While Zach was telling this tale, Asher noticed that Lani's body had begun to hum with excitement. She was like a blood-hound on a scent and it totally turned him on.

"So, when I met him on the island, and he was introduced as something else, it struck me as odd. Especially when he in-sisted we'd never met."

Lani narrowed her eyes. "Did you doubt it was the same person?"

"No, I was pretty sure it was the same guy. He has a fairly distinctive look. Do you know what I mean? Not like you'd mis-take him for a bunch of other people."

Was this a legit lead? Asher glanced at Lani, but her expres-sion remained inscrutable. He wanted to end this meeting with Zach and get her alone so he could figure out what was going on in that big beautiful brain of hers. Hope was tapping on the edge of his consciousness, wanting in. For the first time since his whole world came crashing down around him, Asher re-alized the level of fear he been suppressing. His hands began to shake as the truth of his reality struck him. In the back of his mind, he'd been grappling with going to jail for a crime he hadn't committed. Only now, as it was looking like someone else might be a suspect, did traction set in.

"Well that sounds promising," Asher said, keeping a lid on his excitement as they stood up and headed toward the exit of the Royal Diner.

Before they reached the exit, the chime above the door rang, warning him someone was coming in. Both he and Lani slowed to let the new arrival enter. Deputy Vesta entered, tipping his hat to Lani as she headed out past him. Asher started to follow, but found the deputy in his way. Before he could step aside, Vesta had bumped his broad shoulder hard into Asher's chest as he went by. Although the blow didn't throw him off balance, the hit jolted his ego, reminding him that in the eyes of the town, he was a thief who'd stolen from people who couldn't afford the losses.

In a much more subdued frame of mind, Asher lengthened his stride to catch up with Lani. "Why do you think Billy would've introduced himself as Bond Howard?" he asked, picking up their earlier conversational thread.

"First of all, we're not really sure if this Bond Howard and Billy Holmes are the same person."

Asher appreciated Lani's caution about as much as a pie in the face. He wanted her to leap all over this lead and chase it down to prove she believed in his innocence and would go to any lengths to exonerate him. Instead, she showed every sign of proceeding with her plodding, methodical investigation.

"How do we go about figuring out if they are?" Asher asked, letting just a bit of his impatience show.

He unlocked his car and swung the passenger door open for Lani. She shot him the oddest look before sliding into the car.

"What?" he prodded.

"I can open my own doors."

"Stop being so damned independent," he growled, wishing she understood how much he enjoyed taking care of her. "Let me help once in a while."

Asher wasn't just talking about the car door. He wanted to impress upon her that he was someone she could rely on. She might be too proud to accept financial help from him, but he could be there for her in other ways. As a sounding board to bounce ideas off of. As muscle in case she got into another tight situation like the one with Mika Sorenson's husband.

"Whatever."

She pulled the door shut, leaving him standing on the side-walk, staring at her through the side window. How could this woman be so sensual and yielding in bed and stubborn and prickly out of it? Naked in his arms, she gave every part of herself to the moment and to him. But heaven forbid he fixed her favorite cocktail or made her dinner or—*gasp*—opened her car door, because then she became surly and churlish.

By the time he circled the car and slipped behind the wheel, she had her laptop out and was madly clicking away on the keys. From her extreme focus he might as well not have been in the car at all.

"Where to?" he asked, starting the engine. If it had been up to him, he would've driven straight to Billy Holmes's house and demanded answers.

"Just a second."

Asher was growing accustomed to Lani's ability to block out all distractions when she was investigating and didn't take offense when she put him off.

Still, he decided to do some musing out loud. "Why do you suppose Billy was using a different name in LA?"

"We don't know that it was Billy."

"But Zach seemed pretty sure," Asher argued. "And he was right about Billy's look being distinctive."

Lani made some noncommittal noises and continued to work away at her laptop. With a weary sigh, he put the car in gear, signaled and pulled out of the parking spot. One way to find out about Billy was to ask the guy himself. A tempting move, but he suspected he would do himself no favors if he started confronting people and accusing them of the theft. However he could go ask the suspect's good friend, Asher's brother, Ross.

They were halfway to The Edmond Organization when Lani looked up from her laptop and realized they weren't on their way back to the estate. "Where are we going?"

"To talk to Ross. He's known Billy since college and they've kept in touch all these years. Surely he knows what his good friend has been up before he moved to Royal two years ago."

"Are you out of your mind?" She rolled her eyes. "We can't barge into Ross's office and start asking a bunch of invasive questions about his friend."

"Why not?"

When she didn't immediately answer, Asher glanced her way. Her pained expression was like a knife in his chest.

"Why the hell not, Lani?" he demanded, a sick feeling swirling through him.

"A few months back your brother was struggling financially."

"You don't seriously think that Ross was involved in this embezzlement, do you?"

He couldn't believe what he was hearing. Ross wouldn't do something like that to him. Yet even as he rejected Lani's inference, her logic began eroding his trust. Whom was he supposed to put his faith in? The man he'd called brother since he was a teenager? Or the woman he'd spent a fun-filled summer frolicking with? The same one who was currently investigating him for embezzlement?

"Let's put it this way, I suspect everyone." Her answer was a sharp kick that connected with his head and set his temples to throbbing.

"Including me," he stated flatly, gripping the steering wheel until his knuckles turned white.

"Yes."

Presuming he'd made inroads with her had been too optimistic. Just because they were sleeping together, didn't mean her opinion of him had improved. No. Just as it had been between them five years ago, he was little more than a walk on the wild side for her. She'd been clear from the start that she couldn't take him seriously. He wasn't relationship material.

While he'd been ruminating, she'd gone back to typing. If they weren't heading to the Edmond headquarters, he needed some destination. "So, where are we going?"

If Lani heard the tension in his voice, she made no sign. "I think the best thing is to head back to Elegance Ranch. I have some research to do on this Bond Howard character. We need to figure out if he and Billy are the same guy."

"And how do we do that?"

"Well, we can start with his social media."

"Billy's?" Asher had no idea how that was supposed to help.

Lani shook her head. "Bond Howard's."

Asher gave her space to work as he drove back to the estate. The moments of freedom he'd known while driving during his all-too-brief trip to the Royal Diner left him hyperaware of how little he'd appreciated his freedom until now.

As the estate gates loomed, he had a fleeting but overwhelming urge to turn the car around and head straight for the airport. He knew he wouldn't get anywhere with the electronic-monitoring device strapped to his ankle, but a jittery restlessness had taken hold of him. In the past he had exorcized his demons by indulging in some sort of risky action. That door was shut and barred to him for now. He would just have to face his reality and learn to make the best of it.

The thought actually made him grin. Was this what personal growth was all about? It figured it would take something as drastic as looming imprisonment to wake him up.

"Any luck finding Bond Howard's social media presence?" he asked as the car raced past the main house and made for the stable.

"Hmm."

It really was time for a change, he mused. As much as he enjoyed living close to his horses, he really should put the entire string up for sale and move away from Elegance Ranch.

"There's quite a bit actually," Lani said, clicking away on her laptop. "Turns out he has several online personas."

Asher mulled that bit of news as he parked beside her SUV. Her preoccupation with whatever data she was finding gave him enough time to shut off the car, exit and have her door open before she closed the lid. He smirked at her scowl and went the extra mile by offering his hand to help her out of the low-slung sedan.

The tingle in his fingers shot straight to his groin. He pushed all thoughts of sex from his brain and asked, "How did you find the additional social media profiles so quickly?"

"I have software that allows me to find similar images on the internet. Already the search has yielded profiles for Bobby Hammond and Brad Howell, in addition to Bond Howard."

"That looks pretty suspicious," Asher said, hoping she agreed.

"Maybe." She started for the stairs to the apartment. "We'll need to do some more digging before that becomes clear."

"We'll," he echoed, grinning. "I like the sound of that."

Nine

For days after their meeting with Zach, Lani kicked herself for letting Asher think he was participating in the investigation. It was hers to handle. She shouldn't have involved him at all. And the excuse that she enjoyed his company was too lame for her to acknowledge even though it was absolutely the case. So much for her lone-wolf policy. Maybe she'd been too quick to downplay her need for associates. His determined approach to the task was altering her attitude. Sure, his style was different from hers. But that didn't mean his results weren't sound. Could she let go of her need to control the entire process? *Should* she?

Still, day after day they'd set up their laptops at his breakfast bar. Side by side, typing away in companionable silence. She'd done a deep dive into Bond Howard while Asher researched Bobby Hammond and Brad Howell. Sure enough, Billy Holmes had been living in various parts of the country under different names. They'd contacted anyone who had tagged him in their photos and a picture was beginning to form. The women were quickest to respond. Asher and Lani discovered Billy had left a trail of jilted lovers and unsatisfied investors in his wake. Everyone was angry.

And now he was comfortably ensconced in the Edmond estate, living rent-free in one of the guesthouses and showing no sign of moving on. Lani gazed in the direction of the main house, wondering how a college friendship had translated into the relationship Billy now enjoyed with the entire Edmond family. From what she could tell, he was practically a member of the family. Did Ross know about Billy's multiple identities? She hadn't seen the two men interacting. Was it possible that they'd been working together to bring the festival down?

If so...why?

It was well-known that once Ross's former lover—and their child that she'd never told him about—had returned to town, his relationship with his father had completely fallen apart to the point where Rusty had disinherited his biological son. Would Ross's financial troubles have made him an unwitting pawn in Billy's schemes? Or had Ross gotten in over his head and chosen to frame his own brother for the crime to avoid taking the fall?

Either way they couldn't tip off either man until she gathered more information.

"It's not looking too good for our boy, is it?" Asher's delight broke through Lani's introspection. His lopsided smile had appeared. For the first time since she'd visited him in jail, he looked genuinely relieved.

Although she wanted to reassure him, her instincts warned her to be cautious. "Not at all."

Asher's good mood dimmed. "You don't sound all that sure."

"It looks bad," Lani agreed. "But nothing we've turned up is proof that Billy is connected to anything illegal with the Soiree on the Bay festival. Adopting multiple aliases and convincing wealthy women to invest in his business ideas might be sketchy, but not every venture is successful. Maybe the guy is better at ideas than execution."

"So I'm still the bad guy."

He'd raked his fingers through his hair frequently over the course of the last two hours and several unruly spikes poked up in various directions. She liked his disheveled look. It reminded her of all those mornings when she'd awoken in his bed and watched him sleep. She'd known such joy in those unguarded moments. Anything had seemed possible. Like she could have it all... The satisfying career she craved. A happy life with the man who showed her how to let go and have fun. Lani pushed away the fantasy. These dreams of the perfect future were a distraction she couldn't afford.

"Look, don't give up hope." She set her hand on his shoulder and squeezed. "We'll find something."

Asher took both her hands in his and faced her. His somber expression made her stomach drop. She traced his features with her gaze, absorbing the sensual curve of his lips, the strong bones of his face, the hint of stubble that blurred the sharp jut of his jaw. Naked emotion flickered in his dark brown eyes. Relief. Gratitude. And something...*more*. Her breath caught at the vulnerability she glimpsed in that unguarded moment. She set her palm on his chest. In the stillness that followed, her heart found a new rhythm and beat in sync with his.

A second later he lowered his thick lashes and the link between them snapped. The recoil stung. Neither one of them was brave enough to acknowledge the connection between them for long. Yet each day it grew stronger. The ache more acute when they were apart. And unlike when they'd been together that summer, she was losing the will to resist her longing to be with him. In the sensible moments when her emotions weren't in control, she wondered what would happen when this case ended.

"I hope you realize how much I appreciate that you believe in me," Asher said, covering her hand on his chest and giving a light squeeze. "I don't know how I would've gotten through this without you."

Lani's throat tightened, making speech impossible. This would be the perfect moment to tell him that she still had doubts about his innocence. Her last report to Kingston Blue had been objective and scrupulously professional. Afraid that she was letting her personal feelings interfere with her judgment, she hadn't voiced her suspicions that Asher might have been set up. Once again she had prioritized her career over her personal life and doubted Asher would understand.

Instead of facing her mistakes, she apologized to him in a way that they could both appreciate.

"Hey," she murmured, sliding her fingers through his hair and offering him her best come-hither smile. "I could use a snack."

Asher's sleepy gaze stroked her features. "I'm feeling a little hungry myself."

"You know I'm not talking about food, right?"

His wicked grin said it all. "What did you have in mind?"

She slid off the stool and snagged his waistband, drawing him toward the living room. "It's about time we christen this chair, don't you think?"

"Oh, yes. I'd been thinking that exact thing just an hour ago."

"And you didn't bring it up?" she teased, unfastening his belt, the button on his jeans and the zipper below. With her breath escaping her lungs on a languid sigh, she burrowed under all the fabric and dropped to her knees before him, taking his clothes with her. At her urging, he stepped out of each pant leg, letting her undress him. His fingers brushed a stray lock off her cheek. She knew he would tangle his hands in her hair later, riding the movement of her head as she brought him pleasure with her mouth.

Lani placed her hands on his thighs, palms skimming his hair-roughened skin, past his jutting erection and over the smooth, chiseled plains of his abdomen. There, she gave a gentle shove and he sat down in the armchair with a quiet grunt of surprise. Then she was parting his knees and sliding between them. Her fingers began working the buttons of his shirt. When she had them undone, she spread the fabric wide and leaned forward to press a kiss to his throat. His Adam's apple worked as he swallowed hard and she smiled as she nipped and nuzzled her way to his ear, across his jaw and finally to the corner of his mouth. He turned and slanted his head so their lips met. Their open-mouth kiss was a slow, sultry tease of breath and flicking tongue. Lani's hands tracked down his chest and stomach, savoring the splendid muscle beneath all his silken skin. The man was perfection in so many ways.

With her hot gaze on his arousal, she set to peeling off her own clothes. Stripped down to her underwear, she fondled her breasts through her lace bra before bracing her hands on the chair's arms and bending forward.

"Care to do the honors?"

"My pleasure."

He reached behind her and popped the bra clasp. The fabric fell into his grasp and she bestowed a saucy wink.

"Thank you."

As the ache between her thighs intensified, Lani skimmed her palm down her belly and beneath the edge of her panties. Because he loved to watch her like this, she threw her head back, rolled her hips from side to side and pressed her fingertips against her clit. Wetness soaked her panties. When he made a strangled sound, she opened her eyes and focused on his face.

A moment later she dropped to her knees once more and let her hair down, knowing he adored the seductive slide of the strands against his skin. With a brazen smile, she moved between his thighs and wrapped her fingers around his erection without warning or preliminaries. A breath ejected from his lungs, a startled curse that made her smile.

Lani eased her hold on his shaft. "Too much?"

"No." The single syllable wheezed out of him as her thumb circled the head of his shaft, sliding over the bead of moisture she found there before gliding her fingers to the base. "It's perfect."

Asher clenched his fingers over the chair's arms and settled deeper into the seat, offering his body for her to play with.

She repeated the stroking motion, watching the way his head dropped back and his lips parted. He watched her from beneath heavy lidded eyes, tiny flecks of copper blazing in their depths. While his posture looked relaxed, his expression remained tight with anticipation. She understood. She couldn't wait to get her mouth on him. And why bother holding back when that's what he wanted too?

She licked her lips and lowered them over his blunt head, purring in delight at the salty taste of the velvety flesh. A growl tore from Asher's throat as she flicked her tongue over him, tormenting him the way he had done to her the night before.

"God, Lani."

Her name on his lips was heaven. She decided to reward him. Shutting her eyes to block out all distraction, she hummed and took him in, the vibration making him jerk in reaction. He was clutching the arms of the chair now, bracing to endure the wicked pleasure she was giving him.

Making her lips into a tight circle, she took as much as him into her mouth as she could handle. It was a lot, but she'd learned how to relax and open for him. When the head of his erection hit the back of her throat, his fingers slipped into her hair. He played with the strands, applying no pressure as she withdrew, circled him with her tongue and bobbed backed down again.

His appreciative murmur, punctuated with the occasional hiss of acute pleasure were the only sounds that came from him. He'd let her know when he was close. Communicate if he wanted her to finish him in this way or climb aboard. In the meantime she would make this a night to remember. By alternating between teasing and deep dives, she held him on the brink longer than she expected.

But his willpower was only so resilient and she'd mastered the art of pleasuring him this way. When he cupped her face in his hands and angled her head away from his erection, her body awakened with delight. He covered her swollen lips in a tender kiss that tangled their tongues and said without words how deeply he appreciated her.

"Come here."

He pulled her up off the floor and drew her onto the chair. There was just enough room for her knees on either side of his hips. His long fingers bracketed her hips, moving her into position. His thick shaft bobbed against her thigh, seeking the connection they both hungered for.

Lani gasped as he speared into her dripping heat. Utterly turned on, the full length of him filling her was nearly enough to trigger her orgasm. She was close...so close. Swollen with longing and impatient with need, when his mouth closed over the tip of one breast and sucked hard, she knew there would be no more holding back. Her hips bucked enthusiastically against him, grinding her clit against his pelvic bone, and a heartbeat later, her climax ripped through her.

She clutched his head against her breast, riding him hard, launched even higher at the scrape of his teeth against her nipple. The bliss seemed to go on and on, aided by the length of him driving into her over and over. Lani gasped and cried out, ridiculous incoherent chanting as her pleasure soared higher, so much higher. She could scarcely breathe. Surely she should have plateaued by now. But his persistent thrusts, so smooth and with perfect rhythm, made her muscles tense and coil as she ascended toward the peak of yet another orgasm. He'd done this for her before. Made her come and come and come again.

It's what made her crazy for him. His body, his soul, the heart he tried to protect. He was the one she'd dreamed about before they'd ever met and long after they'd parted. Fate had brought them back together. Now it was up to them to figure out how to make it work. Because this time she didn't want to say goodbye.

Had it only been three weeks since he'd been arrested for embezzling the festival funds? It felt like the threat of imprisonment had been hanging over him for far longer. How ironic that the worst thing that had ever happened to him resulted in something as wonderful as bringing Lani Li back into his life.

The last week together had been nothing short of magic. They'd returned to the playful camaraderie and sizzling passion of five years earlier. There were moments when he was convinced everything would turn out okay, but then he'd bump the electronic monitor on his ankle and the whole miserable mess returned to his awareness in a hurry.

Asher shook hands with the horse trainer who'd arrived to pick up Royal Flush. As they loaded her into the trailer for the journey to California, he walked away with a tight throat and a heart ready for fresh opportunities,

The money he'd gotten for Royal Flush would clear the debt between him and Lani. Sacrificing his favorite mount demonstrated his willingness to grow. As much as he'd loved them, the horses tied him to his old life. They had been his comfort when his relationship with Rusty floundered and offered direction when it came to his life's purpose.

Lani had been right to call him out all those years ago. He *had* been a directionless frat boy. But that had changed once he'd met her. And now that she was back in his life, he intended to evolve even more. New challenges awaited him and Lani was the key to what he wanted to do next.

Smiling, Asher attacked the stairs to his apartment, taking the steps two at a time. He was eager to share his new vision with Lani and see her reaction. She agreed with his assessment that The Edmond Organization wasn't the place for him. Tonight he was taking her to dinner, a celebration of the positive changes he was making in his life since she'd come back into it.

He'd chosen Sheen, not only because the restaurant was known for its exceptional cuisine, but also for being run and staffed by all women of various ethnicities. Ross's fiancée, Charlotte Jarrett, had returned to Royal to oversee the kitchen and had quickly made the restaurant a Royal favorite.

Lani had headed back to Dallas that morning to meet with a

potential client and planned to return by six o'clock. That left Asher an hour to shower and get ready for their date. The word sent an electric zap through him. With his nerve endings buzzing pleasantly, he headed into the bathroom and the large mirror over the double vanity reflected back his goofy grin. He rubbed his palm over his stubbled cheeks, noted the sparkle in his eyes and remarked at the transformation joy had wrought. Damn, he was *happy*. Even to the point where he could appreciate the pain-in-the-ass electronic monitor clamped to his ankle, being charged with embezzlement and wire fraud had brought Lani back into his life.

Half an hour later Asher emerged from his closet dressed for dinner and realized he was no longer alone in the apartment. A cell phone was ringing in the living room. Eager to show Lani how much he'd missed her, he was halfway across the bedroom when he heard her answer the call.

"Hello, Kingston."

Asher slowed his pace as the name registered. Kingston, as in Kingston Blue? An image of the famous singer popped into Asher's mind. Above-average height with an imposing frame and a handsome face framed by long dreadlocks, his open and friendly manner combined with a wide white smile had disarmed and enchanted everyone. But it was his keen brown eyes that had told the real story as his gaze had scrutinized the construction happening at the festival site on Appaloosa Island, assessing the pros and cons before agreeing to headline Soiree on the Bay.

What was he doing calling Lani?

"What's up?" While she came across as calm and professional, Asher detected a wary note.

Moving carefully, he took several steps toward the door leading into the living room, the better to hear the conversation, aware that by eavesdropping he was questioning if he could trust Lani. In a flash he realized he was once again prioritizing his needs first and in doing so causing damage to their fledgling relationship. How could he hope to form a solid connection with her when the first time his faith was tested, he chose to doubt.

"...progress report," came the deep rich masculine voice. Lani must have had him on speaker.

Progress report? What progress report? Asher recalled how she'd avoided answering every time he asked her who hired her to look into the missing money. Was Kingston Blue that client? The man hadn't made all his money with his music. He was a savvy businessman, as well. And obviously one determined to locate what had been stolen from him.

"As I mentioned before," Lani said, "this case is a lot more complicated than it seemed. The money vanished from the bank accounts right after the funds were transferred. The feds think the money was moved offshore, but there's no trace of those accounts on Asher's work or personal computers, his phone or in his house. If he was funneling the money away from the festival accounts, then he was very careful about it."

"If?" Concern deepened Kingston Blue's voice. "You disagree with the feds about Asher Edmond's guilt?"

"I know the evidence points to him. His name is on the house in the Maldives," she said, "and his online signature triggered the wire transfers. But he could've been set up."

A pregnant silence followed her words. Asher's heart hammered. While it sounded like she was defending him, this conversation drove home the fact that she'd ultimately come to Royal to find the missing festival funds. Something he'd conveniently put to the back of his mind.

"I hired you because of your previous relationship with Asher," Kingston Blue said. "I assumed you would use that connection to get information out of him about where the money ended up."

Kingston's words scored a direct hit. Asher set his hand on the wall as his thoughts reeled. All this time she'd been playing him for a fool. While he shouldn't be surprised, that didn't make the emotional blow less devastating. She made it very clear five years ago that her career came first and he was just a reckless playboy without a future. Well, one thing was true, obviously she'd gotten a lot better at acting.

"That's not how I work," Lani said stiffly. "I've been looking into various people involved in the festival and Asher isn't the only one with access to those funds. His brother Ross—"

Kingston Blue interrupted her. "It seems to me you're just offering me excuses why you think your ex-boyfriend is innocent. I'm not paying you to exonerate him."

"Asher was never my boyfriend." Her voice was stark and fervent on that point. "I'm not emotionally involved with him now if that's what you're thinking. You hired me to find the money and if you can be patient with me a little longer, that's what I intend to do."

"By chasing random leads."

"By doing a *thorough* investigation," Lani insisted. "As soon as investigators found the house in the Maldives, they stopped looking at anyone else."

"There's overwhelming evidence that Asher's the one who transferred the funds out of the festival account. Where they went is what I want to know."

"So do I," she said. "But I need to figure out who actually stole the money."

"Asher Edmond."

"Maybe." Lani sounded less than thrilled to be arguing with her client. "But I'm also looking into someone else. Billy Holmes."

"Who is that?"

"Friend of the family. He lives at the Edmonds' estate. I've discovered he has a suspicious background and I'd like to pursue the lead."

Kingston Blue paused before answering as if weighing his options. "You have three days. After that you're off the case."

Asher took several seconds to compose himself before emerging from the bedroom. Lani was standing by the large window that overlooked the extensive manicured grounds between the barn and the main house.

"You're back early," he remarked, crossing the room to pull her back against his body and place a kiss on her cheek. "How'd the meeting with the new client go?"

She stiffened momentarily before relaxing into his embrace. "Good. She hired me."

"Then we should celebrate." Asher headed into his kitchen to pull a bottle of champagne from the wine cooler, and set two glasses on the breakfast bar. "You have a new client. I sold Royal Flush."

"You want to celebrate that?" Lani asked, drawing near. "That's been a big part of your life. I thought you'd be sad that she was gone."

Asher focused on pulling the cork from the bottle rather than look at her. He was still processing the call he'd overheard.

"It was hard to part with her, but she's too well trained to waste away here." Asher pictured the chestnut tearing across the polo field and smiled. "And since her new owner paid me a hundred thousand dollars for her, I can pay you back the money you put up for my bail and compensate you for the time you spent on my case."

This last part he'd added to test her reaction.

"I already have a client." She looked uncomfortable. "You know that."

"Is there some reason you can't have two?"

"I'm not sure that your goals aren't in conflict."

"It seems as if everyone wants to find the money. Including me." He extended a glass filled with bright sparkling liquid toward her. "I'd also like to find out who stole it. I don't see how we could possibly be in conflict."

"I just don't think it's a good idea."

Dismayed by the fact that she continued to let him think that Rusty had hired her, Asher chose not to push any further. No doubt she had her reasons for keeping him in the dark. The fact that they were at odds as long as this case remained open was not the problem. He was more concerned what would happen once everything had been wrapped up.

He lightly clicked his crystal flute against hers before taking a sip. He watched her surreptitiously while appearing to savor the champagne. She looked more miserable than he'd ever seen her. Obviously guilt wasn't a comfortable weight on her shoulders.

"Now that I've officially closed the door on any chance of a comeback as a professional polo player—"

"Was that a possibility?" she interrupted, arching one dark eyebrow.

"Hush. I've been thinking what I want to do next."

Retreating into his frat-boy act was familiar and would serve him better than venting his frustration over the investigation's slow progress.

"Next?" She looked resigned as she asked, "What about your position at The Edmond Organization?"

"I promised Rusty that I'd stick with it for two years. My time is up and after spending these weeks with you, I realize I rather enjoyed investigative work and I think I have a knack for it."

She gave an odd snort and then began to cough vigorously as if the champagne had gone up her nose rather than down her throat. "I'm sorry?" she wheezed. "Didn't you go to work for the family business after Rusty threatened to cut you off? How are you going to support yourself?"

"By partnering with you."

"Partnering...?"

"You're not the only one who can dig up information on people. I checked you out and it turns out your business is in a bit of a slump. It could use someone like me to bring in more high-profile clients."

Lani was staring at him as if had sprouted a set of horns. "Let me get this straight, you want to go into business with me?"

"Why so surprised?" He ignored the negative sweep of her head. "We work well together."

"I think you like dabbling in my investigation because it's a distraction. But once this case is over and if you're exonerated—"

"If?" Her meaning went through him like a hot blade. Without her on his side, eager to prove his innocence, he could still go to jail. Even if the money was recovered.

She continued speaking as if he hadn't interrupted her. "I'm convinced you'll lose interest in the kind of work I do."

Asher needed no further proof of Lani's low expectations about him and the hit blew a big hole in what he thought was developing between them. This constant feeling of not being good enough because he'd made mistakes in the past was getting old. No wonder he'd preferred traveling around the world playing professional polo to sticking around and seeing nothing but disappointment and disapproval in his father's eyes.

"Are you really worried that it's the investigative work I'm going to lose interest in?" he countered, frustration making him strike out at the one person he wanted to make happy.

She shifted her weight backward, a slow recoil from his insinuation. "What else?"

"Or is this about us?"

Ten

Us?

Lani stiffened at the question and leveled her gaze at him. The answer was too fraught with uncertainty to answer. Was Asher romancing her for the sole purpose of using her to change careers? She'd been worried that he wanted her on his side to clear him of the embezzlement charges, but now it seemed he wanted to move in on her business, as well.

"Is there an *us*?" she asked, unsure where to draw the line between reality and fantasy.

"You tell me. Are we going to keep seeing each other once the case is over?"

She could barely acknowledge to herself how much she wanted their sexual connection to develop into deep romantic love much less share that with Asher. Long ago she'd confessed her feelings and he'd rejected them. She couldn't face that same crushing disappointment again.

Lani bit her lower lip and grappled with how to answer him. "I don't know." She wanted to, but once the prescribed proximity of the investigation ended, would Asher even be interested in a personal relationship anymore? His interest in her business seemed to confuse the situation. "You live here in Royal and I'm in Dallas…" It was an obvious dodge given how they'd broken up last time.

"Once you were open to a long-distance relationship," he reminded her.

"And you made it very clear that it wasn't your thing."

"What if I moved to Dallas?"

Hope barreled through her, but she shut it down. Was this about their relationship or a business partnership? Had she let herself be played?

"Are you serious about quitting The Edmond Organization?"

"It's not for me," he told her.

"What about your horse training?"

"I'm already in the process of selling the string." His gaze increased in intensity as he spoke. "I'd like to help you with your business, but it's more important that you want to take a chance on me."

"I tried that once." She could barely get the words out past the lump in her throat. "It didn't work out so well for me."

"So you're saying you can't trust me."

"I don't honestly know. All this is coming at me so suddenly and there's a lot of upheaval in your life right now. Who knows how you'll feel once the case is closed and things settle down." As much as she wanted to trust him with her heart, she'd been devastated last time.

"Don't make this about how I feel," he said, wariness entering his expression. "I want to know how you feel. What are we doing? Is it just casual sex or are we going to turn it into something real?"

"Something *real*?" She tried the phrase on for size, but couldn't find comfort in the fit. "I don't know."

Even though they'd reconnected physically, her resistance to baring her heart put a wall between them. A wall she was loathe to tear down. Sex was one thing—they had explosive chemistry and it was easy to lose herself in the magic of his touch. However, as long as the embezzlement charge hung over his head, he needed her help with the investigation. Once it was over, she would reconsider taking the risk of getting emotionally entangled with him. But for now she couldn't in good conscience commit to that.

"Because you're using me to close your case and make your client happy?"

"I'm *not* using you." That was true even if it had been her plan at the start. Once her old feelings had surfaced, she'd lost the battle with how much she wanted him. "But I really don't know if we can make it work."

"Sounds like you've made up your mind." He stared at her for a long time while a muscle jumped in his jaw. "So, I guess that means you're putting me in your rearview mirror once more."

"*I'm* the one putting *you* in the rearview mirror?" Was she hearing him right? "I recall that I wanted to try the long-distance thing and you thought that was too much of a commitment."

Asher's gaze intensified. "And so you called us done and walked away."

"You didn't give me a whole lot of choice. Basically, it was either give up on grad school and run off with you to Argentina or we were over." Her blood raged white-hot as unresolved resentment flared. A second later fear and panic kicked in. She was on the verge of losing him all over again. "You didn't want to do the long-distance thing."

"Okay, so maybe that was a mistake."

Maybe?

"Or maybe neither one of us was ready for a committed relationship" she said. "And so we did the best thing we could do for ourselves and broke up."

"It wasn't that cut and dry for me."

What did that mean? Lani sucked in a deep breath in an effort to calm her wildly fluctuating emotions. She hadn't expected the fledgling intimacy between her and Asher to be tested so soon.

"What do you want me to say?" *That you were my first love and I never got over you?*

"I want you to be honest with me about how you feel."

"Honest." Her chest heaved as she gulped in a big breath. "Okay, if you want the truth, the reason I don't think it's a good idea for us to become business partners or any other kind of partner is that I'm not sure I can count on you."

From the first she'd recognized that they approached situations completely differently. Where her personality was a bullet shot from a gun, a swift straight line from problem to solution, Asher was like air. A gentle breeze coming at her from one direction. Then moments later a gust of wind that smacked into her blind side, knocking her off her feet.

"You still see me as that irresponsible frat boy." Asher scowled. "That's not who I am and hasn't been for a long time."

Yet he couldn't stick with anything. Not polo. Not the job with The Edmond Organization. Not her.

"Really?" she challenged. "Look at the mess you're in because you didn't take your responsibilities with the festival seriously."

"You have no idea what I take seriously. Yes, I had access to the accounts…"

"And someone—probably Billy Holmes—was able to take advantage of that."

"But it could've been any of us. Gina. Ross. Even Rusty given how close the two of them are. He chose me for some reason I don't get."

Lani heard Asher's sweeping frustration, but couldn't summon the courage to comfort him. "Hopefully I can figure that out. I'm heading to Las Vegas to meet with his mother tomorrow."

But Asher wasn't going to be thrown off topic. "What would it take for me to prove you can count on me?"

She dug her fingertips into the back of her shoulder where

stress was pinching the nerves and gave her whirling brain a moment to process everything that was coming at her.

"I really don't know."

"Well, at least be straight with me on one thing. Do you think I stole the money from the festival?"

"No." At least she could give him a clear, decisive answer on that score.

He gave her a tight smile. "Well, I guess that's something. And the money for my bail. Do I return the hundred thousand dollars to you?"

Lani went cold. The intensity of the question put a hard lump in the pit of her stomach. Was he shooting in the dark or had he overheard her conversation with Kingston? She'd been careless when she didn't realize he was in the apartment.

When she didn't answer right away, he continued, "Or should I wire it directly back to Kingston Blue?"

Damn. Now he knew she'd been deceiving him from the start. "You can give it to me. I'll get it back to him."

His eyes narrowed. "Can I trust you?"

Although she knew it was a big show to get under her skin, Lani stiffened. "Of course."

"I'm not so sure. Knowing how complicated our relationship is, you let me believe my father hired you. How could you let me think he was finally on my side?"

Lani dropped her eyes to the floor. "I shouldn't have done that."

"No," he agreed. "You think you understand how messed up things are between us, but it's worse than you know. It was a big deal for me to believe that he wanted to help me out."

"Why such a big deal now when he's supported you since the day he married your mother?"

A sardonic smile ghosted across his lips. "He supported me. But there were conditions tied to it. Conditions I had no idea about until three years ago." Asher's grim expression made Lani's heart sink.

It was becoming clear that she'd made a huge error in judgment. "What sort of conditions?"

"He and my mother had a little side agreement regarding her alimony. She agreed that since I turned eighteen, any money he gave me came out of the payments he owed her. And as part of the deal, she wasn't allowed to tell me anything about what was going on."

Lani gasped. "Why would he do that?"

"Because he's a miserable excuse for a human being. I don't know if he regretted formally adopting me or if he just wanted to mess with her. A couple years ago, I found out she was nearly bankrupt and I couldn't understand why. She finally broke down and confessed what had been going on. I confronted Rusty and he offered me a bargain. He would pay my mother everything he'd withheld if I agreed to sign a five-year contract with The Edmond Organization."

"Did you?"

Asher kept his gaze fixed on the windows that faced the main house. "As much as I wanted to help my mother, I knew I wouldn't survive five years working for Rusty. Instead, I got him to agree to let me work for him for two and a half years in exchange for fifty-percent of the money he'd spent on me. That, and what I had in investments was enough to get her out of trouble."

"Why didn't you tell me this before?" Lani asked, her heart aching for all he'd been through.

"Why should I?" He shook his head. "When you already had more than enough reasons not to trust me."

He was right. She'd failed to believe him at every turn. And each time she'd been wrong.

"So now you know. I didn't quit polo because I was afraid to be cut off. I didn't join The Edmond Organization because I was trying to win Rusty's approval, and I'm not leaving because I can't stick with anything. I haven't sold off my horses because I'm tired of training. And I don't want to become your business partner as some sort of lark."

Lani had no words that could undo the damage she'd caused by not believing in him. "I'm sorry." It became immediately obvious this was the wrong thing to say.

"Don't be. It's my problem, not yours." With his lips flattened into a thin line, he raked his fingers through his hair. "Look, I don't feel much like celebrating tonight and it sounds like you've got a trip to get ready for. If it's okay with you, I think we should skip dinner and call it a night."

"Okay. I understand…"

And while she stood with her heart a lead stone in her chest, Asher headed into the master bedroom and closed the door behind him.

The morning after his fight with Lani, Asher woke with a headache and a really bad idea.

It was time for a party.

Not that he had anything to celebrate or was in the mood to be social. Lani had let him believe that she was on his side and that he had a reason to dream of a better future with her a big part of it. Nothing he'd done in the last three weeks had convinced her to give him a chance. She still perceived him as someone frivolous and shallow, unable to consider anyone's welfare but his own. Had he really thought by letting her in on his bargain with Rusty that her outlook toward him would suddenly be transformed? He was so tired of fighting everyone's bad opinion of him, of having to prove himself to people he loved.

The realization hit him like a piano falling from a very tall crane.

Damn.

He loved her. He loved Lani Li.

She was the one he let get away. Now he knew she was also the woman he couldn't live without. The one person he longed to spend the rest of his life laughing and fighting and making love with. The certainty had been building for days. It had taken a huge relationship-ending blowout for the fog to clear from his brain.

Was it any wonder he wanted to act out, to wallow in self-sabotage, letting everyone believe he was the same direction-less jerk he'd always been?

He thought back to five years ago when he and Lani had first met. What if he'd been more serious back then instead of letting frivolous pursuits distract him? He could've saved his mother financial headaches and achieved a high level of success in his field. Instead he'd fallen short of expectations and reinforced Rusty's disapproval.

At the time he hadn't realized how he'd given his power away. Not until Lani had come along and opened his eyes to hard work and focused goal setting had he been filled by an optimistic sense of his own worth. How different things might've been if he'd had someone in his corner sooner.

Someone who could've channeled his ability to charm people into positive avenues. Much of what had appealed to him with the Soiree on the Bay festival was the chance to benefit others. How ironic that instead of helping people out, the whole situation had destroyed numerous lives.

Being the guy that everyone hated had been a wake-up call. Using his money and position to benefit others would be so much better than selfishly squandering everything he'd gained. When his accounts were unfrozen, he intended to make changes in his life. He would invest in other people's dreams, focusing his resources, time and energy on helping people.

But that was his future. In the now, the one woman he needed to believe in him couldn't. The agony lancing through his heart pushed him toward self-destructive behaviors. The old Asher would lose himself in fun. And nothing said fun like a lively party with a large group of friends. Since he wasn't allowed to go anywhere without Lani, he would just have to bring the party here.

Since he doubted very many people would show up for his benefit, Asher reached out to Gina for help.

"Call everyone you know. We're throwing a party at Elegance Ranch."

"Are you sure this is a good time?" she countered.

"It's the perfect time. Rusty's out of town and I'm stuck on house arrest."

"It's going to end up being a pretty small affair." She sounded as low as Asher felt.

They hadn't spoken much since he'd been released from jail, but he'd texted her often to check in. Despite still smarting over the way she'd turned her back on him, they were family and he loved her.

"Even if there's only twenty or thirty people, it will be a party." Easing up on the forced optimism, he added, "And I really need this."

"I'll see what I can do."

She grudgingly offered suggestions for a fun-filled, family-friendly barbecue with a guest list including their usual complement of friends from the Texas Cattleman's Club—or at least the ones who were still talking to them—but also those in Royal who'd suffered because of what happened with the festival. Fearing that no one would show up if they thought he was involved, he suggested that she leave his name off the invitation.

Fifteen minutes after he'd hung up with Gina, Ross's number lit up Asher's phone.

"A *party*?" Ross demanded. "Are you out of your mind? This is no time to celebrate anything."

It wasn't a celebration, but a distraction. A way to keep from brooding over the implosion of his relationship with Lani and the bleak future that lay ahead of him.

"I'm stuck here alone with nothing to do," Asher complained.

"You're on house arrest," Ross snapped. "I don't think throwing parties is going to enhance your reputation."

"I'm not throwing a party. You and Gina are."

Asher hadn't really expected his brother to understand. Practical Ross had never related to the restlessness that drove Asher. His identity had always been cemented in being the heir to one of the wealthiest men in the country. That Ross suffered the same neglect as Asher didn't negate the blood bond.

"This isn't a good idea."

"No, it's a *great* idea." And one that Asher hoped would prove to Lani that he would make an excellent partner for her. "Oh, and make sure you invite Billy. It wouldn't be a party without him."

Eleven

Still reeling from the fight with Asher the day before, Lani buckled herself into her seat for the three-hour flight from Dallas to Las Vegas. Her stomach flipped as her phone rang. Hoping it was Asher, she glanced down at the screen but the caller was Kingston Blue.

"Hey," she began as the plane filled up around her. "I'm on my way to Vegas,"

She'd snagged a window seat and watched the grounds crew load luggage under the plane. Since she only needed a few necessities for her quick trip, her own bag sat in the compartment above her head.

"What's in Las Vegas?" Kingston Blue asked, his voice hard and suspicious.

Apparently her people skills were in the toilet. Not only had she damaged her relationship with Asher, but her credibility with her client was dangling by a thread.

"A woman by the name of Antoinette Holmes," Lani explained. "She's Billy Holmes's mother."

A charged silence radiated from the phone. She gnawed on

her lip, imagining the grim tension in Kingston's face. As much as she didn't want to argue with the musician, she believed in her investigative skills *and* in Asher's innocence.

"Look, I know you don't agree with the direction I'm taking the investigation, but you hired me to find the money and I really don't think Asher's your guy." Her voice heated as her confidence flared. "If you want me off the case, I understand, but I'm still going to investigate Billy Holmes."

"How much of this has to do with your personal relationship with Asher Edmond?" While the edge had come off Kingston's tone, he sounded no less dubious. "You were in love with him once. Can you assure me that's not interfering with your judgment now?"

Lani breathed a sigh of relief that her client was willing to hear her out. This she could handle. After all, for the last five years she'd been telling herself that falling for Asher had been a huge mistake and one thing she never did was screw up twice.

"When you first approached me with the job, I wanted him to be guilty. Things didn't end well between us and I thought maybe he was finally going to have to take responsibility for a mistake he'd made."

Initially, she'd intended to demonstrate to her treacherous heart that Asher was a lying, manipulative, selfish jerk who'd toyed with her for fun and thus banish him from her daydreams forever.

"So what changed?" Kingston asked.

"I'm a professional. I approached this case by looking at the facts." Never mind that one glimpse of Asher looking exhausted and defeated in that jail cell had started to change the polarity of her emotions. "Which resulted in me interviewing several people and finding out that Billy Holmes had a sketchy past and an odd fixation on Rusty Edmond."

"But what does any of that mean?"

"I don't know, but I'm hoping to find some answers by talking to his mother."

"Fine. Keep me updated."

Lani ended the call, relieved that the musician appeared appeased for the moment. As the announcement came to stow all electronic devices, her mind went back to the last conversation she'd had with Asher. She recognized that letting him think his father had hired her had been a mistake. When she landed in Las Vegas, she would let him know that she'd spoken with Kingston and relayed her opinion about Asher no longer being her prime suspect.

Not that she believed this would be enough for him to forgive her. She hadn't understood about the strained relationship between Rusty and his adopted son or the pain Asher had felt at being either ignored or criticized by the only father figure he'd ever had.

As the plane taxied toward the runway, she closed her eyes and mentally reviewed what she'd dug up on Billy Holmes.

He'd grown up in Las Vegas, raised by a single mom.

Without any luggage to pick up at baggage claim, Lani secured a rental car and was on her way to meet Billy's mom. Antoinette Holmes was a cocktail waitress at a downtown casino and lived just east of the city center in a second-floor apartment in an older complex.

Lani was careful not to trip on the chipped concrete as she strode past a pool in desperate need of refurbishing. Feeling the heat radiating off the sun-bleached door of apartment number twelve, Lani used the corner of her phone, instead of her knuckles, to rap.

The face of the woman who answered the door looked much older than fifty-nine beneath her heavy makeup. Years of harsh desert sunshine and hard living had taken its toll on Antoinette's skin. Yet Lani could tell Billy's mother had once been a beauty.

"Antoinette Holmes?" Lani spoke the woman's name like a question although she already knew the answer.

"Yes?" The woman rested her left hand on her hip. Her slender fingers were tipped with long bright blue nails adorned with rhinestones. They matched her blue workout pants and matching sports bra. Antoinette's face might've showed her age, but her trim body did not.

"My name is Lani Li. I'm a private investigator from Dallas, Texas, and I was wondering if I could speak to you for a few minutes."

When she had indicated she was from Texas, Antoinette's eyebrows had risen. Now, however, as she raked her gaze over Lani's jeans, pale blue T-shirt and boots, the older woman's expression shifted from surprise to caution.

"What about?"

Not wanting to fidget and give Antoinette any sense that this inquiry was anything other than routine, Lani resisted the urge to wipe at the sweat trickling down her temple. Dallas had been in the upper eighties when she'd left. Las Vegas was already well into triple-digit temperatures and the heat index continued to climb as the sun crept toward its zenith in a cloudless sky of vivid blue.

"I'm doing some background work on your son, Billy," Lani declared blandly. "And I have a few questions only you can answer."

"What sort of questions?" The waitress looked poised to slam the door in Lani's face if she didn't like the answer.

Lani suspected she'd get nowhere if she told the truth. "Did you know your son has been living in Royal, Texas, for the past two years? He's staying in a guesthouse at Elegance Ranch, a property owned by Russell Edmond."

The thing about wearing long false eyelashes was that they called attention to a woman's eyes and what Lani glimpsed in Antoinette's wide green gaze was longing, anger and a trace of fear.

"I haven't seen or heard from that boy in years so I don't know what I can tell you." The older woman studied Lani for a few seconds longer while curiosity and reluctance battled on her face. In the end Antoinette backed into the house with a curt gesture that invited without being welcoming. "You might as well come in. I don't need to be air-conditioning the neighborhood."

"Thanks."

Crossing into the dim interior of the woman's apartment was like stepping back in time. And not in a good way. Years of cigarette smoke clung to the '70s wallpaper and burgundy carpet beneath her feet. As Lani made her way across the grungy patchwork of spills and threadbare spots, she couldn't help but contrast the shabby one-bedroom apartment to the elegant guesthouse on Elegance Ranch where Billy lived.

"Can I get you something to drink?" Antoinette asked, leaving Lani to wonder if she was being hospitable or if a lifetime of waitressing made the offer a habit. "I've got diet soda or water, or I could make some coffee."

"I'll take a soda," she said with a polite smile after glancing at the dishes piled in the sink. Hopefully the drink would come in a can because she couldn't imagine there was a single clean glass in the place.

After Lani perched on the gold velvet couch her hostess had indicated, Antoinette headed into the kitchen to fetch the offered drink. This gave Lani a chance to glance around. Billy's mom said she hadn't heard from him in years. Obviously she hadn't benefited from any of the money he'd swindled as Bond Howard, Bobby Hammond or Brad Howell.

Spying a cluster of pictures on a side table, Lani leaned over to peer at them. What she saw caused her to pull out her phone and snap several images.

These were obviously a collection of Antoinette's most cherished photos. They told her story, starting with a grainy shot of a somber-faced man and his beaming bride on their wedding day. Her parents, based on the fashion and quality of the photo.

Next in order was a shot of a fresh-faced teenage Antoinette, posing in a cheer uniform with two other girls similarly dressed. The trio triumphantly held a trophy in their grasp, indicating Antoinette had known better times.

Lani's favorite of the bunch was a charming image of the woman snuggling a boy of about four or five. From his mother's joyful smile, Billy hadn't lacked affection growing up. But the photo that stopped Lani's breath was the one in a fancy gold frame. It featured a beaming Antoinette and a much-younger Rusty Edmond.

"That's my boy," Antoinette said, handing Lani an off-brand diet soda before indicating a wall of photos from Billy's school years. "The last picture I took of him was the day he went off to college." She gave a bitter laugh that turned into a classic smoker's cough. "First one in my family to go."

"You must be very proud of him..." Lani trailed off, hoping Billy's mom would fill in the details without the need for direct questions.

"It gave him airs." Antoinette stared at the pictures on the side table. "What sort of background check are you doing on my boy?"

Lani resisted the urge to clear her throat. "The man who hired me is very particular about the people he does business with." It wasn't a lie. Kingston Blue had certainly had her checked out before hiring her.

"I haven't seen Billy in five years or so. He never came back much after he graduated college. Just walked away, as all men do...as his father did." Antoinette darted a glance at the man framed in gold. "I should've known better."

"Does Billy have much to do with his dad?"

Speculation gleamed in Antoinette's narrowed eyes. "Why do you need to know something like that?"

"It fills out the picture..."

The older woman assessed Lani's appearance once more. "I've said all I'm going to for free."

She blinked. "I'm sorry?"

"If you're a private detective, you've probably got an expense account." The waitress licked her lips and smiled. "If you want to know anything more, it's gonna cost you."

With Asher's freedom on the line, Lani had a lot riding on this interview, and a photo of Rusty Edmond with Billy's mother demonstrated there was a story here. To persuade the authorities to look at Billy, she needed something that piqued their interest.

Moving with deliberate intent, Lani opened her purse and added up everything she had. Would nine crisp one-hundred-dollar bills be enough to get all the information she needed? Lani pulled out one bill and set it on the coffee table in between them.

"Does Billy see his dad?"

Antoinette's hand shot out and drew the hundred toward her. The bill disappeared into her ample cleavage.

"No."

Trying not to let her impatience get the better of her, Lani plucked out another bill and set it on the table. She made sure to avoid glancing at the cluster of pictures as she asked, "Does his father know about Billy?"

"He knew I was pregnant, but he didn't believe Billy was his."

So the answer to that was no. The photo of his mother with Russell Edmond was the only one of Antoinette with a man. Billy obviously knew or suspected that Rusty was his father. What was Billy up to? Why hadn't he told Rusty that they were father and son?

"Why not?"

Antoinette crossed her arms over her chest and scowled. Another bill appeared in Lani's hand. She set it on the table.

"Tell me about Billy's father." She gestured at the picture in the gold frame. "Is this him?"

"A real charmer with a sexy drawl. He was from Texas like you. An oilman with deep pockets. Good tipper." The waitress purred, "He made me feel like the most beautiful woman on the planet."

While the woman relived what was obviously a high point in her life, Lani couldn't help but notice the similarity to how she'd met Asher. Antoinette waxed nostalgic about Rusty's hypnotic gray eyes and how his deep laugh had given her chills.

Meanwhile Lani pictured how Asher had hungrily watched her through half-closed lids and wore down her resistance with his lingering, sensual smiles. "He liked to come to the casino where I worked and throw money around. He treated me good."

"That's great," she murmured, growing uncomfortable at their parallel experiences.

Yet was it a surprise that when a wealthy man wanted a woman, he used whatever means at his disposal to have her?

"Until I got pregnant," Antoinette said. "Then it was over."

Abruptly Lani felt sorry for the woman. If she and Asher hadn't been careful, that might've been her, pregnant and scared with an uncertain future looming before her. Given his restless nature and frat-boy attitude, would Asher have reacted any better to an unplanned pregnancy than his father had?

At least she knew things would be different today. If she got pregnant, she had no doubt that Asher would not only want to be an involved father, he'd probably insist on taking care of her, as well.

The thought warmed her. Even though she let him believe her opinion of him hadn't changed, the concern he'd shown for those harmed by the troubles surrounding the festival demonstrated that he could care about someone besides himself. And really, if she took a good honest look at everything that had transpired between them that summer on Appaloosa Island, she knew she never would've fallen for him if he hadn't treated her so well. In fact, once she stopped getting in her own way, she'd discovered that Asher made her feel secure.

Lani plucked the rest of her cash out of her wallet and placed it on the table. "This is everything I have. Just answer these last few questions." And then without waiting for Antoinette to agree, she launched into the rest of her inquiry. "Did you ask him for child support?"

"Never thought of it."

That was so obviously a lie, but Lani resisted the urge to challenge Antoinette.

"But you said he was wealthy. I would think you could've proved Billy was his son and benefited financially. How come you didn't run a paternity test?"

Suddenly Antoinette didn't look so eager to keep going. "You ask a lot of questions."

"I paid you a lot of money for answers," Lani countered in aggrieved tones as frustration got the better of her. Asher was counting on her to save him and everything hinged on what she found out. "Why no paternity test?" she repeated, slapping her hand over the pile of cash as the waitress leaned forward to snatch it up.

Antoinette kept her gaze riveted on the money as she mumbled, "There were other men around the same time."

Yet a paternity test would've provided definitive proof of whether or not Rusty was Billy's dad. Unless…

"How much did he pay you to leave him alone and forget about the paternity test?"

"You think you're so smart, don't you?" Antoinette snarled. She glanced at the money again and heaved a sigh. "Fine. He paid me ten grand to drop it and never contact him again. And Russell wasn't the sort of man you crossed."

"So, you don't actually know who Billy's father is," Lani mused.

But Antoinette obviously hoped it was Russell Edmond. The ornate gold frame around the oil magnate's image highlighted how much he'd meant to her. Billy had grown up seeing that face every day. It made perfect sense that he'd believe this man was his father.

Had resentment festered with each passing year? Growing up poor, had Billy become obsessed about his wealthy father living in Texas? Had he planned how he was going to make friends with his half brother and eventually worm his way into the family?

"Does Billy begrudge his father for not acknowledging him?"

"No. Why would he?" But something about Antoinette's answer didn't ring true for Lani.

With one last glance at the photo of Rusty and Antoinette, Lani lifted her hand off the cash and got to her feet. After a quick goodbye and no backward glance, Lani escaped the suffocating apartment with her thoughts whirling from all she'd learned. Finally Billy's motive was clear. Not only had he taken revenge on his father's family, but he'd also pulled off the biggest score of his life.

No doubt he wouldn't be sticking around for much longer. In fact Lani was surprised he'd stayed in town this long. With that thought came a rush of panic. She needed to get back to Royal as soon as possible and convince the authorities to take what she'd discovered and go after Billy. But first she needed to reach out to the one person who would benefit the most from what she'd learned.

This might be enough to save Asher and she couldn't wait to tell him.

But two hours and three phone calls later, Asher hadn't picked up once.

As her plane for Dallas began boarding, Lani ended the last call without leaving a third message. She was determined not to jump to the wrong conclusions as to why he wasn't answering her calls. But even so, anxiety sank its talons into her psyche, making her wince. There were a lot of possibilities for why he wasn't picking up beyond the one currently stuck in the forefront of her mind—that she'd hurt him badly. Badly enough that he wanted nothing more to do with her? Lani desperately hoped not.

Asher couldn't take his gaze off Ross, Charlotte and Ben. He'd never envied his brother as much as he did at this moment. That could've been him with Lani and possibly their own child if he hadn't been so afraid of the changes required to move forward with their relationship. Without offering her any sort of vision of an alternative, better future with him, he'd selfishly asked her to change her plans for grad school and follow him to Argentina and beyond. Was it any wonder that she'd balked? He'd known how driven she was.

If he'd put some thought into a plan, he might have found a better way to convince her than, *I have plenty of money. You'll never need to work a day in your life.*

He'd known immediately that was the wrong tact to take with her. But it wasn't like he could set his heart at her feet, tell her he'd fallen hard and couldn't bear to live without her. What if it didn't last? What if she woke up and realized he wasn't good enough for her? He'd dreaded the possibility that the love shining in her eyes would dim as disappointment set in.

She'd stopped criticizing his lifestyle once they'd started dating, but her desire to help people and her passion for justice was all he needed to recognize that she didn't approve of his lack of direction any more than Rusty did. And at the end of summer, when she left Appaloosa Island to live her mission-driven life, he'd been left wondering why he always seemed to be craving the love and approval of people who could never accept him for who he was.

Lately he'd been wondering a great deal about what might've happened back then if he had changed. Grown up. Become the man Lani needed. Would she have started to take him seriously? Would they have gotten married? Had a child? He'd sure wanted to be with her. To demonstrate what life with him could be like, he'd taken her on a magical journey through the extravagances his lifestyle afforded him. The big boat, fine dining and luxurious suites at the best hotels, a private plane to anywhere they wanted to go... But he'd mistaken her delight in the finer things he offered with a shift in her nature. She might've been able to appreciate the amenities he had access to, but that didn't mean those things would become more important to her than her schooling and the career in law enforcement she'd hoped to pursue.

"It's good to see Ross this happy, isn't it?"

While he's been observing the happy family, Gina had walked up beside him. Despite her upbeat statement, she looked as gloomy as Asher felt. He threw his arm around her in comfort. Over the course of Lani's investigation into the missing festival money, Asher and his sister had made a semblance of peace.

"Obviously fatherhood and being in love suit him." Asher noted a roughness to his voice. He swallowed a hard knot in his throat before musing, "Do you suppose either one of us has that to look forward to?"

"I don't know about you," Gina murmured, "but I'm pretty sure I don't."

"Why is that?" Asher turned his full attention on his sister and seeing her misery, took her hand in his. Squeezing gently in reassurance, he said, "You never know. Mr. Right could be waiting for you to notice him."

She responded with a bitter laugh. "With our family's reputation sullied by the festival scandal, who could possibly want me now?"

"Any man with half a brain would realize what a catch you are," Asher said, surprised by his sister's inability to see her worth. "There's more to you than being an Edmond. You know that, right?"

Not only was Gina beautiful and smart, she was kind and giving, as well. That she failed to recognize all she had to offer wasn't a surprise. None of the three siblings had been showered with the sort of approval and love that would've given them the confidence to take on the world. Rusty never acted as if he gave a damn about any of them. Was it any wonder the three of them struggled to find love and develop successful relationships?

"I really don't," Gina said. "I guess I never realized how much I benefited from being an Edmond until our name got dragged through the mud."

"I'm sorry this happened."

His sister looked stricken. "I know you. Stealing isn't your style. I feel bad that I ever believed you were guilty."

"Don't worry about it," Asher assured her with a warm smile. "The evidence was so damning that there were times I actually thought I had stolen the funds."

"Oh, Asher." She laughed at his joke as he'd hoped she would and his spirits remained high even as she sobered once more. "But what are we going to do about proving your innocence?"

"Lani and I have some ideas on that. In fact, we have a suspect."

Gina looked startled. "Who?"

He'd promised Lani not to tell Ross what they learned about Billy, but he could share the information with Gina without violating their agreement.

"We've been looking into Billy."

"Billy Holmes?" Her voice was louder and sharper than Asher would've liked and he immediately shushed her. "Why him?"

"We found out he's been operating under false names all over the country and getting women to invest in schemes before backing out and taking their money with him."

"Seriously?" she gasped, confusion blanketing her expression. "That makes no sense! He's been Ross's friend since college. I can't imagine him doing something like that or being that type of person without Ross realizing it."

Asher pondered how Rusty had embraced Billy when the cranky billionaire rarely approved of anyone, including his own children. "Well, he's obviously pretty good at charming people to get what he wants. I mean, he *is* currently living in the guesthouse on our estate."

"What does Ross have to say about this?"

"I haven't spoken to him about it and I need for you to promise me that you won't say anything either. I can't risk him tipping off Billy. He's already left a trail of missing funds across the country. Nothing on the scale of what was stolen from Soiree on the Bay, but it has all led up to this moment. And with me in jail, he gets away with it."

Gina's brown eyes grew wider as he spoke and Asher realized his voice had grown louder as he vented his frustration.

"You need to go to the authorities with this," his sister said, her eyes darting toward Ross and his family.

"With what?" Asher growled. "It's nothing but speculation at this point. I have no proof." Then he remembered that Lani had called him before the party started. Still smarting from their last conversation, he'd never picked up her calls or listened to her messages. He pulled out his phone and unlocked the screen. "Or maybe we do. Lani called me from Vegas."

"What was she doing there?"

"That's where Billy's mom lives. She went to see what she could find out. I haven't listened to her message."

"You've been with her a lot. I heard she moved in for a while," Gina remarked, her voice carefully neutral. "Is it all business? I mean, when you two dated before, it was pretty clear she meant a lot to you."

"It's not business on my part," he retorted, his clipped tone exposing his raw emotions. "She just doesn't see a future for us."

"Because…? I mean you were once in love, right?"

"Yes. And my feelings haven't changed on that front." Even though he was confessing to the wrong woman, it felt good to admit how he felt about Lani. "I just don't think I'm the man she wants."

"So become that man." Gina's advice was simple and hardhitting. "That girl looked at you with heart emoji in her eyes. I'm sure if you put in the effort, she'd come around."

With his lungs constricting in reaction to his sister's words, Asher drew Gina into a hug and then hit the Play button on his phone.

Lani's voice came over the speaker, sounding excited and somewhat annoyed. "Will you please stop avoiding my calls? I know you're not unavailable so I guess I'm just gonna have to leave another message. I talked to Billy's mom and it turns out she had an affair with Rusty. He gave her ten thousand and told her to never contact him again. The thing is, she has no proof that Billy is Rusty's son. She never had a chance to do a paternity test and apparently there were several men she was seeing around the same time. I guess that explains Billy why was so unhappy when Ross and Rusty looked like they were getting along and why he set you up. He thinks he's Rusty son and resents the fact that he didn't have all the things growing up that you all did... Well, the plane's getting ready to take off so they're making me shut off my phone. I'll arrive in Dallas in three hours. I'll call you when I land and we can talk more then."

The whole time Lani had been speaking, he'd been staring at the screen. Now he looked up at his sister and saw his shock mirrored on her face.

"Wow," Gina said in awe.

"Wow is right."

"Now we have to talk to Ross. And tell the authorities."

"Absolutely." But his attention was on the dark-haired man making for the exit in a hurry. "Except I think we might be out of time." He indicated Billy's rapid departure.

Gina's eyes rounded. "Do you think he heard us?"

"Maybe." To Asher's relief, Billy's progress was halted by a trio of women. "Can you keep him busy for me? I need fifteen minutes."

"Where are you going?"

Asher thought about his apartment over the barn and the unlocked front door giving access to anyone on the property. "I'm going to search the guesthouse."

Twelve

The distance between the main house and the guesthouse where Billy currently resided was a three-minute jog along a tree-lined winding drive. Asher accomplished it in half the time. Heart pounding, his breath coming hard from the sprint, he trotted up the steps to the front door, keyed in the code to unlock the door and entered.

The house's cool stillness embraced him. Asher knew the housekeeper wasn't home. Anytime there was a party at the main house, she joined the staff, keeping the food and drinks flowing smoothly from the kitchen to the guests.

Still, running into someone was the least of his problems. He had no clear idea where to begin a search and a limited amount of time to execute it. What did he hope to find? A laptop with incriminating information would be great but he'd settle for a file marked *stolen festival funds*.

When they'd landed on Billy as a prime suspect, he'd proposed to Lani that they infiltrate the guesthouse while Billy was away, but she'd shut him down. Her methodical approach didn't involve breaking and entering. But it wasn't really breaking in when he had the code to the front door, right?

Asher made his way into the study off the foyer. He couldn't believe his luck. A laptop sat on the large wood desk and he made his way over to it. Even as he lifted the top and peered at the screen, he had to wonder if this was just a decoy. Surely Billy was too clever to leave a bunch of damning evidence lying around for someone to scoop up and run out the door with.

Seconds rushed by as Asher pulled up the browser history and quickly scanned through it. Asher couldn't see where Billy had used this computer to access any banks. Still, his search had been cursory at best and with time running out he looked around for a place to stash the laptop. If Billy intended to pack up and get out of town, Asher wanted to make sure he wouldn't be able to take this device with him. The quickest, most obvious spot was underneath the couch cushions. He was counting on the man assuming someone had walked off with the computer and that he wouldn't search the room.

The bedrooms were on a level above and Asher headed up the stairs, taking them two at a time. He found an identical laptop to the one downstairs, sandwiched between the box spring and mattress. With excitement pumping adrenaline through his bloodstream, he slid the computer into a laptop case that he found in the closet. With the thrill of the hunt surging, he riffled through the nightstand and dresser before getting even more creative with the search. From their careful concealment beneath shirts and socks, taped to the back of the drawer and even affixed behind the painting over the bed, he unearthed several passports—one with Billy's face but Asher's name that he dropped into his pocket—along with a wad of cash, two burner phones and a handgun.

This was *not* how an innocent man behaved.

Asher glanced at the closet, wondering how many goodies he could turn up there, but heard the front door open. With only one set of stairs leading up to the second floor, he was trapped.

Fortunately he'd left everything except for the laptop where he'd found it. Asher eased out of the master suite and crossed the landing to one of the two guest bedrooms just as he heard Billy start to climb upstairs. With his blood thundering in his ears, he slipped behind the door out of sight and wondered if he dared try to slip down the stairs while Billy was packing.

Instead Asher glanced at the window. Maybe he could try to jump and hope he landed without hurting himself. Moving cautiously, he went to the window and opened it. He hadn't done more than drop the laptop into the bushes below before Billy started cursing. Asher barely had time to press himself against the wall when the other man raced past again.

Deciding this was his best chance to make his escape, and with his ears tuned for the slightest noise, Asher waited until he heard the front door open and close once more. Then he quickly, but quietly, descended to the first floor. After a quick detour to the study to collect the laptop, he headed for the kitchen and the door that led to the side yard. He needed to retrieve the other laptop, but when he opened the door, standing before him was Billy Holmes with a handgun leveled at his chest.

"You."

Asher was not at all flattered at the surprise on Billy's face. "Me."

Billy's gaze went to the laptop Asher held. "Give that to me."

"Or what? You'll shoot me?" He was rethinking his words as the other man smirked. "Fire that gun and everyone at the house will hear. Gina knows what you did. She's probably already warned Ross. They'll lock the gates and you'll never get out."

"I guess I need a little insurance then, don't I?" Billy backed up and gestured with the gun toward the car parked in the driveway.

Unsure what the traitor had in mind, Asher decided to let the scene play out until he saw an opening to act. A suitcase stood beside the car. Keeping a close eye on Asher, Billy popped open the trunk.

"Give me the laptop and get in."

"The trunk?"

Asher took a tighter grip on the laptop, prepared to swing it at Billy's head, but the other man shook his head.

"Don't be stupid. If you make me shoot you, I might not get away, but you'll definitely be dead."

All too aware that would be true, Asher made a huge show of reluctance before handing over what he hoped was Billy's decoy computer.

"Get in," Billy repeated.

"Why? You have everything you need to get away clean."

"Except for a head start. So, to throw everyone into a state of confusion, you and I are going for a little drive."

And before Asher could summon another protest, Billy's hand holding the gun shot out and everything went black.

No three-hour plane ride had ever felt as long as this one.

How could she have told Asher he wasn't the right man for her? *Of course* he was. She loved him just the way he was. She didn't want to change him. Why would she? He was thrilling and adventurous and made her get out of her head and listen to her heart. Loving him was a wonderful chaotic ride and she was ready to spend the rest of her life on it.

The first thing she would do when she saw him again was tell him that she loved him. No matter if he was angry with her or indifferent. She wouldn't hesitate, wouldn't play it safe. If he believed that the only reason she'd been waiting to speak up was to determine if he was innocent, she'd convince him that her change of heart had come the day they'd visited the festival site on Appaloosa Island. She'd just been too afraid to trust her emotions.

As soon as the plane landed, Lani turned her phone back on and watched the screen light up with notifications. She scanned for a message from Asher, but the only names that appeared were Ross, Gina and the Maverick County Sheriff's Department.

Cursing the love of her life for being impossibly stubborn, Lani dialed his number again and groaned in frustration when it rolled straight into voice mail. With Asher out of reach, she turned her attention to the rest of her messages, starting with Gina.

We think Billy overheard your voice mail. Ross and Asher are going to talk to him.

"Damn it!"

Lani's seatmate shot her a dark look and she offered the woman a tight smile and a mumbled apology as she checked the time stamp and saw that it had come in an hour earlier.

And as if that wasn't bad enough, she had three messages from Ross, each one worse than the last.

Billy knows we're onto him and he's running.

Asher went to the guesthouse to stop him.

I'm not sure what's going on, but Sheriff Battle just called to say that Asher is on the run.

What the hell was going on? Lani dialed Ross's number, but after several rings it rolled to voice mail the way Asher's had. She scrolled through her contacts and located the one for the Maverick County Sheriff's Department. Tapping her fingers against the armrest, she waited for someone to pick up.

"I'm looking for Sheriff Battle," Lani said when the receptionist answered. "My name is Lani Li and it's about Asher Edmond."

"One moment."

With hold music playing in her ear, Lani stared out the window as the plane taxied toward the busy Dallas/Fort Worth terminal, stopping repeatedly to let other planes pass. Her heart thudded hard against her ribs as her agitation grew by the second.

What had Asher been thinking to go after Billy? Didn't he know he was already in enough trouble? He and Ross should've called the sheriff and let the cops sort everything out. But sitting idly by when there was something adventurous to do wasn't Asher's style.

"Sheriff Battle." The man's calm, booming voice did little to soothe Lani's wildly fluctuating emotions.

"Sheriff, this is Lani Li. I've just landed in Dallas and I think I know who embezzled the money from the Soiree on the Bay festival and set up Asher Edmond to take the fall."

"I don't think you've heard, Ms. Li, but Asher Edmond is running."

"He's not running because he's not guilty." Lani couldn't imagine what had possessed Asher to take this sort of risk. What was he doing? This might ruin everything. "I think what he may be doing is trying to stop Billy Holmes from leaving town and disappearing."

"What does Mr. Holmes have to do with any of this?"

"I went to Las Vegas to visit Billy's mother. I found a connection there to Rusty Edmond."

A moment of silence followed her words, and then Sheriff Battle said, "Maybe you'd better fill me in…"

By the time she finished explaining everything, the plane had reached the terminal and the woman in the seat next to her was openly goggling. Lani ignored the eavesdropper and willed the passengers to disembark at a faster pace.

"So, you can see why Billy Holmes has to be stopped and questioned," she added, completely out of breath. "It's why Asher is chasing after him."

"If that's true, then they're both heading to the airport," the sheriff said.

"Billy can't get away." If that happened, the money would be gone forever and Asher's name might never be cleared.

"I'll get ahold of the special agents in charge of the case and my deputy that's following Asher and fill them in."

Lani hung up the call and got to her feet. As she joined the line of disembarking passengers, she chided herself for not calling the investigators before boarding the plane in Las Vegas. Yet how was she supposed to know that Asher would do something as reckless as go after Billy on his own? She ground her teeth as the people in front of her slowly shuffled off the plane. When she got ahold of Asher, she was going to kill him. Or kiss him senseless.

Once she reached the terminal, Lani looped her bag over her shoulder and began to jog toward the security gate that led to the arrivals area. She had no luggage, and no reason to follow the crowd to baggage claim. Besides, if Billy and Asher were on their way to the airport, the most likely spot to find them would be at the ticketing level. Only as she passed the doors leading to the shuttle that circled the five different terminals did the magnitude of the search area sap her hope. How could she hope to find Billy amongst the dozens of airlines and thousands of people checking in?

She was racing toward the arrivals area, scanning the faces around her, when she spied a familiar figure exiting TSA. Although he was wearing sunglasses and a baseball cap, she recognized Billy Holmes.

She angled in his direction, moving fast to intercept him. It wasn't until she stepped into his path that Lani realized she hadn't considered how to stop him.

"Billy Holmes."

To Lani's relief, he stopped.

His icy blue gaze darted in all directions before coming to rest on her. "Do I know you?"

"I'm Lani Li. I've been hired by Kingston Blue to look into the missing funds from the Soiree on the Bay festival."

His upper lip lifted in a snarl. "Good for you."

"I'd like to talk to you about your connection with the Edmond family."

"I'm sorry, but I have a plane to catch and don't have time to—"

Billy side stepped as if to go around her, but Lani was prepared for his evasion and kept herself in his path.

"I visited your mother today," she told him, hoping if she delayed Billy long enough, the police might catch up to him. "I know her connection to Rusty Edmond."

Billy shrugged. "They had an affair. So what?"

"So, you think he's your father. You think he abandoned you and your mother and you wanted payback. That's why you stole the money from the festival and blamed Asher."

"That's ridiculous. Asher stole that money. Everyone knows that." He gave her a cocky smile, but tension rode every line of his body.

"I also know about Bond Howard, Bobby Hammond and Brad Howell."

"Who?" Billy continued to regard her as if she were out of her mind, but Lani saw she had his complete attention.

Her cell phone began to ring. Hoping it was Asher, she glanced down at the screen, but realized it was Ross Edmond. She answered the call, but by the time she glanced back up at Billy, he was gone.

"Damn it!" she growled.

"Lani? Is that you?" Ross sounded upset and confused.

"Yes. Where's Asher?" she demanded, searching all around her for Billy. She couldn't spot his tall figure anywhere. It was as if the man had vanished.

"He's being arrested."

Anxiety banished all thought of Billy Holmes from her mind. She had to get to Asher. "Where are you?"

"Outside Terminal A."

As luck would have it, Lani's plane from Las Vegas had landed at the same terminal.

She ran outside and gaped at the mob scene. Four police cars surrounded a sedan parked by the curb with its trunk open. They had one man down on the ground as another argued and waved his arm toward the terminal. It took her a second to realize that Ross Edmond was the one gesticulating wildly and Asher was face down on the pavement, his hands cuffed behind his back.

She ran over and added her voice to the cacophony. "Billy Holmes is in the terminal. I just saw him. He's getting away."

Ross turned to her with a relieved expression. "That's what I'm trying to tell them," he said, "but they're not listening to me."

Two cops lifted Asher to his feet. One wore the insignia of the Maverick County Sheriff's Department, the other was a state trooper.

"I was kidnapped," Asher protested, eyes widening as he spotted her. "Hey, Lani."

As she rushed toward him, the state trooper stepped in her way and stood with his feet planted shoulder-width apart, hands on his gun belt. "And you are?"

"Lani Li. I called and spoke with Sheriff Battle when I landed." She glanced at the deputy's name tag. "Deputy Vesta, didn't the sheriff get ahold of you? You have the wrong man."

"I don't think so," the deputy said, jerking his thumb at Asher. "He's trying to get away." His vehement glare suggested that there was something personal in his dislike of Asher.

"Look, I wasn't trying to escape." He tipped his head to one side, showing a bloody gash on his temple. "The bastard bashed me on the head and dumped me in the trunk."

"You weren't in the trunk when we pulled up." The state trooper pointed out.

"Because the car had finally stopped and I figured it was safe for me to get out."

"The man you're looking for is Billy Holmes," Lani put in, tearing her gaze from Asher's wound. She hoped it wasn't as serious as it looked.

"Don't know anything about that," the trooper said. "We re-

ceived a BOLO from Maverick County that this guy was skipping town."

Lani glanced at the car the police cruisers had surrounded.
Its open trunk seemed to substantiate Asher's claim.

"He wasn't skipping town because he's innocent," Lani
fumed. "You need to go after Billy Holmes. I ran into him in
there. He's getting away."

The trooper glanced toward the door leading into the terminal. "Who's this Billy Holmes character?"

The deputy started dragging his prisoner toward the police
car. "Let's go."

"Can't you wait just a second," Asher protested, resisting. "I
have something to tell Lani."

Heartsick, she moved to go after them, but the trooper caught
her arm, keeping her in place. She glanced around the police
officer, trying to keep Asher in sight.

"Let me go with him."

Was that her voice sounding so desperate and anxious? Suddenly it had become crucial that Asher hear that she loved him.

"They're taking him back to Royal. You can see him at the
sheriff's station."

"Please," she pleaded with the cop. "There's something he
needs to know."

"Fine. Make it quick."

The Maverick County deputy was already urging Asher into
the back of his patrol car when Lani drew near. The deputy had
his hand on the door and was about to slam it shut when she
spoke up.

"Wait." Irrational panic had seized her and wouldn't let go.
"Just give me a second with him."

To her dismay he just smirked at her and started to close the
door. A fraction of a second remained for her to confess the
three words that had been hiding in her heart. Terrified, where
she'd been bold moments earlier, Lani locked eyes with Asher
and sucked in a breath for courage. But as she began to speak,

Asher clearly had something on his mind as well and there wasn't time for both.

As the car door swung on its hinges, an instant before glass and metal blocked their words, their overlapping messages reached their targets.

"I love you."

"I got Billy's laptop."

Thirteen

Asher lay on his back staring at the damn jail ceiling once again. His head was throbbing beneath the hastily applied bandage on his temple. He'd stopped pacing an hour ago and resigned himself to spending the night. At least this time he wasn't worried about being stuck here indefinitely. He'd been told that they'd found Billy's laptop where he'd hidden it and the forensics team was combing the hard drive in search of the accounts where the funds had been sent. Thanks to Lani, a clear picture had formed of Billy's notorious past, stemming from his mother's affair with Rusty that suggested a reason for him to destroy the Edmond family's reputations and set up Asher to take the fall for the missing festival funds.

Unfortunately, in the midst of the wild and completely out-of-control scene at the airport, Billy had escaped into the crowds and it appeared as if he'd vanished into thin air. No doubt he had several different identifications to go with his aliases and with the festival funds squirreled away, he had the means to go just about anywhere.

But none of that mattered anymore. What preoccupied Asher

was that he was stuck in here while Lani was out there doing who knew what. He was on pins and needles waiting to be released. And after he was set free, then what? He and Lani hadn't sorted out their problems. Before leaving for Las Vegas, she'd made it clear that she still didn't trust him.

As the hours passed without any word from her, he grew almost frantic with worry. Over and over his mind replayed those moments before Deputy Vesta had shut him into the back of the patrol car. Once again Asher had screwed up. While Lani was confessing her love, he'd been bragging about securing Billy's laptop. She was sure to think that he was only worried about saving his own ass, not that he'd done it for her so that she could find the missing money and solve the case.

And now she was avoiding him, no doubt guessing that he didn't love her in return. Would she ever give him the chance to explain? Or was it already too late? Maybe she wasn't busy with the authorities. Maybe she'd already gone back to Dallas, putting him in her rearview mirror once again.

Nor could he blame her for leaving him to rot. Hell, if he'd confessed his love to her only to discover she was solely focused on saving her firm, he'd be pretty messed up too. Hopefully she would give him another chance. He would shower her with I love you's from now until eternity if she would just show up.

The door leading to the rest of the police station opened and Asher's heart gave a painful wrench. He was on his feet and across the small cell before realizing his visitor wasn't Lani, but the stocky deputy who despised him.

"Hello, Deputy Vesta," he said in his most droll tone. "I thought you'd forgotten all about me."

Vesta shot him a disgusted look. "Someone's here to see you."

Asher grabbed the bars and held on as relief washed over him. His head spun as Lani slowly advanced into the room. Strands of dark hair framed her exhausted features and her shoulders slumped as if burdened by an enormous weight. She looked as if the news she'd come to share was so bad she couldn't bear to speak it.

"What is it?" he demanded. His stomach knotted. "What's happening?"

"You look like hell," she said, stopping halfway toward him.

Her unwillingness to meet his gaze coupled with her delay in coming to see him made his heart plummet. Either she'd been unable to convince the authorities that Billy was the true thief or her part of the case was concluded and this was goodbye.

"Well I've been locked up in jail for…" without his watch or a clock to gauge the time, he'd lost track of how long he'd been in this cell "…a while now," he concluded wearily, wondering how he could possibly convince her they had a future if he remained locked up. "You, on the other hand, look glorious."

Her lips flattened into an unhappy line. "I'm tired and in desperate need of a shower so…"

More than anything he needed to touch her, to crush her in his arms and deliver his heart into her keeping. But this time he knew he needed more than his easy charm. She needed—deserved—the honest message of his heart.

"About what happened at the airport," he began.

"Billy got away." She shook her head. "We're not sure if he's actually Rusty's son, but it's clear that he believes that's the case and that he wanted Rusty—your whole family, really—to pay for abandoning him and his mother."

Asher could care less about Billy Holmes or the damned case. All he knew was that his future happiness was slipping through his fingers. He needed to be clearer, to make her understand how mad he was at himself for screwing up again. Hopefully it wasn't too late to make her understand that he regretted not speaking from his heart. It was what *she'd* done in that tense, chaotic moment. Would she believe him now?

"I don't care about that right now," he insisted, wishing she'd stop staring at his chest and see his earnest expression. He blustered on, "I want to explain about what happened when you said

I love you and I told you I got Billy's laptop. What I was really trying to say was that I love you too."

After flicking her gaze to his face, she took a single step closer. Her bowed head and tightly clenched hands gave her a look of uncharacteristic uncertainty and Asher took that as his chance to spill all of it.

"I've loved you since the first time you called me frat boy," he rushed on, baring all his fear and regret, his joy and hope. He needed his sincerity to reach her, to encourage her to give him—*them*—a chance.

He stretched out his arms as another slow, shuffling step brought her almost within reach. She continued to remain silent, but her willingness to hear him out gave him hope.

"From here on out, I'm at your command," he declared, the words tumbling out of him. She'd given him this chance and he would not fail. "Whatever you need. Whoever you need me to be. I'm that guy. I swear you will never be disappointed in me ever again."

She'd moved near enough that he could wrap his fingers around her jacket lapels and pull her forward.

"I love you," he murmured, putting his whole heart into the phrase.

Lani caught his wrists as he tugged her toward him, but to keep her balance rather than to resist him. Still, it was pretty obvious that more kept them apart than the steel metal grid between them.

"I love you just the way you are," she whispered, lifting her gaze to his at last.

The amount of anguish in her mink-brown eyes made Asher catch his breath. Throat tight, he cupped her cheek and cursed the mess he'd made of things. If only he'd been able to find the courage years ago to give her his heart.

"But I'm already different because of you," he said. "Being with you that summer five years ago changed me. Oh, I resisted. I was still an arrogant ass, asking you to give up on your dream when I wasn't ready to grow up and take responsibilities for the decisions I'd made." He shook his head in disgust. "Looking back, I was so stupid to persist in trying to win Rusty's approval, too caught up in my resentment when I couldn't."

"We both had a lot of growing up to do." Her smile was both sad and filled with regret. "With grad school ahead of me, I wasn't ready to be in a serious relationship. I didn't think I could have it all. A successful career *and* you."

Optimistic that she hadn't barred her heart to him, the knot in his chest eased slightly. "Maybe I'm reading this wrong," he teased, "but I'm not sensing you thought being with me was gonna be a picnic."

"Oh, it would've been a picnic, all right," she muttered with a quiet snort. "Including fire ants and an unexpected thunderstorm."

"You're not wrong." He accepted the accuracy of her claim with a wry smirk. "Being with me won't be without its surprises."

When it came to consistency and predictability, he would not be her ideal choice. They approached things in completely opposite ways. She was methodical. He was spontaneous. Yet they both loved a challenge and never let fear stop them from engaging in thrilling adventures.

"At least it will never be dull." She thrust her knuckles into his stomach. The jab didn't hurt, but her message was clear. *Don't make me regret this.*

"I swear I won't," he murmured, pressing his face into the gap between the bars, but finding her lips remained out of reach. "I don't suppose there's any way you could get me out of here so we could seal our new partnership with a kiss."

"Oh," she said with a playful lilt in her voice. "Did I forget to mention that you're free to go?"

The news shot through him like a lightning bolt. "This is the second-best news I've had all day."

Her left eyebrow lifted. "And the best news?"

"Deputy Vesta promised me meat loaf for dinner."

As her eyes blazed, Asher was really glad to have the protection of the cell bars between them. A second later, however, before she could voice the murder flashing in her eyes, the aforementioned deputy reentered the room and unlocked the cell door.

"See if you can stay out of trouble this time," Vesta grumbled, looking as if he'd tasted something really bad.

With a cheeky smile for the deputy, Asher grabbed Lani's hand and pulled her toward freedom. This time, his incarceration had only been a few hours, but while waiting for Lani to come visit him, it had felt like an eternity.

He intended on making a beeline for the front door, but Lani resisted. When he looked back at her, she shook her head.

"We need to get that off first," she said, indicating the monitoring device on his ankle. "You are officially no longer a suspect in the theft of the festival funds."

Asher wrapped his arms around Lani and swept her off her feet. As he whirled her in a tight circle, she wrapped her arms around his neck and laughed merrily in his ear. Nothing had ever felt as good as her body pressed up against his, her breath warm on his neck, her joy filling him with giddy delight.

When he set Lani back on her feet and dipped his head to hers, she rose up on tiptoe to meet him half way. Her lips parted on a groan and he sent his tongue dancing forward to meet hers. They clung together, the fierce, thrilling kiss making his head swim. His throat tightened on a rush of joy. This woman in his arms was all the contentment that had been missing from his life.

"I take back what I said earlier," he declared, breaking off the kiss. "*This* is the second-best news I've heard all day."

As he spoke, he towed her toward the room where the electronic device had been attached a month earlier. Half an hour later he emerged into the humid evening and sucked in a breath of fresh air.

"We have to celebrate my freedom," he said. "Where should we go? New York? Buenos Aires? Tahiti?"

"How about we go back to Elegance Ranch and start figuring out how this new partnership of ours is going to work."

"When you say partnership..." He held his breath, wondering what she had in mind. Did she mean a business partnership? Or a personal one?

"I've been thinking about hiring an associate and I could use someone like you with the sort of connections that could bring in a better paying clientele." Her fingers tightened on his as she added, "It doesn't pay well, but if you work really hard, we might be able to grow the business."

"I appreciate your willingness to mentor me," he teased, drawing her toward the parking lot, eager to get her alone and show her without words just how much he adored her. "And I am grateful for your faith in me, but..."

"But?" she prompted, doubt creeping into her tone.

"But..." They reached her SUV and she reached into her pocket for the keys. "I have a little different take on our partnership," Drawing her into his arms, he lowered his forehead to hers. "One that involves rings and vows and kids. To summarize, it's us living happily-ever-after."

Lani chewed on her lower lip for several suspenseful seconds before her lashes lifted and she met his gaze. "Are you sure you're ready to take on that sort of partnership?"

"I've been thinking about it a lot. Someone needs to keep me in line. And I think you'll agree that no one is better at it than you." He grew serious as he stared into her eyes, willing her to see the fervent truth of his love. "And then there's the part where I adore you and can't bear to live without you. I want us to have kids and be a happy family."

The words came faster and faster as her muscles tensed. She seemed reluctant to take him seriously and his breath grew ragged as a tight band around his chest kept his lungs from fully expanding.

"I know this may seem like it's coming too soon. What can I say to convince you I can't live without you?" A lightbulb went off in his head and he dropped to one knee before her. Taking her hand in his, he offered her solemn sincerity. "Lani Li, I offer you my heart. Will you accept?"

To his dismay, she began to laugh.

"What's so funny? I'm trying to be all romantic."

"This is you being romantic?" She twisted her features into a skeptical expression, but a slight twitch at the corner of her mouth hinted at a smile.

"Give me a chance," he rasped. "Marry me."

For several heartbeats the only sound between them was the harsh, irregular pattern of their breathing. As he waited out the silence, Asher knew this wasn't the moment that would make or break them. He wasn't going to give up if she said no. She was too important to him to so readily accept defeat. He would fight for her. Fight for the amazing future they would have. But when her words came, it became clear that any battle she intended to wage would be at his side.

"Yes. I'll marry you."

Relief slammed into him. Leaping to his feet, he banded one arm around her waist and startled her with a quick spin and a dip. "At last you'll be mine."

"I've always been yours," she gasped. "Now, can I please get up?"

He set her back on her feet, but kept her in his arms. Setting aside all levity, he cupped the side of her face. "I'm done with running away because I'm too scared to face rejection. I intend to stay put and put in the effort."

"I love you, Asher Davidson Edmond." She framed his face with her palms and set fire to his blood with her earnest gaze. "I'm sorry I didn't give us a chance five years ago. I was afraid to choose you over my career because I didn't trust what we had could be enough. I never even considered fighting to have both. I know now that my life isn't fulfilling without you in it.

Let's make a life together. With kids and a successful business."
A brilliant smile bloomed. "We can have it all."

"We absolutely can." He brought his lips to hers. "And we will."

* * * * *

Keep reading for an excerpt of
Texas Outlaws: Jesse
by Kimberly Raye.
Find it in the
All He Wants anthology,
out now!

1

THIS WAS TURNING into *the* worst ride of his life.

Jesse James Chisholm stared over the back of the meanest bull this side of the Rio Grande at the woman who parked herself just outside the railing of the Lost Gun Training Facility, located on a premium stretch of land a few miles outside the city limits.

His heart stalled and his hand slipped. The bull lurched and he nearly tumbled to the side.

No way was *she* here.

No frickin' *way*.

The bull twisted and Pro Bull Riding's newest champion wrenched to the right. He was seeing things. That had to be it. He'd hit the ground too many times going after that first buckle and now it was coming back to haunt him. His grip tightened and his breath caught. Just a few more seconds.

One thousand three. One thousand four.

"Jesse!" Her voice rang out, filling his ears with the undeniable truth that she was here, all right.

Shit.

The bull jerked and Jesse pitched forward. He flipped and went down. Hard.

Dust filled his mouth and pain gripped every nerve in his

already aching body. The buzzer sounded and voices echoed, but he was too fixated on catching his breath to notice the chaos that suddenly surrounded him. He shut his eyes as his heart pounded in his rib cage.

Come on, buddy. You got this. Just breathe.

In and out. In. Out. In—

"Jesse? Ohmigod! Are you all right? Is he all right?"

Her desperate voice slid into his ears and stalled his heart. His eyes snapped open and sure enough, he found himself staring into a gaze as pale and blue as a clear Texas sky at high noon.

And just as scorching.

Heat swamped him and for a split second, he found himself sucked back to the past, to those long, endless days at Lost Gun High School.

He'd been at the bottom of the food chain back then, the son of the town's most notorious criminal, and no one had ever let him forget it. The teachers had stared at him with pity-filled gazes. The other boys had treated him like a leper. And the girls… They'd looked at him as if he were a bona fide rock star. The bad boy who was going to save them from the monotony of their map-dot existence.

Every girl, that is, except for Gracie Stone.

She'd been a rock star in her own right. Buck wild and reckless. Constantly defying her strict adoptive parents and pushing them to the limits. They'd wanted a goody-goody daughter befitting the town's mayor and first lady, and Gracie had wanted to break out of the neat little box she'd been forced into after the tragic death of her real parents.

They'd both been seniors when they'd crossed paths at a party. It had been lust at first sight. They'd had three scorching weeks together before they'd graduated and she'd ditched him via voice mail.

We just don't belong together.

For all her wicked ways, she was still the mayor's daughter, and he was the son of the town's most hated man. Water and oil. And everyone knew the two didn't mix.

Not then, and certainly not now.

He tried to remember that all-important fact as he focused on the sweet-smelling woman leaning over him.

She looked so different compared to the wild and wicked girl who lived and breathed in his memories. She'd traded in too much makeup and too little clothes for a more conservative look. She wore a navy skirt and a white silk shell tucked in at the waist. Her long blond hair had been pulled back into a no-nonsense ponytail. Long thick lashes fringed her pale blue eyes. Her lips were full and pink and luscious.

Different, yet his gut ached just the same.

He stiffened and his mouth pressed into a tight line. "Civilians aren't allowed in the arena." He pushed himself to his feet, desperate to ignore the soft pink-tipped fingers on his arm. "Not without boots." Her touch burned through the material of his Western shirt and sent a fizzle of electricity up his arm. "And jeans," he blurted. "And a long-sleeve shirt, for Chrissake." Damn, but why did she have to keep touching him like that? "You're breaking about a dozen different rules."

"I'm sorry. You just hit the ground so hard and I thought you were hurt and…" Her words trailed off and she let her hand fall away.

He ignored the whisper of disappointment and concentrated on the anger roiling inside him. "You almost got me killed." That was what he said. But the only thing rolling over and over in his mind was that she'd put herself in danger by climbing over the railing with a mean sumbitch bull on the loose.

He pushed away the last thought because no way—no friggin' way—did Jesse care one way or the other when it came to Gracie Stone. He was over her.

Finished.

Done.

He held tight to the notion and focused on the fact that she'd ruined a perfectly good training session. "You don't yell at a man when he's in the middle of a ride. It's distracting. I damn near broke my neck." He dusted off his pants and reached for his hat a few feet away. "If you're looking for City Hall—" he shook off the dirt and parked the worn Stetson on top of his head "—I think you're way off the mark."

"Actually, I was looking for you." Unease flitted across her face as if she wasn't half as sure of herself as she pretended to be. She licked her pink lips and he tried not to follow the motion with his eyes. "I need to talk to you."

He had half a mind to tell her to kick her stilettos into high gear and start walking. He was smack-dab in the middle of a demonstration for a prospective buyer who'd flown in yesterday to purchase the black bull currently snorting in a nearby holding pen.

Because Jesse was selling his livestock and moving on.
Finally.

With the winnings and endorsements from his first championship last year, he'd been able to put in an offer for a three-hundred-acre spread just outside of Austin, complete with a top-notch practice arena. The seller had accepted and now it was just a matter of signing the papers and transferring the money.

"Yo, Jesse." David Burns, the buyer interested in his stock, signaled him from the sidelines and Jesse held up a hand that said hold up a minute.

David wanted to make a deal and Jesse needed to get a move on. He didn't have time for a woman who'd ditched him twelve years ago without so much as a face-to-face.

At the same time, he couldn't help but wonder what could be so almighty important that it had Lost Gun's newly elected mayor slumming it a full ten miles outside the city limits.

He shrugged. "So talk."

Her gaze shifted from the buyer to the group of cowboys working the saddle broncs in the next arena. Several of the men had shifted their attention to the duo standing center stage. "Maybe we could go someplace private."

The words stirred all sorts of possibilities, all treacherous to his peace of mind since they involved a very naked Gracie and a sizable hard-on. But Jesse had never been one to back down from a dangerous situation.

He summoned his infamous slide-off-your-panties drawl that had earned him the coveted title of Rodeo's Hottest Bachelor and an extra twenty thousand followers on Twitter and eyed her. "Sugar, the only place I'm going after this is straight into a hot shower." He gave her a sly grin he wasn't feeling at the moment and winked. "If you're inclined to follow, then by all means, let's go."

Her eyes darkened and for a crazy instant, he glimpsed the old Gracie. The wild free spirit who'd stripped off her clothes and gone skinny-dipping with him their first night together.

But then the air seemed to chill and her gaze narrowed. "We'll talk here," she said, her voice calm and controlled. A total contradiction to the slight tremble of her bottom lip. She drew a deep breath that lifted her ample chest and wreaked havoc with his self-control. "A fax came in from the production company that filmed *Famous Texas Outlaws.*"

The mention of the television documentary that had nearly cost him his livelihood all those years ago was like a douse of ice water. "And?"

"They sold rights to a major affiliate who plans to air the show again and film a live 'Where Are They Now?' segment. They're already running promos for it. Sheriff Hooker had to chase two fortune hunters off your place just yesterday."

His "place" amounted to the burned-down shack and ten overgrown acres on the south end of town that he'd once shared with his father and brothers. As for the fortune hunters, well, they were out of luck. There was nothing to find.

His lawyer had been advising him to sell the property for years now, but Jesse had too many bad memories to want to profit off that sad, miserable place. Ignoring it had been better. Easier.

He eyed her. "When?"

"It's airing next Tuesday." She squared her shoulders, as if trying to gather her courage. "I thought you deserved fair warning after what happened the last time."

His leg throbbed at the memory. "So that's why you're here?" He tamped down the sudden ache. "To give me a heads-up?"

She nodded and something softened inside him.

A crazy reaction since he knew that her sudden visit had nothing to do with any sense of loyalty to him. This was all about the town. She'd traded in her wild and wicked ways to become a model public servant like her uncle. Conservative. Responsible. Loyal.

He knew that, yet the knotted fist in his chest eased just a little anyway.

"I know you just got back yesterday," she went on, "but I really think it would be better to cut your visit short until it's all said and done." She pulled her shoulders back. The motion pressed her delicious breasts against the soft fabric of her blouse. He caught a glimpse of lace beneath the thin material and he knew then that she wasn't as conservative as she wanted everyone to think. "That would make things a lot easier."

"For me?" He eyed her. "Or for you?"

Her gaze narrowed. "I'm not the one they'll be after."

"No, you're just in charge of the town they'll be invading. After all the craziness the last time I think you're anxious to avoid another circus. Getting rid of me would certainly help." The words came out edged with challenge, as if he dared her to dispute them.

He did.

She caught her bottom lip as if she wanted to argue, but then her mouth pulled tight. "If the only eyewitness to the fire is MIA, the reporters won't have a reason to stick around. I really think it would be best for everyone." Her gaze caught and held his. "Especially you."

Ditto.

He sure as hell wasn't up to the pain he'd gone through the first time. The show had originally aired a few months after he'd graduated high school, five years to the day of his father's death. He'd been eighteen at the time and a damn sight more reckless.

He'd been ground zero in the middle of a training session with a young, jittery bull named Diamond Dust. A group of reporters had shown up, cameras blazing, and Diamond had gone berserk. More so than usual for a mean-as-all-get-out bucking bull. Jesse had hit the ground, and then the bull had hit him. Over and over, stomping and crushing until Jesse had suffered five broken ribs, a broken leg, a dislocated shoulder and a major concussion. Injuries that had landed him in a rehab facility for six months and nearly cost him everything.

Not that the same thing wouldn't have happened eventually. He'd been on a fast road to trouble back then, ignoring the rules and riding careless and loose. The reporters had simply sped up the inevitable, because Jesse hadn't been interested in a career back then so much as an escape.

From the guilt of watching his own father die and not doing a damned thing to stop it.

It wasn't your fault. The man made his own choice.

That was what Pete Gunner had told him time and time again after the fire. Pete was the pro bull rider who'd taken in thirteen-year-old Jesse and his brothers and saved them from being split up into different foster homes after their father had died. Pete had been little more than a kid himself back then—barely twenty—and had just won his first PBR title. The last thing he'd needed was the weight of three orphans distracting him from his career, but he'd taken on the responsibility anyway. The man had been orphaned himself as a kid and so he'd known how hard it was to make it in the world. Cowboying had saved him and so he'd taught Jesse and his brothers how to rope and ride and hold their own in a rodeo arena. He'd turned them into tough cowboys. The best in the state, as a matter of fact. Even more, he'd given them a roof over their heads and food in their stomachs, and hope.

And when Diamond had nearly killed Jesse, it had been Pete who'd paid for the best orthopedic surgeons in the state. Pete was family—as much a brother to Jesse as Billy and Cole—and he was about to marry the woman of his dreams this Saturday.

That was the real reason Jesse had come back to this godforsaken town. And the reason he had no intention of leaving until the vows were spoken, the cake was cut and the happy couple left for two weeks in the Australian outback.

Then Jesse would pack up what little he had left here and head for Austin to make a real life. Far away from the memories. From her.

He stiffened against a sudden wiggle of regret. "Trust me, there's nothing I'd like better than to haul ass out of here right now."

"Good. Then we're on the same page—"

"But I won't," he cut in. "I can't."

A knowing light gleamed in her eyes. "I'm sure Pete would understand."

"I'm sure he would, but that's beside the point." Jesse shook his head. "I'm not missing his wedding."

"But—"

"You'll just have to figure out some other way to defuse the situation and keep the peace."

And then he did what she'd done to him on that one night forever burned into his memory—he turned and walked away without so much as a goodbye.

Subscribe and fall in love with a Mills & Boon series today!

You'll be among the first to read stories delivered to your door monthly and enjoy great savings.

WE
SIMPLY
LOVE
ROMANCE